Captain Rum

A wondrous adventure

Edited by
Professor H.D. (Bert) Lampluck

John Perrier

Title and copyright notice

"Captain Rum: A Wondrous Adventure"
Edited by Professor H.D. (Bert) Lampluck
By John Perrier

Published by JP Publishing Australia
Copyright 2015
ISBN 978-0-9875694-2-4
Historical fiction/adventure/maritime

Also available as an E-Book
ISBN 978-0-9875694-7-9

Please see the end of this book for:
More titles from JP Publishing Australia
Ways to connect with us

"I hereby undertake not to remove from the Library ... any volume, document or other object belonging to it...."

Part of the *Reader's Pledge*, which everyone must take before entering the Bodleian Library at Oxford University. Thankfully, I accidentally broke this rule, or this extraordinary tale might never have been discovered.

Prof. H.D. (Bert) Lampluck

One rainy morning in September 2011, I was browsing through the 'Rare and Fragile Books' section of the Bodleian library at Oxford University. I was researching my main area of study, prehistoric art, when I stumbled upon an inconspicuous little book. It immediately struck me as unusual because it had neither the author's name nor a title on its cover. I hoped that it contained unseen discoveries on Mayan sculpture.

After wiping the dust from its brown paper jacket and delicately prising open its covers, I discovered that it was a hand-written diary. A quick browse confirmed that it was a ship's log, written by Captain Fintan McAdam in 1821. I was initially disappointed because such diaries are common in historical archives, and are usually very dull reading. A few weeks later, I would wholeheartedly change this opinion.

In hindsight, I was lucky to have stumbled across it at all, because it was incorrectly filed in the art/sculpture section, on the bottom shelf of the farthest aisle. Judging by the dust on the cover, I doubted that anyone had read it before.

I intended to return the book to the front desk so that the librarian could file it correctly, so I tucked it into my library bag and continued browsing. By lunchtime, I had gathered enough books for my research and returned to my office. I threw myself into my work, and amongst the hustle and bustle I quickly forgot about the little journal at the bottom of my library bag.

Two thousand years ago, when a Mayan labourer was constructing a drainage pit at the Temple of Uxbenka in South America, I doubt that he realised that his labour would one day help to uncover the incredible tale of "Captain Rum". How did this happen? Six weeks after my library visit I was assisting on an archaeological dig at that very temple when I stepped on what I thought was solid earth. It wasn't. The ground collapsed into the previously mentioned drainage pit and I tumbled in, resulting in a fractured ankle. On medical advice, I could not walk for a month.

If injury had confined me to bed in Oxford, I would have happily used the time to study. However, I was isolated on a remote dig site in South America with only a few books and, Heaven help me, *no internet access*. By the third week, having exhausted my supply of history books, I chanced upon a nondescript book in the bottom of my library bag. At first I was confused as to what it was - after 35 years of study my mind remains sharp in some ways, but unfortunately even Oxford professors suffer from occasional absent-mindedness!

A glance at the opening pages of the Captain's log prompted my memory, so I wrote myself a note to return the book to the library when I returned home. With nothing else to occupy my time, I browsed through a few entries. McAdam's diary quickly drew me in and I finished the remainder of my rehabilitation fascinated by the adventures that unfolded from its fragile pages.

When I returned to Oxford, I was so excited about the journal that my first visit was not, as you would expect, to the Faculty of Fine Art Studies, but was instead to the Dean of Maritime History. Even someone with the Professor's unique experience was fascinated by the diary. We agreed that the mysterious Captain deserved further investigation.

It took me only a month to uncover some basic facts about the author, Captain Fintan McAdam. He was born in 1794 as the only child of shipwright George McAdam and his wife Elsie. Young Fintan stayed at school until he was nearly 14 years old, indicating that he was an above-average student, for it was rare for children born to working class parents to study beyond a few token years.

Fintan then took an apprenticeship in his father's shipyard, where he steadily progressed to tradesman. Sadly his mother passed away of tuberculosis[1] in 1812, after which McAdam, no doubt heartbroken, enlisted as a crewmember on a Merchant Navy voyage to East India. He returned to find that his father had passed away in his absence. Now very much alone, Fintan joined a second year-long spice run to the East Indies.

After returning from his second voyage, McAdam's luck must have improved, because in February 1816 he became engaged to Miss Elizabeth Heath. But fate was not done with him yet. In a sad conclusion, *The Times* of August 1818 listed Elizabeth's name, unfortunately in the "Deaths Register".

---

[1] In the 19th century this disease was known as *consumption*

More bad fortune followed. Soon after his wife's death, McAdam was sentenced to three months jail in Shepton Mallet prison[2] for theft. He escaped after two weeks, injuring a guard in the process, for which a more serious arrest warrant was issued.

McAdam fled to Liverpool. We know this because in 1820 his name appeared on a pamphlet advertising *The Wandering Bards: For Song, Dance and Poetry to Enliven One's Evening.* The flyer pictures a marquee style tent and advises an entry fee of one penny.

Writer. Ship builder. Sailor. Escapee. Actor. Our captain was certainly multi-talented!

After these brief mentions, the historical record of McAdam ran cold. Until now. I was excited that the journal was historically important, but because of the amazing nature of its tale, I was concerned that it might be a well-crafted fake. With the help of a technical team from the Art Department, I conducted some tests. First, I performed a microscopic analysis of the paper, which showed that its source was probably the paper millers *William Smedley and Co,* who manufactured at that time in nearby Wales. Second, I analysed and dated the ink, which proved that it was from squid, which McAdam could have easily obtained and applied via a feather quill. The text, like the paper, was approximately 200 years old.

Finally, I performed the simplest and perhaps most important test of all: the book smelt of the ocean and had a salty taste. Yes, I did lick it! These tests indicated that the journal was a genuine 1820s ship's log, and an authentic record of the travels of Captain Fintan McAdam.

Now for the first time I humbly present the journey of Captain Rum, in his own words, for you to enjoy. It truly was a wondrous adventure. Bon voyage!

---

[2] Shepton Mallet prison was built in Somerset, west of London, in 1625. When it ceased operating in January 2013 it was Britain's oldest prison. At the time of closing it held 189 life prisoners.

A note from the editor regarding the transcription

As the editor of this manuscript, I had the responsibility to decide what material to include and what to omit. I must confess to slightly altering the original document, rather than transcribing it with literal precision. While some readers might feel that this detracts from its original charm, the changes greatly simplify the text's readability.

Specifically, I updated the spelling of all words to their modern equivalents, as it was often difficult to decipher McAdam's phonetics – for example, he once wrote "cleaoothesse" for "Clothes". I also replaced formal words (such as 'thou') with their modern equivalents (in this case, 'you').

Similarly, I updated McAdam's grammar where I felt it would improve readability without altering meaning or nuance. As one case in point, McAdam universally used the verb "be" without using other forms such as *am, is, are, was, were*, or *been*. Instead of 'I am happy today but I was sad yesterday', he would write 'I be happy today but I be sad yesterday'.

I also admit to sneaking in some extra punctuation, particularly periods. In keeping with the style of the time, McAdam constructed long, convoluted sentences, often running to 100 words or more. At times they made my eyes water. I also inserted paragraph breaks where I felt it was appropriate.

To demonstrate the scope of my editorial changes, I have included below:

(1) A digitally enhanced copy of a small section of the original text

(2) a literal transcription, and

(3) the text as presented in this volume.

I trust that this excerpt gives you the flavour of the original text, and helps to justify my adulteration. I hope that the reader trusts my editorial judgement, but those doubters who wish to view the original log should apply in writing to:

The Librarian in Chief (LIC)
Bodleian library
Broad St, Oxford   OX1 3BG
United Kingdom

*

Finally, I am indebted to my academic colleagues for checking many of McAdam's assertions, for they often seemed fantastic beyond belief. I discovered that the truth of the natural world is often far more peculiar than anything that this writer could invent!

Our research uncovered a host of fascinating facts and historical notes that I have included in footnotes and appendices, which I hope you find an interesting addition to the tale.

H.D.L.

Digitally enhanced copy of original text

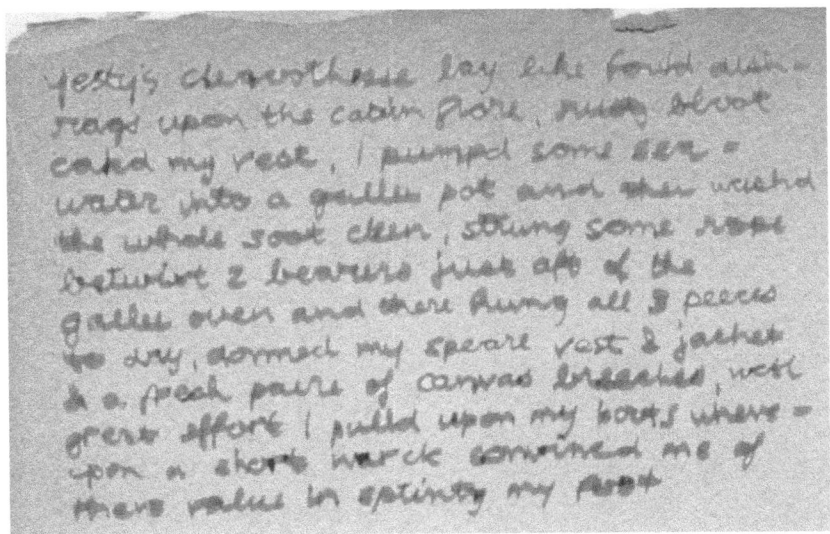

Literal transcription

Yesty's cleaoothesse lay like fould dish-rags upon the cabin flore, rusty bloot cakd my vest. I pumpd some sea-water into a gallee pot and then washd the whole suit cleen, strung some rope betwixt 2 bearers just aft of the galley oven and there hung all 3 peeces to dry, donnd my spaere vest & jacket & a fresh paere of canvas breeches, with great effort I pulld upon my boots where-upon a short warck convincd me of there value in splinting my foot.

Text as presented in 'Captain Rum: A Wondrous Adventure"

Yesterday's clothes lay like fouled dishrags on the cabin floor. Rusty blood caked my vest. I pumped some seawater into a galley pot and then washed the whole suit clean. I strung some rope between two bearers, just behind the galley oven, and hung all three pieces to dry. I donned my spare vest and jacket and a fresh pair of canvas breeches. With great effort I pulled on my boots, whereupon a short walk convinced me of their value in splinting my foot.

The Journal

Tuesday February 13, 1821

Although I was not yet at sea, today seemed like a good time to start a record of my voyage. Every journey begins with a single step, and mine was this morning into the office of *Winterbottom's Maritime Brokers*. I had spotted a ship for sale and wanted to make some enquiries.

For the past year, I had harboured growing thoughts that a long voyage across the oceans would help to clear my mind. A few seasons of salt air in my lungs might not only expel some demons, but shake the plod[3] off my tail as well. Yesterday, as I was taking a chilly mid-morning walk along the Thames River, I spied a run-down sloop for sale, and the old sea-dog inside me could not resist. Some enquiries led me to Winterbottom's brokerage, and I was soon inspecting the vessel herself[4].

At first sight she was a tired old girl, and was clearly in need of a shipwright's attention. Yet her design was everything I could have hoped for: she had a tall central mast of Conifer Pine, and a shallow drafted keel that would allow me to explore estuaries and shallows. True, she was small, and most sailors would consider the galley and quarters below deck to be cramped, but for a crew of only one the space was ample.

As it was with my dear departed wife Elizabeth, I fell in love with the little sloop immediately. I quickly decided that she was the one to partner me on my voyage, and to the surprise and delight of Mr Winterbottom, I left £5 as a deposit. I doubt that he had ever earned his commission so easily.

My mind since then has been a swirling current as I dream of the adventures that await me. But I must remain rational because I have a long list of tasks to complete before casting away, and must do it without alerting the plod that I have returned to London.

---

[3] The *Plod* was common slang for the police
[4] Tradition dictates that a sailor's ship is always referred to with feminine pronouns.

Wednesday 14 February

After a fitful sleep – for my mind was already full of nervous anticipation - I arose to a breakfast of eel in pastry[5]. I donned a large duffle coat against the cold wind, for the river was still frozen, and then set out for the Bank of England. In time, I passed the mooring at which my ship (yes, *my* ship) lay idle, patiently awaiting my attention.

Ambling onward, for it was an hour before the bank would unlock its gates, I continued along the Thames. Despite my heavy coat, I shivered as I passed the Clink, where the wail of a prisoner drew horrid memories of my time in Shepton Mallet prison. I remembered the stench of the night bucket, the swill that passed as rations, and the nights that froze your fingers, your lips, your feet, and then finally your bones.

At least I endured that cesspool for only 14 days. The thought of serving the remaining 76 days of my sentence - plus another five years for my escape and ten for injuring the guard - was unbearable, so I remained alert for the plod. Once my ship was seaworthy and provisioned I would cast away, and would be forever free of their unjust law courts and cold shackles.

I crossed the Thames at London Bridge, dodging the hawkers and touts as I did. I had no interest in their offers today because I had a purpose. Also, a fortune that would double a swipe's[6] lifetime take weighed down my pockets, so I entertained no distractions. After a short walk, I arrived at the Bank of England where I made myself known, and I was soon ushered to the office of Mr J.W. Peathorn, the manager.

I opened proceedings by introducing myself as Mr. Fintan McAdam. This simple introduction would not ordinarily seem out of place, but since returning from Liverpool I had lived under the false name of Mr. J.W. Smith to divert the attention of the plod, who still searched for that man who escaped from Shepton Mallet from under the peaks of their bobby caps. But in order for the sloop be registered and for Lloyds[7] to

---

[5] Eel was frequently eaten in the 1800s as it was one of the few species of fish that could survive the polluted waters of London's Thames river. Eel baked in pastry (so that it could be eaten by hand) was a common workers' meal. This snack was the forerunner to today's meat pie.

[6] A *swipe* was a pick-pocket

[7] Lloyds insurance began in Mr Lloyd's Coffee shop on Tower St, London, in

accept my insurance proposal, I had to present my original documents; I had no choice but to return to my baptised name of Fintan McAdam.

"So, in summary, you wish my bank to redeem your valuables in exchange for a promissory note[8], Mr McAdam?" he confirmed after I had explained my business to him.

"Yes, Mr. Peathorn, that's exactly what I am after. I have a purse filled with gold sovereigns that are surely worth a few pennies. I'd be most obliged if you would kindly exchange them for a note."

He peered at me through his little round spectacles and down past his long, pointy nose. Whether it was because of my rough, weather-worn jacket or my unshaved chin, his look was one of disdain.

"I'm curious, Mr McAdam, where...."

He paused and propped his spectacles even higher upon his nose, folded his arms and then continued. "I am curious as to where a, where a..." he searched for a term, "...where a *working man* would obtain such treasures."

Now I know that I wasn't born a Lord and that I don't have a seat in parliament. Nor would most people consider me a gentleman. But this man, this pea-brained Peathorn, was suggesting that I was exaggerating my wealth, or maybe even that I had acquired my riches by ill means. If he only understood the long months at sea that I endured to earn these rewards - suffering with scurvy, fighting pirates, and clinging to nothing but hope and Providence[9] during savage storms - he might not have treated me like I was nothing but a toad. If he could have seen my father, sweating during the summer and trembling during the winter at his shipyard, scraping together the hard-earned pennies that he

---

about 1688. This venue was popular with sailors and other merchants, and it soon became the place to visit for anything maritime. Businessmen gathered there to listen to sailors' insurance proposals, from which grew the Society of Lloyds. Today Lloyds of London transacts insurance premiums of about $50 billion per year. Not bad for a company that started in a coffee shop!

[8] A promissory note was much like a modern cheque.

[9] McAdam uses the word *Providence* to mean "sound judgement and foresight, combined with good luck and some help from above". He routinely capitalises the word and refers to it with female pronouns, indicating that he attached a degree of quasi-religious significance to this provider of good fortune.

ultimately bequeathed to me, then he would not have dismissed me with such disdain.

I felt my temper welling inside me, and heat rising into my ears, so I forced myself to stay still and silent so that I did not lash out at him. Even though he richly deserved a flogging, I did not want to attract the unwelcome attention of the law.

"You look more like a navvy[10] than a Naval Captain," he added down his nose.

I shot to my feet, now failing to contain my rage. I leaned forward across his desk and fixed him with a stare. Had he been nearer I may well have fixed my hands around his throat as well.

"My money is as good as the next man's," I growled. With that I upended my purse, scattering dozens of gleaming coins across his desktop. His balding head jerked with surprise and he looked up, startled, trying to utter what might have been an apology if I had let him speak. "And the next bank's note is as good as yours. You've just lost £20 commission, £10 more in exchange and maybe a £5 gratuity had you been more of a gentleman. I trust that your stockholders do not hear of your failure, although they very well might. Good day, Sir." I scraped the coins into my purse, and without pausing to hear his feeble apologies, I stomped out the door.

Without care as to my direction, I banged down the nearby streets like an empty tin can buffeting in a gale. I stomped down King William Lane past the Martyrs' Church and soon found myself in Billingsgate market. It was crammed with stalls – foods, beverages, merchandise - and no doubt swilling with swipes. I kept my wits about me and my hands tightly around my purse to guard my fortune. By and by[11] I wound my way to the riverbank, where a long rest allowed that pompous dung-beetle Peathorn to fade from my thoughts.

I sat alone as the sun rose above the bridge, and enjoyed a minute of warmth. Then, clutching even more tightly at my purse, I ploughed deep into Billingsgate market, this time with newfound purpose. Soon I spotted a familiar red-and-white striped pole signifying that a barber was attending his chair[12]. He stropped his razor with fearsome speed,

---

[10] *Navvy* was a term for a rough labourer.
[11] *By and by* was an old term for "eventually" or "sooner or later".

then lathered my face with a soaped brush, and was soon scraping the beard from my chin with practiced dexterity. He was a happy fellow who entertained me with jokes and stories while he shaved away my growth.

"And a haircut, Guv'nor, I beseech thee," I asked with mock pomposity.

"Certainly m' lord," he replied in a cockney accent, playing along with my too-polite request. Soon my chin was smooth and my hair was neatly trimmed. Leaving three pennies - including a whole penny as a tip, for he was a jolly fellow and was well skilled in his craft - I walked onward through the crowded market. I bought a new blue jacket and a hat, and then had a final stop near the gate, where for a ha'penny a young lad polished my shoes to a looking-glass[13] sheen.

Then I headed to the Royal Bank of Scotland. Those people who say that Scots are tight with their money are right, for the manager, Mr. McAllister, would redeem my precious coins for only £445, 2s and sixpence. But I received a far better reception than at the English bank, and a mug of hot sweet tea as well. He even complimented me on my haircut! When I departed, with Mr. McAllister wishing me Godspeed[14] for my travels, I had in my pocket a promissory note (payable to Mr. R.W. Winterbottom, for £295), 20 five-pound notes and 50 crisp one-pound notes. Mr McAllister even paid me the sixpence in silver pennies rather than the new copper ones. Before the sun set that evening, I was the proud owner of the sloop. Mr Winterbottom even addressed me as *Captain* McAdam as I departed his brokerage.

I am anxious that three men - Winterbottom, Peabody and McAllister - now all have the name *Fintan McAdam* on their documents. Mr J. W. Smith – your days are few. My urge to weigh anchor grows stronger with every tick of the clock.

My ship does not yet have a name. Mr Winterbottom suggested *George IV* in honour of our new King, or perhaps *George III* to pay tribute to the recently departed. Whenever this question comes to my mind, I can

---

[12] To this day some old-fashioned barbers still use a red-and-white pole outside their shop.

[13] "Looking glass" is an old term for a mirror

[14] *Godspeed* is an expression still occasionally used to wish somebody a safe journey.

think of no answer other than 'Elizabeth', which would honour my departed wife. But if I followed this thought then the pain of her passing and the horrible nightmares of that day would pursue me across the seas, which would defeat the purpose of my journey. I sat for a while to ponder the question, and to let the little ship inspire me. No appropriate names came to mind, but I have decided with finality that it will not be *Elizabeth.* I must forget her.

Thursday 15 February

I awoke this morning on my sloop. I had not intended to stay on board, but had simply drifted to sleep as the gentle lapping of the river on her hull lulled me with its rhythm. The water's sound was very relaxing, and I looked forward to it singing me its lullaby on my journey. However I was not so naive to believe that every day would be as calm as this one— I am sure that I will encounter a blow or two along the way.

Last night I had a dream in which evil, angry seas tossed my ship about. She was rolling like a cut log and yawing[15] like a boy's top. The ocean was deep - deep and black - and was spitting white foam over the gunwales[16]. The storm's ferocity grew with every passing moment, and the wind tore at her sails until they were just flailing canvas rags. Just as it seemed she could take no more, two giant waves careened into either side of her. But instead of crushing her, the waves transformed into a pair of giant wings. The wings pulled themselves free of the sea and then flapped in steady beats, like that of a dragon. Slowly, my little sloop lifted herself above the waves and flew away to safety.

Ordinarily such a nightmare would worry me, because dreaming of a storm before weighing anchor is known to bring bad luck. But this dream, with its wings of water, had the opposite effect. It told me that Providence was on my side for this adventure; no matter how deep my problems, I would find a way free. I welcomed her support, for even the

---

[15] *Yawing* means to spin around a vertical axis (...like a boy's top). Along with *rolling* (like a spinning log), a ship can also *pitch* from front to back like a see-saw.

[16] The *gunwale* is the upper edge rail of the side of the ship. The word is pronounced 'gunnel'.

best-prepared ship in the Kingdom could not compete against even a pennyweight[17] of bad luck.

Skipping breakfast, I scampered about my ship from the bottom of the bilge to the top of the mast. I pulled at planks and banged on beams, and exposed every ill-fitting board or loose joint. I unfurled and inspected both sails inch by inch, for I had decided that even a single fraying thread would not escape my attention. I checked the caulking between the planks and discovered that it was deficient on the aft[18] of the hull. I examined every piece of rigging and discovered to my dismay that the previous owner had left knots tied in their lengths, causing them to rot. The galley[19] was ... well, let me say that there will be many displaced rats in the days to come.

By and by I had cast my eye over the entire ship, and compiled a long list of repairs. In writing the list my quill tip was busy and buzzing, like a dragonfly over a summer pond, dipping down here to add a note and there to amend another. I look forward to my hammer being as active as my quill.

The sun crept across the southern sky and finally dipped behind Blackfriars Tavern. The sight of this public house[20] reminded me that I had not eaten all day. With my work completed, I retired to Blackfriars where my threepenny special included Turkey soup, roast mutton with potato cakes and a delicious bird's nest pudding. I felt justified in succumbing to one of the seven sins – gluttony - as rationed days lay ahead, and it would pay me to hoard some surplus weight now, which I could call on in leaner times. Soon the heaviness of the day's work fell upon me, and I was barely prostrate before my dreams began.

Saturday 24 February

For nine days I have worked on the hull, and I am pleased with my progress. Getting my ship into the dry dock was an ordeal because the

---

[17] A *pennyweight* was an old unit of measuring weight. One pennyweight was equivalent to about 1.5 grams.
[18] *Aft* means 'toward the back'. In contrast, *fore* means 'toward the front'.
[19] The *galley* is a ship's kitchen area.
[20] A *public house* was a tavern; the term is still frequently used, but these days we simply shorten it to "pub".

pumps were not in the mood to stick at their task. Maybe it was too cold for them to work, but work they must, because I was increasingly anxious to depart before the plod became aware of my presence. My heart skipped every time I saw a pair of them marching along their dockside beat. For one, I didn't trust that bank manger Peabody. Although he did not know my prison story, he did know my name - and he was the type for tattling.

After propping my sloop firmly onto dry timber bearers, I commenced tarring[21] her hull. Frequently the cold locked the tar solid, meaning that I had to make regular trips to the boiling pit. I also scraped away the vessel's fading name badge, for I intended on re-christening her, although my mind still wandered on this choice.

Sunday 25 February

Today was the Sabbath[22], so the docks were nearly deserted. However, many passers-by, dressed in their Sunday finery, ambled toward the cathedral to attend a service. I am not interested in Church matters, and preferred to concentrate on my repair tasks instead. However I knew that working on the Sabbath could offend some people, so I laboured inside so that I didn't attract unwelcome attention for dishonouring the day.

Yet I still cannot understand how any god would decree that I should be damned for working on a Sunday, when he does not stop the oceans. How could this god demand that I rest, when his seas do not[23]?

As the cathedral bells signalled the end of the service, I climbed the short ladder onto deck for some clean air, for the cabin was stale. The parishioners milled about in the nearby square, talking earnestly – as usual, a little too earnestly, for it seems to me that most of them

---

[21] Tar, a sticky black substance, was used as a water repellent on a ship's timber hull.

[22] A weekly religious day of rest, taken as Sunday for the Christian England of the nineteenth century.

[23] In his journal, McAdam ignores convention by using lower case letters rather than capitals to begin the words 'God' and its associated pronouns 'He' and 'His'. I have reproduced this error faithfully as it gives a hint of his attitude towards matters of faith.

attended the Sunday service for the chit-chat rather than for the piety and preaching.

One fine filly in a lace dress caught my eye. As she turned, I saw a dark ringlet of hair fall over her cheek before she flicked it aside. That one small action reminded me of my dear Elizabeth. Try as I might, I could not forget Beth and her pale skin, Irish green eyes and tinkling laugh. For a minute my reverie was a happy one but then, as always, the vision turned ghastly. I quickly looked away to banish the sight of Beth in her dying throes, but the nightmare would not let me go. Despite it being nearly three years since that day, my memory of her was still raw.

The vision, like always, was so powerful that it seemed like Beth was dying, yet again, before my eyes. This was not just a distant imagining, but was a ghost-like presence that appeared in front of me. Even though some deep part of my mind knew that it was not real, the sight of my beloved, lying in front of me covered in blood, still rattled me to my core.

When the vision finally ceded, I retched over the side of the ship. After that I headed directly for Blackfriars, for I knew that some strong liquor would calm my nerves. But because it was the Sabbath, I had to rap on the back door until my knuckles were red, and then drink outside the window[24]. Eventually I had enough rum inside me to wipe the horrid pictures from my mind, and to steel my trembling limbs.

By late evening the fog was thick, and the rum had gathered clouds inside my head as well. I could not find my sloop through both fogs, and so ended up falling asleep on the riverbank until the deep cold woke me. By and by, I somehow stumbled back to the pier and collapsed into my bunk, shivering as if I was still locked in Shepton.

Monday 26 February

My hands were bloodied and bruised this morning– perhaps I fell on the way home, although I also have a distant memory of hitting a lout who tried to swipe my pockets while I slept on the riverbank.

---

[24] Public houses were closed on Sundays. Some patrons, particularly if they were well known to management, were able to access sly grog by knocking on the back window.

Today the sun never truly dawned. It seemed as though the whole city stayed in bed all day under an overcoat of a thick pea-souper[25]. Even at noon, the sun was barely as bright as the moon. The heaviness of my rum-soaked head and the warm comfort of my blanket pulled me to my hammock like a loadstone[26] draws a nail, and if it wasn't for my worries that the plod would send me back to prison for 15 years then I may not have roused at all.

By and by I rose, and stoked the galley stove for a mid-afternoon pot of tea to soothe my aching temples, to warm my swollen hands, and to fortify me against the damp, damp cold. I passed the afternoon away in this moribund state, and by and by simply let the lodestone blanket win its influence over me.

Tuesday 27 February

I awoke freshly at dawn, and once about, I was pleased to complete the hull. Every board was tarred solid and she was as watertight as frog skin. Satisfied, I asked the dock master to slide her into the water, which he achieved with the help of only eight men and two pounds of soap[27]. Soon my ship was bobbing like a new cork.

Since acquiring my sloop, I had worked deep past sunset on most days, pressing myself onward under lamplight until I felt dizzy with fatigue. By then, the pulling power of my hammock had been so strong that I had often fallen asleep onboard, meaning that I had spent only three nights at my rented bedsit. With my lease soon due for renewal, I felt it was an opportune time to make the sloop my home. This move would not only spare me a long walk after each day's work and then a return journey the next morning, but would save me a shilling per week on rent. Although my funds were holding for now, I had no income, and still much provisioning to be done.

I walked along the Thames bank, turning north at the mill toward Chancery Lane. I walked onward past the agricultural fields, the hen houses, and then past the sty. I passed by the woods - even now my memories here are very raw, and I still cannot take the short cut along

---

[25] A *pea-souper* was a very thick fog; literally as thick as pea soup.
[26] A *loadstone* is a magnet
[27] Presumably the soap was to lubricate the rails that held her.

the woodland path because of what occurred there three years ago. But today I stayed strong, because I knew that I would soon be at sea and able to leave this forest - and its memories of that horrible, horrible day - behind me.

I trembled only for a few minutes. The remaining walk to my bedsit helped me to calm myself, even without the aid of rum. By and by I fully steadied myself, and knocked upon the door of Mrs Harlesden, the proprietoress of the small inn that had been my home since I had returned from Liverpool the previous spring.

"Good afternoon, Mr Smith," smiled Mrs Harlesden as she opened her front door.

It pained me to hear that sweet lady address me by this false name. However, my lie had been necessary, in case my lease documents had fallen under the gaze of an overzealous official with the plods' arrest list in his hands.

"Your rent remains in credit for another two days, Mr Smith. Would you like to pay further in advance, or have you come on other matters?"

I told her that I had another issue to discuss, and soon we had settled over a cup of tea and a helping of her delicious pumpkin cake. (I cannot understand why this vegetable usually ends up in pigs' troughs, when, with the addition of graham flour[28], creamy milk and a little sugar, such delicacies can be created.) After tea, I reluctantly told Mrs Harlesden that I was ending my tenure and moving out, at which she appeared genuinely saddened.

I told her of the adventure across the seas that I was undertaking, at which she, like a mother-figure, expressed concerns for my safety. I reassured her that two years in the merchant navy had prepared me well to handle sea life, and that my apprenticeship in papa's ship yard had given me the experience to ensure that my vessel was sound. I must have sounded earnest, because her brow slowly unwrinkled as her concerns faded away.

After another cup of tea, we simply chatted about the weather and such. My ears sprang forward when she mentioned a visitor, Sergeant

---

[28] *Graham flour* was an early type of whole-grain flour

G. Jones, from the London Police Constabulary, who had enquired about a man called *McAdam*.

Nothing came of it, as dear Mrs Harlesden did not have to feign innocence- she truly didn't know anyone of that name. My false name of Mr J.W. Smith had served its purpose. But her story confirmed my fears that the plod were closing in on me, and reinforced that I should depart as soon as possible. After I cast away the plod can search all they like, but they will not find me north of the Cape of Good Hope[29].

Before leaving, I slipped Mrs Harlesden a shilling, asking her to keep my mail until I returned from my journey. She graciously agreed, but only on the condition that she could return my shilling at once, saying that my handiwork on her premises during my stay was ample payment. In response, I thanked her for her goodwill and then, while pretending to pocket the coin, I slid it under the chair cushion. With luck I'll be rounding the Cape before she chances on it.

I had soon packed my simple belongings into an old cart: a chest of good carpenter's tools, two tallow lanterns[30], ten books (three in Spanish), a spare hat and an old suit. I also retrieved my scimitar from its hide above the closet. Curiosity bound me to unsheathe it, and I gazed in wonder at its smooth, carved handle and, of more importance, its gleaming edge. The sword was a precious keepsake from my second spice run, in which a band of Corsairs[31] had attempted to capture our ship. Fortunately they were a rabble, so only one pirate made it aboard. We quickly overpowered him and I was lucky enough to pounce on his disengaged sword. He was summarily dropped like a sounding lead[32] over the stern. I had treasured the gleaming scimitar from that day onward, and although no pirate had yet felt its sting, it was comforting to know that I could play that hand if needed.

---

[29] The Cape of Good Hope is the southern tip of Africa.

[30] Tallow was a substance extracted from the fat of sheep and cattle, and was used in the same way that wax is used in candles.

[31] *Corsairs* were Caribbean pirates

[32] A *sounding lead* was a heavy lead weight attached to a long thin rope, which was dropped over the side of the ship to measure the water's depth. A sailor could affix a portion of wax to the bottom of the sounding lead, which would bring up a small sample of the ocean bed.

As I bid Mrs Harlesden goodbye, she offered me two wrapped slices of her pumpkin cake. I accepted immediately, repaying her kindness with a kiss on her hand. Turning quickly to avoid seeing her blush yet not so briskly that she would see that this was my intention, I was soon peddling my rickety cart toward the dock. Before nightfall, I had settled into my new home.

Thursday 1 March

The weather has turned brighter, and the ice has melted from all but the stalest parts of the river. But the turning of the new month reminds me that I should depart as soon as possible. The unwelcome attention of Sergeant G. Jones is chipping away at my mind like a sculptor at his marble.

This afternoon I headed north of the river to Holborn's High Street. Despite the long list of errands and tasks that I had already completed, my mind continued to dart like a hummingbird in search of missed necessities. I hoped that a wander down the merchant row might prompt some useful yet unimagined ideas. My walk paid a good dividend.

I had just arrived at the bottom of Holborn Hill when I passed the premises of *Mr T. Hill and Son, Makers and Purveyors of Fine Optical Equipment*. I introduced myself to Master Hill, who was a plump young lad – I suspected he laid the lard too thickly on his bread[33]. Nevertheless, he was very knowledgeable on optics, and drew my attention to a range of naval telescopes. One model caught my interest - its mahogany barrel was beautifully carved, and even papa would have not have found any flaws with the lathe work. The sight tube contained three glasses and a brass finder scope at the near end. I tested it only once before asking the lad to crate it for me. He also gave me a lint for polishing, and quipped that it would spot me a mermaid from 20 furlongs[34] if I kept it in good condition.

---

[33] Lard is the congealed fat from cooked pork. It was used to moisten bread in much the same way as we use butter today.
[34] A furlong was an old unit of measurement that was close to 200 metres. Its use survives today (just) in the horse racing industry.

He also suggested another device that I might find useful on my travels: a burning glass. With firm tropical sunlight and the right tinder (I must pack some dry pine cones) Master Hill assured me that it could produce a flame in less than two minutes. He explained that it worked like a magnifying glass, focusing the sun's rays and collecting its heat to a point. He declined my joking request for a demonstration, citing the condition of the sun over London which he described as 'weak from an illness but missing the fever'. I purchased the burning glass too.

Rarely would a sailor have need to enter *Whittow & Harris's Art and Stationery supplies* [35] but as I passed the shop front, I spied a set of small journals that I felt would be perfect for a captain's log. Blank, white pages such as these readily intoxicate me; such a sight draws forth the anticipation of not only the words that will soon fill them, but also the adventure that will provide the words.

After I mentioned to Mr Whittow that I was about to embark on an ocean voyage, he asked his lad to cover each journal in brown paper rubbed with wool fat[36]. This wrapping, he assured me, would help to keep the damp at bay.

(I write in the first of these journals now. In order to keep my story together in one volume, I will transcribe my musings so far into this journal over the next few days. I intend on taking the opportunity to improve on my grammar and penmanship as I do.)

My arms fatigued as I walked back toward my sloop with two heavy crates. On the way, I passed a public house called Ye Olde Mitre Tavern[37], where I paused for a rest and an early supper. Just as I finished my meal of pork chops fried with apples, a young lady sat near me, alerting me with a smile as to her intentions. She quickly aroused my interest. But just as I moved across toward her, a vision of Beth thrust itself into my mind so firmly that it was like a scene playing out in front of me. I tried

---

[35] George Harris (1756-1838) was the son of a butcher. In 1779, he became apprenticed as an artist to Benjamin Whittow. They formed an art supply company in 1803, which traded until 1826.

[36] The wrapping obviously worked well, because it remained intact until I stumbled across this very journal in the Bodleian library.

[37] This tavern, situated at 1 Ely Place, London, still trades under the same name to this day.

my best to focus upon my present company, but I could not escape Beth's ghostly face as it imposed itself over that of the girl.

As usual, the vision started serenely enough: on this occasion I saw myself meeting Beth for the first time. She flashed me a coquettish smile as I handed her a ha'penny for a newspaper. While accepting the coin, she confessed surprise that a shipyard worker could read. As always happened in my visions, the sound of her voice was muffled and distant, as if emanating from behind a wall. Yet another part of my mind could understand her insinuation perfectly. I grinned at Beth, for I had heard such thoughts from others before, and promised to teach her the alphabet if she wished. She gifted me an even broader smile that entrapped me like a rabbit in a snare. The memory of our first meeting had sustained me through many dark days, but now I looked in vain through the vision for the bar woman's face, knowing from experience what was about to happen. But I could not shake the vision. I was compelled to watch in horror as Beth's smile contorted into a wretched face with lips that twisted in agony, and her chilling screams filled my head. The transformation was so complete that it did not seem like a trick of my mind, but instead that Beth was sitting, in abject agony, on the bar stool next to me. I hurriedly excused myself outside where I lowered myself unsteadily to the ground. I sat until a score of slow breaths eventually steeled me.

When, oh when, will these apparitions leave me alone? I hope that a long stretch at sea and the experience of adventure will dull these ghastly flashbacks, for I can no longer face a woman without succumbing to their evil.

I waited outside the Old Tavern until the bar wench departed, for another encounter might provoke further visions. After that, I returned inside, where I doused my rawness with many mugs of medicinal rum.

Just after the last orders bell, I glanced up from the bar to see a young rogue running away with my crates. Although my internal compass was rum-addled and my wheels were wobbling, the heaviness of the crates slowed the boy, and I caught him after a chase of less than a furlong.

My Papa used to tell me not to beat a man until you had given him three chances, for anyone could make a mistake or two and should be forgiven. But the rum had me in no mood to obey old sayings. Enraged, I gave the boy several hard clips – perhaps too strongly, but my nerves

24

were still threadbare from my earlier visions. The boy wasn't moving when I left him. Blood was flowing freely from his head, I think from a cut above his right eye, and probably his nose as well.

I retrieved my crates and returned to the Old Tavern for more rum, but they had closed the doors. No amount of thumping would change the barkeep's mind. I was livid at the time, but am now pleased that the barkeep stood his ground, for I had consumed ample liquor by then. By and by I relented and angrily returned to my ship, where fatigue eventually overpowered my anxiety and I passed out.

Friday 2 March

I slept restlessly and awoke early, with a pained head, as I always do after the visions. I roused myself, and although it was still dark I ventured toward the Olde Mitre - not to drink, but to check if the lad was still there. Although the scoundrel deserved punishment, I felt that I had given him too firm a beating, and I was worried that I may have killed him. I saw brown pools of dried blood on the ground, but was pleased to see that the boy had gone. I hope he recovered.

On my return through the docks, I saw a fishing boat that had a strange contraption hanging from its mast. I asked the vessel's Captain about it, and he told me that it was an instrument to predict the weather. This roused my interest, for although a good sailor can ride out a storm, a wiser sailor avoids it.

The Captain directed me to the merchant, a nearby purveyor of already-used navy equipment. Once at the *Naval Surplus Supply Company*, which was adjacent to the docks, I described the device to the store-keep. He showed me a brass tube with quicksilver[38] floating freely inside. He called it a "barometer". At first glance, this device reeked of trickery and magic that only a simpleton would believe, and I thought to pass on it. But the store-keep gave me a pamphlet explaining its uses, and after reading it I thought that it was worth a try, even though its science escaped me. I handed over sixpence, and then returned to my sloop where I fixed the barometer firmly on the mast, just below the mainsail boom[39], for convenient observation.

---

[38] *Quicksilver* was the old term for mercury, which is a liquid metal that was used in thermometers and barometers.

The hanging barometer prompted me to consider what other equipment I might need to access quickly, for I had packed everything tightly in the hold. I quickly realised that an enemy did not have to give warning of his approach, so it was important to store my weapon where I could quickly find it if needed. I duly mounted my scimitar discreetly near the base of the mast, from where I could access it in a trice[40].

I hope I don't ever need it in such a situation.

Tuesday 13 March

Today, I proudly declare that my ship is seaworthy, and is fit for any adventures that Mother Ocean cares to throw at her. For weeks I have laboured and have now completed my original list of tasks.

❖ I re-spliced the sheets and halyards[41] and refurbished the mast rigging.
❖ I rebuilt the galley oven brick by brick and added a small chimney to the main deck, which I crowned with a tight scuttle cap. The sloop's prior owner did not even try to keep the galley free of grease and smoke, so the addition of the outlet will keep the cooking quarters far cleaner.
❖ I created a safe area under the floorboards in the hold, into which I stashed my valuables.
❖ I even polished the bell.

I compiled a chest of bibs and bobs that I might need for repairs while at sea: plenty of spare rope, wire, leather, timber, nails, glue, canvas, &c[42]. I also packed an extra hull plank and even a spare bearer, although I hope that I do not need to use it; such a situation would be unthinkable.

---

[39] The *boom* was the horizontal spar to which the mainsail attached at the bottom. By moving the boom, the angle of the sail could be adjusted.
[40] A *trice* is a very short period of time; an instant.
[41] A typical ship has many ropes, each of which has a specific name. In fact the term "rope" is rarely used on a ship. For example, the *mainsheet* adjusts the angle of the mainsail by pulling on the boom, and a *halyard* lifts a sail up the mast, setting it in place.
[42] Etcetera

I also purchased a chest – a tarred waterproof box– in which I stored my tools after I had greased them and wrapped them in oilskin cloth. Now that my sloop was shored against the elements and prepared for all situations, I had just one remaining task: to make a name plate. But before I could formally christen her I had to choose a name. Perhaps *George IV* will do.

Wednesday 14 March

This morning, my water-wings dream returned. As before, a tar-black ocean pounded my sloop, but she did not crack. In my dreams, I stood on the deck as the full moon illuminated the crashing waves, their white tops lathering like a mad barber's foam before he swipes it away with a cold cutthroat[43]. I stood brazenly on the foredeck, braying at the storm, safe in the knowledge that my sloop was a fortress. Then the seething waves transformed into giant dragon-like wings and beat my little ship above the mutinous sea.

But then, just as the hull cleared the water, a colossal wave, larger than St Paul's dome[44], hit my sloop flush on her starboard[45] hull. The impact jolted me from my feet and I tumbled over the gunwale. As I plunged into the black ocean, dozens of giant sharks – those scourges of southern waters - surrounded me, menacing grins upon their evil faces. I had seen these creatures on my previous journeys through the oceans, so I had no wish to stay in the company of those devils any longer, not even in a dream. Mercifully, I awoke just before they attacked me.

Despite the cool of the morning, when I finally awoke my blanket was moist with sweat. As I lay uneasily, I wondered at the significance of my dream. It must have been another message from Providence that I

---

[43] A cutthroat was a straight edged razor (looking much like a modern knife) that folded into its handle. It was the standard implement for shaving until the invention of the safety razor by Mr. King Gillette in about 1900.

[44] McAdam was referring to St Paul's cathedral, which was by far the largest building in London at the time.

[45] The starboard is the right side of the ship when you are facing forward (i.e. toward the bow). The port side is on the left. In modern times each side is marked with light that is coloured either red (port) or green (starboard). These conventions can easily be remembered by the question "Is there any *red port left* in the wine cellar?"

should not ignore. After rising from my hammock and settling my uneasy condition with a bowl of oatmeal and several strong mugs of tea, the meaning of my dream slowly become apparent: I realised that I must remain vigilant of sharks. Many sailors have warned me of the dangers of these sea-devils in warmer waters, for they could cut a man in half with just a single bite of their ferocious jaws. I have heard that some of these monsters are longer than a horse and carriage.

After a month of work, I felt that I deserved some leisure time, so this morning I lay in my hammock until the dockers outside had stopped work for their mid-day bread. Later, I called on Mrs Harlesden for tea and she rewarded me with a healthy serving of pumpkin cake. While chatting I casually inquired about her visitors. She mentioned a few but none, thankfully, from the constabulary. As I departed she offered a warm hug, knowing that I might not return for years. I winced when she bid me "Goodbye, Mr Smith."

She is a beautiful lady, and I shall miss her dearly. She is almost like family to me.

After that I headed for the bridge, for despite my wish to depart soon, I felt I had earned half a day of rest. The sun had drawn the touts and lags from their holes and Billingsgate sprouted them like poppies on a summer field. I allowed them to draw me into their web, and even tipped a ha'penny into a tramp's hat in return for a recitation of two poems – ten stanzas of Coleridge[46] by my request, and a Shakespeare sonnet of his choosing.

In time I passed a small canvas tent. It was a bedraggled affair, threadbare and torn, but held the promise of a show of sorts inside. I parted with a silver penny, and took my seat on a wooden bench alongside two dozen other patrons.

The show was most entertaining. The performer, who called himself *The Astonishing Andrew, Amazing Animal Talker*, was accompanied by a dog called 'Smiles'. Thankfully this dog was not mangy, like the mutts who scavenged old soup bones from rubbish heaps, but was clean and

---

[46] The Coleridge poem was no doubt *The Rime of the Ancient Mariner,* an epic poem about a fantasy sea voyage. McAdam would not have known at the time, but his poem was an inspired choice - his journey would turn out to be just as fantastic as the old sailor's adventure.

sound. The performer called a series of instructions to the dog, who responded in kind. He was able to sit when asked, roll over, and even lie down. He correctly pointed his paw at a ball when asked, and then identified a pipe, a penny, and a handkerchief among items collected from the audience. At the end of the performance the dog calmly bared his teeth, thereby performing an impression of his name. I had never seen a wild animal perform such feats.

I was already satisfied that my penny was well spent, but The Astonishing Andrew had another act to follow. After a short interlude, he returned to the stage with a large grey bird perched on his shoulder. The bird was, he told us, from distant Africa, and was named 'Perty the Parrot'. The Astonishing Andrew then started talking to the Perty, whereupon the parrot replied in a human-sounding voice, much to the delight of the small crowd. To happy applause, The Astonishing Andrew carried on a conversation with Perty, with the bird responding to his questions. In hindsight I suspect a ruse, for the bird only uttered simple words such as *Yes*, *No*, *Perty want nuts* and *I'm Perty*. Yet by using only a dozen such bird phrases, The Astonishing Andrew maintained an amiable chatter with the bird, culminating in Perty declaring to the audience *I love you all*. The gratuity jar was filled by a dozen extra ha'pennies by the show's conclusion.

I passed the rest of the afternoon compiling a fishing kit. During a search through the market I found two bamboo fishing poles with wooden reels. I had time to engage in a lengthy haggle, and my patience was rewarded by a spool of trace wire for no extra cost. By the day's end I had also purchased a tin box complete with sinker moulds, lead sheets, 25 barbed hooks and a sharpening stone. From the same vendor I picked out ten Aberdeen flies[47] of various sizes, while from his neighbouring vendor I purchased two spools of Chinese silk fishing thread[48]. Although each line cost a hefty shilling, I could not break it

---

[47] The flies mentioned are artificial baits for fishing. They were traditionally made from small feathers, hair and beads tied around a small hook. When pulled through the water, the flies resemble baitfish or small insects. Aberdeen, which is on the mid-eastern coast of Scotland, is an area famous for fly fishing.
[48] Silk is one of the strongest natural fibres. Although it loses some strength when wet, it is very durable. Most 19th century attempts to raise silk worms in England failed, meaning that the British had to import their silk from China, making it very expensive.

with my arms, so at least my extravagance had value. A large fish can feed a man for many days, so hopefully my purchase will pay me back many times over.

The constituents of Mrs Harlesden's cake had long since passed, so I turned my attention to dinner. I started at a market stall with two small pork rolls. Just as I finished the second, I noted a delicious aroma from a nearby stall where a dark-skinned man was frying beef on a hot griddle. As I approached him the aroma grew, and soon overpowered even the nearby tannery. It was a sublime and unusual smell.

I asked him about the recipe and he told me that it was a blend of Indian spices called "Curry Powder". Although I had earned my keep transporting spices across the seas for many months, I had never smelled them combined in such harmony. I bought a plate of beef cooked in his "Curry Powder" with a spoonful of white rice, and enjoyed the fire and flavour it brought to my palate.

I returned to my sloop with the sun not yet dipped, but stopped short of the vessel at the sight of a uniformed plod at the dock head. I feared it was Sergeant G. Jones, who had enquired after me at Mrs Harlesden's bed-sit. For want of business I purchased *The Times*[49] and sat on a bollard[50]. Eventually the plod moved on. I still do not know if he was looking for me or not.

Thursday 15 March

My ocean-storm dream returned again last night – not twice but three times my nightmares repeated themselves. Throughout my restless sleep I battled the tar-black waves, hollering inside as I fell into the shark-infested water. Many times I stared deep into the manic jaws of those vile predators, waking with a gasp of air as they closed their razor-like teeth around me.

The dream returned for the fourth time as the first morning gull's cry echoed through the docks, and I watched as the wings finally grew from

---

[49] *The Times* newspaper was first published on 1 January 1788. It is still published today, and is now owned by the multinational media company NewsCorp.

[50] A *bollard* is a short, thick post for mooring boats

my ship and carried me away from the prowling sea devils. Suddenly I felt a sense of urgency. I sat up at once, sharply awake. My stomach was churning. I knew from the feeling in my bowels that I had barely a moment to get to the dockyard pit, which I made with only a trice to spare. As I squatted over the pit with the sickness leaving me, it came to me: a name for my ship. True, the setting for the revelation was most unromantic, but an ideal moniker was suddenly as clear as the southern skies in May.

By and by I completed my ablutions and returned to my sloop. Ceremoniously, I stood to her port side and proudly, like a father with his first-born, laid my right hand upon her hull. I then loudly stated: "I now christen thee... *Maris Alarum*". After splashing the bow with water, I added: "In the Latin of our forefathers, I declare that you have Wings of Water... *Maris Alarum.* "

Although there was nothing more than a puzzled tern looking on, I paused in showman style before adding, "May all who sail in you know good Providence, may you enjoy Mother Ocean's freedom, and most importantly, may your Water Wings set you free from your past."

Maris Alarum. Wings of water – just like in my dreams. Already I have grown to like it. "Maris" is almost a female name – it is admittedly not as sweet as is Elizabeth (I must stop thinking of her!) but is certainly more like a maiden's moniker than a knave's name. Yet her name barely matters, because my ship would be just as solid and beautiful if I had named her *Rotten Raven's Guts*.

The morning was still young, and my constitution had returned, as I registered my ship's name at the Maritime Authority. I signed my mark hesitantly, for the name Fintan McAdam now had a certified home, giving yet another clue as to my whereabouts for any plod looking to avenge their brother, the fallen warden.

Friday 16 March

Today I focused my energies on procuring equipment and provisions for my journey, for when this task is complete I can cast away; the sooner that occurs the better. I needed charts and navigational instruments, weapons, medicine, food and water. If I was able to find a provedore to

31

sell me a casket of good fortune – well, I would barter for that with everything except my soul.

Actually, I would not trade it for the *Maris Alarum* either. (In hindsight I see that my quill has made the same pledge twice for, like any true sea captain, my ship is now part of my soul and cannot be separated from it.)

I hailed a carriage and rode across town to the establishment of Mr P. Dollond[51], who was reputed to be a fine craftsman of navigational instruments. As soon as I strode through the doorway to his display room my eyes sprang wide and my jaw dropped, for it looked more like Aladdin's treasure cave than an instrument shop. I was like a child set free in Hamley's.[52]

Rows of shelving contained instruments laid out like museum antiquities, yet these pieces were not ancient but were shining, polished and new. Mr Dollond, no doubt acquainted with such a reaction, was not the least upset by my curiosity, and permitted me plenty of time to browse his goods before he introduced himself and enquired as to my purpose. Again I hesitated to use my birth name, particularly as the plod had shown his hand at the dock. But with my departure now so close at hand I felt that the slow machinations of the law would not catch me now, and I did not wish to confuse myself with my own moniker any longer.

"Mr McAdam, at your service."

---

[51] Peter Dollond (1731 - 1821) was an English maker of navigation instruments, who passed away soon after this very meeting with McAdam. He was most famous for his telescopes, which were admired worldwide for 150 years. Admiral Lord Nelson owned one, as did Captain James Cook. Dolland's business, started with his father John in 1750, merged in 1927 to form Dollond & Aitchison, which made spectacles. This company was eventually bought out by Boots Opticians in 2009, which currently has about 700 branches in the United Kingdom. Thus a pair of Boots eyeglasses can be traced back to the man who served Fintan McAdam in 1821!

[52] Hamley's is a famous toy shop that opened in 1760 on Holborn high St, London. It still operates today, and is now reputed to be the world's oldest and largest toy store.

"A pleasure to meet you, Mr McAdam," he replied in a slow voice, and added a bow so low that I could see the detail of his white hair. "Let's have some tea while you tell me of your needs. Robert!"

A boy appeared and was despatched for the brewing pot. He duly served us tea as I set about listing my requirements to my learned companion. He listened carefully, nodded occasionally and asked some questions regarding my ship, her intended route, and my expected departure and return dates. He stopped when I mentioned that my journey had no firm chronology. I would return, well, when I returned. He then seemed puzzled.

"What is the nature of your cargo?"

"Well, there's no specific haulage, Mr Dollond."

"Is the trip for scientific discovery? The likes of Mr Banks[53] have done famously well from their discoveries. Or are you chart making?" I slowly shook my head. "Then you must be a member of the Royal Geographical Society? Or are you chartering a wealthy benefactor to the antipodes[54]?"

"No, Sir," I replied, now feeling foolish for the general lack of endeavour to my plans. "I have no sponsor, nor am I a member of the Society."

Mr Dollond's brow now became more stern – an unwelcome development, for he had been very convivial until now.

"So your voyage is neither a cargo haul, nor a scientific voyage, nor for charting and you have no benefactor or sponsor. I pray then, Mr McAdam, please advise me as to the purpose of your travels."

I shifted in my seat, uneasy not only at his questions but at my sparse replies. I mumbled for the right words but could not formulate a clear answer. After an uncomfortable pause he stood from his chair and faced me, low and directly.

---

[53] Mr Dollond was referring to Sir Joseph Banks, a botanist who travelled on the southern voyages of Captain James Cook.
[54] *Antipodes* (pronounced an-tip-o-deez) means "the opposite side of the world".

"I ask you, Mr McAdam," he said in a low but firm voice as he looked squarely into my eyes, "to produce your privateer's licence or to leave at once[55]."

A-ha! My mind now formed some sense from the hubbub. He thought I was a pirate!

"Mr Dollond," I replied. "I'm not a privateer, and I promise you that I'm not a pirate either. I can see why you might have guessed this, but you must believe that my journey is simply to see what adventures Mother Ocean presents me."

Mr Dollond stood taller and straightened his tie. After a few ticks of the corner clock he sat, now a little easier, yet he still seemed unconvinced of my motives. "Go on."

The clock struck the quarter hour and then the half as I replayed my life at sea for this gentleman. My words flowed steadily, like a full river over a high waterfall. My desire for Mr Dollond to know my truth was so strong that my words tumbled out with rare freedom.

I told him of my years in the shipyards, tailing my papa with his tool bag, and how the sailors' stories in the timber yard had cultivated my yearning for the ocean. I recounted my two spice runs, originally as a deck hand and then as first mate, and confessed that these journeys had helped to soothe my soul after the untimely deaths of my parents. However I skirted mentioning my prison break and my subsequent flight to Liverpool as if they were jagged rocks in the shallows. Nor could I bring myself to tell him about Beth and the horrible visions that I hoped to escape. My story finished with the reminder that I was not a pirate and had no inclination towards that life, but that I simply now wished to see the wondrous world for its own sake.

Mr Dollond's red-rimmed eyes fixed me with a low stare. In my rough duffel coat, with no hat and old boots, I was now feeling like I did when I sat before that dung-beetle Peabody at the Bank of England. Mr Dollond rubbed his chin. Would I regret telling my own name and tale with such honesty? I sat unmoving, not wishing to bump the mood with even a sip of tea.

---

[55] A *privateer* was a sailor who was authorised by the government to do battle with the enemy, or to take riches from other vessels for the "benefit of the kingdom" - in other words, a "legalised" pirate.

"Your tale is charming, Mr McAdam."

I stilled my shoulders so that my sigh would not betray my relief.

"It will be gratifying to do business with such an open heart as yours, knowing that my instruments will find a good home. Let us now provide for ... I am sorry, but what is the name of your ship?"

I again felt sheepish, for no-one (except a single tern) had yet heard my sloop's name.

"It's the *Maris Alarum*."

"Wings of Water," he replied after a short pause in which to think; he was clearly familiar with the old Latin. "Wings of water to fly you across the oceans. A fitting title."

We smiled, for we now understood each other's position. So it was, as the clock struck four, that I left Mr Dollond's suite carrying three crates.

The pride of my new collection was a fine sextant[56]. This magnificent piece was more like an artist's creation than a navigation tool. It had a green lacquered base and a handle carved from rich elm. Mr Dollond assured me that with skilled use I could make my latitude[57] to within three furlongs, and that with this sextant in hand I would never be lost. I hope he is correct.

We had a lengthy discussion on my options for measuring longitude. Mr Harrison's chronometers[58] had proved their worth. His timepieces lost

---

[56] A *sextant* was a navigational instrument that allowed the user to measure the angle of a celestial body - such as the moon, sun or stars - from the horizon. This angle, when combined with other data, could be used to plot the ship's position.

[57] *Latitude* was the ship's north-south position. By contrast, it's *longitude* was its east-west position. Latitude was relatively easy to determine with a sextant, because when a celestial body was directly overhead it was at the same latitude as the observer, which could be read off a chart. However, longitude was devilishly difficult to establish and it took centuries, and some of the greatest scientific minds, to develop a reliable method.

[58] John Harrison (1693 – 1776) was an English clockmaker. He invented the marine chronometer, the first device that kept accurate time at sea. Having a sea clock on home-port time was vital because it solved the problem of establishing a ship's longitude. By referring to the clock when it was noon locally (i.e. when the Sun was at its highest) and comparing to home-port time

only one second per day at sea and were barely as big as a dinner plate! Unfortunately my dwindling purse meant that I had to pass upon a Harrison clock, or even a cheaper imitation. Mr Dollond also mentioned Maskelyne's[59] lunar method but, with four hours calculation and innumerable charts to consult to establish a position, it seemed too complex for a simple adventurer. In the end we decided that it would be best to estimate my longitude by dead reckoning[60]. To this end I purchased a log float and a sandglass timer[61].

I also purchased other navigation aids that all bore the fine workmanship of Mr Dollond: a mariner's compass with an extra loadstone, a sounding lead for measuring depth, and a chart of the world that included the tracks of Captain James Cook's voyage - he was such a master cartographer that I am assured of its accuracy.

I tipped the carriage driver a full penny, for he was very helpful in unloading the boxes. I carefully stowed them in the port hold, because it is well known that a docked ship that tilts to starboard foreshadows an unlucky voyage.

After that I retired to Blackfriars for a meal. What a fine spread it was: slices of oatmeal-stuffed hog's head, potatoes and even some green beans. My belly is thickening by the day.

---

you could determine your position. The problem of establishing time at sea was so important that in 1714 the British Government offered a prize of £20,000 (about US$5 million today) for a solution. Following a protracted battle, and after producing four versions of his incredible clock, Harrison finally collected the prize in his 80th year.

[59] Nevil Maskelyne (1732-1811) was a British Royal Astronomer who devised a complex method of determining longitude at sea using precise observation, many calculations and complex charts. He was also trying to win the longitude prize, but was trumped by Harrison's clock.

[60] *Dead reckoning* was simply measuring the speed and direction of the vessel and then charting the outcomes, giving an estimate of position. It was simple but very inaccurate, especially over long journeys; once you lost your position it could not be pinpointed until a known landmark was sighted..

[61] A *log float* with a thin line attached was thrown over the stern of the vessel. As the boat sailed away from the float, the navigator could determine its speed by measuring the length of line payed out in a given period, as measured by a sand glass timer. To facilitate this measurement the line was knotted at intervals, which gave rise to the maritime term for speed: *knots*.

Monday 19 March

I took a long morning walk to the Covent Garden Square[62]. Over the previous three days, I had sourced food and other provisions for my journey. I estimated that a three-month supply would be sufficient, with wild game, birds and fish supplementing my stores. I had not purchased any goods so far but had instead debated the quality and price with merchants, and intended to place orders once I had settled all other preparations. That day was rapidly drawing near. Using a graphite and clay pencil (I have never used such an implement before - it is very handy – I will pack one for my voyage[63]) I steadily compiled a list of suppliers and merchants.

I found prices agreeable at Covent Garden Square, especially when compared to the scoundrels at Brick Lane and Camden. By noon I was satisfied that my requirements had been met, and so I placed orders with more than a dozen merchants.

I ambled back to the riverbank and was content to lie on a grassy slope and watch the terns and gulls scrap for food. By and by I was heartened by the sun's appearance through the fog, sporting enough authority that I could even remove my jacket. As I did an unexpected shilling piece fell from its pocket. Mrs Harlesden - the reverse swipe!

Unfortunately my quiet rest drew out a memory: *Beth reclining upon this very riverbank. Her dress is white, and her dark hair curls across her cheeks. She laughs at my anecdote –her tinkling, cascading laugh – but as always in my dreams the sound is muffled, as though she was laughing from under a blanket. For the first time I realise that I love this woman.* The memory amplifies, and becomes a vision. Suddenly Beth is lying next to me, here and now. The vision is so sweet that I hesitate to let it go, but I know what will happen next: *her face contorts in pain and I hear her screams. I see her lying on the leafy woodland floor as her lips turn blue...her blood pooling on the ground around her....*

---

[62] Covent Garden is now a busy market area in London. In 1821 the market stalls had just started establishing themselves.

[63] Although crude forms of the pencil had been around for many decades, they did not become practical until the early 1800s.

I stood quickly, and focused my energies on the gulls and terns to rid myself of the horrid visions. I fought for many ticks of the clock before the apparition faded, and after much angst I steeled myself to move onward, away from that grassy bank forever.

But I know it is only a chime of Big Ben before another vision assaults me. I cannot relax in London, for every landmark has a memory attached to it, and every memory soon turns into a nightmarish apparition. At sea, there will be nothing to strike these evil dreams. At sea, I will be at peace from her ghost. At sea, I can forget her forever.

To douse the pain I headed straight to Blackfriars, at times breaking into a run such was my haste to wash out the agony of Beth's death. I shunned food, for my mind needed calming more than my belly. I quaffed a good few measures of rum in succession, and then stayed on imbibing slowly for many hours before I fell asleep at a table. I didn't wake even as the barkeep dragged my slumbering body to the roadside and dumped me there, he later told me, like an old bag of charcoal. The morning gulls were about their business by the time I awoke, freezing, and staggered my way back to my ship. I must have fallen, because I now have a large bloodied lump on my head, and my left shoulder and wrist are painful and bruised.

Tuesday 20 March

I took an afternoon coach ride to the premises of Mr Edward Jenner, apothecary[64]. He was an old man who moved very slowly, but he nevertheless assisted me in compiling a chest full of medicines. Unfortunately he had no potions to cure an over-indulgence of rum (I could have used some immediately) but for my journey he suggested a new concoction called *quinine*[65]. Mr Jenner put a small drop on my tongue - it tasted vile - but he assured me that those in the far empire

---

[64] An *apothecary* is an old term for a pharmacist. Edward Jenner (1749-1823) was instrumental in the early development of vaccines, having been involved in research on smallpox and cowpox.

[65] *Quinine* was a drug treatment for malaria. It first appeared in medicines in the 17th century and remained the drug of choice until the 1940s. Originally dispensed as ground bark from the *cinchona* tree, it was isolated and named only in 1820, demonstrating that Mr Jenner was very up-to-date in his knowledge.

had used it to prevent malaria, and suggested that I should take five drops in sweetened water every day. Perhaps, he offered, I could mix a little with some gin[66].

He also recommended a medical almanac written by Dr G. Blane[67] that I could consult if sickness overcame me on my journey. While returning in the coach with my purchases, I chanced upon a page in Dr Blane's book with a recommendation on scurvy. It said that the Captain of the *Suffolk* in 1795 had dosed the ship's rum with lemon juice and had not a single case of the malady on the entire journey.

Heeding the good doctor's advice, this afternoon I procured eighteen four-gallon jugs of rum. I also purchased five lemons, quartered them, and then pressed a slice into each rum jug. To the amusement of the barkeep at Blackfriars, who suggested that I was heading for a lousy Wednesday morning, I also bought six large crocks of gin. I divided the quinine and tipped an equal portion into each gin crock. The taste of both the rum and the gin was unpleasant, almost stinging, but if they prevented my teeth falling out from scurvy, and halted the rigors from the ravages of malaria, then I would just have to take my medicine.

By the early evening my condition had improved, so I walked to merchants *Tatham and Egg's* under a dark wintery sky. After a short wait I was attended by Mr Egg, who wasn't a chicken farmer as his name suggested, but rather a weapons merchant[68]. Perhaps he came into this line of work to defend himself from slurs and insults, for his bald head did in many ways resemble his name.

Although his strange accent made him difficult to understand, Mr Egg was an agreeable fellow. He sold me two fine pistols with which I could defend myself from pirates if necessary. Their stocks were carved from

---

[66] Quinine was often mixed with sweetened water to hide its bitter taste. English colonials drank this "tonic water" to ward off malaria, and later started mixing it with gin. This drink quickly gained widespread popularity, and is now known as, of course, *gin and tonic*.

[67] Sir Gilbert Blane (1749 –1834) was a Scottish physician who initiated health reforms in the Royal Navy. In 1795, on his advice, the entire navy used lemon juice to prevent scurvy. For the return journey they sourced limes from the Caribbean. For this reason, "limey" became a slang term for a British person.

[68] Mr Durs Egg (1748–1831) was a Swiss-born British gun maker. He was most famous for his flintlock pistols.

walnut while their muzzles, cocks and triggers were cast in iron. To prevent rust I would have preferred silver components, but my purse was already stretched too far. Mr Egg also sold me 1600 pennyweight[69] of black powder and ten cases of cast iron shot. He demonstrated a method in which he pre-loaded both pistols with powder and shot, and then tied them to either end of a scarf before hanging them around my neck. This arrangement would allow me to fire two shots in succession before having to repack the muzzles.

Mr Egg told me that he had, on order, a pistol that held six shots in a revolving caddy that did not require re-packing. When I expressed my scepticism, he explained that the black powder was actually held within the shot. Incredible! He called it a *revolver*[70], and added that if I wished to return in 60 days he would be demonstrating its use to a gathering of gentlemen. Unfortunately I had to decline his kind invitation as my cast-off was imminent.

I signed my mark for the pistols, now using McAdam by default. I am increasingly worried that my name is about the town on too many papers. I must cast off soon, for to delay any longer is to invite the devil to dinner.

Wednesday 21 March

From the first hint of light in the dawning sky, I was busy organising my provisions. It did not go well. My cussing began before sun up and continued without a pause until sunset. Of the dozen or so suppliers with whom I had placed orders, most failed to deliver as promised.

❖ The butcher had supplied 60 lbs of pickled pork in jars, rather than salted in crates. He should have known that glass jars are ill-suited to ocean life, for the swaying and clanking of a vessel can crack them.

❖ The baker supplied 50 large loaves, not small buns. Even worse, he charged me for the large loaves even though I did not order them. What am I to do with 50 large loaves? They will be stale and mouldy before I have eaten a fraction of them. Only the baitfish will be pleased with this scoundrel of a baker.

---

[69] 1600 pennyweight is about 1.5 kilograms.
[70] The first revolver was made by Elisha Collier in Boston in 1814.

❖ The flour was poorly ground and milled, and was stored in a sack so worn and threadbare that not even the dullest weevil would have trouble in bypassing it.

❖ The oatcakes[71] were as succulent as a London brick. I shall need to boil them in brine before eating them or I will surely crack a tooth.

❖ The yeast arrived poorly packed, and would surely have gone off before time. To remedy this I encased it in many layers of greaseproof paper, each tied with string and wiped with a coating of lard, to keep it dry and viable.

Only the beef, salt, vinegar, tea, oil and sugar arrived as requested. The sauerkraut was passable, but I nevertheless added a gallon of vinegar and a pound of salt to the crocks. From Billingsgate market I procured some raisins, cheese and peas, and a half-pound jar of Curry powder from the dark-skinned merchant.

I purchased six large sacks of coal from a vendor near the dock so that I did not have to pay a carriage driver to cart them, even though they cost sixpence extra.

I paid three lads a full penny each to collect and cut me a dozen crates of stout timber braches, as I planned to use wood rather than coal for simple fires to boil water and the like, especially during warmer months when the cabin had no need for heating. They also collected a large box of pine cones for tinder. However the firewood was green, and when I split some of the braches they oozed sap, and most of the pinecones were so fresh that they were still closed, with their seeds still inside. I shall have to dry them for a month before they are useful.

Twice I traipsed to Covent Garden Square to remonstrate with a merchant. On the next occasion that I sail the oceans I will use a good provedore, for my boot leather, like my temper, is frayed from the exertion.

Thursday March 22

---

[71] *Oatcakes*, also known as hardcakes, were a staple food on many early sea voyages. These plain, tough biscuits were made from oats, fat and salt, and despite their poor taste they had good longevity and provided nutrition.

Despite the aggravation of the yesterday's labours, I slept as soundly as a winter fox. I therefore knew that my preparations were complete, for the sleeping heart often perceives what the awakened mind cannot.

With my main tasks now finished, I made one final bow to the mother country and to Providence: I scooped a good portion of earth into an oilskin cloth and tied it tightly, sealing a small part of England to take with me upon my journey. Not only would this provide an extra ounce of luck, but would remind me where my heart lay no matter how far the winds pushed me from home.

I informed the harbourmaster of my imminent departure, which I planned for the first northerly change, hopefully within a day or two. With the wind at a firm sou'easter, I had the morning at my leisure. While wandering around outside the dock, I passed the *Naval Surplus Supply Company* from which I had purchased the barometer. A chance view through the window landed my gaze on a display reading: *Fisherman's Friend now available*. I was a sailor and adventurer, not a fisherman precisely, but if this "friend" was a better mousetrap for sea creatures then I was happy to loan it a minute's attention.

I greeted the shop keep as an acquaintance, and he enquired if I had managed to understand the barometer. I told him that it was proving itself very useful (not quite true) and asked him about the 'Fisherman's Friend'. It turned out that the device was simply a thick corset of cork, which, when strapped around the chest, allowed the user to float on the water[72]. A fleeting glimpse of the wicked black ocean and spitting whitecaps from my dreams convinced me of its value. I parted with a hefty five pennies for the Fisherman's Friend. It was soon to prove that even five pounds would have been a bargain.

Although it was only March, I then headed to a nearby bath-house[73]. Once I set sail, my opportunities to bathe would be limited, so it made sense to have a long cleansing tub before my departure. The proprietoress expressed surprised that a customer was knocking at her door so early in the year, and remarked that I was her first bather for the season. It took her some time to heat the water, during which I

---

[72] In England in 1821, virtually nobody was able to swim.

[73] In the early 1800s, most people bathed only once or twice per year, usually at the start of spring in April or May. This practice gave birth to the tradition of May weddings.

enjoyed a whole plum cake at Blackfriars. After finally immersing myself in the warm waters, I wallowed in it until my fingers were furrowed like raisins.

After the tub, I planned to return my Fisherman's Friend to the *Maris Alarum,* and then retreat to Blackfriars for a long game of whist. It wouldn't matter if I lost because my remaining pound notes were of little value on my travels, yet if I won it would provide one last measure of good luck. But as I entered the shipyards, the sight of a uniformed constable scuppered my fine plans.

"Good day, Sir," said the plod as I passed him at the entrance.

"Good day to you, Constable," I remarked and doffed my hat.

"Might I have a minute of your day?"

"Of course you may, good Sir," I replied, wishing that my throat could form any words but those.

"Might I enquire as to your name?"

"It is Smith, sir. Mr John William Smith. And please tell me, Constable, your name."

"Sergeant Gareth Jones, from the London Constabulary."

My heart flapped like a fish in a bucket, then stopped, and then flapped again.

"Your papers?"

"I don't have them with me, Sir, as I am just retiring for lunch. If you have the patience I can fetch them for you, although my lodging is some distance away."

"And where is that?"

"I live in a bedsit at Mrs Harlesden's Inn, across the fields from Chancery Lane." As soon as those words left my throat I wanted to suck them back, but alas, one cannot withdraw what another has already heard. Sgt Jones, I am sure, sensed my lie, and he stepped sideways to locate himself across the dockyard gates to bar my exit.

"Just yesterday I enquired after Mr J.W. Smith at those very premises, but was informed that the gentleman had terminated his lease. Are you the same Mr J.W. Smith, or should I consider it fate to have met a man with the same name who moved there only today?"

My mind caught a glimpse of Shepton Mallot: the guard's arm cracking as he fell in my pursuit ... the shots ricocheting off the wall as I scrambled over it ... the posters of my likeness that adorned the lamp-posts for the next month ... my eventual dash to the relative freedom of Liverpool. The fish inside my chest flapped again.

Jones stepped closer to me, and became terse. "Mr Smith," he said, now with his head arching back at a small tilt, "do you have the acquaintance of Mr Fintan McAdam?"

If I needed a sounding-lead weight I could have ripped out my heart and used it instead, for it now felt so heavy that my knees nearly gave under the load. But in the face of this pressure I called upon my days as an actor in Liverpool, and put on a performance of innocence.

"No. Not at all, Sir. I have never heard of McAdam, I'm afraid. But I bid you a pleasant day, Sergeant Jones, for my stomach tells me that I am late for lunch."

He paused, and looked at me with clear misgivings.

"Do you have any knowledge of the vessel *Maris Alarum*? I understand that she is docked close to here."

"I'm sorry, Sergeant Jones, but I haven't heard of this vessel, although I applaud her Latin name. She would be called *Wings of Water* in the King's English." I hoped my high language would demonstrate my intellect, and therefore make him more inclined to believe my story than if I was a common street scoundrel.

"But you've never heard of this ship?"

"No sir."

"Well then, sir, I wish you good-day."

Good day? I borrowed my whist-playing face and stilled my eyebrows in case they revealed my game, because an obvious sign of relief from me now would surely heighten his suspicions. Sergeant Jones did not move from the gate, so, rather than rock the rowboat, I wished him good day and walked further into the shipyards. My breathing slowed with every step but I dared not look back in fear of prompting more conversation.

"McAdam!"

I heard my name yelled loudly and turned on instinct. Before I had barely twitched I realised my error, but my sudden movement had revealed the truth. Jones, if not before, now knew my lies. He started toward me, brandishing his truncheon and hollering like a navvy.

"Halt! In the name of the King, I command you to halt!"

I had no intention of halting. I bolted through the shipyards dodging bollards, rope coils and old crates. The shrill screech of Jones's whistle rang out across the bay, alerting nearby plod that a criminal was at large. Quickly my options for escape narrowed, so I turned left toward the dockyard wall, hoping for a break in its length. I followed the wall for a furlong, and although it was constructed to keep the night-time rascals *outside* the shipyard, it did a fine job of keeping me *inside*. I turned to see that Jones had gained ground on me. Clearly the name *plod* was a misnomer because Jones scooted like a hare.

Bereft of better options, I scampered down toward the riverbank, along the line of piers, hoping to flank around Jones and head back toward the exit. The sight of three blue uniforms in the distance soon upended this plan – I had no chance of escape through the dockyard gate. The plod now had me truly cornered, so I turned seaward onto the nearest jetty. I don't know why I did this, because it went nowhere but toward the icy Thames, but in the flame of the moment it seemed a better route than toward my pursuers.

I pressed further out along the jetty like a rat up a blocked drainpipe. Jones slowed to a walk, for he knew that I had nowhere else to run. I glanced across and could see the *Maris Alarum* at the next pier, patiently awaiting my return. But she may as well have been in the Antipodes, for I had no way of reaching her except to walk on the water. If only she could sprout her wings now!

Jones now had me trapped at the far head of the jetty. He stood at its foot, barring my path to liberty. His backup soon arrived and all four men advanced toward me, brandishing their truncheons with menace and grisly smirks upon their faces. The plod did not look kindly upon those who broke the arms of their kin.

If I descended from the heights of the Heavens to the depths of Hell, I could scarcely fall further than the fate that now awaited me. To be but

45

a northerly puff away from sailing the open leagues of the oceans, but then to be incarcerated in a clink where freedom is measured in feet - no man has yet been born who could handle the stop at the end of that fall.

But how to escape? I could not swim or walk on water. I could not run. I could not fly. So my only chance was to wrestle the four large, armed policemen who were now just yards away. I was fair with my fists, and could handle myself in a stoush, but my chance of winning this battle was nil. But I knew that I had to fight like a rabid fox hound, for the stakes – my freedom, my future, my life - were impossibly high.

I glanced about for a weapon – perhaps some cast off timber, or a rusty yard of chain. It was then that I saw, in my own hand, wrapped in a brown paper bag ... a possibility. It would not make me fly nor walk on water, and although I could not swim it *would* make me ... float.

I quickly strapped the Fisherman's Friend around my chest. With barely a moment to spare, I plunged over the jetty into the freezing Thames below. An icy flare hit my heart. My lungs were shocked to a halt and only started, by and by, with a groaning gasp of air. My legs were instantly as stiff as an old lead pipe and my arms cramped, twisting into my chest. The plod taunted me from the pier.

"Are you swimming to Van Diemen's Land[74], McAdam?"

"Is your bath quite warm?" shouted another.

I had seen on my travels some natives, those in the Antipodes especially, who had learnt to swim through the water like fish. Unfortunately, I was not one of those people; I swam like an anchor. But with the cork brace around my chest at least I did not sink like a sounding lead, and could breathe. I forced my arms free of my chest and then moved them, as I had seen the natives do, to propel myself away from the dock.

I did not know if it was the movements of my arms or the eddy currents through the dockyards, but I slowly put some distance between the jetty and myself. The plod continued to laugh and seemed content to wait at the pier, knowing the water would conquer me soon.

---

[74] Van Diemen's Land was an early name for the Australian island of Tasmania.

"Your game is up, McAdam," yelled Jones. "You'll soon drown. Or freeze. I'd rather see you in the clink for ten winters than flotsam[75] upon the Thames." With that he cast a rope in my direction. "Take the rope and we'll haul you in. It's a better fate than what awaits you in Hades[76]." I had no more thoughts of grabbing that rope than of voluntarily putting my neck through a hangman's noose.

I soon figured that if I floated on my side, I could propel myself by reaching out through the water and then pulling down my arms. My chest was heaving and my feet were numb, but I knew something that Jones and his cronies had not yet reckoned: the *Maris Alarum* bobbed just 100 yards away, patiently awaiting my arrival like a trusty steed. Harder and harder I pulled my arms, as the plod, like a drunken posse, grew more rambunctious as they sensed me weakening from the struggle.

"Take care of the eels, McAdam."

"Is your name McAdam, or McMad-man?"

"Your corpse will make fine fodder for the Thames crabs, McAdam."

Although they cast the rope again, I ignored it, for my freedom for the next 15 years was the price to pay if I grasped it. I distantly heard them planning to row out to collect my corpse. Although my arms now felt like they were made of junket[77], I continued to grab and pull my arms through the water as though I was climbing a ladder: reach out right, reach out left, pull down right, pull down left. I repeated this mantra with every stroke: Reach right, reach left, pull right, pull left. Slowly and without further fanfare from the plod, I made my way across the harbour.

My legs were pained and numb, but I found that by keeping them fluttering it helped my course. My breathing became as heavy as a labouring sow, but I dared not pause because I feared that I would seize like a greaseless motor. Instead I turned onto my other side and continued stroking against the water. My mind could now countenance nothing but this rhythm. Reach and pull. Reach, pull. Reach. Pull.

---

[75] *Flotsam* means wreckage floating on the water, for example after a ship wreck. In contrast, *jetsam* is what has been thrown from a sinking ship.
[76] *Hades* is another term for Hell.
[77] *Junket* is milk jelly

My memories of the next few minutes are foggier than a pea-souper. My head spins and my sensibilities fly away like an autumn kite. I hear yelling, and I see a blue blur of plod start to run along the dockyard foreshore. Jones yells at me again, but his words are grey and distant. I reach and pull, reach and pull. Now they turn toward the pier. Whistles blow. I pull, I reach. My lower legs cramp and lock tight. I cannot use them. Despite the Fisherman's Friend, my head bobs below the surface like a dunking apple. My lungs inhale not air but the fetid Thames water. I roll onto my back. I cough out brown fluid, and then suck in some wheezing air.

Reach and pull. My left arm curls to my chest and refuses my orders for further service. With my right arm, I reach and pull. I yell inwardly: reach and pull.

Suddenly, I am bobbing below the pier. *Maris Alarum* is close. With a spinning head, I seek a timber bearer. My hands slide off. I pull again and with hidden strength I drag my carcass onto it. I cling to a post and wrench myself to sitting. My head collides with a post and a large splinter digs into my cheek. I feel the warm blood course down my neck.

I must stand. I reach for the pier deck and my right arm finds a bollard. I cling to it like a barnacle, but my feet kick freely through the air. I pull against the bollard, but do not have the strength to lift myself up, even if a shark was snapping at my toes. I pull again, but rise not even an inch.

My feet kick the pylons and I gain a little traction in a nook. I jam my boot into the crevice and then push down. My ankle turns sideways, but I load my weight upon it anyway. I hear my foot crack, but strangely I feel no pain. I stand on my twisted foot and pull again on the bollard. Somehow, I roll onto the pier.

The plod have turned and are now on the jetty. I now see a many-legged creature charging at me. A blue-grey monster. It is angry.

The blood from my cheek wells up in my eyes, and my lids stick together. I can barely see. Crawling, I make my way across the pier to my ship's stern tether. I feel for the rope - it is tied around a cleat. My numb hands work to loosen the knots, but in their cramped and frozen state they just will not work. Two half hitches, I tell myself, just two half hitches. I fumble. I curse. I fumble some more. My fingers work but cannot prise the knot. I am two half hitches from freedom, but to my blue fingers they are like Gordian knots[78].

The jetty-boards vibrate with the hoof beats of the plod-monster as it gallops nearer. Through bloodied eye-slits I see it hurling and seething and cussing. I now see its separate heads and arms.

I lurch forward and tumble over the gunwales onto the deck. My last chance. I reach out blindly, swinging my arms through the air. Soon they thud against the boom and I follow it to the mast, where my hands grope until they close around my scimitar. I pull it from its sheath. Its hilt feels good in my palm. It gives me strength.

I force my eyes open. The plod-monster now has separate legs and arms and heads and eyes. I turn and find myself at the bow. Two hacks and the *Maris Alarum*'s bow tether is gone. Her bow drifts from the dock as I tumble to her stern. I have one more rope to cut. One short rope stands between me and the freedom of the sea; between me and years of the stench and savagery of Shepton. I collapse forward, my whole body thrusting down through the scimitar, down through the rope. The force of the impact knocks the sword from my hand. I find the strength to look up. The final tether has been cut.

I lay. Exhausted. Unable to move. The current drifts the ship a few yards from the dock. The plod-monster arrives, splitting into four separate ogres. One jumps. He hits the gunwale and plunges into the Thames. Hollering. Howling. A rope is cast. The *Maris Alarum* drifts another few yards. A baton hits the deck beside me and clatters across it. Another hits my leg, hard, but I see this, not feel it.

In a blind daze, I tug at the halyard rope and somehow raise the mainsail. A puff of breeze swells it. *Maris Alarum* yaws. I crawl to the whipstaff[79] and turn her to the east. The plod scream and cuss. The Thames current courses me away. The cussing fades and fades and fades. It is gone.

I lie upon the deck, nothing visible but a red slit of sunlight, and listen to the sound of the loose sails flapping in the breeze. I swear I can hear the

---

[78] The Gordian knot was a mythical knot that was reputedly impossible to disentangle. Alexander the Great eventually "solved" the puzzle of the knot by simply cutting it with his sword.

[79] The *whipstaff* was the stick used to steer the vessel

beats of giant wings. Giant wings, beating, and flying me away to freedom. I am leaving London - the plod, the prison, and my pained memories - behind.

Friday 23 March (Ed: see footnote below[80])

Lat: (R) 51.28°N Long: (R) 1.78°E   Heading: W

It was light when the sharp pain in my cheek finally awoke me. I lay in my hammock, naked except for the blanket that covered me, with vague memories of my escape cascading through my head: desperately trying to stay awake to steer my ship out through the Thames ... waking up, freezing, my hand fixed so tightly around the whipstaff that it pained my fingers ... bawling shouts as the *Maris Alarum* drifted from a true course, twice into other vessels and once, I have a vague notion, into a bridge pylon.

My slumber was more misery than rest: the cold was deep and wet, and a searing pain stabbed my cheek every time my head moved even an inch. At the time I thought the pain was an evil impost, and I flailed at it many times in my dreams. But now I see that it helped my cause by waking me often, ensuring I steered a truer course than had I slept soundly.

The stars had told me it was near midnight as I sailed past Southend-on-sea and into the channel. I did not have the wherewithal to adjust my bearing, but simply dropped the running anchor in the middle of the North Sea and slept.

The midmorning sunlight was radiating through the hatch. My body felt painful all over, and I was so tired it was as if I had not slept at all. Yet a sense of liberty swelled within me, fuelled by the knowledge that the plod could not catch me here. They would be better to search for a grain of salt at the Blackpool beach than one little sloop on the seven

---

[80] Each of McAdam's log entries at sea begins with date, position and heading data. The (R) symbol prefacing latitude and longitude readings stands for "Reckoned" i.e. estimated, as opposed to (Obs) for observed with a sextant. McAdam deduced longitude by extrapolating his speed and bearing and hence was usually reckoned, except when sighting known landmarks. McAdam's entries also routinely included weather and other nautical observations, which I have omitted for simplicity.

seas. Emboldened by that thought, I felt it was time to set a proper course and to formally embark on my journey.

That task, of course, required that I leave the confines of my hammock. But the instant my right foot hit the cabin floorboards I knew that something was wrong. At first it felt like my ankle had driven itself into a loose nail, but a closer inspection revealed severe purple bruising, reminding me of the searing crack as I had hauled myself onto the pier.

Wincing, I hobbled toward my medicine kit and set about making a compress. What a poor first taste of liberty! After consulting Dr Blane's almanac, I combined, in equal parts, chloroform, sassafras oil and alconite root[81]. I added a dash of iodine and then shook the mixture in a stoppered flask. I soaked a rag in this liniment and then went to bandage the compress to my swollen foot, but discovered that in the haste of my departure I had forgotten a supply of crepe cloth. I limped to the general spares and rummaged out a bolt of canvas, from which I cut half a yard. By tearing it into strips that I sewed together with a round sail-makers needle and some Chinese silk thread, I formed a serviceable bandage, and soon had the liniment compress in place.

My attention now turned to my cheek, which had throbbed throughout the night. The tin looking-glass in my quarters reflected the grisly truth: my face was splattered in black-brown blood, with a splinter the size of my finger lodged upward into my right cheek. A mere inch of soft flesh separated me from a life with a pirate's eye patch.

I hobbled to fetch a pair of pliers, on the return downing a full mug of rum. The spirit soon did its duty and I was suitably fortified. With one sharp pull the splinter was out. I dipped a sail-makers needle into the remaining rum and scraped it around the wound, removing three shards. Then I dipped a rag into the liniment and held it over the laceration for a count of twenty. The concoction was far more painful than the original splinter, but I knew that it was necessary to kill the poisons, so I persisted. By the time I had finished my treatment, my brow was sweating as if it was a summer's day in Hyde Park[82].

---

[81] Such ingredients were common in first aid kits of the day. A medicine-soaked compress was seen as the cure for most conditions, regardless of their origin.
[82] Hyde Park is a large garden park in central London. It opened to the public in 1637.

Yesterday's clothes lay like fouled dishrags on the cabin floor. Rusty blood caked my vest. I pumped some seawater into a galley pot and then washed the whole suit clean. I strung some rope between two bearers, just behind the galley oven, and hung all three pieces to dry. I donned my spare vest and jacket and a fresh pair of canvas breeches. With great effort I pulled on my boots, whereupon a short walk convinced me of their value in splinting my foot.

I gingerly climbed the ladder to the deck. My right leg was little help – it could bear no more weight than a fleeting touch - and my arms felt blue and green from yesterday's exertions, so the climb was that of an aged widower. When I finally emerged upon deck I creaked myself upright, although I tilted to starboard because of my foot.

The sun poked out from behind a cloudbank. It revealed that it was already after noon, meaning I had missed the sun's zenith for my first observation of latitude. Already my navigation is untidy!

A fortuitous nor'-easterly wind change caught the mainsail and it filled to billowing. I pulled upon the headsail halyard and set it wing-to-wing[83] with the mainsail, sending my sloop skimming across the white tops. Although my body was wracked with pains from crown to base, I felt as grand as a Lord in his castle. For I was now truly *Captain* McAdam, commander-in-chief of the *Maris Alarum*. I set the rudder for sou'-west, destination adventure. Despite my deep fatigue, my spirits soared as I left London, and its achingly awful memories, behind.

Saturday 24 March

Lat: (Obs) 49.45°N   Long: (R) 0.4°E   Heading: SW

I headed down the French coastline, making good progress. The *Maris Alarum*, with her newly tarred hull and not even a barnacle to stall her, sliced through the water like an eel through the Thames.

---

[83] A *wing-to-wing* sail configuration is used when sailing directly downwind: the mainsail is set on one side of the boat and the headsail at the other. This configuration is now more commonly known as 'butterfly wing'.

Most of the day I spent in the galley, for in the haste of my departure I had left a few tasks unfinished. I organised the provisions so that usable portions were readily at hand so that I did not have to retreat to the holds for every small convenience.

I anchored overnight about half a league[84] from the Normandy port of Le Havre. I had no desire to go ashore, instead just wanting a good night's sleep more than boisterous company, particularly as that company spoke a foreign tongue.

Sunday 25 March

Lat: (Obs) 49.45°N   Long: (Obs) 2.52°E   Heading: SW

I woke after a long and restful sleep. By and by I weighed anchor and made for the Island of Guernsey.

My foot and cheek still pained me, but by the afternoon the ache was leaving my arms. I had not yet changed the compress on my foot, mainly for the fear of removing my boot. Twice daily I bathed my cheek in the liniment; this was an awful task because it stung like a devil's pitchfork, but I persisted because I did not want the poison to flower.

Once I had set my sails, I retreated below to continue some simple chores. I sorted the firewood and tinder so that the driest pieces were near the top of the heap, with the greenest below. I stored the young pine cones aside in a wooden crate, for they would not be dry, or even open, for a month. I propped open the scuttle so that the breeze would help to flush the dampness from the wood, or my meals will all be smoked, not grilled.

I ate pickled pork with lots of bread, for I had a vast mound of loaves and could better use the storage space. I tried a fresh crust with the curry powder but found it distasteful, even with a dash of oil. I tried the curry spices with some boiled beef and it combined more pleasantly.

With fair going I made St Peter's Port by sundown. I am not sure if it was the cold weather or because it was the Sabbath, but the trip to shore was a waste of my rowing. Even the public houses were as battened as a

---

[84] A *league* is equal to three miles, about 4.8 km

hatch in a storm. It was a shame to return to the *Maris Alarum* with not so much as a mug of warm cider in my belly.

Monday 26 March

Lat: (Obs) 49.45°N   Long: (Obs) 2.52°E   Heading: Docked

In the morning light I rowed my tender[85] to shore again, hoping for a more open reception than the previous evening. My arms had regained their strength and I found it bracing to be across the still port waters in the cool morning air. I did not feel like a long walk as my foot still hurt when I put weight on it, so I just ambled about the harbour and watched the town awaken.

Later, in a narrow lane, I came across a vendor selling some fine tomatoes. However he would not accept my pound notes as payment, no doubt distrusting me for the bloodied scar upon my cheek. I did not have the energy to row back to *Maris Alarum* for some bread to barter, and so I left without the produce.

In the same lane I chanced upon another vendor selling coffee beans, which gave off a rich and delicious aroma that hinted of cocoa. Such fine coffee was not what I had expected in Guernsey; the purveyor told me that he had shipped the beans from the Caribbean. I desperately wanted the beans, for they would add variety to the mundane fare aboard my ship. But no, the purveyor would not accept my pound notes either, even when I offered him double his price.

My head battled itself: a long dinghy-row to fetch ten loaves of bartering bread verses my desire for fresh coffee beans. Some minutes later I encountered a second vendor of tomatoes who was thankfully agreeable to my pound notes. Although they were very ripe, I purchased two bushels, and had soon bartered one for a small sack of coffee beans. I returned to the *Maris Alarum* content with my morning's trading and spent the remainder of the day packing away one third of the tomatoes, cooking some into jam and pickling the rest. My salted beef and fresh tomato loaf that night tasted more like a meal than the

---

[85] A *tender* was a small row boat that was used to go ashore in shallow waters. It was usually stored on deck and lowered via ropes and pulleys to the water, but was sometimes towed behind the main vessel.

usual boot leather. I was happily content to finish my dinner with a fine Caribbean coffee.

Thursday 29 March

Lat: (Obs) 48.07°N   Long: (R) 5.8°E Heading: SW

For three days I have sailed with fair winds, maintaining a true sou'-westerly course. My sextant has proved itself a fine tool for determining latitude, with my positions matching those recorded by Cook to within an arc minute[86] or two.

I took it upon myself to learn the workings of the barometer. The pamphlet said that when the quicksilver dipped below 29 inches, a storm may be soon arriving, but when it rose above 30 inches, it was more likely to be calm. How such trickery worked was beyond my thinking. I read the science of M. Pascal[87], but I still could not fathom how a tube can measure the heaviness of air when it clearly weighed nothing at all. But for now the mercury sat at 30¾ inches, foretelling fair sailing ahead. So far, both the barometer and the weather had been my friend.

Today I caught a sea bird. It sat upon the deck for too long, giving me time to fetch my net. True, it was only a morsel of meat, but it was tender after broiling. I have dragged my fishing lure for two days but so far I have caught only one simple fish barely worth the frying.

Monday 2 April

Lat: (Obs) 47.06°N   Long: (R) 6.7°E Heading: SW

I now feel set on my trip, and have eased into the life like it is a goose-down pillow[88]. My days roll by at a tepid cadence. In the cool morning sun I usually sit on the deck, sipping coffee or tea. I often read, including one book in Spanish that I have completed twice in an attempt to

---

[86] An *arc minute* is 1/60th of a degree.
[87] Blaise Pascal (1623-1662) was a French mathematician and scientist. He performed early experiments with atmospheric pressure, essentially inventing the barometer.
[88] *Down* is the layer of fine feathers underneath a bird's tough exterior feathers. Goose down is particularly soft and warm, and is used to stuff luxury pillows.

improve my vocabulary. All the nearby ports are Portuguese, and I hope that this language is similar enough to Spanish that I will be able to communicate with the local people. On most days it is warm enough to remove my vest by noon, and at times even my shirt! I am pleased to take such pleasure from this simple life. Already I can feel my mind letting go of my past.

My foot was less painful to stand on, but its sinews had tightened. I fashioned a walking stick by splitting a spare hull plank, and then using a rasp and spoke-shave[89] to form the curves - an endeavour that took me almost two full days. In London this trivial task would have been a heavy waste of the clock's ticking, but at sea it was a pleasant diversion.

Such is the life of a sailor, and I enjoy its tranquillity. For the want of some company it is perfect - yet the close quarters on a small ship can incite cabin rage, so there is a price to pay for conversation.

Tuesday 3 April

Lat: (Obs) 41.14°N   Long: (Obs) 8.66°E   Heading: Docked

After nearly a week of free sailing I docked pre-dawn in the Portuguese town of Oporto[90]. The harbour was sensibly designed with a protected quay and the waters were calm, so I expected a comfortable stay.

After spending so much time on my ship, I felt that a morning countryside amble was in order. I also hoped that the exercise would free the sinews in my ankle. Some low tree-studded hills surrounded the port, so it was for them that I headed.

The sun had not yet risen and the harbour was near-deserted as I set off. By and by I left the port behind, and set my sights on the top of a nearby hillock. The walk was most pleasant - until I spied something unexpected that changed the entire direction of my day: there, lying on the path in front of me, was fresh deer dung.

Suddenly, a nightmarish vision hit me with more ferocity than a runaway horse. *Beth, anguished cries bawling from her blue lips.*

---

[89] A *spoke-shave* is a woodworking tool designed to plane and shave curved surfaces
[90] This town is now known as *Porto*.

Screaming. Beth was dying, *again*, in front of me. My legs gave from beneath me, and my chest constricted until I could barely breathe.

Deer. I had not expected to see any here, and so was not prepared for this intrusion into my mind. The mere sight of the dung had been enough to precipitate a vision of *that day*, of that stag wandering down the path as we waited with hushed breaths as it stepped over the lasso, of Beth lying in a pool of her own blood on the forest floor, of.... *that day*.

It took until the sun pushed its heralding rays above the horizon until I could rid my eyes of it. But then what could I do? To return to my ship was to surrender, but to walk onward would invite the terrors again. I wanted to fight this evil, but how could I attack something that was inside my own head? Paralysed with anxiety, I simply sat with my head in my hands for a long while.

Slowly I summoned my strength. By and by I vowed that despite the rasping rawness of Beth's final moments, I would refuse to bow to it; it was better to re-mount a cantankerous stallion that has tossed you than to concede it victory, or on the next mounting it will be emboldened further. I vowed not just to walk among the deer, but to capture one as well. To slaughter a big stag would prove medicinal – I could not fight my own mind, but to take down a buck might provide a small measure of sweet vengeance.

With strengthened resolve, I returned to my ship and fetched two short lengths of rope and my scimitar. Many local workers were now about their business, so I sheathed the sword under my breeches so as not to attract unwelcome attention, for a stranger in town with a gleaming weapon is rarely a friendly sign.

Soon I was back among the trees. After taking some further time to steel myself, not against the hill, but against what assailed me from the past, I set off in pursuit of the herd. I inched along a path, staying downwind of where I felt the deer might be, following a well-trodden pad[91]. By and by I encountered both the purpose, and the nemesis, of my walk: of a small herd of grazing deer, including a single large stag.

---

[91] A *deer pad* is the path that the deer form through the forest by repeatedly travelling along the same route.

At first sight, the stag stole my wind from my chest, so powerful was the memory that its antlers provoked. But I thought again of the cantankerous stallion and renewed my vow. I owed as much to Beth. I quietly followed the path and soon found an ideal section in which to set a trap, and despite it being three years since I had done so, I laid the ropes with well-practiced dexterity. A stout sapling nearby provided a firm spring, so I attached a rope to the highest tip of its trunk proper and heaved on it until I had bent it near sideways. Then I anchored the spring-line around a large rock and tightened it using a haymaker's hitch, locking the sapling flexed in place.

The spring was set. Next I tied a snare. A simple rolling hitch created a slip knot, from which I formed a wide lasso. I laid the loop, hidden by loose leaves, across the deer pad, and then placed a scavenged mound of berries inside it as bait. Then I lay hidden behind a rock, with my scimitar firmly in my palm, and waited. I calmed my mind from the past by distracting myself with thoughts of a thick venison fillet upon my plate.

By now the sun was warm, and the deer were less inclined to travel, so my wait was long. I did not fret about the delay because my time was free. However, my stillness gave evil thoughts another chance to enter my head, and it took all of my concentration to keep them out. I repeatedly reminded myself that I must forget Beth and wipe all thoughts of her from my mind, because I know from experience that although at first the memories are sweet, the finish is bitter.

The sun was bathing the forest and I was about to surrender when an odd little animal wandered along the pad. It had the face of a squirrel, yet the body of a cat, and a long bushy tail. Its coat was deep grey with a white blush across its breast. I had not seen an animal like this before and did not know what to call it[92]. Yet its flesh looked thick and firm, which raised my interest even further. I lay still and silent as the squirrel-cat crept closer to my snare, and I held firm even as it sniffed the bait. I knew that I would have just one chance to ensnare the creature, for it had no horns like a deer around which the lasso could tighten. The moment of capture had to be precise. So I waited.

---

[92] McAdam's description suggests he may have sighted a Beech Marten, a common relative of stoats, wildcats and weasels.

Fatefully, the squirrel-cat stepped across the loop. Immediately I slashed my scimitar down at the taut spring-rope, cutting it, allowing the sapling to pull the lasso tight around the creature's torso. An unholy cacophony of shrieks ensued. I leapt from my hide and within seconds had silenced the screeching beast with a swift swipe of my sword. Its congealing blood turned my mind in awkward directions, but I focused upon coiling my ropes and then determinedly skinned and gutted the animal. Soon I felt proud enough to pat my own back, for although I had not slaughtered a stag I had survived a trip into the woods without capitulating. I had remounted the cantankerous stallion. Hopefully next time it will not be so bold.

I retreated down the hill to my ship where I lunched on fried squirrel-cat with curry powder. Then I took a few large drafts of rum to help settle my jangled nerves. Initially I was pleased to have battled the demons, but as the afternoon passed from my galley chair, my anguish over the visions of Beth intensified. Why, oh why, was I unable to let her go? That horrible, horrible day had replayed itself again; I could not wipe it from my eyes. I had removed myself from London, but already, barely 10 days from Southend, Beth's ghost had already caught up to me. Yes, I had escaped the plod and those unjust judges who would throw a man's life away for but a moment of drunken ribaldry, but how could I escape from something that was inside my head? I turned to the rum even harder to fight off the demons, and emptied a crock as I fought myself through the afternoon.

My recollections of the evening are dull, but I faintly recall setting off toward the hillock, seething and cussing aloud, with a rum bottle in one hand and my scimitar in the other. I have a vague feeling that I was attempting to bring down the stag. However I didn't get far, as I fell when trying to negotiate a gangway from the quay, and tumbled into waist-deep water. I emerged up the harbour bank muddy, suddenly more sober, still angry at the world, yet somehow still clutching both the rum bottle and my weapon. A distant shred of common sense somehow emerged from my addled mind and I staggered back to my ship. Later I fell asleep in the galley, bottle and weapon still tightly in hand.

Wednesday 4 April

I spent the morning cleaning my mud-caked self, and washing my stinking suit. After that I slept again and achieved nothing until mid afternoon. Upon awakening I finally felt well enough to venture into the town. My cheek was healing with no sign of redness or pustules, so I felt more comfortable showing my face than I did in Le Havre.

Three moneychangers soon apprehended me in turn. Some brief conversations using my broken Spanish demonstrated that they were all scoundrels, and I was determined not to concede to their meagre offerings. One fellow so insulted me that I nearly cuffed his ears, and it was only that I felt sheepish from my previous night's mischief that saved him a beating. But, by and by, my resolve weakened and I changed three shillings for a piece of eight and a few reales – barely half a fair price.

After sunset, I chose a cafe for evening supper. The barkeep had a fine selection of meats that hung from the cloister and for three reales he provided a plate with a small portion of each, along with some bread, olives, oil and a slice of cheese. It was excellent fare that tasted far fresher than the hearty but stodgy meals of a London public house. The barkeep called it *tapas*. I also had a delicious carafe of sweet port wine, of which I shared a glass with an *alcoholico* at the bench.

After I finished the port wine, a troupe of three began playing music in the corner. They had a type of lute, a wooden whistle and a peculiar looking drum. The drum looked like a large crock-pot with a skin stretched over its rim, with a rope extending from the centre of the skin. The player worked the rhythm by strumming and tugging upon the rope, producing an agreeable beat.

"Que e?" I asked, receiving the reply that the drum was called a *Zambomba.* I could have guessed as much by repeating its sound: zam-BOM-ba, zam-BOM-ba.

Most diners rose to dance, but because of my foot I stayed rooted to my chair. Instead I tapped my stick along to the rhythm and joined the band in hollering *Ole!* Later in the night a girl with deep brown eyes and white teeth rewarded my enthusiasm with a beautiful smile. After that I couldn't avert my eyes from her, because she was pretty indeed.

Unfortunately she departed soon thereafter. I hoped that I would meet her again.

Thursday 5 April

Lat: (Obs) 41.14°N   Long: (Obs) 8.66°E   Heading: Docked

I spent the morning in dock attending chores, and took a long walk in the afternoon. I had sighted a fine cathedral[93] from the top of the hillock and wished to explore it from closer range. In broken Spanish I asked a lad for directions. Although he was a Portuguese native he nonetheless understood my request, and I was soon on my way.

My foot felt looser from the previous day's exertions, so I walked up the stairs to the top of the cathedral's bell tower. After the evening bells – which were so loud that they continued ringing in my ears for hours - I returned to the little cafe. The wine-drinker was there again, but not the girl with brown eyes. I again feasted upon a plate of meats and produce. Today was a different selection – it included *tostadas*[94], vinegar-pickled onions, two cheeses and two meats.

After devouring that fine meal I ordered a bottle of the sweet red wine that I had tried the previous evening. The *alcoholico* hovered about me like a mangy dog at a scrap heap, and by and by I succumbed to his presence, relenting with a half glass. He tried to talk with me but I waved him away, for I was of no mood for broken natter with a drunkard tonight. Instead I sat alone, watching the passers-by, hoping for the brown-eyed girl's return.

Just as I drained the last of the port wine, she arrived. She glanced across the room and flashed a shy smile at me, at which my heart kicked like a trapped rabbit. I returned her smile and watched her as she sank onto a small corner stool. Emboldened by the wine, I ordered two glasses of *vinho branco*[95] from the barkeep and moved toward her.

I sat nearby and slid a wine toward her. She looked across, perhaps a little suspiciously, but did not take the glass.

---

[93] The Porto Cathedral, a magnificent building completed in 1737, still stands today.
[94] Toasted bread
[95] *Vinho branco* is Spanish for "white wine"

"*Esto es para ti,*" I said, offering her the drink more formally. "For you." I am not sure whether she understood my broken Spanish or my English, but she nodded and shyly accepted my gift. I was pleased.

"*Hola,*" I said. "*Mi nombre es McAdam.*" I paused for effect. "*Capitan McAdam.*" I tried to appear as gentlemanly as possible, but suddenly became aware of the scar on my cheek. I raised my wine and took a swig of wine to hide it.

"Hola," she replied. "Hola, Capitão McAdam."

My belly tingled, for her reply meant that she not only understood my greeting, but that she regarded me more highly than a common bar slug. Then, just after she had addressed me, she awarded me a little sideways smile. Just like ... Beth's.

Slowly, inexorably, Beth's apparition materialised over the brown-eyed girl. I was not giving substance to shadows, for the image was as real as the chair on which I sat.

At first Beth's face was pretty, smiling and laughing. She gestured toward me with a curling finger, beckoning me closer. I slid across, unaware if I was alive or in a dream. I looked in Beth's eyes, and they drew me forward. *Our first kiss. My first kiss. It was warm. Warmer than I expected.* Unable to draw myself away from this comfort, I looked into Beth's soft green eyes for more. I moved forward to kiss her again, and as our lips gently touched I noticed the aroma of her perfume; that sweet fragrance still echoes through my head. But then, as always in these nightmares, her face changed. Her eyes widened in fear, and her lips turned purple and spasmed into a warped twist. I jolted back, horrified. I shook my head to rid myself of the vision, but it remained. I closed my eyes, twice, but both times I reopened them to see not a brown-eyed Portuguese woman but a cold, deathly visage of Beth – blue skin, smeared with black-brown blood, her green eyes wide open in panic....

I reached for my wine to douse my anxiety. Trembling, I knocked over the glass, shattering it and spilling the wine over the brown-eyed girl's white tunic. Now irreparably anxious, I scampered from the bar and did not look back.

How can a man rid himself of such nightmares? I was convinced that time at sea would help me to forget her, but so far Beth's memory has remained as sharp as a cutthroat razor, and has assailed me twice in just two days. When will her ghost leave me in peace?

Friday 6 April

Lat: (Obs) 40.25°N   Long: (R) 10.1°E   Heading: Due SW

I went to cast away immediately upon my return to the *Maris Alarum* last night. I needed the open and featureless ocean that had nothing to remind me of Beth; even Oporto was flaying me with memories. But I demurred, for the barometer had dropped a full half an inch, indicating that foul weather was approaching. Instead, I sat with a mug of gin trying to calm my heart, which was pounding like a Zambomba drum. After downing a half a quart[96] of this mind medicine, I rechecked the barometer, hoping that it has risen in the interim. But the mercury level had dropped another eighth of an inch – a huge fall in just one day.

Logic told me to stay in dock with the sails furled, but each glance across the ship's deck toward the town of Oporto, with its demonic deer and that brown-eyed Beelzebub, told me that I was better off at sea. I needed solitude. I needed to look out over the gunwales and see nothing; nothing but endless ocean. After another draft of gin I decided to cast away, cursing at the barometers black magic as I did. The sun was a long way from rising as I tacked my way out of the harbour. I did not even glance back in case the brown-eyed girl was about.

I did little for the rest of the day but sleep and sail, for my head was heavy indeed, weighed not just from tiredness and the acrid effects of the gin, but also from the knowledge that Beth's ghost was following me across the seas.

Saturday 7 April

Lat: (Obs) 39.76°N   Long: (R) 11.4°E   Heading: SW

Wanting solitude, I headed southwest, away from the coast. Although I was rapidly leaving the coastline, the birds remained thick in the air.

---

[96] A *quart* is an imperial measure of volume roughly equal to one litre. Half a quart of spirits is an extremely large amount to consume in a sitting – McAdam would have been very intoxicated.

Large flocks of white gulls dived for fish on both my port and starboard. Thinking that this was a sign of good fishing, I tied an Aberdeen fly onto a hook and cast my line over the stern. I trolled for only a few lazy winds of the spool when a fish struck the lure. I was pleased that I had bought such strong silk line, for this fish was mightily strong.

The bamboo pole was bending almost onto itself such was the fight. For a long while I could not make any line and twice had to let the fish run. But I held fast and, by and by, the fish tired more than I did, and I was able to gaff it aboard[97]. I had seen this species of fish before: a blue-fin tuna. It was as long as my arm and heavy with flesh. I was thankful that I could leave the pickled pork in its jar for a few days.

Sunday 8 April

Lat: (Obs) 39.53°N   Long: (R) 11.9°E   Heading: SSW

I continued on a sou' westerly heading and put a good few leagues between the *Maris Alarum* and the coast. I was concerned that the barometer had dropped again - it now read $29_{1/2}$ inches. I considered returning to the mainland – I even contemplated Oporto - but demurred, for my ship was equal to any foul weather and my health was fine. I would rather battle Mother Ocean than any demonic apparitions from within, which Oporto would surely ignite. I was sure that we could handle a blow; in fact I would welcome the argument to keep my mind focused.

I steaked the blue-fin and ate two portions, fried with oil, salt, pepper and a little sauerkraut. The vinegar in the cabbage tasted fine alongside the fish flesh. Sauerkraut on its own was an ordeal that I usually swallowed only under protest from my tongue, but alongside the fried tuna it was palatable.

Monday 9 April

Lat: (Obs) 39.13°N   Long: (R) 12.2°E   Heading: SSW

---

[97] A *gaff* is a pole with a sharp hook at one end used for retrieving objects or fish from the ocean.

I continued sailing away from Oporto. My journey had again settled in to a rhythm and I was now feeling more content than when I departed. My foot felt fine, and I discontinued use of the walking stick and removed the compress. I had a myriad of petty tasks that I carried out steadily and to the full, for their activity occupied my mind and their completion gave me warmth.

My only worry was the barometer, which continued to drop, and was now at 28 ½ inches. However I was beginning to doubt its science, because apart from the strengthening wind, which I welcomed, the weather remained fair.

Mostly I now feel happy, for whenever the salt air is in my chest and the sun is on my back, I feel like I am flying as high as the gulls that glide beside my ship. I thought back to the louts and laggards who lined the London alleyways: every man owned such a pair of wings, but it was a pity that most men had not discovered how to fly with them.

Tuesday 10 April

Lat: (Obs) 38.51°N   **Long: (R) 12.3°E**   **Heading: SSW**

Today I discovered some rats in the galley. I had seen one before but thought nothing of it, but today there were three rodents that scurried with high agitation and carted away every loose crumb. I checked the provisions in the hold and found signs of gnawing on the bread, meat and flour. I set both my traps with bread in the hope of capture, because I will have a big problem if the rats breed.

I again trolled for tuna, and was rewarded with a strike after barely an hour. Judging from the bend in my pole and the fight it took to the reel, this fish was even larger than the last. My arms ached from the scrap by the time it tired. But just as I hauled the fish near the stern, the load lightened and the line slacked. Had the fish spat the hook? A few more turns of the reel revealed the truth: the fish's head was still attached to the line but its body had been bitten clean in half. Was it a shark?

A pang of fear coursed through me. During my spice runs I had heard many stories of these sea-devils. I knew of a fellow jack-tar[98] who had lost his leg to these prowlers. In the antipodes I had even witnessed, at

---

[98] A *jack-tar* was slang for an old sailor

close range, the menacing grin of a striped tiger shark as it lunged for a baited hook. I had no desire to remake my acquaintance. I did not know if such beasts existed in these relatively cool northern waters, but felt that, for once, ignorance was the better path than knowledge. I saw myself as strong enough to confront whatever Mother Ocean dealt me on this voyage, yet I conceded that the mere thought of a shark attack rocked my core.

I pitched the severed head back to the ocean as far as my arm could cast it. I went down to the galley and poured a mug of rum. By and by, my shaking ceased. I hoped that the sharks did not return to my dreams again, and took another draft of rum to be sure.

Wednesday 11 April

Lat: (Obs) 38.04°N   Long: (R) 12.7°E   Heading: SSW

Thankfully I slept soundly; the shark-devils left my nightmares alone.

The barometer had again dropped a quarter.

At mid morning the gulls disappeared. I did not know why, but it seemed that Beelzebub himself had chased them away, such was the haste of their departure. Did these birds know something that I didn't? Perhaps a blow was near. However I temporarily gained some new company: a pod of dolphins swam by, arcing their backs above the steadily-growing waves. They were headed on the opposite bearing to the *Maris Alarum* but stopped as if to survey her. I tossed them the leftovers from the first tuna, which they appeared to receive gratefully.

I also discovered that raisins soaked in gin, rather than water, provided a fine accompaniment to bread and cheese. The raisins imparted a sweet flavour to the gin, making it more palatable. I was pleased to have found a tasty way to avoid malaria.

Thursday 12 April

Lat: (Obs) 37.49°N   Long: (R) 12.9°E   Heading: SSW

The gulls had not revisited the *Maris Alarum* again - perhaps they had returned to land for rest. The weakly landlubbers! Yet the rats continued their frantic dance in the galley and at times I could hear them scurry about at night. I removed only one rodent from the traps.

My foot ached intensely while I was lying on the hammock in the evening, but I could not understand why because the blueness had long gone. I searched Dr Blane's book and found a small entry saying that stiff joints often ached before a storm, so my suspicions were heightened that a bluster was close. After reading the doctor's advice I reapplied the compress.

The barometer had dropped again. The pamphlet told me that below 29 inches of quicksilver in the tube was an indicator of rain, and below 28 inches a storm, but even though mine showed only 27 ½ inches I had no great fear[99]. I was sure that both me and my ship could handle a spray.

---

[99] 27 inches of quicksilver equals 914 millibars. Standard pressure at sea level is 1013 millibars, so the atmospheric pressure was *far* below normal levels.

Friday 13 April

Lat: (Obs) 37.04°N **Long: (R) 13.2°E** **Heading: SSW**

Even at sun up the rats were busy. At least I didn't need to clear away the scraps from my cooking, because the rodents carted every morsel away as if they were silver sovereigns. Why were they so busy? Were they preparing to desert the ship? Despite all this activity, the traps caught nothing overnight, so I added some pork rind as bait in the hope of better hunting.

As was my habit in the morning I sat on the deck, but the wind soon made it very unpleasant. It blew from the east at 30 knots[100], so I had to work the whipstaff and sails hard to keep the south in my bearing. A squall was knocking on my door, which I welcomed, for no jack-tar ever learned to sail by floating a tub on a millpond. A heaving sea would advance my skills, which I could use later when even more spiteful weather struck.

The impending foul weather may have explained why the gulls departed in such haste. However, it was not so easy for me to glide above the clouds back to land – except, of course, with the Water Wings of my dreams - so I stayed on course.

I am pleased that Friday 13th passed without poor Providence. That I negotiated the devil's day without major problems augurs well for my future, for if Lucifer intended to strike me down he surely would have acted on his day.

---

[100] One knot equals about 1.85 km/h. 30 knots equates to about 55 Km/h, which is classed a 'near gale' force wind. Below this ranking are winds that are classed as *calm, light, gentle, moderate, fresh* and *strong*.

Saturday 14 April

Lat: (Obs) 36.90°N   Long: (R) 13.6°E   Heading: SW

I awoke early after a fitful sleep. My sloop rolled and pitched awkwardly throughout the night, such was the strength of the wind, which I reckoned at about 40 knots[101].

My foot was aching and swollen, so I mixed some more medicine from the chest - this time also adding some sulphate of zinc and tincture of myrrh - and massaged it in. I was surprised to see that the rats had gone from the galley. I have heard that it is an indicator of an approaching storm when the rats hide, and also conceded Dr Blane's truth that a stiff joint swells before a squall. The barometer had dropped another quarter inch, so all signs indicated that Mother Ocean was about to test me.

Due to the sharp pitching of the ship I didn't brew a coffee, but climbed to the deck anyway to survey the ocean. She was grumpy – not as malevolent as a woman scorned, but certainly one irritated. White caps sprayed from the wave peaks. The overcast skies dulled the ocean to a leaden grey. Although I was confident that the *Maris Alarum* was stout and strong, I doused the headsail as a precaution, for I was a long way from the sanctity of land if trouble struck.

*

It is now after noon on the 14th April. The wind grows ever stronger and now has enough whip to blow away my hat had I not strapped it firmly around my chin. I have cleared the decks and furled the sails, lashing the mainsail to its boom and stowing the headsail below deck. The sky grows darker, as do my fortunes. The quicksilver in the barometer sits at 26 ¾ inches[102] but I don't need this reckoning to know that a massive storm is at hand. I can only hope that it passes quickly.

---

[101] 40 knots equals roughly 75 Km/h, considered a 'gale' force wind. Above this lie the classifications *of strong gale, storm, violent* and *cyclone*.

[102] 26 ¾ inches of mercury equates to about 900 millibars. This reading, if accurate, is one of the lowest readings of atmospheric pressure ever documented, telling us that it was truly a massive cyclone.

I do not ask Providence for a light load, for such mercies are for those who stay in port, but I do ask her to grant me a strong back with which to bear it.

Sunday 15 April

Mother Ocean is in a vengeful mood. I now sit inside the cabin with the hatches shut tightly, with a small tallow lantern as my only comfort. Just once I ventured onto deck; my head had barely passed through the hatch when the wind nearly blew my hair off my head. The rain did not fall downwards but speared sideways, stinging my face and eyes like birdshot. It was only by turning my eyes to the lee of my own head that I could see at all.

One glance at the ocean set my heart at a fast clip, from which it still suffers. Wave after wave of black walls are bearing down on the *Maris Alarum*, rising higher than the ship herself. The whitecaps are not rolling but are *ripping* off the waves, then arcing upwards with a vicious spray. My ship's bow is pitching so high that at one moment I see nothing but angry clouds ahead, until the next instant, when she plunges down the next face so steeply that I am staring into Mother Ocean's black heart. At times everything except the mast-top is swamped under the surging torrents.

Fork and chain lightening crack to the bow and stern. Vast sheets of white light shoot across the heavens, sharpening the whitecaps to a steel glint. The noise! I have never experienced its equal. Thunder booms, claps and then rolls into the distance, then claps and booms and rolls again; I can feel it shaking my belly. And how can it be that wind can scream? The air has no throat or mouth or lips, but it howls and shrieks like a demented demon. Yet the holler that came from my own mouth was ripped away before it even reached my ears.

I now sit in the hold on a sack of flour, which provides cushioning of sorts from the relentless pitching and pounding that grows ever more violent. When, oh when, will this relentless squall end?

I have already experienced this scene in my nightmares, except that this reality is far worse than my imaginings. I wish that *Maris Alarum* would sprout her wings and fly me away, for this night brings me no joy at all.

*

My tallow lamp burns low. I must write with the lead-and-graphite pencil, because the ship's pitching and rolling make using the inkpot impractical. I remain tucked in the hold, clinging to the flour sack, bruised and battered despite the cushioning. My ship's movement is so furious that even my head is in danger from the bearers. I had hoped that nightfall would bring some respite, but the ocean's anger mounts and mounts. I know the *Maris Alarum* is stout, but I fear that she cannot withstand this onslaught.

Despite my precautions, her wild rolling has emptied the galley cupboards above. With every turn the contents clatter from port to starboard and back again, smashing mugs, breaking pots and causing an unholy row. I can hear the heavy cast iron pots above all else, and can only hope they do not crack a plank.

The sound of the waves pounding upon the hull is like the whipping of a dragon's tale. I tell myself that I tarred the planks thickly, but I fear that not even a mighty elm tree could withstand this pummelling without breaking a bough. Every creak or crack brings a thump to my heart, because the ocean is so ferocious that I fear that the keel will split.

*

Those who talk of Hell as a boiling pit of fire and brimstone have not experienced a storm at sea like this one.

I would not have thought it possible, but the storm has turned even more violent. In all my days I have not experienced its equal, or even its younger sibling. From the hold, I can hear nothing but the screaming wind and the relentless pounding of waves on the hull. At times the *Maris Alarum* rolls so far that her mast must be dunking below the water. I fear she may capsize.

Although no mere mortal would be able to assist me in this hour of damnation, it would be a comfort to have another on board to share my fear. I do not understand why, but having another person feel the storm's wrath would soften its bite. Even if my Elizabeth were here I would draw strength from providing her comfort.

Oh, that this night would end.

Monday 16 April

I am not a praying man, but many times today I found myself beseeching the god of the church, the Roman gods, Providence and Mother Ocean herself for mercy.

If this storm is punishment for injuring the prison guard, then it is like flogging a guinea pig with a bull whip. Surely the gods know that the guard's cracked arm was just an unfortunate side effect of my escape and not the purpose of it?

I asked the gods if they aimed for me alone. But for what other reason they have brewed this storm? Surely I am the only creature, man or beast, within its vengeful reach.

*

Perhaps the gods listened, because my ears tell me that the wind has dropped. Judging from the pitching, the waves also seem lower. I think, and hope, that the storm has now blown past. The *Maris Alarum has* survived, although her captain will need a few good drafts of rum to sleep this evening.

My ship still yaws about the ocean, slowly spinning as if she is trapped on a fairground carrousel, but compared to her previous vitriol this movement is like Mother Ocean giving the *Maris Alarum* a warm hug.

*

Gradually my heart has slowed, and is now at a steady thump. I do not know the time and although the lightning and thunder continue unabated, the wind has calmed even further. I now feel that the worst of the tempest is over, but I hesitate to commit to this as truth, for it is easy to convince myself when my want is so great. I must look outside before I can truly relax.

*

I poked my head through the hatch. I felt a breeze, not from the east like before but from the west. It stiffened. I looked at the spinning sky, where the black clouds were rotating like a giant whirlpool. I peered up the mast and followed its line to the heavens, where there was a clear spot in the clouds, with a sliver of crescent moon looking down through it like a winking eye. Fear instinctively raised my hand to my mouth. I have heard of such swirling maelstroms: a dreaded typhoon. The storm was not over. *I was in its eye.*

My ordeal was only half complete.

I returned to the galley, battened the hatch and then further retreated to the hold. I could think of no helpful actions and so I simply lay clinging to the flour sack, with my eyes closed, as the ocean surpassed even her earlier fury.

I now lay, no longer pleading for mercy but instead just wishing for the end - one way or another. My wish is for my life to continue as before, but I know that I am only a penny-flip away from damnation. If I am to die tonight, then I want it to be soon.

I think of Beth. For once I do not try to wipe her from my dreams, but hug her blue and bloodied body with all my mind. Perhaps I will be with her soon.

*

I don't know the hour, or even if it is day or night. I have just been aroused by a noise louder than a cannon shot. It was not lightening or thunder, but had a sound of even greater menace. The *Maris Alarum* now lists so far to port that she lumbers almost on her side. I cannot walk on the floor, but instead will have to slide and slip and crawl across to the scupper. Although I fear what I will discover, I must inspect the damage immediately. My ship cannot stay afloat at this tilt.[103]

*

From the galley I crawled across the ladder, which was now angled with the listing ship; it was not vertical, but lying as though it was resting on a wall. As I unbattened the hatch, a fierce gale ripped down through the hole, forcing me to retreat. With a sense of foreboding I donned the Fisherman's Friend, knotting the chest strap tightly. I didn't pause to think what benefit it would provide if I were swept overboard, for it would just prolong my suffering until the malevolent sharks took me. It simply felt wiser to don it than not.

---

[103] It was clear from the almost illegible text in this section that McAdam wrote these journal entries under great duress.

Again I raised the hatch, forcing it against the gale, and peered across the ships lilting deck. At first I could see nothing through the driving rain and the black night. But then a bolt of lightning shocked across the sky, illuminating the horror.

The mast had snapped in half.

It had been truncated near its base, leaving a spar no higher than a man. The rest of the mast was caught up by the rigging, and trailed in the ocean like a giant sea anchor, pulling the *Maris Alarum* sharply onto her side. If a rogue wave were to strike now, my ship would surely splinter, sending her and her captain to a wet burial. I had to cut the mast free, or my journey, both through the oceans and through life, was over.

If I tried to walk across the sloping deck it would end in a slippery slide into the oblivion of the howling sea. I hastily retreated to the galley and, tripping in the dark over cracked and ruined provisions, I groped aimlessly for a knife. Despite sifting through all that I could get to hand, I couldn't find anything that would cut through ropes and rigging. For the want of a knife, my ship remained dragged onto her side - a perilous state even on a hamlet pond, but deadly in the maelstrom outside.

Then, a thought: *my scimitar*. I hoped to all the gods that it was still fixed to the base of the mast.

I crawled to the general stores and somehow retrieved some rope. Fumbling in the blackness of the cabin, I lashed the cord tightly around a stout bearer, played out as much as I thought would take me to the mast, and then looped and fastened the rope firmly around my chest and shoulders.

My tallow lamp was long since extinguished, but I needed no light to know what happened next: a colossal wave smashed into the port side of the *Maris Alarum*, sending the cracked end of the mast through the top of her hull, like a medieval battering ram through a flimsy fence. The hull cracked and splintered, leaving a gaping hole. Water poured through the fissure, flooding the cabin with a surge of brine. A lightning bolt flashed through the hole, illuminating the unholy kerfuffle in the galley. Then, as the next wave hit, more water poured in through the hole.

The *Maris Alarum* was sinking.

I had to cut the mast free to right her, and do it immediately, for with every passing moment my hopes of survival dropped. With no other option, and seawater now flooding the galley, I clambered onto the windy, slippery, rolling deck. Below me, just a few arm-lengths away, was the mast stump. But how to reach it?

I had no time to think. I simply released my grip from the top rung of the ladder, and dropped myself down the sloping deck. I slid down its surface like a greased pig, and careened into the mast stump. I clung to it fiercely. After steadying myself for a few pitching rolls, I sat on it legs astride, as if I was riding an unbroken stallion.

I felt for the tag end of the rope around my chest, and frantically looped it about the mast stump and finished it with a quick hitch. Now, riding that bucking horse, I grasped forward along the mast stump, feeling for my scimitar.

If I could meet with the pirate who dropped his weapon for my gain I would shower him with riches, for although the seas rolled and the waves struck and the wind blew, my mighty little sword sat snugly in its scabbard.

Once I had its hilt firmly in my palm I thrashed out at the rigging, slashing wildly like a bird caught in a spider's web. I hacked, cut, and sliced ferociously, all the while rolling up and down with the monstrous seas. With each cut, the remaining ropes tightened, bearing more of the load. Then, at last, with a whip-like crack, the final rigging snapped. The mast slid into the churning sea.

With the weight of the collapsed mast now unburdened, the *Maris Alarum* suddenly righted herself. I was flung back from my sitting position so that I was now lying on my back on the deck, my legs up around the mast stump like women in childbirth. I cut my tether from the stump, and then hastily crawled and scrambled back down into the galley.

Lightening arced into the galley through the broken hull, but at least the righting of the ship had cleared it from the sea. An occasional rogue wave still sent a splash through the hole, but not enough to send the *Maris Alarum* to Davy Jones' Locker[104]. I sat and watched the angry sky

---

[104] *Davy Jones's Locker* is an old term for the bottom of the sea – the ship's graveyard.

through the hole. I had no way to monitor the passing of time, but it felt like it was many hours before the storm waned. By and by I crawled to my hammock and lay there, jerking in and out of slumber, until day broke over the grey and heaving ocean.

For the first time in my life, I wish nothing except to be on land.

Tuesday 17 April

Not since that fateful hunting trip with Beth had my countenance veered so low. After only three weeks at sea, my journey and my plans were scrambled like a breakfast egg. The storm not only crushed the life from the *Maris Alarum* but drained my spirit of its endeavour as well.

My mind harkened back to the Thames shipyards, the day after my purchase of this proud little sloop. I had marched on her with pride, my quill at the ready, noting all that I had to do to prepare her for adventure. Today I performed the same task but with neither satisfaction nor delight. Although the list of repairs was much longer, my quill moved far slower. Whereas before my hands darted excitedly about the page like a summer dragonfly, they now lumbered from letter to letter, sluggishly transcribing the labour that will soon fill my days.

Morning's first light revealed the worst: the mast had snapped clean away. The only salvation was that the mainsail remained lashed to the boom, mercifully spared in the truncation. But with not even a man's height of mast remaining, even the most determined rigger could not hoist a sail of any substance. The *Maris Alarum* simply bobbed on the sea, aimlessly floating around the Atlantic Ocean like cast-off bottle.

The hole in the port hull was as big as a bull's head. It was in need of urgent repair. The *Maris Alarum* took on a lot of water; the bilge was flooded, as were the holds, so she was sailing very low in the water. I had a bilge pump aboard, but had not yet had the heart to fetch it from amidst the debris below.

During the storm the flour sack had split, casting its contents about the hold. The water inundation had formed an ungodly white paste, which now coated everything with a pale crust. The galley, provisions holds and my quarters were like a jumbled child's puzzle. Such was the omnipotence of the storm that nearly everything was cracked, dented or ruined. Even my prized sextant now had two large bends, rendering my observations of latitude as mere guesses. And I had no knowledge of my longitude at all, as the storm has made my previous reckonings useless. With no land in sight, I was lost like a child in the jungle.[105]

Today I had no appetite for work, and could bring myself to do nothing other than sit on the deck and stare at the broken mast. If this is what Mother Ocean did to those who professed to be her friend, what atrocities would she commit on her enemies?

Wednesday 18 April

In the morning, without enthusiasm for my task, I set about repairing the hull. First, I cut some spare planks, and then glued and nailed them from the inside. The crack was high enough on the hull that I could then lower myself over the port gunwale and tar it from the outside. At least now the water would stop splashing into the galley.

The sun was tracking downward in the western sky by the time I had finished, and the warmth was fast leaving the air, so I climbed below deck and lit a wood fire in the galley oven. I shivered, and craved for coffee. Although the pot holding the beans had smashed, I was able to retrieve a handful from its remainder. By scrounging amongst the debris, I collected a second handful. I located my pestle, and by and by I located my mortar – it was aft of my hammock. I ground enough beans for a weak brew, but a brew nonetheless, which I fortified with a large splash of rum. The coffee was a small mercy amidst the carnage, and it helped fleetingly to fortify me against the drudgery that lay ahead. I took the mug to the deck to again peruse the broken mast, for I had not yet figured out how to repair it.

As I finished my mug, a large log of driftwood floated past on my starboard. A strange bird was perched on the log: it was as large as a falcon, perhaps eighteen inches high[106], and had the blue and red

---

[105] During the storm, McAdam lost his true position, and some of his navigation equipment. He therefore ceased including his latitude, longitude and knot speed in his log entries. However, he continued adding his heading, as well as weather and other nautical observations, to each entry. As previously, I have omitted this information for simplicity.
[106] Eighteen inches is about 45 centimetres

colours of a parrot, and a long curved beak. It was clearly exhausted and looked close to death, like both the Maris Alarum and I. Then, as it passed the stern, it flapped it wings and flew - so tired that it was as ungainly as a chicken - and thumped, spent, onto the deck. And there it sat.

I had a mind to kill and eat it, for the typhoon had ruined most of my provisions. But then I thought that this bird had not only survived the storm that nearly sank the *Maris Alarum,* but it had somehow dodged the sea-devil sharks as well; we were brothers, of sorts. The bird looked at me with huge eyes that were set into its round owl-like face, and I knew that I did not have the heart to slaughter it.

The body of a falcon, the plumage of a parrot, the face and eyes of an owl, and a long curved beak like a macaw[107] – I have never seen such a curious bird in all my travels. It reminded me of the squirrel-cat in Oporto in the way that it seemed to be pieced together from various other creatures.

"Hello parrot," I said aloud. "Welcome to the good ship *Maris Alarum.*"

The bird twisted its neck about like and owl, and then returned its curious gaze to me.

"I trust that you enjoy your stay, for we have the finest sailing vessel in His Majesty's kingdom at your service. She is just lacking a sail."

Again the parrot-bird widened its owl-like eyes[108], stared at me intently, and then emitted a loud carking sound. I left the bird, and returned to sit in front of the warmth of the galley stove, where I took many long drafts of rum to help me sleep.

Thursday 19 April

I had no appetite for work today, and found it difficult to rouse myself from my hammock; the squalor repelled me back to bed each time I

---

[107] A *macaw* is a type of parrot found in South America, which has a large powerful beak.

[108] Some birds such as parrots are able to control the widening of their irises. This action is called 'pinning'. Birds pin their eyes – i.e. open them widely – when concentrating, confused, or occasionally when frightened.

lifted my head. To see my little sloop in such a state did not make me angry, nor sad, but just *heavy*. I felt as though thick molten lead ran through my veins, from my eyelids to my ankles.

By and by I talked myself up. I emerged on deck to be greeted with a squawk from the strange bird. I was not surprised to see that it was still there, as it was clearly exhausted from fighting the typhoon. I am sure that it did not feel like flying any more than I felt like working. Perhaps molten lead ran through its bird-veins as well.

"Good morning bird."

The bird looked at me, its deep eyes seeming to study my every nuance.

Aaaark, aaaark, it squawked. Our pleasantries exchanged, we both simply sat, building our respective energies for the tasks that lay ahead.

By and by I set about emptying the bilge. I located the pump in its store and unbattened the scuttle into the hold. To say it was "filthy" would belittle the word, for my provisions were spilled, soaked, coated with flour paste, and generally in an unholy cacophony. I opened the lower scuttle into the bilge, which was filled high with brine, and soon had the pump in place and primed. I fed the hose up through the deck and, with a labour that lasted until the sun was low, I pumped the bilge clear. The whole afternoon the owl-parrot-falcon simply sat looking at me with its big black eyes. If only it could have helped work the pump-arm.

After completing the pumping, I inspected the bilge. A dead rat, no doubt drowned amidst the turmoil of the storm, lay at its bottom. Not wanting the stench of rotting flesh to further insult to the hold, I fetched it out by the tail. I returned to the deck with the stinking rodent, intending to cast it over the side. However I noticed the bird sit up, its alert eyes following every swing of the rodent in my hand.

"Are you hungry?" I asked it. The bird did nothing. "Would you like rat?" I held up the rodent by the tail. "Rat. Nice tasty rat? Yes?"

The bird made no sound, but followed the pendulum rat with swinging owl-like eyes.

"Dinner is served," I said with mock pomposity, and flicked the rat toward the bird. It needed no second dinner bell, and launched its talons upon the rat in a trice. Its large beak quickly dissected the rodent and it was soon gulping down slivers of pink flesh. No doubt it had eaten very little since the storm, and it looked ravenous.

I thought of a useful task for the bird. Many farmers in the home country kept an owl in their barn as a ratter. Perhaps the parrot-owl-bird would be useful to keep the vermin at bay on the *Maris Alarum*. I fetched my fishing net from the store and cast it over the exhausted bird; it squawked and screeched as I tied a thin cord around its talon to prevent it from flying away during the night. I then removed the net, and retreated to the galley to summon supper from amidst the squalor.

Friday 20 April

I awoke to a fine calm day. Normally such fine weather would provide a lift to my mood, but today I had wished for dreariness and rain so that I could lie guiltlessly under my blanket without my tasks calling at me ever more loudly. By and by I rolled heavily from my hammock, grabbed a handful of breakfast raisins from a battered tin pot, and emerged into bright sunshine.

"Good morning, bird," I mumbled. "Did you sleep well?"

It looked at me, unblinking, through its saucer-like eyes.

Aaark Maark, it cawed.

I threw it a raisin, which it quickly gobbled. It watched me as I slowly picked through the rest of the fruits, but I could spare it no more for my rations were thin. This thought eventually prompted me to action, for I had yet to sort through my provisions. Although the task was onerous, any further delay would make it even harder.

My attention first turned to the galley. Laboriously I picked up all that the typhoon had strewn about, slowly forming three piles.

The first heap contained things that were still in good condition: the cooking utensils and iron pots were fine, and yes, I even found my knives in good order. Most of the tools and spares, which had been stored in a separate hold, were serviceable. My small oilskin pouch of Earth, scavenged from the Mother country before I departed, was whole; if only it was large enough to stand on, for at present I would trade this slovenly ship for just one square foot solid land.

The fishing kit was scattered fore and aft, but after methodical collecting and repacking, it had enough components to hopefully catch me a meal. By some magic my telescope had survived – the padded mahogany box was bruised and dented, but the looking glasses inside were intact. The sounding lead was fine, as was, surprisingly, the burning glass. The timer for the log roll was shattered but this did not worry me, for I had little use for it now. There was little value in knowing my speed and bearing when my current location was as vague and vast as the Atlantic Ocean herself.

The second pile contained items that I could mend, or that were partly serviceable. My sextant was dented in two places, but could still give a rough reckoning. The compass glass was smashed, but the needle rotated freely, and my charts and books were wet but might be usable if dried carefully. My journals were less affected, for their greased paper wrappings had helped to protect them. My pistols were wet but intact, as was the shot, but I would have to sun-dry the black powder. But I was worried that the weapons were now vulnerable to the ravages of rust, no matter how diligently I dried and oiled them.

Finally, I made a heap of everything that the storm had ruined beyond service. The barometer had shattered, but I felt no further need for it anyway, for even with forewarning I had little way of averting a storm, of which the filth and confusion before me were testament. Crock pots, glass jars and other such containers had shattered, their contents spilled into a grisly sludge on the galley floor. The medicine chest was still sealed, but my hopes of its contents being whole were soon dashed, with most of the flasks being broken and empty.

The provisions in the holds were in a wanton state. The pickled pork was strewn about and flecked with shattered glass and pottery, ruined. The crocks of cooked tomatoes were just a smear across the floor, although some whole fruits survived, bruised, but still holding nutrition. I washed and packed some whole fruits into a surviving salt jar in the hope of preserving them. The bread loaves were sodden lumps. The sugar had all but dissolved in the inundation, and the spare pickling vinegar was gone. Even my precious jar of curry powder was no more.

Thankfully the cheese, peas and dried beef were fine. The oat hard-cakes were sodden (but perhaps improved by the dousing), while the raisins were just a little plumper. The yeast was still wrapped and I hoped dry, but without any flour it was useless. My sack of tea was wet, but I hoped the leaves would recover some vigour once dried. One tub of sauerkraut sat defiantly upon the shelf, the only container still in its original place. Overall, my provisions were depleted by three parts in four. I now had barely enough food for a few weeks, even on tight rations.

The storm had cast the Caribbean coffee beans from bow to stern and coated them in flour paste. At first I tried to scavenge them, and began placing each bean in a pot. But against the vast face of my overall task my patience soon waned, so I shovelled them away with the rest of the detritus.

Thankfully I had stashed my water and rum tightly in the lowest hold, so I lost no water and only four gallons of the spirit. However, the gin bottles had shattered, giving the hold a piquant aroma. I had better avoid mosquitoes now that my malaria medication was gone.

Onerously, I carried the ruined provisions to the deck and cast them over the gunwales. I emptied the ruined flour over the starboard rail, retaining the sack for a rag. It was then that I discovered the full dishonesty of the Camden grain miller: in the lower reaches of the sack he had ground the flour so poorly that it contained whole kernels of wheat - husks and all. Much of it looked as though the seeds had just been plucked from the ear. That miller will feel my fist upon his chin when I return to London.

I shared a sodden bread loaf with the owl bird.

"Bread and water for supper, my friend," I said.

I sat and watched as the bird gulped down the mushy meal. The lumpy bread reminded me of Shepton prison and made me cringe. I felt sudden remorse for incarcerating the bird with a tether about its ankle. I had no right to hold this creature of the skies against its will any more than the English plod thought it just to jail me for rescuing a neglected rowboat from a lazy owner. We, the storm survivors, were more like brothers than master and slave. While the bird pecked at the bread, I slid across and, amidst a flurry of feathers and squawking, unknotted the string.

"Fly and be free, my feathered friend," I said. To my surprise the bird did not move, but simply continued to gullet down the bread.

"I can trap my own rats."

At this, the owl-bird turned its head. It looked at me with earnest eyes, but did not move.

"Fly. Fly away," I intoned, giving an impromptu lesson by flapping my arms.

The bird seemed to understand. It flapped its wings and lifted from the deck for a moment before settling back into place. Perhaps that was the extent of the strength in its wings, which were doubtless still blue from its long fight against the tempest.

"You're free to leave, bird. But you're welcome to stay and feast upon the galley rats if you wish. By my reckoning there's at least half a dozen."

Again the colourful parrot bird tilted its head, but did little else. I returned to my chores, and by and by I settled to my quarters. No doubt the bird will soon regain its strength and fly away.

Saturday 21 April

Despite four days of labour, my ship remained more slovenly than a West End bordello[109]. After breakfast consisting of just a single slice of cheese, I returned to my cleaning tasks, for despite now having little to do and a vast expanse of time in which to do it, I wanted the job completed quickly. The mess gnawed at my spirit. I trudged about for a few hours, mainly cleaning the flour paste off everything. At mid morning I surfaced to the deck.

To my surprise the bird was still aboard, perched on the port gunwale. Despite the stodginess of the fare, it must have appreciated the board and lodgings. (In truth it was probably still fatigued, but it did look a little stronger today.)

"Good morning bird."

The bird studied me as if I was a book.

---

[109] The west end of London is currently one of the most vibrant and exciting parts of the city. However in 1821 it contained many bordellos and other houses of ill repute.

Gaark Maark, it carked.

"Are you hungry?"

The bird sat still, its feathers ruffling in the breeze. I wanted to feed it a few titbits of food but I could not spare any rations. I had no reckoning how long it would be until the ocean currents carried the bobbing *Maris Alarum* to salvation ... it could even be midsummer, or beyond. Then I thought of the rat traps below.

"Would you like a rat for breakfast?"

The bird twisted its head and looked directly at me. I could swear it nodded its head, agreeing with my suggestion. I smiled at myself as I retreated to the hold; was I crazy to enjoy the company of a bird?

I emerged minutes later proudly swinging a near-dead rat by the tail.

"As promised, a rat, good sir." I pitched the rodent forward and the owl-bird intercepted it before it hit the deck. It made brief work of the meal; it must still be very hungry. When it had finished the bird sat tall, stretched its neck and then turned to look at me, eye to eye.

Raaaaarrrt, it squawked.

"My pleasure," I replied mockingly.

By and by I returned to my tasks, and by nightfall the holds and galley were a passing grade of tidy. In light of my diminished provisions I set two lures on trailing fishing lines, but had no strikes. After a morose supper of hard-cakes and a little beef, I checked the rat traps. They were empty. I cursed myself for discarding all of the spoiled pork and bread, for I had to sacrifice two pieces of cheese for the traps.

I now sit at my galley table with my third mug of rum at hand, to fortify me against my despair. I have repaired most of the storm damage in five days, but I still must find a way to repair the mast, for without it I bob aimlessly, at the mercy of the currents. This is not adventure, but instead is a tepid wait for ... for what? I am now going to the deck to have another draft of rum.

Sunday 22 April

I woke with only vague memories of the previous evening. Accompanied by several mugs of rum, I had talked to the bird for many hours. Sometimes rum sets the tongue too far from the brain and I suspected that might have happened during that evening. At least the bird did not come at me with its fists for some unintended slur, or lock me out to sleep in the stable.

I wasn't hungry, but I pined for a rich mug of coffee. But the storm had taken it from me, so I settled for weak black tea. After that I checked the rat traps, finding not one but two rodents. I hoped the bird was still on board, and a minute later was pleased to see it sitting upon its perch.

"Would you like some rat, my friend?"

Raaaart, it screeched.

"Come here, Bird" I said, motioning him closer. "I will give you some rat."

The bird looked at me, and then took a timid step closer.

"Here," I intoned quietly.

The bird looked at me intently again, but stayed motionless. I left one rat upon the deck and retreated two steps. Slowly, with hesitation, the bird inched its way along the rail, and by and by it pounced down onto the rat. I sat close by and watched it devour its prey.

When it had finished I held up the second trophy.

"Would you like another rat? Come." I held the rat out in my outstretched palm.

This time the bird was less hesitant; its need for food carried greater weight than its fear of me. It hopped across the deck and surprised me with its candour by plucking the rat directly from my grasp, and was soon tearing into the freshly killed flesh.

Raaaart.

"Thank you? You're welcome."

Raaart, it squawked again.

It was as if we were having a conversation.

Raaart.

I smiled weakly. It was nice to have someone to talk to, even if it was just a bird.

My motivation for activity remained low, but, by and by, I turned my attention to the mast, for I urgently needed to set sail for land. My provisions were low and fishing was unproductive, so I had to replace the mast as soon as was possible. But how could I conjure a mast from little more than air and water?

By and by, I had an idea. My original mast was keel-stepped.[110] Papa, before he passed, told me that some shipwrights were now affixing the mast directly to the deck. Perhaps I could remove fixing plate from the keel and reposition it onto the deck, thus lifting the mast a good few yards? However, on closer inspection it was quickly evident that this would not be possible; the fixing plate was designed merely to keep the base of the mast from slipping sideways, not to hold it vertically. Furthermore, the deck timbers were far too thin to hold a heavy load under such leverage and pressure, even if I shored them up with spare planks. I would have to find another way.

My next thought was to build an extension to fit atop the existing mast stump. But what could I use? The longest length of timber on board was the boom, but it was as vital as the mast and could not be sacrificed. I had a few spare hull planks that were too thin to be of service, and one spare bearer. Perhaps the bearer could be shaped? I scrambled down to the farthest hold and located a thick plank of elm. With great effort I dragged it to the deck for inspection.

The original mast had been ten yards high, a single trunk of conifer pine. The remaining stump was less than two yards high and the spare plank just three yards. If I somehow joined them at their ends I could create a mast five yards high – barely half the original and weaker as well. I thought of, but rejected, a few other ideas – pulling off a longer existing bearer, or binding two hull planks together – before settling upon my original plan. With luck a half-mast would get me to land, where I could search for a tall stout tree to form a more suitable replacement. It was a poor solution, but none other would cultivate itself in my mind.

---

[110] *Keel-stepped* refers to the practice of fixing the mast to the keel, at the bottom of the ship. Many modern yachts are, by contrast, *deck-stepped*.

Driven by ghastly imaginings of a slow hungry death, I fetched my tools from the hold, unwrapped them, set aside the oiled cloths, and with a deep sigh I ordered myself to work. First, using a galley chair as a horse, I sawed the entire plank end to end. I write this sentence easily, but in truth the labour was long and dogged. I cut it at a slight angle, forming a five-by-three-inch profile at the thicker end, tapering to three-by-three-inches at the top. I paused mid morning, and again at noon, to sharpen the saw. When fatigued (four times) I checked the fishing lines, finding them empty.

All the while the bird sat patiently upon its perch, watching me with its inquisitive gaze. At times when I moved about the deck it hopped after me, following me like a duckling trailing its mother. It seemed to be quite fond of me!

Finally, the plank split along its length. I adzed the square edges off and then used a spoke-shave to finish it like a pole. Then I sawed around its bottom end to a depth of about an inch and chiselled away the surplus timber, leaving an elliptical tenon three by two inches in area and six inches high, and then gouged a mortise of the same dimensions in the original mast stump[111]. This labour took me long past sunset. I hoped that soon I could fit the new extension atop the old mast stump, and sail away from this fishless ocean desert.

At night I sat in the galley, utterly exhausted, with the bird for company. I nibbled some salted beef and a slice of cheese, occasionally casting some crumbs for the bird. It was becoming very familiar - once it even perched on my forearm. It was heavier than it looked, and its talons were sharp and dug into my flesh, although not so deeply as to draw blood. I could feel the rough under-surface of its toes gripping against my skin.

I collapsed into my hammock early, under the weight of heavy fatigue. I slept soundly – not out of contentment or satisfaction, but utter exhaustion.

Monday 23 April.

---

[111] A *mortise and tenon* is a woodworking joint consisting of a protruding knob that inserts into a matched hole

The day was hot and still and the seas were calm, so I was again without excuse to shirk my tasks. After a poor breakfast of tea and sauerkraut, I checked the rat traps – empty – and the fishing lines – also empty.

"Morning bird,' I mumbled, for my day had started poorly.

Gaar Maar, the bird warbled back.

"More work today, bird," I said, gesturing at the mast.

Raaart. Raaart.

"Hopefully we'll be sailing again by tomorrow."

The bird twisted its head, ruffled its hackles[112] and squared me in its penetrating gaze.

Raaart. Raaart.

I sighed. "I might as well be working as talking to a mangy squawking bird," I said aloud. However, I soon felt glad that it could not understand my language, for the thought had come from my tired head and not my heart.

I recommenced the mast repair, being chiefly concerned with whittling the tenon on the mast extension and rasping the mortise on the stump until they fitted each other precisely. Due to the extreme forces on it when bearing a hoisted sail, I would not tolerate any play in the joint. The bird watched me closely as I worked - at one point I brushed it aside, for it had flown to my shoulder and was squawking in my ear. *Raart raart raart.* (I shall hear that noise in my dreams tonight, I am sure.) The bird, although a handsome creature, was becoming annoying.

In the afternoon I fashioned eye-bolts[113] and other mast fixtures from wire, nails and other assorted spares. I also fixed two spare pulleys to the very tip of the mast, ready to accept the mainsail and headsail halyard ropes. After a miserable supper of oatcakes – there were still no fish on the lures – I turned to the rum to soften my dismay.

---

[112] The hackles are the feathers at the back of a bird's neck. Some birds lift these feathers when anxious or under duress, giving rise to the modern term "to raise one's hackles".

[113] Eye bolts are bolts with a hole – en eye – at the end, allowing for ropes or clamps to be fed through them.

Tuesday 24 April

I awoke late, with my stomach green from last night's final mug of rum. Perhaps the ache in my head was from the second last draft, and my rasping dry mouth from the third-to-last.

Maybe I have doused my despair with too much rum lately? But when my chores are done, and the heaviness returns to my bones, it seems the only way to get through the evening.

I had only faint recall of proceedings, for the spirit had taken a firm hold. I sported a bruise on my shoulder and a deep cut above my left eye. Hazily I recalled spinning about as the ship rolled, before bouncing off the galley bench and thudding to the floor. I remembered the bird cackling at my misfortune.

I was pleased that my tin looking glass was dull for the want of shining, for I had no desire to face myself this morning. To view my own hanging cheeks and to gaze into my own red eyes would have filled me with nothing but self-pity. Thankfully, the dull reflection from the grimy metal let one small part of my denial remain, allowing me just enough wind to keep my own flag aloft, even though it was a bedraggled cloth hanging limply at half mast.

My day again started late, with the lasting effects of the rum still coursing through me. Throughout the morning the bird squawked its incessant *Raart raart* at my ear again and again, prickling my mood. Eventually I lost patience and tried to clip it with the back of my hand. Try as I might, it was too quick for me to land a telling blow. By and by I relented; barely an hour after rising I was prostrate in my hammock, and slept sporadically until mid afternoon.

Eventually I roused, and cursed myself for losing the greater part of a day's work. Angry, I set to my tasks fervently, and by evening I had fitted and glued the mast extension into place. I was pleased to note that the mortise held very tightly about the tenon, with not even a sixteenth[114] of play. I hitched some temporary stay-ropes[115] in position.

---

[114] A sixteenth refers to one sixteenth of an inch – about 1.6 mm. McAdam was obviously a fine craftsman.

[115] The *stays* are the ropes that keep the mast upright. Today they are more commonly referred to as *shrouds*.

Tomorrow I will set some permanent rigging. I keenly anticipate the surge of the keel through the brine as the wind fills the sails.

Wednesday 25 April

Once I assured myself that my carpentry was sound – the mortise and tenon was holding the extension neatly to the vertical, and had very little wobble (my papa would be proud, although he might not have said as much) - I set out to fix the mast stays in place. My first task was to feed the stay ropes through the eye-bolts at the top of the mast. However I had not carved footholds nor affixed pegs to the mast for fear of weakening it, so the ascent was proving mightily difficult. I was also worried that my weight, when combined with the lurching of the boat, would prove too much of a load for the repair to tolerate, meaning that my efforts were hesitant, and tempered by anxiety.

I had attempted more than a half-a-dozen times to climb the mast, but could not haul myself to within an arm's reach of the top eye-bolt. The climb was all the more strenuous because I also had to carry the stay-rope over my shoulder, rendering one arm as a poor contributor. I quickly earned three large splinters for my efforts.

Cursing like a navvy, I berated myself for not having looped the stays in position before erecting the mast. By and by, I managed to climb within reach of the mast tip, but as I stretched out my arm to feed the stay through the eye-bolt, the rope slipped from my grasp and fell, landing in a crumpled coil on deck. Cursing loudly, I slid down the mast, earning a fourth splinter as I did, before regathering the rope and climbing back up once more.

I was lathering like a flogged horse by the time I finally looped the stay through the eye-bolt, descended, and then knotted the free ends of the stay rope to the fore and aft pad-eyes[116]. Two stays were complete, but I still had the port-side stays to fix. Throughout the whole vexing exercise the bird had observed me with barely a movement, except of its head, which bobbed up and down, following my exertions.

---

[116] A pad-eye was a plate with a small raised loop it its centre, which was screwed or bolted into the deck. It served as a firm anchoring point for rope.

Again I attempted to climb the mast. Again I fumbled the rope as I reached for the eye-bolt, and had to descend to retrieve it. During my next attempt, I witnessed the bird do something that I had never seen before.

I had just dropped the rope for the second time as I reached for the eye-bolt. The bird, who had been pensively observing my activities, suddenly emitted a loud squawk. I looked down to see it hop toward the coil and grasp the tag end of the rope in its talons. At first I was alarmed that the bird might abscond with one of my best ropes. But then, without further ritual, the bird flew upward, close enough to me that I was able to retrieve the stay from its talons! Thanks to the bird, I was able to feed the rope through the eye-bolt and was soon on deck, shaking my disbelieving head.

My mind harkened back to the show at Billingsgate market, where *The Astonishing Andrew's* canine performed tricks, and a bird responded to his utterances. I also knew that some farmers kept dogs as workers, and had trained them to do menial tasks, so it was clear that animals could be taught simple manoeuvres. However, I have never heard of a creature, be it bird or beast, to assist a man without prior training. But I had to believe my eyes, for they had never lied to me before, and there was no-one else to bear witness to the bird's astonishing act. Perhaps, I thought, the bird had a familiar ritual in its own habitat, such as fetching vines from the forest floor to weave a nest. Regardless, the bird's action saved me a frustrating task.

I was relieved that I did not have the energy to clip the owl-parrot with my hand yesterday, for it was a good bird. Yesterday's anger was only the rum tiredness talking; the cussing had not come truly from my heart. Grateful, I fetched the bird a slice of salted beef. It had earned its keep today.

Thursday 26 April

I was pleased to see a rat in the trap this morning for it meant that the bird could have a feed without weakening my stores. I emerged onto deck holding the captured prey in my outstretched hands. The bird needed no invitation, and without any hesitation it perched on my forearm and had soon devoured its meal.

91

Raart, raart it screeched between beakfuls of flesh, wolfing down the rodent like a Viking devouring a sheep's shank.

I set myself to the task of hoisting the sails. Soon I encountered the same problem as yesterday: how could I loop the halyard rope through the pulley at the top of the mast? My fingers were splintered and blistered, so I did not wish to repeat my near-futile climbing efforts of the previous day. Instead I fetched some thick rope, cut it into short lengths, and knotted each tightly around the mast at intervals of about one foot, forming a ladder of sorts. I hitched the stays as tightly as possible to hold the mast firm, and then, clenching the mainsail halyard between my teeth, I inched my way up the mast-ladder. I had learned that mast climbing was a far harder task than it appeared, so I was pleased to thread the lanyard through the top pulley on my first attempt. Just the headsail halyard remained before I could truly call the *Maris Alarum* a sailing ship. Again I ascended the mast on my makeshift ladder, but then fumbled the rope as I reached to thread it through its pulley. As the halyard fell to the deck, I looked to the bird: could it repeat its heroics from yesterday?

It did not move.

"Fetch," I called to the bird. "Fetch the rope."

The bird sat motionless, pitiless to my plight. I called to it again, but soon realised that I was unrealistically optimistic to expect a repeat of something so incredible. On previous occasions in Blackfriars Tavern I had gambled a few pennies on the draw of a single card and won, but never had I succeeded twice in a row. Miracles did not come in pairs.

I retreated down the mast, retrieved the rope and lumbered back up the splintered pole. With only a small measure of further frustration I eventually threaded the halyard, and with great relief lowered myself to the deck. I tightened and tensioned the last of the rigging, rechecked that all was in good order, and then it was finally time to turn my bobbing bathtub into a sailing ship once more.

Without ceremony, I hoisted first the mainsail and then the headsail. Even though they were lax, and less than half of their normal height, the weakly fluttering and flapping sails were a joyous sight for my rundown eyes. I was pleased to see the fruits of my long labours performing as intended. Even though she was lacking in grandeur, the *Maris Alarum* was now a sailing ship again, and not a giant death casket bobbing upon the ocean.

My reckoning was that the mast would tolerate no more than 15 knots of wind – a moderate breeze at best. My going would be slow and tedious, but at least I now had some control over my direction. I set a course of east-south-east, reckoning the African coast to be the nearest port of salvation.

I spent the rest of the afternoon resting on deck, simply enjoying the movement of my ship through the ocean and the joy of the salt air through my hair. I talked often to the bird; if I had seen someone else doing this I would have thought them half mad, but somehow, out here in the middle of a vast and empty sea, it seemed a normal undertaking. At first the bird moved little, just staring at me intently with its deep owl-like eyes, as was its habit. Later it began cackling and garbling, almost like it was replying to my soliloquies. It really was a strange little creature, but I was beginning to like it.

Friday 27 April

I emerged this morning in lighter spirits, for the wind was in my sails again. Although I knew the mast was far from stout, it was holding the canvas at a slight billow. Perhaps within a few weeks the *Maris Alarum* would touch land. I could then limp south to the Cape Town, where I could replenish my flagging stores, replace my makeshift mast and start my journey afresh.

I looked for the bird, and was pleased to see it flying level with the deck, stretching its wings and occasionally flying low along the water, occasionally dipping its talons under, perhaps hunting fish. Clearly it was regaining its strength. When it saw me, it landed softly down on its rail perch.

Gaar maar, it cackled; its warble sounded softer and more mellifluous than its previous carks and caws.

 "Good morning."

Raart. Raart.

Ah, now that was more familiar.

Raart.

I set about my business, until suddenly I was struck by thought. Perhaps this squawk was not but a dumb bird's cackle, but instead a request. A request for....

Raart.

I retreated to the galley and checked the traps. One snare had entombed a tiny rodent. Quickly, I returned to deck and held up the prize.

Raart, raart screeched the bird, flapping its wings excitedly. I tossed the rat in the air. The bird launched after it, its blue and red plumes shooting through the air, and nearly guzzled the rat whole before it hit the deck.

"Raart" for rat? Had the bird learned to repeat my utterances?

I knew it was possible, for I had heard with my own ears The Astonishing Andrew's parrot repeat its master's tongue, and even act as though it was answering his questions. I wondered if I could teach the bird to do the same. It would prove an interesting amusement while we sailed our way slowly to land – wherever and whenever that might be. I decided to try.

I started with the names of foodstuffs, for each morsel would provide a simple reward if the bird named it correctly. As I fetched small portions of various provisions from the galley, I smiled at the memory of the tapas plate in Oporto, which I had now recreated in simplistic form for the bird. I sat crossed legged on deck, opposite the bird. It looked at me intently, then at the food plate and then back at me. I picked up a shred of salted beef.

"Beef," I intoned.

The bird said nothing, but simply stared at the morsel of meat in my fingers.

"Beef."

Its eyes widened, but again it said nothing. I tried again a few more times, but was met by nothing but silence. I put the beef on the deck and instead tried a slice of cheddar.

"Cheese."

Nothing. The bird's eyes followed the cheese, occasionally darting back to the slice of beef lying on the deck.

"Cheese. Cheese. Cheese." I repeated the words slowly and at length, but did not receive a reply. I picked up a raisin and tried the same approach.

"Raisin."

The bird turned its head like an owl, ruffled its blue neck feathers and looked down at the salted beef slice again, but still it said nothing. The sun methodically rose in the eastern sky as I tried to coax the bird to talk. I tried teaching it the words for peas, oat-cakes and even sauerkraut, but not a caw passed its beak. Although I had little else on my card for the day, by and by I tired of the lessons. Perhaps I had again been too optimistic; teaching a bird to talk might not be as easy as I had imagined.

Feeling hungry, I devoured the cheese and raisins. The bird sat looking at me, clearly waiting for a morsel, but with rations so tight I could not be lenient, for it had not repeated the words. Savouring every bite of my 'beggar's tapas', I shelled and ate the peas and then the sauerkraut. I was picking my way through the final shards of beef when, in an off-hand way, I waved a sliver before the bird's owl-like eyes and said *beef*. The bird flapped its wings, lifted itself perhaps a foot above the deck, then settled back to its spot. Then it flapped its wings again; seemingly satisfied that it now had my attention, it looked at me and cawed:

Beeeeef.

Then it looked at the shred of salted meat in my hand and then back at me.

Beeeeef.

Had there been just a breath of wind, it would have blown me over like a top out of spin.

"Very good, bird," I exclaimed aloud. "Beef?" I asked.

It looked at me squarely and carked again.

Beeeeef.

I shook my head to rebalance my senses, for to hear a sound that passed as English from a bird's beak was a surprise, even though it was exactly what I had been hoping to hear. As a reward I held out the meat, which the bird quickly snatched away.

Aaark.

"You're welcome, good Sir," I replied with mock pomposity. I broke to a broad grin and laughed. Yes, I laughed: the simple joy of this success had snuck in through a door that I didn't realise I had left ajar.

In the evening, I carried the bird on my forearm to the galley where we shared supper, for its achievement deserved a simple celebration. I also enjoyed a draft of rum, but for once this tipple was more festive than medicinal.

Later, after much word repetition, the bird learned the word for the spirit, and later kept cawing *raarm, raarm, raarm.* It sounded like it was ordering three drinks from a bar-wench at Blackfriars!

I smiled as I bunked down for the night. After weeks of sorrow and desolation, a simple bird had changed my mood. I hoped that it stayed on board the *Maris Alarum,* for it was a welcome distraction from this otherwise Doldrums-like sail[117].

Saturday 28 April

The wind was slight today, which suited the mast. The old jack tar inside me was very confused, for I found myself wanting a light breeze rather than a stiff wind –the opposite of my normal wish. But mostly I was pleased to see that the top and bottom sections of the mast remained vertical, and in one piece.

After breakfast and completion of my morning chores, I set myself to teach the bird some more words. I chopped up some provisions into morsels – tiny portions, for I had little to spare – to use as rewards. So far the bird had mastered three words (*rat*, *beef* and *rum*), and I hoped to teach it another one or two today.

---

[117] The *Doldrums* was an area of ocean in which the prevailing winds were slight, meaning that sailing was slow. The modern expression 'in the doldrums', which refers to feeling bored, tired or listless, has its genesis in this nautical term.

I started with a repeat of yesterday's lesson, but this time focusing upon the words *cheese* and *raisin*. I held up a sample of each, simultaneously saying the word. At first the bird was silent, but after an hour or so I finally managed to coax the bird to repeat a single word: in this case, *raaaarzin*. I rewarded it with a juicy titbit of the dried fruit.

That success buoyed me to continue, but I had to rest often, for the bird would lose interest in my tutelage. During these periods, I busied myself with chores, or with trying (but failing) to discern my position. Then I would tempt the bird back to my forearm with a morsel of beef, before settling onto the deck for another lesson. After midday I coaxed the bird to repeat a word for cheese – *kreeese.* It seemed to find the "ch" sound difficult to pronounce.

Later in the evening, while we sat under the cool cloudless sky on the deck, I decided to set the bird a challenge. From a crock of sauerkraut I scooped a goodly portion and held it in front of the bird's wide eyes.

"Sow-er-kraut," I said slowly.

The bird sat, staring with its owl-like eyes at the pickled cabbage, but said nothing.

"Sow-er-kraut," I repeated.

The bird seemed disinterested and preened its blue and red wing feathers with its beak, seemingly to demonstrate its feelings to me. I tried again and again but could not get the bird to repeat the word. By and by it looked at me and carked *Raaaarzin*.

"No, this is a raisin," I replied, holding up a tiny fruit. "This," I shook the pickled cabbage, "is *sow-er-kraut*."

The bird suddenly pitched forward and snatched the raisin from my fingers before I had even flinched. The thieving spiv! It had not earned that reward. I lashed out on instinct, clipping it across its wing with a short backhand blow. It screeched and then took flight.

Instantly I realised that I had reacted poorly. In my past, many men have deserved of a swipe from the back of my hand, but this bird, who had simply taken a morsel of food to sate its hunger, was not one of them. I turned to placate it but it had flown to the top of the mast.

"I'm sorry bird," I hollered, but even as the apology escaped my lips I knew that it was futile, for it would not understand my words. I proffered three plump raisins in my outstretched palm but could not coax it down. By and by I tired of cajoling, and retired to my quarters for the night, leaving the raisins on the deck as a form of apology.

As I lay in my hammock, my mind harkened back to my childhood schooling at Reverend Butler's[118] classroom for boys – that grim, foreboding place. True, I was in many ways fortunate, for my papa and in particular my mama saw rare value in reading and writing, whereas most lads were ordered to work from 10 years of age. I was also fortunate that Reverend Butler himself was a writer of sorts[119], and that he pushed my faculties to the full.

But it was my memory of Bible readings that stuck in my craw the most firmly: we pupils stood in a semi-circle reading obscure Bible passages in turn, with the Reverend prowling behind us ready to strike with six cracks of his birch should anyone mispronounce even a single word. Quickly I came to not only abhor the Bible but the teachings of its Church as well. It was clear to me, but unfortunately not the Reverend, that flogging was a poor way to impress faith or knowledge into a young mind.

With Reverend Butler as my reference, I vowed that I would not strike the bird again. I only hoped that it had not taken flight from the indignity of my swipe. As for the word for *sauerkraut* - well, perhaps the bird did not speak German!

Sunday 29 April

I sat with the bird perched on my arm, enjoying the firm sun and the movement of the *Maris Alarum* through the water. My morning gift of a small rat appeared to have healed our rift. Later, once my chores were

---

[118] McAdam's schoolmaster was Reverend Thomas Butler. Butler was a clergyman, but he harboured an open desire to join the navy. Perhaps this yearning helped to bond him with the young Fintan McAdam, whose family was steeped in shipping. The Reverend's father, Dr Samuel Butler (Snr) came from a long line of tradesman but distinguished himself with his scholarly talents, much like McAdam. Such a transition was rare at the time.
[119] Reverend Butler's son, Samuel Butler (Jnr) became a famous novelist. He was no doubt encouraged down this path by his scholarly father and grandfather.

complete, I set myself to teach the bird more words. Its vocabulary had increased by two words yesterday, a total I was determined to expand upon. The bird's tongue was quickly becoming the focus of my days, and while I realised that the pursuit was trite, I was glad to have something, anything, on which to focus while I sailed slowly east.

I had a tin mug full of shredded food scraps as encouragement. Rather than teach the bird more words for foodstuffs, I decided to introduce it to some nautical terms. I placed the bird on its favoured perch on the port gunwale and then pointed to the sail.

"Sail," I slowly enunciated, while holding a crumb of cheese where the bird could see it. "Sail."

Kreeese.

"No, *this* is cheese," I said calmly, pointing at the cheese. "*This*....is a *sail*."

The bird tilted its head and widened its eyes, gazing from one to the other. It seemed perplexed, if it is possible for a bird to look as such. I repeated the words for each item – cheese ... sail ... cheese ... sail –in confluence with its shifting gaze. Then I pointed at the sail again, clearly identifying it. Still the bird just looked. Slowly and calmly – for I was determined to hold both my temper and the back of my hand– I repeated my actions and words. Nothing.

To break the frustration, I reverted to an earlier lesson, and simply pointed at the cheese.

"Cheese" I said.

Kreeese.

"Good bird," I mumbled, feeding it the sliver. Quickly I retrieved another slice from the mug and pointed at the sail.

"Sail."

Kreeese.

"No, *this* is a sail."

Kreeese.

"Sail."

Aaark. Simple displeasure.

Calmly: "Sail."

The bird shifted its gaze between the morsel in my fingers and the large expanse of flapping canvas, and then back at me. "Sail," I said yet again, firmly but with measured tone. It was after two dozen more firm but patient repetitions that the bird finally opened its beak correctly.

Saaaarl, it cawed.

Yes! Yes, it had done it. The bird had learned a new word.

"Good bird, good bird," I whispered, and quickly supplied its reward.

I held up a different reward, this time a shelled pea, and pointed to the sail, intoning the word as I did. The bird simply sat in silence.

"Sail," I offered again, slowly repeating the word until the bird carked back *saaarl.*

"Well done bird, you've earned your pea," I said, stroking the bird's neck plumage as I fed it the tiny treat. It almost seemed pleased with itself. Emboldened, I encouraged it onto my forearm and carried it amidships, pointing at the mast.

"Mast," I said, using a slow and clear tone. This time I had not shown the reward to the bird. Would it respond without such encouragement?

I would like to report that it was easy, but that would be a falsehood. It took at least a dozen more lessons, each intertwined with periods of rest, chores, navigation and eating, not to mention many dozen repetitions of the word, before the bird finally responded in kind. *Maaaarst.*

I dug about the mug until I found a raisin, which seemed to be the bird's favourite treat, and fed it directly into its beak. We practiced for a while longer, but soon the bird lost interest. Despite the drawn out drudgery of the day I was quietly pleased, for the bird now knew seven words. Already we were closing in on Perty the Parrot and The Astonishing Andrew!

Monday 30 April

It was clear that with patience I could teach the bird to repeat my words. But today I wondered whether it was simply mimicking my words, or if it truly understood their meaning? This afternoon, with my tasks completed and the sun cooling in the west, I sought to find out.

I lined up three morsels of food: beef, cheese and a raisin. When I had the bird's attention, I directed my gaze toward the rewards. Without saying anything, I pointed to the beef and looked at the bird expectantly. I wanted it to name the food without my prompting to see if it could remember and say the word by itself. But the bird simply sat, staring longingly at the titbits, with not even a tweet passing its beak.

I pointed at the cheese, then the raisin, but the bird remained quiet. I repeated this exercise many times as the sun worked its way downward. At times I proffered "what is this?" but I admit this was to quell my mounting frustration rather than to assist the bird's understanding. As the sun touched the horizon my patience wore thin, so I retreated to the galley for a calming mug of rum, allowing the bird to follow me.

After slowly finishing and refilling my mug, I continued the bird's lesson at the galley table. Again, I arranged the titbits, pointing to each in turn and waiting for the bird to reply. Many times I wanted to break the impasse by naming the morsel for the bird to repeat, but knew that this would not help my cause.

By and by the bird lost interest in proceedings. It began preening itself and then hopped about the galley. Later, as I sipped on my second mug of rum, the presence of the food morsels lured it back. It dared not touch the food without my permission (so perhaps yesterday's backhanded cuff, impetuous as it was, had served a purpose). I urged myself to remain patient, and continued pointing, but as the pink light from the sunset above dulled to grey, I capitulated. For many hours my frustration had waged a battle with my patience and was now winning the confrontation. It seemed that the bird did not really understand the meaning of the words, but was simply repeating my sounds. Perhaps I had expected too much from a simple animal.

I reached for my mug, and proffered it toward the bird in a false show of good manners.

"God bless you," I offered as I took a gulp.

Suddenly the bird let out a loud cark.

Raarm.

I looked at the bird, surprised. Had it just named the spirit without prompting? I fed it a raisin and held the mug out toward it, also pointing with my free hand.

"What is this, Bird?" I asked expectantly. "What is this? "

Raarm, screeched the bird again.

I fed it another titbit. I pointed to the rum again and received the same reply from the bird: *raarm*. Had it finally understood? Did it understand that the mug held rum, rather than simply repeating my sounds?

I arranged some food scraps on the table and pointed at a sliver of meat, occasionally prompting it with simple phrases such as "What is this?" After only half a dozen attempts, the bird widened its eyes, then shook its feathers before carking *Beeeef*. I let out a short whoop. Such was my sense of achievement that I fed it two large shards, even though I had precious little to spare.

Enlivened, I spent the hour before supper pointing to different foodstuffs in turn, and by the end of the session the bird could name each one correctly without verbal cues. After tea we climbed to the deck, where it repeated the words for *mast* and *sail* using only the prompt of my pointing. In contradiction to my earlier thoughts, it now seemed that the bird *could* understand the meaning of the words. This was a significant revelation; like a trained dog taught to *sit* or *roll over*, the bird was able to conceive simple meanings from words and not just repeat sounds.

This realisation added a new level of purpose to our lessons. Perhaps I could teach it to perform some simple tricks as well. I was not sure if this was possible, but if a dog could be taught to respond to basic commands, then I could not see why this clever bird could not be trained as well. But, I decided, I would leave this task for another day.

As I lay in my hammock that night, I realised that not once today did I fret about the mast, Africa, my low provisions, or my increasingly hungry belly. I had drunk only a few modest mugs of rum, and nightmarish visions of Beth had not attacked me for many days. It seemed that occupying my time with the bird, and gaining simple pleasure from our achievements, was allowing other real problems to fade into the background hum of my mind. I was content to simply focus upon my pet bird and leave the sailing to the *Maris Alarum* and the fortuitously steady westerly breeze.

Was this a good thing? I wondered. Was it wise to ignore my problems for a token few days of enjoyment?

I think so. I know that the bird's words are nothing more than a diversion, and that they serve no purpose other than my entertainment. But I won't allow this realisation dim my pleasure, for I have encountered very few agreeable moments in recent weeks; Mother Ocean had not gifted them very generously. To rebuff this satisfaction because it was trivial would be self-denial for no reason. I have suffered too much in my recent past to allow any such deprivation.

As I drifted to sleep, I noticed that my lips were set in a small, contented smile.

Tuesday 1 May

I spent the morning reviewing the previous day's lessons with the bird. It had a good memory, and soon consolidated its knowledge.

In the afternoon I taught the bird a verb. (There is a sentence that I did not foresee writing in my log!) It took some time, but after much persistence – and undeniably some irritation – the bird grasped the concept of 'fly'. In the initial stages I helped it to understand by nudging it into the air from my forearm in synchronicity with my command. It soon learned to flap briefly around the deck before docking back on my forearm to claim its reward. By and by I only needed to issue the command and the bird would take to the air, even if was perched on the gunwale at the time.

By nightfall, the bird's sharp talons and rasping skin had welted my forearm with a train of small scratches. I bathed the lesions in salted boiled water, and wrapped them in the canvas bandage that I had used earlier on my broken foot. I decided that I would henceforth use the wrapping whenever the bird perched on my arm, for I had no medicine to prevent the small wounds from becoming poisoned.

After my evening meal, as I sat out on deck with a simple draft of rum, it struck me that the bird did not yet have a name. It had shown no inclination to depart so I felt – and, I confess, hoped – that it would stay on as my pet. As a pet, it needed a name, for "the bird" was lacking in familiarity.

Drawing upon my schoolboy Latin, I tossed possible names through my mind: *Tempastus Avis*, for Storm Bird; *Callidus Avis*, for Clever Bird; or even *Magna Psittacus*, for Big Parrot - certainly the bird was all of those things. But each moniker seemed too starched for such a bright and happy creature. But when the Latin word for 'Owl' came to mind I knew, instantly, that the name would fit the bird like an old boot. I pointed at the bird.

"Bubo."

The bird seemed confused and tipped its head sideways.

"You *Bubo*."

Again I was met with silence. Even after perhaps two dozen repetitions the bird did not seem to grasp the concept of its own name. By and by I tried another method, pointing to the mast.

"Mast"

By and by came the bird's reply: *Maarst.*

"Sail."

After some time*, Saarl.*

Then I pointed at the bird again.

"Bubo."

The bird twisted its neck and looked again at the mast and sails. Then it tipped its neck, as if to look at itself. Then, in a quiet cark, it said its own name.

Boooooo-bo.

"Yes, you're Bubo," I beamed."Bubo, the cleverest bird on all the seven seas."

The bird sat tall, flapped his[120] handsome wings and trilled his own name again, this time loudly. *Boooooo-bo!* The bird's gaiety - for I am

---

[120] Henceforth McAdam uses the pronoun 'he' when referring to Bubo, rather than 'it'. While it is unclear if McAdam was able to identify Bubo's sex, the use

sure that he was displaying pleasure - was joyous to observe. Now, perhaps, the bird could learn my name. I pointed at Bubo and then at myself, and slowly intoned the words:

"You, Bubo ... me ... Captain McAdam."

Bubo studied me carefully with his large owl's eyes.

I repeated the names while pointing: "Bubo ... Captain McAdam ... Bubo ... Captain McAdam...."

Caarptaarn.

"Yes! Yes, Captain."

Captaarn.

"Captain *McAdam,*" I repeated as I pointed at myself.

I failed to appreciate that I was holding a mug of rum close to my chest, and that Bubo looked at this cup each time I pointed. Suddenly, his confused, wide black eyes contracted, almost as if he understood something. Then he looked at me again, then back to the mug, and then me once more before finally lifting his wings and cawing:

Captaarn Raarm.

Before I could react he flapped his wings and took to the air, squawking *Captaarn Raarm* in full voice.

"No Bubo," I hollered, now aware that he had mistaken my gestures. "I am Captain *McAdam,* not Captain Rum."

Captaarn Raarm.

I tried correcting him again but my pleas fell upon obstinate bird ears. Clearly he had christened me with his own moniker: Captain Rum.

I should have named him *Cucule insolens:* The Cheeky Bastard.

Wednesday 2 May

In between my usual chores, my futile attempts to discern my longitude, and several cups of weak tea to ward off my mounting hunger, Bubo and I spent another day in lessons. Buoyed by our

---

of this pronoun does suggest increasing familiarity.

previous successes, I decided to teach him to respond to another instruction. After spending the morning in training - which involved a game with small rewards that I hid under mugs, first side by side, but then around the deck – he mastered the command *find*. By the end of our session I could instruct him to 'Find Beef' or 'Find Raisin' and he would go to where he had seen me secrete that morsel and root it out.

Later, as I was dropping through the hatch in the galley, I thought to test Bubo's intuition with a different command.

"Find rat," I instructed, while pointing into the galley where I had seen two rats only that morning.

Bubo tilted his head sideways, but apart from that twitch he did not move. I tried again. "Find rat." I pointed down the hatch. "Rat," I repeated. "Find rat." By and by he seemed to grasp my intent and dropped himself below deck. I sat in the breeze, smiling and listening to him scurrying around below. Eventually he emerged from the hold with a small rat's tail protruding from his mouth. After gulping it down, he looked at me and cawed *Raart*. I may be over-interpreting Bubo's expression, but he did seem to be proud of himself.

I recalled from my natural history lessons that some birds have surprising intelligence. Aesop's crow raised the level of water in a pitcher by dropping stones into it until it was high enough to drink[121]. Also, a farmer from Sussex had observed a crow stealing bait from a rodent trap by pushing it with a stick held in its beak. I guessed that Bubo's intelligence was at least equal to those crows, if not higher. Certainly his language repetition skills were superior. Perhaps he was even as clever as a dog.

I hoped that Bubo would stay with me for my entire journey, for he would provide great entertainment to people in port– maybe I could start a travelling tent show with him, like The Astonishing Andrew. If he stayed with me all the way back to London then he would also provide great insight to students of natural history in the Society. Perhaps I could even arrange an audience with Mr Banks[122].

---

[121] *Aesop* was an ancient Greek writer who is most famous for his fables. Modern researchers have confirmed that crows are intelligent enough to understand the physics of water displacement as mentioned in Aesop's tale.
[122] *The Society* refers to the Geographic Society, while Mr Banks is no doubt the

After completing Bubo's lessons I took stock of my provisions, which were perilously low. Some of my earlier generosity toward Bubo was warranted as I considered him my responsibility, but I now realised that I could not dole my rations with impunity, for with my weak sails I was covering barely two leagues per day. Landfall could yet be a month away.

The total food on board was as follows:

- ❖   Salted beef: six pounds.
- ❖   Raisins: Only four dozen or so remained
- ❖   Cheese: Less than half a pound
- ❖   Peas: Half a box unshelled.
- ❖   Sauerkraut: half a crock
- ❖   One small jar of bruised tomatoes in salt
- ❖   Tea: three parts in four of a large sack; weak but plentiful.
- ❖   Oat hard-cakes: plentiful but now with some mould. The oat seed in one biscuit had even sprouted a tiny shoot, no doubt a result of its previous dousing. The lousy Billingsgate baker clearly did not bake them sufficiently - he was as much a scoundrel as the lazy miller who prepared my flour with such haste that some of it contained whole wheat kernels.

I still had an unopened packet of yeast, but I had no use for it without flour. Thankfully my water was abundant, although it now tasted stale. I had just eight gallons of rum and lemon remaining. In all I had only seven days rations, perhaps another day or two if I was strict. But I had no spare food for Bubo.

I was sure that Bubo was capable of catching his own fish, but very few seemed to be about. I checked the fishing lines regularly but had caught nothing. Did the typhoon drive all the creatures from the ocean? Perhaps when the *Maris Alarum* was nearer to the coast the warmer currents and rocky habitats would provide richer pickings, but out here, in this vast and featureless ocean, the marine life was sparse. So my hunger grew and my belly shrank. I hoped that Bubo could find enough rats to keep himself fed, although I feared that they, too, were now in short supply.

---

aforementioned Sir Joseph Banks.

The westerly wind had turned and mellowed, so I spent much of the afternoon on deck, actively working the sails and whipstaff, trying to extract another yard from every puff. In between I taught Bubo a new word (*pea*) and tried to ignore my mounting hunger pains. In the evening I studied my navigation charts and tried to plot my latitude from the stars. But I could not make my position truly and had no knowledge of my longitude at all. Never have I been so utterly lost.

Thursday 3 May

I awoke to a fifteen-knot breeze, which was the strongest wind I had encountered since the typhoon passed over. I wanted to test the mast repair, so I set the headsail and mainsail wing-to-wing. However I soon regretted my confidence, for the mast developed a kink at the join. I shored it with extra timbers that I bound tightly over the joint with cord. I also set two extra mast stays, bringing the total to six. The extra stays will cause inconvenience about the deck, but if they helped to keep the mast true then I was prepared to suffer a skinned shin or two.

Before setting the stays I trained Bubo in a task. It took most of the day, and a small portion of beef and raisins– in truth, more than I should have spared – but eventually Bubo mastered the skill of passing a rope through a the hole in an eye-bolt. I began this lesson by first teaching him the word for *rope*. When I was confident that he understood the word, I demonstrated the instruction *thread rope* by repeatedly feeding the rope through a mock mast & eye-bolt, and then encouraging Bubo to attempt the task using his dextrous talons and beak.

Although I wrote the above words in just a few minutes, in truth this task was long and tiresome, particularly on the frequent occasions in which Bubo tired of my repetition. But I held fast to my goal, and although it consumed a lot of my patience, I hoped that Bubo could use this new skill for a purpose. As the setting sun tipped on the horizon. I placed a stay rope in his talons, and then instructed him to *fly*. Once he was aloft I commanded him to *thread rope*.

I was inordinately pleased that he completed his set task on only his fourth attempt. I conceded that the teaching exercise took far longer than had I simply completed the rigging myself, but Bubo had now learned a task that might prove useful in the future. I also saved myself two climbs up the mast, which, besides holding a promise of more splinters, may have weakened the mortise and tenon joint even further.

By nightfall both extra stays were in place and I had tightened them with haymaker's hitches. Despite the additional stays and the extra timber around the joint, I reckoned that I could not trust the mast at any breeze over a gentle push. My onward journey would be slow and painstaking.

I was pleased that Bubo remained on board because – I hope that this does not sound like I am touched by a fever - I enjoyed his company. I talked to him often, even though he could not possibly understand me. The simple chatter kept my mind from idle wandering down unhappy paths. My nightmarish apparitions had diminished in both intensity and frequency since Bubo arrived, and I wished for it to stay that way.

But he, too, was growing hungrier by the day. Although he found one small rat last night, even after a thorough root through the hold today he did not discover any prey. I feared that the earlier traps might have worked too well. Had I known that Bubo would remain on board I would have bred the rodents in a cage. Once or twice I saw him plunging his talons into the water after fish, but I have not seen him catch anything of size or substance.[123] I checked the fishing lines three times per day but caught nothing. This ocean was as barren as a Glaswegian winter garden.

I am now subsisting primarily on tea and hard cakes. However, the cakes are deteriorating and what I don't consume in the next few days will be unpalatable.

Friday 4 May

I took my telescope and scanned the horizon in the warm light of morning, hoping to sight land through the clear light of the rising sun. My scope was a fine one and showed the wave tops with clarity, but

---

[123] Many birds typically eat nuts and seeds, but are opportunistic omnivores, and will therefore eat small animals, including fish, if necessary. A student from the veterinary department assures me that it is even safe to feed fish to domestic parrots.

alas that is all it sighted. I regularly scanned for bird flocks or a suggestion of a fish school, but sighted nothing of consequence.

Again my lures attracted no fish. I kept a net handy upon the deck in readiness should I spot a passing school of krill or the like, but so far to no avail.

Bubo has not eaten for two days. Our lessons have slowed, for he was annoyed with me and persisted in squawking for beef or cheese. I could not help him. I took to locking him on the deck while I ate because he was now trying to pull the food scraps from my hand.

I make a dozen cups of tea each day as they provide me some spark and kept the pangs at bay. My breeches[124] have been falling to half-mast, so today I suspended them with two cords crossed over my shoulders.

My mind often harkens back to my final days in London. I can taste the delights of Mrs Harlesden's pumpkin pie and her molasses pudding. I yearn for a seat at Blackfriars Tavern with a bowl of hot Turkey soup and a bold plate of roast mutton at the table, but instead I pour another cup of tea. How I regret not scavenging more of the Caribbean coffee beans that I had bought in Guernsey. After the storm, among the squalor and rabble, retrieving the beans one by one from amidst the debris seemed a petty and wasteful undertaking. Now I would labour twice as long for just one cup of warm rich coffee to break the monotony on my palate.

Likewise, I should have salvaged more of the pickled pork. At the time it seemed little more than swill, and below the station of a captain's plate. But in these desperate times such decisions return against me, goading me with my own impetuousness, like a prize ring fighter taunting a glass-jaw[125]. Should I have scavenged more pork? Packed more food to allow for such occurrences? Used a stronger sack for the flour? To these questions and many more, I answer *yes*. But, like a glass-jaw, I can retaliate only with frustration; my counterpunches connect with nothing but air. The pork, coffee and flour are long gone. At best I can ignore my regret, but not reverse, or even repair, my actions.

Saturday 5 May

---

[124] Trousers
[125] A *glass-jaw* was a term for a fighter who was easily knocked out

I ate a full oat cake for breakfast in the hope that my stomach would spare me the growling. However, I felt green soon after and retched it into the sea. I shall have to fry them before eating from now on.

Although I tried many different combinations of fly, hook and sinker on my fishing lines there was no change to my fortune. If only I could find a vein or even a single school of fish then my hunger would be satiated.

I tried to continue with Bubo's lessons but my patience was thin and his concentration span was low. We made some small gains: he now recognises his own name, and comes when called. He has developed an instinctive understanding that the nodding and shaking of my head mean 'yes' and 'no' respectively. I did not teach him this specifically; he seems to have acquired this knowledge on his own.

When talking to Bubo, I often find myself using full sentences, even though most words must be incomprehensible to him. But he can obviously pick out key words that he knows, for he usually comprehends my message if I talk slowly and repeat it often enough. I am also getting to know his moods by his reactions and bird-gestures.

I noted that some of the scratches from Bubo's talons on my forearm had turned red. Several of them were very tender, and had pustules accumulating on their edges. I scraped the puss out, washed the wounds with boiled salt water, and dried them in firm sunlight. It was a shame that my medicine chest had not survived the storm, for a tincture would have helped to kill the poisons more readily. I planned to scrape and bathe the cuts every day until they had healed, for smaller scars have killed a man.

Yet more poor news with the mast. Despite the extra stays it appeared the tenon inside had cracked, and the whole joint was now dependant on only the outside binding for support. I lowered both sails even further, leaving a canvas barely a man's height to catch the faint breeze.

At dinnertime Bubo and I sat on the deck, without food.

Beeeeeeef.

"There is no beef, Bubo," I lied. (There was a smidgen left.)

Kreeeeese.

"There is no cheese Bubo."

By and by I relented and fetched him a quarter of an oat cake. He quickly devoured it but carked on much the same. He tried to perch on my forearm, but I would not allow him to because of the redness. Nevertheless he continued to squawk.

Beeeef. Kreeese.

"Quiet Bubo. There is no beef. There is no cheese."

Raarzin.

"There are no raisins."

He hopped up to my shoulder and carked again: *Beeeef. Kreeese. Raarzin.*

He would not have understood that his proximity to my ears amplified his sound, making it even more irksome. I asked him to be quiet many times, but he continued his incessant carking until I felt my redness rising. Without thinking I slapped at him with an open palm. My hand hit his front and flung him backward, off my shoulder. Suddenly, in a flurry of wings and feathers and talons he was onto me, scratching and biting and screeching like a stuck swine. I batted him away furiously for the bird seemed intent upon tearing out my eyes.

"Stop Bubo!" I screamed, but he continued even more ferociously. "It was nothing but a timid tap."

Parrying him away furiously, I retreated to the hold and pulled down the hatch. The bird was rabid. How could he have turned on me so quickly? I had shared my scarce food with him and nursed him from near death. I had even allowed him in my quarters, and spent many hours teaching him words. But he had turned on me like a wild cat for the want of a shred of beef.

I spent the rest of the day brooding, with angry rum as company.

Sunday 6 May

I awoke late, feeling green and rusty. My knuckles were sore and red but I could not remember why, for the rum stole away my last hours. I brewed a pot of tea as strong as the weak leaves would surrender, and fried a little salted beef and a hard-cake on the griddle. After slowly

112

chewing my way through the tough meat and leathery oats I picked out an entire oat cake – a peace offering to Bubo.

I emerged from the hatch to an unwelcome sight. Both sails flapped in lumpy heaps upon the deck, useless. I scurried across to inspect the damage and soon found two frayed halyards, one from each sail. Instantly I knew how the damage had occurred, for the ropes bore the marks of a sharp beak. Sitting atop the mast, far from my reach, was that wretched bird. I quickly relinquished my wish for peace.

"Bubo!" I yelled, furious. "Bubo, come here."

The bird, of course, did not do as instructed. He simply sat on the mast top, stationary, with his hackle feathers raised high.

"Bubo, come here!"

Again he ignored me.

I went red and waved my fist at him. "Bubo bad bird. Bad Bubo." My temper welled inside me, but I could do nothing but thump my fist into the mast. I hollered at that cantankerous bird again, but he did not even turn toward me. I tried to climb the mast, but I was too weak to lift myself beyond a couple of yards. I fell and thudded onto the deck, bruising both my arm and my pride.

"You are my pet. I am your master," I yelled. "Come here now." Bubo just ruffled his feathers, but otherwise did not move.

"You would have died without me. I saved your life and shared my food with you, yet you hurt me and my ship for a shred of beef." Yet even as the words left my lips I knew that they were futile, for he could not understand my exhortations.

My stomach swam from last night's rum. The glare from the morning sun seared through my eyes and my mouthed felt parched and sticky. I needed water. Still seething and unable to gain any retribution, I lowered myself down through the hatch, slammed it shut and battened it tightly. I spent the rest of the day in my hammock, for my dwindling strength had been wasted in anger on the bird.

That bird could fend for itself today. I would make no more peace offerings.

Monday 7 May

When I awoke in the early morning I remained annoyed with Bubo, but the height of my rage had soothed. I recalled my earlier vow not to hit Bubo; true, although it was just a minor slap, and his incessant carking had piqued me to a temper, it was a promise broken just the same. Bubo had not eaten for days and would soon be very weak if we did not make our peace. After calming myself further over a mug of tea, I fetched two lengths of spare rope to repair the halyards, and some food for Bubo: two oatcakes and a small handful of the remaining raisins. Bubo was perched on the port gunwale, but when he saw my hat protrude through the hatch he quickly flew to the mast top. I held out the raisins in one hand, the hard-cakes in the other.

"I have raisins Bubo." These words, I knew, he would understand, particularly the last two. Yet he did not move. I tossed Bubo a large crumb of hard cake that he ignored, and it pitched into the ocean, a wasted morsel. But I did not chide him, for we had experienced enough angst.

"Come, Bubo." I said calmly. "Captain Rum has raisins." I proffered the raisins again. This time he at least turned his head. "Captain Rum has oatcakes for Bubo." Another head movement, but nothing else.

"Come here Bubo," I tried again. "Come here." I waited patiently for a minute, but he did not even ruffle a feather. "Captain Rum is sorry, Bubo. Captain Rum is sorry he hurt Bubo."

I left the hard cake and raisins on the deck, tossed the spare ropes aside and returned below deck before my very shallow well of patience ran dry.

*

I spent more time poring over navigational charts trying to discern my position, and then calculated best and worst case scenarios. Assuming my continued slow sailing, I was either four days from the African coast, or still yet forty. Of course I had yet to re-mend the mast, so even 40 days could be a fanciful wish.

Outside, I could hear Bubo clambering about on deck. He had evidently come down from his mast-top perch and was no doubt gulping down the titbits of food. I hoped he was eating well for although I was hungry, he must be close to starving. By and by the cluttering above ceased.

I packed away my instruments and climbed heavily up through hatch. There, perched in his usual spot on the port gunwale, was my pet bird. I looked at him and he at me. He folded his wings across his belly in a way I have not seen him do before. Then, this little bird amazed me yet again. I followed him with my eyes as he flew up toward the top of the mast. There I spied the two ropes I had left on deck: they went upward, through their respective pulleys and then down toward the sails. Bubo had threaded the replacement halyards! I was stunned beyond belief, and for a minute I could do nothing but stare.

Bubo flew over and perched on my arm, and despite the pain of my raw skin, I rubbed his neck feathers. I must admit, although I am of strong disposition, I could do nothing but whimper in amazement at this truly wondrous bird. But show me the man who would not feel emotion at such a natural display of kindness and I will show you an empty soul no longer fit for this world.

Together we completed resetting the sails, and soon they were working as before. Our quarrel was over as completely as if it had never started.

That afternoon I made a leather patch for my forearm. I fastened two canvas strips to its edges so that I could tie it in place, ensuring that Bubo could perch on my arm whenever he desired without cutting my skin. I also constructed a simple perch for him in my quarters, for he was now welcome to sleep inside. He had earned the right.

Tuesday 8 May

Bubo was still asleep when I awoke. Although my stomach called loudly at me for breakfast, I lay in my hammock waiting for him to awaken.

Constantly now my body yearns for food – I would now consider even a serve of lumpy turnip mash as a banquet. Yet although I felt constantly famished, my sapped strength caused me the most anxiety. I had little energy for anything but lying in my hammock in my dank quarters. This sloth and slumber is not how I envisaged my grand adventure. A stale oatcake could not provide a man sustenance for a day's work. I felt as weak as a new lamb. (Ah, lamb - I would give my kingdom for a juicy leg.)

In time Bubo awoke and we climbed slowly to the deck. Unfortunately the mast had kinked further overnight, and was now as upright as a Blackfriars Tavern drunk at the Last Orders Bell, and wobbled just as much. I knew that we had to sight land soon; land with tall and stout trees, for if it was filled with just bushes and shrubs then my plight would not change. If that land had some berries that I could nibble, or some fleshy roots to make a stew, then I would feel obliged to Providence for her graciousness. I realised that my chances of such a find were low, as I did not even know my position, meaning that my compass and charts were useless. My course was no better than that of a blind man in the dark.

I continued observing through my telescope for land, school fish or bird flocks but sighted nothing but endless leagues of deep blue water. However when I later checked the fishing lines a thought crossed my mind that I hoped might help my situation.

"Bubo," I called out to my bird. "Come, Bubo."

Bubo responded to his name and flew to me obediently. He was soon perched in his now familiar position upon my forearm, with the new leather patch protecting my tender skin.

"Find fish," I instructed him.

Bubo tilted his neck and widened his eyes: I had come to realise that this reaction meant that he didn't understand.

"Find fish," I repeated, pointing at the trailing lures.

Bubo flapped off my arm and hesitantly flew to the stern. He dove into the water and emerged with a fishing lure between his talons.

"No, that's a *lure*, Bubo," I said, shaking my head. "It is not a fish."

Bubo dropped the lure back into the sea where it continued worthlessly trailing the ship.

"Bubo find *fish*," I repeated firmly, but with kindness in my voice.

Bubo stopped flapping and dropped to a low glide. He landed gently upon the stern railing and looked at me quizzically, with his colourful head tilted to the side. Then it occurred to me: damnation! - I had never taught him the word for 'fish'. How could I have missed such a basic word? Now I had another problem: how to teach him something to which I could not point. I tried waving my hands through the air like a fish swimming through the water.

"Do you understand, Bubo? Fish."

I pointed at the sea, still making the waving motion. Bubo merely tilted his head further. In desperation, I lay on the deck and swam on it like a simpleton. Bubo carked loudly.

I stood up, my embarrassment causing further frustration as I cursed myself for missing such an important lesson. Checking myself to rein in my temper, I stood upon the deck, breathing calmly and patting Bubo's neck. A sound that passed for a purr rumbled from his beak; he seemed to enjoy the stroking. But my problem remained. How could I communicate the concept of 'fish' to Bubo? Solving this problem quickly became paramount, for my hunger and weakness were mounting daily, if not hourly. Soon I might not have the strength to work even if I found land. My survival might hinge on the outcome of the lesson.

I retreated to my quarters and retrieved this journal. On a blank end page I drew my best impression of a fish[126]. I called to Bubo. Perhaps hoping for another stroking of his neck plumage he quickly clambered and clattered his way down through the hatch, traversed the galley and then flapped his way into my quarters. I held up the picture before him.

"This is a *fish*, Bubo. *Fish*."

Bubo studied the likeness. He cocked his head, first to one side, then the other. His shook his head then looked squarely at the picture again. Nothing. I admit that I am no Constable[127] but surely my rendering was recognisable as a fish. I had even drawn a dorsal fin and added scales for effect. But no matter how long Bubo looked at the picture he was no nearer to its meaning. When I subsequently tested him with the instruction to "find fish" he simply pecked at my journal.

---

[126] A picture of a crudely rendered fish survives on the final page of the journal. A copy is included in appendix two.

[127] McAdam was no doubt referring to the well-known English painter John Constable (1776-1837)

Sometimes I felt that Bubo was more intelligent than some of the bar laggards at Blackfriars, but even the dullest, most brain-battered drunkard would recognise this picture as a fish. However it seemed that Bubo could not realise that the picture was not *the* fish, but instead that it was a drawing *of* the fish. He seemed to think that a journal with some dark curved lines on the page was a fish. I would need another way.

By and by Bubo flew out of the cabin, no doubt to sit upon his perch in the gentle breeze, as was his penchant. I retreated to my hammock in order to conserve my strength. But just as I had pulled the thin blanket around my shoulders I had a thought: even though Bubo could not connect between a picture and its true embodiment, perhaps a solid rendering would help.

I fetched a thick scrap of green firewood from the bottom of the heap and whittled it with a sharp knife. Steadily I carved the body, then the tail and finally the head of a fish. I gouged three narrow slots into the body and inserted shaped chips of wood to represent pectoral and dorsal fins. When the likeness was to my satisfaction – I wasn't sure if it was a cod, tuna, or some other species, but it mattered little – I scampered up to deck. Bubo soon settled on my patched forearm, whereupon I held out the likeness of the fish before him.

"*This* is a fish, Bubo. *Fish.*"

His head was still but I could see his eyes darting laterally as he studied my coarse sculpture. I pitched and rolled it up and down to represent swimming. "Fish, Bubo." I pointed to the water. "Fish swim in the ocean."

Then his black eyes flared widely but then quickly contracted tightly, and he straightened and lifted his head. He cawed a word that I just recognised: *fik.* (It seemed that he could not pronounce the "sh" sound.)

"Good Bubo," I said quietly while I patted his neck. "Now, Bubo *find* fish. Find fish." I pointed out to the seas and swept my arm about its expanse. "Bubo fly. Bubo fly, Bubo find fish."

He understood. With one large sweep of his blue and red wings he launched into the air, and was soon circling the mast with his sharp eyes scanning the water below. He flew in ever-increasing arcs, gradually increasing his sweep, and by and by he flew so far away that I could no longer see him. Then I tracked him with my telescope but eventually lost sight of him altogether as he ducked and bobbed above the water. I hoped he would soon return with dinner.

*

I wish it had been so easy. I sat on deck for many hours waiting for Bubo. By and by the warm sun had sunk low in the west, yet Bubo had not returned. I increasingly feared for the safety of my little pet as the skies deepened, for although the wind was light, his strength was low. I hoped I had not inadvertently set him a task that would prove his undoing.

The skies grew pink, and then red. They say a red sky at night is a harbinger of good fortune but tonight it reeked of gloom, for it meant that darkness was approaching while Bubo remained at sea. I trained my telescope around the horizon searching for even a flicker of flashing wing, but could see nothing in the low light. I called Bubo's name in my deepest, loudest voice, progressively to the east, west, north and south, but I heard not a cark in reply. How could I steer my pet home? Perhaps a little rum would aid my thinking. *No. I must stay strong.*

Soon Venus poked herself above the horizon and began her slow planetary waltz across the sky. Sirius[128] came out, at first timidly, but then glinting like cut glass before a fire, but still Bubo remained absent. I remembered when he had first drifted by the *Maris Alarum*, a sodden lump of wet feathers clinging to a half-sunken log. Since then he had grown stronger, learned to understand more than a dozen words and had shared much with me. He was a fine pet who kept my mind from turning toward troublesome thoughts.

But our sparse rations had weakened him. Now he had flown heedlessly across vast reaches of Mother Ocean searching for food for us both. The tyranny of the unforgiving distance might send Bubo back to where he started: a bedraggled mess of feathers clinging to some passing driftwood... if he could find some driftwood. Even if he had the strength to fly back, he might not be able to find my ship in the blackness of night.

I had not partaken of a drop of rum in three days, but now it called at me from the galley. I resisted its wanton invitation because I wanted to

---

[128] Sirius is the brightest star in the sky.

stay alert to aid Bubo's return. As tiredness settled over me on that dark and suddenly very lonely deck, my worries grew, and soon encompassed far more than just my pet bird. My mind tortured me with all manner of misgivings - my lack of food, the broken mast, and the increasingly high probability of dying at sea.

A waning gibbous moon[129] rose. I shivered crudely from both fatigue and cold as the damp air dropped colder by the minute; although the season neared summer, the nights remained cool. Perhaps, I thought, Bubo would appreciate warmth upon his return, so I stoked the galley fire to a blaze and then returned to deck.

Two more stars dipped below the western horizon. I grew colder, weaker and more tired. My anxiousness mingled with my fatigue, exacerbating both. Still the rum called out for me. I tried to ignore its siren but in the end I decided to partake of just one small draft to quieten its nagging and clear my mind. I climbed through the hatch to fetch a mug.

I cursed aloud, for the galley jar was empty. I struggled my way down the scupper, into the hold, where I tripped past the firewood heap as I stumbled toward the rum store. I stepped on a cut branch but it did not even crack - even after six weeks at sea it was still green and sappy, and would be fit only to smoke a pig, not to cook one. (Ah, but I wish I had a pig.)

As I reached for the rum crock, an idea coursed through my mind like a fork of lightning across a black night sky, temporarily emancipating some energy from deep within me. I turned back to the firewood heap and rooted through it, gathering only the greenest branches. With as much strength as my weary legs could summon I climbed to the galley, and thrust the sappy timber into the burning oven. The fire spat and cackled, and the green branches smoked like tobacco as the flames reduced their milky sap to black smears.

---

[129] When describing the moon, the terms 'waxing' and 'waning' refer respectively to its increasing and deceasing size. A new moon is a dark moon, which, as it *waxes*, becomes a *crescent* moon, *half* moon, *gibbous* moon, and finally a *full* moon. It then *wanes* back through the same pattern. The moon, like the sun, always rises in the east.

I climbed to the deck and was satisfied to see a thick cloud of white-grey smoke billowing from the chimney. The plume curled its way toward the moon, reaching like a high flagpole above the bobbing *Maris Alarum*. It was like a lighthouse in a storm to guide Bubo home from afar.

Emboldened by renewed hope I stayed on deck, steering my ship in the direction of my last sighting of Bubo. Then, determined to do whatever I could to help, I repeatedly called Bubo's name to each of the cardinal points in turn. I scanned the seas by eye and with my scope in case he was floating. I vowed that I would stay all night if necessary.

By and by the smoke dwindled, so I returned to the hold for more green timber. I re-stoked the fire and fanned the flame with a tin plate, for its heat had dropped. The gentle cracking of the fire lulled me, and exhaustion again began to win its battle. I returned to deck where I hoped the cooler air would keep me alert.

I dreamed a menagerie of thoughts as I fought to stay out of slumber: that I was lying in a sweet, soft mattress at my old bedsit; that I was eating a tender shin of beef and a sweet plate of treacle pudding; that I was having a ribald whist night at Blackfriars, drinking measure after measure of rum while my gaming pennies piled higher. I thought of Liverpool, of London ... of the markets and the rivers and the open fields. Then, without the strength to resist it, I dreamed of Beth.

As I wafted between asleep and awake, I thought of her more, and more again. Then, with my defences down, the thoughts morphed into a stark, unforgiving vision. She wears white, again. Where are we? The setting is hazy. Slowly, St Paul's Cathedral materialises in the background, and to the fore is matted grass upon which we sit. Now I recognise the occasion: a luncheon on the grass. I watch myself as I fumble about in my pocket. Yes, the ring is there. Beth is speaking but I do not hear her words because I am inwardly practicing a short speech to her. Satisfied, I take a breath and nervously pull the ring from my vest pocket, but clumsily spill it from my grasp.

I try to recover it quickly but the silver band and emerald stone (to match her eyes) flashes brightly in the midday winter sun. I see her hand rise to her mouth in shocked acknowledgement, but under that hand I see a trembling smile. I try to go on one knee and attempt to stammer out a proposal, but it is too late: she is already nodding her head, already crying tears of joy, and soon she is sobbing 'yes' into my shoulder in response to my unspoken question.

But then her soft sobs amplify, and turn into harsh shrieks. *No, not again.* The apparition changes and instantly, as I draw back from the embrace, we are in the forest lying in a hide, next to our deer trap. I smell the musty, damp leaves of the undergrowth, mixed with the gentle sweet fragrance of her perfume. I hear the faint snap of a twig under a heavy hoof, and turn to see the stag wander down the pad, its broad antlers spread wider than a man's reach, each tine[130] sharp and menacing. It pauses to nibble the bait and I see myself – my own hands - cut the spring rope, and watch as the lasso encircles the stag's broad antlers. Beth leaps up in excitement. *No!* I try to yell, but my throat is tight, closed. I see the stag twist and kick and pull. *Watch out Beth! Come back!* I hear a loud crack, that awful crack, as the spring sapling breaks. The stag flays it head. I see its antlers, but only in a blur of movement....

A creak in the mast mercifully jolted me awake. I cursed myself aloud for allowing that wretched nightmare an open pass into my mind. I tried to quieten my ragged breathing, and focused on the dark areas of sky between the stars to try to still my vaulting mind. But the panic inside me continued, and I knew that I needed some rum to soften the landing. I needed that rum quickly.

I hurriedly fetched a four-gallon crock from the hold. I needed just a quick draft to settle my nerves, and then I planned to return to the deck to call for Bubo again. Just one draft. Bubo needed me ... and I needed him. I could not desert my pet in his time of angst. I fanned the fire a little more, and then quickly downed a second short draft of rum while I waited for the flames to take hold. I would have just one more measure before going back to my lookout....

Wednesday 9 May

I awoke with a start and took a moment to register my surroundings. Through foggy eyes I saw the galley stove was before me, its coals now white ash. The rum crock sat on the floor, half empty, and the dawn sun

---

[130] A *tine* is the pointed branch of the antler

slanted through the hatch. I had fallen asleep in front of... Bubo! Where was Bubo?

I climbed to the deck, cursing myself for capitulating to the lure of the rum. I had fallen asleep, and in doing so I had failed Bubo. My gaze went immediately to his favourite railing on the port gunwale but it was vacant. I peered up toward the mast and riggings, hoping he was perched high, taking in the morning breeze, but to no avail.

I fetched my telescope and scanned the horizon looking for any hint of movement in the low sky, but I saw nothing but uneven waves upon a moderate ocean. Methodically I trained the scope over the whole of the heavens, encountering only wispy clouds. I knew that Bubo could not have flown throughout the night, for he was far too weak and hungry. I felt impotent, for what could I do now?

Nothing. It was too late. Last night had been my opportunity to help, but my taunting memories had forced me onto the rum. I had failed. Now I could do nothing but sail onwards in the hope of chancing on Bubo floating on driftwood as before. Yet as the *Maris Alarum* sloughed her way through the endless, unforgiving ocean, I knew that this was nothing but the mollifying wish of a guilty man. Had the rum cost me the life of my pet?

"Bubo" I bellowed to the horizon. I yelled again and again in my loudest voice, but I knew that it was forlorn, for Bubo's hopes had faded more completely than London snow in May. It would have been impossible for him to stay aloft in his poor condition for an entire night. It pained me to realise that I would not see him again. I sat on deck – I simply sat – and cursed myself aloud. I called to him again, many times, but saw nothing with either looking glass or eye.

By and by I heard a clatter to my aft. I turned sharply to see Bubo clambering out of the hatch. I rushed across, picked him up, and soon found myself hugging the little bird so dearly that I nearly crushed him. He emitted a sharp cark of annoyance.

"Welcome back," I said, despite knowing that he did not understand my words. "Welcome back, my little friend." As I petted him with relief, the realisation came to me that Bubo had returned to the ship during the night, and he had simply bypassed my slumbering carcass on his way to his perch in my quarters. He had been sleeping the whole time I had been out on deck fretting over him! Not for the first time I thought: you cheeky bastard.

He perched on my forearm with his talons piercing my unprotected skin, but the sharpness of the pain did not worry me for it reminded me that he was here, and not ... out there. I petted his neck feathers, which elicited a low grinding sound from his beak akin to a rumbling purr[131]. He bowed his head, seemingly to direct my soft strokes to the back of his neck as I talked to him quietly, telling him in a gentle voice that I was pleased that he was back on board, and that he had done a fine job of finding fish.

Without warning, Bubo's eyes suddenly pinned closed and he tipped back his head. I had got to know that this gesture meant that he understood a concept, and so wondered what thought had grasped his mind. I spoke to him again, encouraging him to speak words, and allowed plenty of time for his reply. By and by, between neck-feather rubs, I coaxed him into warbling out four words: *Bubo ... fly... find ... fik.*

I could not be sure if he was attempting to convey a message, but it certainly appeared so when he later flapped his way to the stern, where a small sardine lay forlornly on the deck.

Find fik, he trilled again.

"That's wonderful Bubo. Good bird." I petted his neck feathers again. "Bubo must eat this fish with me."

Aaark - his universal negative answer.

"Bubo eat fish with Captain Rum," I repeated, hoping that he understood at least some of my sentence.

However he simply *aarked* again, and then flapped across to the hatch and flew down to his perch, no doubt to continue his rest; his labour had earned him a full summer's hibernation if he so chose. It occurred to me that he had probably eaten heartily from the sardine school that he had discovered, for a sardine was always found within a multitude.

---

[131] Beak grinding is a natural habit of many parrots. They make this sound by sliding their rough tongues against their upper beaks. It indicates pleasure or contentment, much like a cat's purr.

Satiating my hunger suddenly became my dominant emotion, so I retreated to the galley and in a trice had cooked the fish. I wolfed it down whole - head, tail, eyes and all. I then took to my hammock – true, I was tired, but a part of me also wished to be near Bubo. He perched beside me with his head tucked under his wings as was his usual manner when sleeping.

I was not only pleased with the ration of fish that Bubo had delivered, but also amazed at his use of words. He had conveyed a simple but complete message to me, rather than just repeating individual words, surpassing my already high opinion of his intelligence. All animals used voice to communicate: dogs barked in different ways, such as growling, whining and whimpering, to convey emotions; whales were known to sing complex songs underwater that travelled for many miles to talk to another. But I had never heard of an animal that could not only imitate human sounds, but also use them to construct a meaningful phrase. [132]

As I lay watching him, my mind continued to play with last night's problems, especially concerning food. Yes, Bubo had found a sardine school and had eaten to satiety. But he could not carry more than one fish at a time back to my ship, so the returns for me were meagre. And I would not risk him flying so far again, for the dangers outweighed the cargo. I tossed ideas about my head but no solution seemed apparent.

When I was not thinking logically of how to obtain more food then I dreamed of it. Today on my reverie menu was pork chops with stewed apple, oatmeal-stuffed hog's head, and a plate of curried beef from the dark man at Billingsgate markets. It was difficult to think of anything but food.

---

[132] McAdam was understandably amazed at Bubo's linguistic abilities. While it may seem extraordinary and even paranormal to the reader, similar bird intelligence has been documented in scientific studies. One 30 year old African Grey Parrot called *Alex* (co-incidentally the same breed as *Purdy*, the Astonishing Andrew's performing bird) had a vocabulary of over 100 words and understood their meanings. He could distinguish 7 colours and 5 shapes, answer complex questions correctly, and appropriately use concepts such as 'bigger' and 'different'. More information on this Bubo-like bird, including some fascinating video, can be found by searching 'Alex the Parrot' on-line. If you find yourself doubting McAdam's account (as I admit I originally did) then I urge you to do this research.

By and by Bubo emerged from under his wing.

"Good morning again, Bubo."

After a pause, he offered some words in a similar vein to his earlier message – *Bubo fly* - but this time I sensed (I cannot say how or why, but it was simply a reckoning) that he was making an offer, not reporting an achievement.

I shook my head. "No Bubo, it's too far. You might get lost and I won't see you again."

Captain Rum.... Find fiks.

"No Bubo. The sun is hot. You can't fly far again. You stay on ship with Captain Rum. I will eat oat cakes."

Aaark. Simple frustration.

But then, without awaiting further instructions, Bubo flapped his way through the hatch and onto the main deck. "Stop Bubo" I hollered after him. "Wait!" I hurried after him as he flew to the bow, where he perched briefly on the gunwale.

I lurched forward to try to hold him, to prevent him from possibly losing his life for the reward of a single sardine, but he was already away. Clearly I had no simple way of restraining Bubo. Even though I worried that he was flying to his death I was powerless to catch him once he took flight, for the sky, air and clouds were his world, not mine.

Then, just as my thoughts were vaulting between frustration and despair, Bubo stopped his advance away from my ship and hovered in mid air, stroking his blue and red wings just firmly enough to stay aloft. It seemed as though he was waiting for me. I retreated to centre deck and adjusted the meagre sails for a more southerly bearing, following Bubo's path. As I approached him he again flew away, but paused again when he was only a furlong away from the *Maris Alarum*. I recalled his simple words - *Bubo fly, Captain Rum find fish* - and I suddenly deciphered his game: he was directing *me* to find the fish! I grabbed the whipstaff and steered my sloop as best I could manage, following this handsome bird. Who needed a compass when such a fine navigator was leading?

I followed Bubo for hours. Although the low sails and poor rigging made the going painfully slow – barely two or three knots – at least I had purpose. Sometimes Bubo flew high toward the sun for a longer view, and once he ventured beyond the range of my unaided eye, so I followed him through my telescope. Once satisfied that he was on course, Bubo returned to my vessel. Once more, perhaps an hour later, he again soared very high and then came down to lead me further to starboard.

Just as the sun began dipping into the horizon, Bubo docked on my leather-patched forearm. He hooted quietly *fiks.* I looked ahead. At first I could see nothing but the glinting orange of sunset waters, but by and by a darker patch appeared, agitating the surface. As we sailed nearer, the patch grew in size and clarity until I could discern the silhouettes of fish as they leaped through the air, evading predators. Before sundown we were among a frenzied school.

From the stern, I cast a lure with my bamboo rod. Barely had it hit the water when a fish took it. I reeled it in and was overjoyed to find a sturdy salmon on the line. I would eat like a King tonight! Bubo enjoyed the fracas, repeatedly swooping along the water and snatching sardines between his talons. I lurched joyously from port to starboard between my two rods, pulling in large fish and re-casting my line. By dark, a dozen writhing salmon covered the deck. I laughed wildly, for I would eat heartily tonight.

Thursday 10 May

In the morning, Bubo and I did little but eat fresh fish, and rest. Already my constitution was returning, as was Bubo's. Having all but finished the sauerkraut, I reserved the vinegar and pickled as many large chunks of salmon as would fit into the crock. I now had food for another week at least, and more importantly, a method by which Bubo could find us fish when needed.

My returning strength enkindled a renewed wish to move onward; my journey was lacking adventure and I still yearned for the ribald voyage of my dreams, but reality was presently blocking its way.

In between chores I spent time with Bubo on lessons, which he seemed to enjoy again. He learned two new words, including (with the opportunity provided when I accidentally pierced my forearm with the sharp point of a set of dividers[133]) the word 'hurt'.

With my hunger problem at least temporarily abated, my most urgent task was again to find land and fix the mast, for today the old repair cracked even further. I dropped the headsail altogether, leaving only the mainsail at one third of its usual height, so my speed over the water was laborious. Such was the limpness of my single sail that I did little more than bob upon the ocean, and my carriage was so poor that the currents affected my bearing more than the wind.

I spent the morning poring over my charts again, but my protractor and ruler were wearing thin at the edges, for I had already repeated this exercise many times. I could not make my longitude at all, had only a reckoning of my latitude, and so was still ignorant as to my true position. If only I could find land, any land, then I could map it out and compare it with a chart. If only I could find land....

I paused. *Find land*....

Of course! I clambered upon the deck. Bubo looked up, seeming to sense from the quickness of my movement that I had something urgent at hand.

"Bubo find land," I instructed.

But before long Bubo had tilted his head, signifying that he didn't understand. Swiftly I realised that I had the same problem as with the fish: Bubo did not know the meaning of the word "land." Again, I was faced with the conundrum of teaching him a word that I could not easily demonstrate.

I showed Bubo a large nautical map, indicating the vast expanses of water while repeating the word 'water'. I then intoned 'land' as I indicated the shaded brown masses on the chart. But even after a long and exasperating lesson Bubo was not even close to grasping my meaning. He lost patience quickly, and resorted to asking for beef when I did not reward him as much as he evidently felt he deserved. I should have predicted that this attempt would fail, for if he could not imagine a fish from a picture then he had no probability of deducing the meaning of 'land' from a chart.

---

[133] Dividers are a common navigation instrument resembling callipers. The distance between points on a map could be determined by locking the tips of the dividers onto the map points, and then transferring the dividers to a scale ruler, from where the distance could be read.

As I retired to my hammock, my mind spun on how I could convey the meaning of the word 'land' to Bubo. If only I had carried England with me on my ship I could have solved this problem in a trice.

Friday 11 May

The morning star had not yet risen in east, and the sun was still an hour from awakening, when the answer came to me. Through a mumble of my own curses I located my tallow lamp in the dark and then searched for what I had packed on my journey as a lucky talisman, which may now prove as much: my oilskin sachet of earth from Mother England.

My anxiety would not allow me to wait for Bubo to awaken, so I roused him from his perch and carried him to the deck. When he was fully alert, I pointed to the ocean and said its name. Then I unfurled the square of oilskin, revealing the handful of English dirt inside.

"Land," I said, pointing. "This is *land*, Bubo." Now adept at his lessons, Bubo replied after just a dozen repetitions. *Laaarnd.*

"Good, Bubo. Good bird." I rubbed his feathers. "Now, Bubo *find* land."

Bubo looked at me, and after I had repeated the order only a few more times he assimilated my request. *Bubo find land.* As simply as that, he was up and away. His body, strengthened by two days of abundance, beat his long wings powerfully as he flew south into the still-dark sky, with my optimism flying pick-a-back[134] with him.

*

The afternoon sky had its first blush of crimson when I sighted him. At first Bubo was just a wriggling black speck on the horizon, like a midge on a millpond, but soon the full grandeur of his majestic wings became clear. He glided into deck, landing heavily on the rail.

No ... land.

I was ever so disappointed.

Saturday 12 May

---

[134] *Pick-a-back* was the original term for riding "piggy back".

I awoke early, just before dawn, to discover that Bubo was absent from his perch. Nor was he on deck. It is said that the first bird feeds on the fattest worm; Bubo must have instinctively understood this saying and was already attending his duties. That he could hold this task in his memory overnight further amazed me. What a fine first mate he was turning out to be.

I busied myself with menial jobs, particularly taking stock of my provisions. My original stores were now almost exhausted. All I had left was:

❖ three pounds of salted beef
❖ a handful of dry peas, still in their shells
❖ half a crate of oat cakes, which now are virtually inedible due to the thick green mould that has grown across their surfaces
❖ an unappealing jar of salted tomatoes that I was saving for emergency rations
❖ half a sack of tea
❖ a crock filled with pickled salmon.

Finally, I had about two dozen raisins. I was not sure why I kept so few of them, but I was now saving them like a miser hoarding his last few ha'pennies. Despite the fleshiness of the salmon, I knew that my diet needed more, and that I would soon fall ill if I did not find fresh food. All of the rum and lemon in the Kingdom would not change that.

Yet my food shortage was merely a symptom of the real problem: my cracked and weary vessel. So I again called upon Providence to grant me a sighting of land; land with tall and true trees, for without them I could not repair my mast and I was captain of an oarless rowboat. If I could just hoist my sails then I could mitigate all other problems, but without means to capture the wind I bobbed aimlessly, and all other problems grew, like the oatcakes' green mould, thicker and more problematic each day.

It was late afternoon before Bubo returned. Eschewing his normal smooth glide in to his perch, he thumped heavily into the deck. His fatigue reminded me of the day we first met. Yet he had energy for his beak, for as he sat upon the deck, he cawed quietly *Bubo find land*.

Land! My fingers clenched into fists and punched the air. Salvation was close. "Good Bubo. Good bird." I ruffled his feathers and lifted him into my arms.

"Where is land Bubo?"

He twisted his heavy head and looked left of the setting sun. "South west?" I confirmed. Bubo simply nodded his head, having learned this gesture from me. He also knew the cardinal points – north, south, east and west - and all four between, and incredibly could navigate them without reference to a compass. It was as if he had a loadstone in his mind[135].

Carrying Bubo in my arms like a child, I set the ragged sails and rudder on course. Then I took Bubo to the galley where we devoured a large portion of the fish, for what was left over after today would soon spoil, as I had no spare vinegar for preserving.

Bubo was clearly exhausted, so I carried him to my quarters and set him on his perch. He didn't awaken all night. I slept only in brittle pieces, for my anticipation was high for landfall tomorrow. What would I find? Fresh food? Meat? Would there be timber and men to help me repair my ship? And women – would there be women? I pushed the thoughts of Beth from my head and tried to sleep.

Sunday 13 May

My sleep was poor, and as lacking in substance as a threadbare old blanket; so thin as to be translucent. I sailed all day, following Bubo's navigation. My mind swam with exotic visions of the land: a friendly port with a shipwright's dock, and a vibrant tavern with buxom women. So when, just upon dusk, Bubo warbled *land,* my mind raced. But a scan through my telescope soon showed a truth that failed in every way to match my expectations. It was not the mainland but instead a scrawny island, little more than a rock. I could see no trees or other useful

---

[135] McAdam was very close to the truth when he wrote this. Modern biologists now know that many birds have chemical compounds in their eyes and brains that help them detect the Earth's magnetic field. This special sense allows the birds to accurately navigate over long journeys.

features. It looked even more barren than the luckless ocean in which I had been sailing.

As we approached the island, I confirmed my initial guess that it was little more than a black stone edifice jutting above the waves. The whole mass was only 100 yards wide, and had steep, rocky, unwelcoming sides. Nevertheless, I judged that it was worth my while to explore it further, for it might contain something of value within its rocky interior, perhaps crabs, meaty lizards, or even some useful flotsam.

However the hour was late and Mother Ocean was grumpy, so I anchored in the lee of the island for the night. I dropped the sounding lead and found it to be 15 fathoms deep[136] – a surprise, for I had guessed that it would be less than five or six fathoms to the ocean floor this close to land. The seabed must drop away very sharply. I surmised that the island was the tip of a deep ocean-bound mountain, perhaps even a dormant volcano. But I had plenty of spare anchor rope to extend the chain, and so despite the depth, I made fast.

Bubo flew across to the island. He did not return for supper, but I did not worry, for I was sure he was resting well. I spent the evening trying to locate the rock on my maps but to no avail. It was so scrawny and remote that perhaps no man had yet marked it on his charts. Perchance no man had ever stumbled across it at all.

I sat in the galley until late. Without Bubo to talk to, my mind soon drifted toward unwelcome thoughts, so I drafted a small mug of rum, and then another, to ward off any evil. By and by I dropped to sleep in front of the fire. I awoke later and stumbled groggily to my hammock. But then, an unknown time later, Beth pulled me toward her again.

At first I felt her presence next to me, in my hammock on the *Maris Alarum*. In a state between asleep and awake, I opened my eyes to see her soft, smooth cheeks almost touching mine, with a stray ringlet of dark hair the only blemish to the powdery silkiness of her skin. I can smell the delicate fragrance of her face powder. I pull back to marvel at how pretty and utterly serene she looks. To wake her now would be like breaking a wondrous enchantment.

---

[136] A fathom is a measure of depth. One fathom is six feet, or 1.82 metres.

I sit up and look around the room, and am surprised to see not the cramped quarters of a vessel, but a fanciful boudoir, complete with curtains and even patterned paper covering the walls. I do not see this vision from above, but with my own eyes. I see Beth's cast off dress. It is white, lacy white - her wedding dress. The simple pink rose, which she had carried throughout the ceremony, sits proudly in a mug of water above the hearth. I gaze down at Beth, and cannot help myself but to gently place a small kiss on her cheek. I lay back beside her, feeling as content as a man can be.

I look again. The soft white pillow changes to a pile of leaves. *No.* Suddenly we are in the forest, lying, waiting, and watching as the stag wanders toward the trap. Then I see the stag, ensnared, tossing about its broad neck. I am excited by the catch, but then, fatefully, I hear a crack. The sapling breaks and I watch, helpless, as the beast lurches toward Beth. I watch in excruciating detail as its right antler's longest tine pierces Beth's white blouse just below her heart. *Please no. No more.* The stag twists and casts Beth sideways to the ground like an urchin's rag doll, her blood pooling red and brown and black about her. She screams. Just screams. I try to get up, I try to yell for help, but I can neither move an inch nor utter a syllable. The stag turns and bolts, dragging the broken sapling roughshod behind it. Elizabeth looks toward me – her face is frozen in fear and drained of blood, a ghostly, whitish blue. It is a face I cannot forget no matter how hard I try. I push my fingers forlornly into her pulsing wound. Oh, oh no. *Stop! Make it stop!*

I tumbled from my hammock, jolting me awake and mercifully banishing the vision. Suddenly I was back on the *Maris Alarum*, but my heart continued to race like it did that day. As I lay, trembling, breathing into my hands, my mind turned with the question: why had she not shared with me her secret? I staggered to the galley chair and hit the rum bottle with a vengeance.

Monday 14 May

I awoke on the galley floor, stiff and aching. My stomach turned, and the back of my head felt as though it had been clubbed with a shovel. I retched up my first cup of tea, and then retired to my hammock. Perhaps my medicine was causing more symptoms than it alleviated.

It was almost noon before I roused again. This time I managed to keep down two cups of tea, but I still felt poorly and so decided against exploration of the island. I had very little to gain from an expedition to a barren crag that would sap my reserves of strength, so instead I climbed to the deck in order to cast away. The wind and the sails could do the work today, for I was in no mood for labour.

My plans unravelled almost immediately, because Bubo was not on his perch. He must have still been on the rock. I called to him loudly and repeatedly, escalating the thumping pain in the back of my head, but he did not return. After two further cups of tea I grew wearily impatient, for I wished to weigh anchor and set my sails. I begrudgingly launched my tender and rowed the furlong to the island. I told myself not to scold Bubo too harshly for his truancy, for although he was very intelligent for a bird, his understanding of mankind's ways was less than a child's.

As I rowed closer a musty, pungent odour filled the air. I had not experienced this smell before; it was like the smell from a pigs' sty combined with a waft of old eggs. It struck my senses firmly for I was accustomed to clean sea air with no taint other than a fine spray of salt water.

I searched for somewhere to beach my tender but there was no natural harbour. With my impatience rising like a tide, I completed a circumnavigation but was none the wiser for a landing site. I rowed again, focusing upon any reach where the rock wall was less steep or high. By and by I picked the best of a poor selection of berths and tethered my tender to a protruding rock knob. With much mumbling and low cussing I scrambled up to a ledge. A shift in the wind amplified the island's smell, which filled my nostrils with the strong egg-and-manure-like stench. The wind shift also brought an unexpected sound to my ears: a dull chatter in the distance, like a noisy choir of summer crickets. Perhaps some band of insects had made a home on this most desolate and unlikely of outposts.

I set about climbing the rock face, for it was a steep haul of perhaps thrice my height to the top. Once I almost tumbled, but I managed to arrest my fall before copping a wetting, with the sharp imaginings of a waiting shark redoubling my efforts to avoid the water. With my brow sweating from exertion in the afternoon heat (and also, I concede, from the lingering effects of the previous night's rum) I eventually pulled myself over the ledge and scrambled upright to better survey the land. I received a great surprise, on many counts.

I had expected the interior of the island to be nothing but jagged and jumbled rock. Instead its steep rocky sides were more like the rims of a giant pot, with the interior being smooth and flat and filled to the brim with odd, white ashen soil. I guessed that the island was the remnant of an old volcano whose crater had since filled with the ashen earth, but I could not even guess where this odd fill came from. Sadly there was no vegetation, no fruits or berries and certainly no trees with which to repair my mast. Just a bare grey surface, as flat and featureless as the moon. Except, that is, for the birds.

Packed against the far side of the crater in the lee of the surrounding wall was a flock of a hundred or so squat birds. The birds quacked and cackled continuously, and it was soon clear to me that they were the source of the chirping sounds. Each was about two feet high and had a white breast, a grey-black tail and long talons. Their wings were tiny, and I doubted that they could fly. Their clearest features were their long, thick yellow beaks, which curved to an ominous tip. I have not seen their like before, even in natural history books.[137]

My next thought regarding the birds arose not in my head but my stomach, for each bird, although scrawny, would feed a hungry man for a day. I could not help but imagine a roasted bird browning in the galley oven, basting in fatty juices and filling the *Maris Alarum* with a deep aroma. I resolved to wrench the neck of the first bird upon which I could lay my hands, and made my way across the plateau with this aim.

Suddenly, the birds became aware of my presence and turned toward me. A trice later I heard an ear-shaking sound as the birds squawked at me in unison, like a tribe of marauding Celts. Those birds that had been sitting now rose to face me and emitted further warning shrieks. Clearly I was unwelcome.

---

[137] A Professor from the Ornithology department at Oxford was unable to identify the birds by McAdam's description. He suggested that they were most likely an island-dwelling endemic species of *Columbidae,* and therefore distantly related to the extinct *Raphus Cucullatus,* otherwise known as the *Dodo.*

At first I held my ground, for a wholesome meal would reward my steadfastness. However I quickly relented as the flock marched toward me like mangrove soldier crabs at tide turn. I rued not bringing along my scimitar, for with a decent weapon I could have slain half the flock with just a few wide swipes. But I was bare-handed and so thought my best strategy was to retreat. Although I was far larger, the birds numbered like a swarm.

As I withdrew the flock advanced further, and my discomfort rapidly escalated. I could not see even a stray branch with which to defend myself. My options were limited: further retreat was difficult because the steep rock wall dropped away behind me (with sharks and other such demons waiting in the ocean should I stumble), to attack bare-handed would be futile, yet to stay still seemed an even greater folly. I waved my arms wildly and shrieked like a stuck swine, but my aggression did nothing to halt their advance. Was I to end my days on a remote rock as the hen-pecked fodder of a flock of feral turkeys?

Suddenly a flash of blue and red feathers caught my eye above. *Bubo*. He emitted a sharp hoot and then some loud yarking sounds as he landed gamely in front of the advancing flock. What a brave bird! A few birds uneasily halted their march. Bubo screeched again and then, after some more rabbled cackling, they quietened a mite further. He turned to me.

No, he screeched, with unusual venom. *No! No! No!*

Although I am not usually a man to take orders from a subordinate (particularly that of a bird!) I quickly acquiesced. Bubo had provided me with a moment in which to retreat and I rapidly realised that I would be wise to take it. I clambered down the rock face and tumbled into my tender. Despite his short tone toward me it was heartening to know that Bubo, like a good guard dog, had developed instincts to protect me.

I rowed to the *Maris Alarum*. Already I was planning to return the next day with weapons and take a brace of birds for salting. I would eat well for a month.

With a few hours of firm light remaining in the day and my plans to depart now deferred, I took the opportunity to inspect my ship's mast. I de-rigged the sails, stripped away the supports and examined the timber joinery. The problem was soon obvious, and was as I had guessed: the protruding tenon knob had snapped under load. To repair it properly I would have to carve a new, thicker tenon. But this would entail thinning the walls of the mortise in the stump. So to pay one I would have to thieve from the other. I doubted the mast would hold another repair.

My kingdom for a tree.

Tuesday 15 May

Bubo did not return to my ship overnight. He must have slept upon the island again. I hoped that the birds had not hurt him, although with his advantage of flight I was confident that Bubo could defend himself from any attacks. Over a cup of tea I considered his vehement exhortations to me yesterday, virtually ordering me to leave the island. I had not heard that urgency in his voice before. Clearly he wished to protect me from the birds; they did indeed look threatening.

Before I return to the island I must reassure him that I have no fear, for my pistols and sword will make short work of the marauding birds.

With a view to hunting on the birds' rock in the afternoon, I spent the morning on mast repairs. I decided to try a rebated joint instead of a mortise-and-tenon joint for the repair. This method would be weaker laterally than in the fore-aft direction, but it provided a better chance of sharing the load between the mast stump and its extension. As such, I spent the morning cutting away the old joinery and then chiselling opposing six-inch recesses into both stump and mast.

By and by I finished rasping the mast rebates and set about joining the pieces together. To this end I used four long screws, which held the posts initially in place. The next step was to drill three large holes through the clamped joint, into which I hammered stout wooden pegs. I then bound the whole joint tightly in hundreds of turns of strong Chinese fishing line, ensuring that there were no gaps between the threads. Over this thin but strong binding I nailed the original four clamping boards, and then further wrapped the whole assembly with black cord. I had nothing else at my disposal to strengthen the mast further. If it broke again I would be in peril, for the timber would not take another mend.

An hour before dusk I abandoned the final riggings and the hoisting of the sails, for the call of an island turkey on tonight's dinner plate gained sway over chores that I could complete tomorrow. I rowed for the rock with my pistols packed with black powder and tied with a scarf about my shoulders (as Mr Egg had shown me in London) and my scimitar hanging from my belt. I planned to take a brace of birds as quickly and quietly as possible, scamper from the island, and then treat myself to a supper of whole bird.

I affixed my tender to an outcrop below the eastern ridge, downwind of where I felt the birds would be. I crept up the rock face with stealth and deliberation, ensuring each foot and hand-hold was firm before committing to it. By and by I reached the ridge top, and with the manure-like stench filling my nostrils, I stole a glance across the plateau. The flock had gathered where I had expected: in the lee of the western wall. I could see Bubo's blue and red plumage standing out amidst the grey and white of the flock, his gay colours contrasting against the dull flock like a garland of roses on a gravestone. Obviously he had made peace with the natives. A few poorly looking birds sat on the periphery, and it was to them that I turned my attention, for every hunter knew it was prudent to cull the weakest animals first and to leave the robust for later.

I wished to maintain my cover until I struck, for alerting the flock to my presence would invite hostility. Their beaks looked sharp, even from this distance. Rather than walk openly across the plain, I climbed, like a welsh mountain goat, around the outside face of the steep island walls. It was slow going and a labour for my arms, unaccustomed as they were to this type of climbing. I had to reverse the orientation of my scarf so that my pistols hung over my back rather than dangling over my belly, for they clanked noisily against the rocks. But slowly, without alerting the birds to my presence, I crept closer.

I had scrambled to within 20 yards of the birds when I encountered a trickle of water cascading down the rock face. Thirsty, I climbed higher to investigate, and discovered that the water was overflowing from a small shaded pool. A large rock that protruded up from its edge concealed this area from the birds, so I pulled myself level with the pool, and once I found firm foothold, paused for rest.

I sucked in a mouthful of water. It was cool, fresh, and not the least salty; it must have arisen from a spring. Alongside newly-killed meat, fresh clean water was the first entry on a sailor's list of provisions, so this discovery was most fortuitous. Providence, if not smiling at me, was at least now glancing in my direction.

I drank more of the sweet water and then quietly bathed my head, enjoying the cool freshness as it trickled down the back of my neck. After another long pull, I hardened myself for the final phase of my attack. I would creep just 10 yards closer, then haul myself over the ridge, take out a bird with each pistol and another couple with my sword, then hustle across the plateau to my tender. The birds, with their stubby wings and long talons, would be lagging far behind by the time I rowed away with my brace. Then, just as I set myself for my final push around the cliff edge, something unusual caught my eye.

It was a dull shine, reflecting the last of the afternoon sunlight, emanating from deep within a rocky crevice. It was only by fate that the crack aligned with the setting sun that I could see it at all.

A shining object in such a location immediately heightened my curiosity, for it was an unusual sight. Perhaps, I hoped, it was mother-of-pearl or some other valuable natural substance, so despite the proximity of the flock, I judged that this oddity warranted closer inspection. Remaining hidden, I pulled myself over the ledge and slithered on my elbows and knees like an eel toward the source of the reflection. It took many firm tugs to dislodge it, for the object was fixed firmly in its place, but soon I had the strange item in my possession and lay low to examine it. It wasn't mother-of-pearl, but something possessing far greater fascination. Something man made.

It was an old pewter bowl or plate that had been squashed flat. As I turned it over I received another surprise, for on the obverse face were feint scratches that appeared to form letters. It seemed that the plate had been fashioned into a rough plaque. I rubbed at it with my sleeve to dislodge the grime and tarnish but was still unable to discern any words, for the markings were in poor condition.

A thousand thoughts filled my head, sending a blast of anticipation through my sinews. This etched pewter was evidence that someone had visited this island before. But why? For what purpose? And where did he, or they, go?

I tried to reset my mind to the task of hunting the birds, but the plaque had aroused my curiosity so intensely that I could not ignore it. I temporarily forgot about the birds; hoping to discover further artefacts, I thrust my arm deep into the rock crevice. But alas, even after a thorough forage I found nothing. The surrounding earth was flat, bare and clearly held nothing of immediate interest, so I gazed further, focusing on the holes and seams in the surrounding rock walls.

By and by, I spotted something unusual lodged into a fissure between two large boulders. I could not confidently identify it from a distance - perhaps it was an old pot. However to retrieve it would break my cover and the birds would discover my ruse. My mind bent itself about a choice: to quell my curiosity and retrieve the pot, or sate my hunger by taking a few birds?

Perhaps I could manage both tasks. First, I would claim the pot and then, if a chance remained, slay a bird or two. If I failed with the second part then I could easily return to the island tomorrow. My mind now set, I sprung into action. I leapt up and scampered across the plateau to the crevice, keeping as low as a spider across its web. Despite my low gait, the birds quickly detected my presence; they became animated and shrieked loudly. Bubo sprung up, carking loudly, perhaps trying to settle the rabble. I thrust my hands into the rock's seam and tugged firmly at the pot. After three frenetic pulls, it gave way. I barely glanced at it as I thrust it into my breeches pocket.

I quickly turned toward the flock. Each bird now faced me, shaking its hard yellow beak with intimidating rhythm. Bubo flew above them, carking loudly, but his exhortations were unheard, or ignored, amidst the rabble. I took a loaded pistol into my palm and aimed it at the nearest bird. Just I was about to bend my finger on the trigger I heard Bubo screech above the flock.

No!

Surely he could see that I was not in danger.

No hurt!

My mind took a vault. Until now I had assumed that Bubo had wanted me away from the island because he was concerned for my safety. After all, a good guard dog will bark - and bite if needed - to protect its master. Now I realised that he wasn't protecting me from the flock - he was guarding the *birds* from *me*. Confused by this sudden realisation, I withdrew my pistol's aim, but held it at the ready nonetheless. But the birds continued shrieking, and some of their braver warriors advanced toward me.

I decided to get off the island as quickly as possible. I fired a shot above the flock. The sharp crack of exploding powder had the desired effect, shocking the birds and halting their advance. I turned on my heel and ran for my tender. I scrambled down the cliff face, grazing my hands and bruising my knees such was my haste.

It was only when I had docked at the *Maris Alarum* that I fully gathered my wits together. I took a quick gulp of rum to settle my nerves and then, in the last of the afternoon sun, I examined my intriguing discoveries. I turned the pewter plaque about in my hands. It was most curious. It held five rows of text, each containing about half a dozen words, but the poor light would not reveal their meaning.

Next I examined the small urn; what a strange little trinket it was! It was narrow, and about the height of a man's outstretched hand, and was sealed with a cork stopper that was rotted and barely viable. Two handles had once adorned the upper edges of the pot, although one had cracked off as I had reefed it free from its lodging. Perhaps its original task had been to contain oil or spices for cooking.

It was a weatherworn thing, with its glazing flaked away from all but a few small patches. I crumbled away the spent cork stopper and then received another surprise, like a child discovering an egg buried in an Easter hay basket: the crock contained a rolled off-cut of canvas.

I unfurled the canvas - perhaps a remnant from an old vessel's sail – and pressed it flat on the galley table. I imagine that my eyes bulged with amazement, for the canvas was covered in words. In truth the letters were faded to a dull purple-grey colour and blotched almost beyond reading, but it was nonetheless clear that the canvas contained a message from someone long since passed.

Could it be directions to a concealed fortune? Perhaps some distant pirates or buccaneers had hidden riches on the island, or lodged a cache of weapons for later retrieval? My mind leapt like a frisky morning colt with possibilities. I tried to discern some meaning from the writing, but the low light was again my enemy. I stowed both the plaque and the canvas note carefully. A thorough examination of both will be my priority at morning's first light.

Wednesday 16 May

I was awake early, for my mind trawled ceaselessly through the night as to the meaning of the artefacts. True, I had found just an old plaque and a square of canvas – not the Ring of Eluned the Fortunate[138], I concede - but a remarkable and very unlikely discovery nonetheless. Perhaps ... perchance ... I dared to dream ... the writings might lead to unimaginable riches.

Unlikely suppositions or outlandish fantasies didn't normally tempt me into their web, but in this case my dreaming was justified. Why else would any man lodge such objects on a barren and desolate citadel such as this if they did not contain directions to a greater fortune? I could think of no explanation more likely, and so allowed myself the luxury of excitement and anticipation, and revelled in it like it was a warm May bath.

Using a galley rag, I scrubbed the pewter plate, which was very tarnished. After my elbow had returned the plaque's lustre I took it to the deck, where I felt the bright morning sun would help clarify the etchings. However they were so feint that even under bold light they were devilishly difficult to discern. Nevertheless I slowly, painstakingly, managed to decipher a few words.

On the left corner of the top row I read the number 12 and perhaps the word "April". Some indiscernible runes followed, then the number 1436. It appeared the writer had dated his piece: 12th April, 1436. By extension the plaque had lain in the rock crevice, undisturbed, for nearly 400 years. I felt humbled to be the first man since to lay eyes upon it.

---

[138] A mythical Celtic treasure, the Ring of Eluned was said to confer invisibility upon the wearer

On the second row I could read little except perhaps the word "order". The third row was just a mumble of lines and letters; an "R" here and a "G" there, but not enough to commit to a word. The fourth row was more legible: it began with the word "Infant" - a baby. But why?

Soon after was the word "Duque[139]". Was this plaque a directive to the riches of royalty? If so, then I was sure that the treasures were plundered from Portugal, for that was the final word on the last line. *Order. Infant. Duke. Portugal.* I had just four words with which to decipher a message written nearly 400 years ago. My mind whirled like a typhoon sky with possibilities, most of which involved treasures concealed for the later benefit of a young Portuguese Duke.

Suddenly I heard a loud clatter beside me. I started. Turning quickly I saw a familiar sight: Bubo. He had finally returned from his island excursion. Although my mind was soaked like a sodden sea sponge with thoughts of the Duke's treasure, I was nonetheless pleased to see my pet bird again.

"Good morning, Bubo."

I expected a garbled greeting in return, as was his learned habit, but instead received a terse *aaark*.

"Captain Rum found a plaque on the island," I said, showing him the shining plate. He barely twitched, and was clearly disinterested in my artefact. Not surprisingly, he could not appreciate the ramifications of such a discovery and the riches that it possibly – nay, *probably* - held within it; riches that I hoped it would share with me through its scratched and tarnished message.

Nevertheless I gave him a quick pet on his neck feathers, for I had missed this gay little creature, but then quickly returned to my examination of the trinkets that had so enraptured me with their potential. The pull of an easily-gained fortune drew a man's attention even more surely than a comely woman beckoning from behind a bedroom door. There was a long silence, before Bubo again carked.

---

[139] McAdam correctly interpreted these letters as the word *Duke*. Hereafter I have corrected the spelling to its modern equivalent, but in this instance, for reasons the reader will soon understand, I felt it important to represent the plaque's text with literal accuracy.

No hurt bird.

"Yes, Bubo," I said, holding the plaque to the light on the hope of illuminating some further letters.

Bird no pea - no doubt his way of saying that the flock had no food.

"I'm hungry too, Bubo. Are you hungry? Would Bubo like some fish?"

Bird no pea, he repeated. I understood his short message, but I felt no sympathy for the birds, for they had attacked me twice already. I would kill one in a trice and think nothing of it. The birds had declared the battle open, so I was entitled to bring about its end. Yet I relayed none of these thoughts to Bubo for my attention again focused upon the plaque, leaving little room for other musings. Was that a name – *Henry* - just after "Infant" on the fourth line?

No hurt bird.

"Ok Bubo. Captain Rum promises Bubo he won't hurt the birds."

Bubo sat for a while, perhaps not understanding my answer. I repeated my promise in simple terms: "Captain Rum no hurt bird", I said clearly while shaking my head and gesticulating to support my meaning. With that Bubo seemed satisfied. Perhaps sensing, correctly, that I was in no mood for nattering, he departed soon thereafter.

I continued studying the lines scratched into the soft metal, but apart from identifying a few extra letters I made little advance. Bereft of further ideas for deciphering the plaque, I fetched the canvas. I lay prone on the deck with the message before me to examine it in detail.

The cloth itself measured from my shoulder to the tips of my fingers, and was almost as wide as my double hand span. It was threadbare and yellowed, particularly the bottom, which was on the outside when it had been folded lengthwise and then rolled. The edges of the cloth had been torn roughly, rather than cut, from what I was now certain was once a sail.

The print was very small, faded and smudged, with watermarks in many places. I counted 49 lines of text, with about 20 words per line. It was organised in six separate sections. By and by I realised that each division was headed by a date – April 10 to April 16, 1436. Clearly the same writer had produced both the plaque and the canvas letter before me. What, I wondered, was his message? Despite the canvas's untidy cursive, some individual letters were clear, but they did not form sensible words.

To aid my understanding I fetched a quill and a square of paper. I transcribed all recognised words and their locations. By noon, I had the poorly total of five.

- The word "plant" appeared on lines five, six and sixteen.
- Line eight began with, I believe, "indefinite", and toward the end I noted the name *Henri*, which was also mentioned on the plaque.
- Line 21 had the name *Jesus*. Perhaps this was a religious homage. I would be most disappointed if this was true, for I remained expectantly hopeful that the message pointed to secreted treasures and riches. If this was a document aimed at pleasing the Lord then I was sure that Reverend Butler (wherever he was) was ready with his birch to treat my misreadings.
- Finally, line 23 mentioned Portugal, confirming that the plaque and the document shared their paternity.

Plant, *indefinite*, *Henri*, *Jesus* and *Portugal*. I had no inkling of the meaning of this message. I studied it again but the letters would not reveal their secrets. Perhaps the message was encoded. Deflated and for now defeated, I headed to the galley for a meal, yet again, of fish.

Thursday 16 May

Upon awakening, I had another examination of the artefacts, but decided to leave them until the sun was higher. Instead I decided to row to the island to hunt some birds, and began making preparations. But as I whetted my scimitar on a grinding stone, I reflected upon my conversation with Bubo yesterday. Had I promised him not to kill the birds? I had only a vague memory of this conversation, because my attention at the time had been on decoding the text. But despite this flippant vow, I remained intent on taking some birds for my larder.

Yet soon the pewter plate and canvas note, with their promise of riches, called so loudly at me that I demurred again. I had plenty of pickled fish remaining, and the birds, with their stubbed wings and poor condition, were going nowhere. I could hunt later.

As I studied the pewter plaque, a strategy came to mind for a truer reading of its etchings. Across its face I smeared a thin veneer of squid ink, then without pausing I wiped away the blackness, leaving traces of ink embedded in the scratches. This contrast heightened the plaque's legibility and allowed me to discern extra letters. With this newfound recognition I deciphered another name: Diogo de Silves. I also clearly identified some more letters and perhaps the word "name" in the last line. My interpretation of the plaque now read:

E?, Diogo de Silves, p? order?

D. J..., ... R ... gr...., ?

Infant Henri..., Duque ? V...,

ve... re..... ?? name(?) ? Portugal.

Despite my progress, I was no nearer to grasping the plaque's full meaning, but I was now forced to concede that it wasn't directing me to buried gold or gemstones. Possibly its words pointed to the canvas note, which I still hoped held such instructions, so I turned my attention to the script-covered sail scrap.

But even under the bright light of a mid-morning sun, its tiny letters soon defeated me. They were simply too small, faded and smudged to be discerned with an unaided eye. If only I had a glass with which to magnify....

I paused. My telescope. Could it enlarge the script? I quickly fetched it from my quarters and turned the focusing knob to its closest position. I stood back and peered hopefully through the eyepiece.

Alas, the telescope was useless. It was only after I had retreated half the deck that the canvas came into relief at all. True, this fine scope could spot a mermaid from 20 furlongs, but unfortunately Mr T. Hill and Sons did not have script reading in mind when they shaped its glass. Even the brass finder scope attached to the barrel proved worthless for such a task. I would need another way.

Heavily and with a sigh I climbed down the hatch to store the telescope away. Frustration pushed so firmly from within my chest that I beat at it with my fist. I felt like a thirsty traveller, who, having crested a hill above a river-filled valley, was unable to find a path down. To have travelled so far through this ragged ocean, and to now have such a secret within sight but beyond my grasp, was a cruel impost indeed.

As I replaced the scope in its mahogany box, I remembered back to when I had purchased it on Holborn High Street. How full of hope and spirit I had been! I had foreseen a challenging and difficult journey, but, I concede, not to the level that I had endured so far. I recalled chatting gaily to Master Hill and his jocularity about the London sun and its feeble attempt to provide warmth. Even with the magnifying effect of the burning glass.... I stopped, stunned by my own recollections. *The burning glass*.

I leapt to action like a child's jack-in-the-box. I quickly located the burning glass, and such was my anticipation that I virtually vaulted through the hatch to deck. Using the magnification of the burning glass and abetted by the bright sun, I quickly discerned what my lone eye could not see. Letters appeared where only smudges had existed previously.

After just a few minutes I identified enough letters that I could spell out a name on line three – Fernando Martinez. Perhaps he was the author. But what was Fernando trying to tell me? I peered at the enlarged smudges for another hour but although I could discern many letters I could not make any sense of the words. Nevertheless I transcribed them to the paper. Were the letters encoded? If so, I had little chance of solving this puzzle, for I had no method of unlocking its deception.

I spent the rest of the morning alternating the canvas examination with simple chores. I even caught a fish from the stern; its flesh tasted white, if one can eat a colour, and was as sweet as nectar. Bubo had not returned from the island. I was becoming concerned for him because he was spending much time with the flock, for which I had little regard.

I had not yet rigged the sails. This task called loudly to me, for I knew that I still had to test the new mast repair against the wind. But each time I started this job I demurred, for Bubo was not around to help; I had spent a day teaching him how to thread a rope through halyard riggings and wished to harvest the fruits of my endeavours. But this unfinished task was not worrying me, for my time was free. I could do it tomorrow.

Throughout the morning I returned frequently to the canvas message, but it continued to frustrate me because although I identified many more individual letters they evoked no meaning. It was as if they had been written to confuse, not inform, the reader.

Suddenly, in mid afternoon, the key to interpreting both the plaque and the document hit me like a cast iron cannon ball to the chest. Even a simpleton could have solved this riddle in a trice, yet I had missed it all along. The names – Diogo de Silves and Fernando Martinez ... the references to Portugal. Of course! The message was not written in code, but in *Portuguese*.

I could not speak the tongue and my command of Spanish was only fair, but the two languages were close enough to be siblings. I re-examined the plaque using every advantage I could eke: the magnifying burning glass, ink-emboldened text, and now armed with the knowledge that I was searching for Portuguese words and not the King's English. With these techniques at my disposal my task was far less exasperating than previously. I made fine progress and by the time the sun was dipping I had eked out a rough translation:

I, Diogo de Silves, by order of John, (??) gracious King and Prince Henrique, Duke of (V?), I claim this island (? in the) name of Portugal. [140]

Although I had missed a few words, the plaque's meaning was clear: Diogo de Silves, the sailor and scribe of the plaque, was claiming the birds' island for his King and Duke. But what, I wondered, was his fate? I set my eyes to the canvas document, which I felt confident held details of his exodus from the island and hopefully directions to his fortune. But the fading light again prevented me from further translation. I slept fitfully during the night such was my anticipation of Senor de Silves' message from the past.

Friday 18 May

---

[140] The word "infant", which McAdam had earlier gleaned, translates to "Prince" in Portuguese. The other words he had previously noted – *order, Duke (Duque)* and *Portugal* - were those whose Portuguese form is similar to their English translation.

I was up with the rising sun, keenly anticipating a day of revelation. I was pleased to discover that Bubo was on deck when I exited the hatch. *Gaaard Maaarn*, he cackled - his usual morning greeting that he had learned by imitating my "good morning" salutation. Clearly his mood had improved compared to his previous visit.

"Good morning Bubo," I said and proffered a thumb-sized portion of pickled fish and a crumb of fried oatcake that he quickly accepted. As we chewed our miserly breakfast, Bubo carked quietly.

Bird ... no pea.

I was aware of the birds' plight but had no answers. My own rations were pitifully short. I barely had enough food for myself, and certainly not enough to share with a mangy flock of turkeys, not even to fatten them up for later cooking.

"Captain Rum can't help the birds. I have no spare food."

Bird hurt.

This seemed to be his way of telling me that some birds were dying; certainly the poorly ones that I had previously sighted on the outer edge of the flock looked close to death.

"I'm sorry Bubo. I feel sorry for the birds," I lied. "But I cannot help."

I looked at him and simply shook my head. He must have understood the meaning of my simple gesture, for with that, he wearily flapped his handsome wings and flew off into the dawn sky. A skewer of remorse flitted through me, for I had no wish to see him in anguish over his kin. But a flashing memory of those menacing yellow beaks soon assuaged my guilt.

Without even pausing for a cup of tea, I used the burning glass to study the canvas document, with my eyes sensitised toward Portuguese inflections. Unlike previously, words now materialised from the document where before I could see only jumbled letters. Painstakingly I recorded each word on a page, leaving gaps where the text was illegible. I worked through the morning, repeating known words aloud to suggest possibilities for the missing ones. Before the sun was half way to its zenith I had translated the first paragraph.

10th April, 1436

A storm wrecked our ship upon this rock. 25 dead. Only two survivors – (? crewman) Fernando Martinez (?....) and myself. Fernando's head (? cut) bleeds profusely.

From just one stanza it was clear that this canvas contained an account of a shipwreck. Yet I clung to the chance that later entries may lead to wealth, for it was likely that the riches of the broken ship were interred here.

I immediately felt kinship with my unknown forebears, for we had much in common: we were sailors, and in all likelihood were the only men to have stood on this secluded outcrop. But what most drew me to Diogo de Silves, like a tide toward the high water mark, was that he cared to record his adventures in a journal, which was an undertaking kindred to my spirit. I felt like he was a brother.

I continued with my deciphering of the text and soon had translated another sentence:

There are many (? no flying, ? flightless) birds that eat seeds, fruits and berries. Tall grasses and green plants grow in abundance.

Seeds, fruits and berries? Abundant grass and green plants? I was so surprised by these revelations that I rechecked the letters, and my translation, twice. I found it hard to accept that Senor de Silves was observing this same barren outcrop when he penned those words. What had become of the vegetation? Why had the island turned into such a wasteland - barren, grey and stinking? My mind did not wander upon this riddle for long, for there was an answer in the very next line.

(?...) in one corner of the island the storm was so (? ferocious) that it washed all plants off the island and into the ocean. This area is grey and barren.

I paused to reflect. If a storm had washed away a section of plants from the island four centuries years ago, then it was clearly possible that last month's typhoon, that tyrant of all tempests, had completely robbed the island of all plant life. The account continued.

I have discovered a fresh water spring. With so much food and water I can survive here indefinitely. I have (? gathered) wood for a signal fire. I expect (?...) Henrique to send another ship within the year.

It seemed that the good sailor might have been rescued. I was pleased, for I already felt that I knew this man. With the account of April 10 now complete I retreated to the galley for sustenance, for I had partaken of neither food nor water since dawn.

Saturday 19 May

I spent a good portion of my day on translations from the canvas, and was disappointed as it steadily became clear that it was *not* a directive to buried riches. It was the dream of every sailor to discover such a message, and believing that I held one in my palms had set my nerves jangling like Sunday bells. Even though those bells were now fading, I was pleased to have heard them a few days, for even a short tune that ended quickly gave a man more joy than muffled silence.

Yet the story of Diogo de Silves still engrossed me. What else could this canvas log tell me of his time on this rock? Although written nearly two centuries ago, his words connected with me as if he had scribed them yesterday.

11th April 1436

Fernando lays still. He cannot talk. I fear his head wound will take him.

I discovered a pewter (? plate ? bowl) in the (? destruction, ? wreckage) and used it to (?) Fernando with fresh water.

I ate a green fruit off a tree today. It tasted fibrous and I suspect provided (? a) little sustenance. I suffered no ill effects.

I watch the birds. They do not fly or swim. They eat only plants, seeds and fruit. I caught one with my bare hands, (? twisted) its neck, cooked it on a small fire and feasted upon it. Very tough. I fed Fernando some bird lard, but he could barely chew.

My brother-across-time's message dismayed me, for he again referred to the plants, seeds and fruits that were no longer available. It was now clear to me that the recent storm had destroyed all plant life on the island. Protected by only low rock walls, the loose ashen soil would have been at the mercy of the towering waves and ferocious winds. From the decks of the *Maris Alarum* I had observed some waves that were twice the height of this outcrop, if not thrice. It was a miracle that the birds survived the maelstrom at all.

151

Diogo's account continued.

12th April, 1436

Fernando passed today. I (? buried) him (? to) the earth. May the Lord have mercy on his soul and may Jesus, the Christ child, (? show) him to everlasting life. Now I (? remain, ? permanently) here alone.

I hammered the pewter (? plate,? bowl) flat with a rock to form a plaque. On it I (? scratched) a message that claims this island for Portugal and her King. I hereby proclaim it "Rock of the Birds".

I finished eating the bird and also ate another green fruit. Some bushes are thick with purple berries. I ate six of these to test their nutrition. They tasted very bitter.

This translation took me until evening. As I retreated to the galley for supper it occurred to me that Bubo had not visited me all day. He was no doubt happy with his kin upon the island, but I did miss the little fellow.

Later, as I lay on my hammock, thoughts meandered through my mind with regard to the island rock. When the typhoon's enormous waves washed away the plants, it would have also removed the top layers of the soil, meaning that the dormant seeds within that earth would have been lost to the ocean as well. That empty plateau held little chance of regrowing to its previous lush state and would most likely stay as a desert-like wasteland forever. It followed that the survival of the turkey birds was perilous. They would gradually die and would cease to exist as a species.

At first, this thought disturbed me a little, but I soon chastised myself for my softness. I decided to stock my larder with some salted birds, for they would soon die by nature's hand anyway. I hoped that if I explained this to Bubo he would see the sense in taking some birds for sustenance, rather than letting them starve to death for the benefit of no-one.

I drifted into an uncomfortable sleep.

Sunday 20 May

When I emerged onto deck in the morning, my eyes first went not to the canvas in my hands but to the port gunwale, Bubo's favourite perch. Alas, it was empty again. He was still on Bird Rock. I trained my telescope toward the outcrop and was relieved to see his grand wings beating as he flew above the island's walls. Twice I saw him plunge downward, no doubt diving for fish. At least Bubo was eating well, even though the yellow-beaked-turkey-birds were starving. They must have deteriorated to a poorly condition by now.

My attention soon reverted to my brother Diogo's letter. The remaining sections were short and my skills were now adept at interpreting the messages, so I quickly transcribed it.

13th April 1436

I awoke with nausea and sickness in my belly. I am thankful for the fresh water spring, for my mouth is dry. I ate another of the green fruit, but I shall not eat the purple berries again.

14thl April, 1436

Although this island is as green and rich as Eden (?), my stomach can hold no food. Whatever passes my mouth soon (? retches) back up. My (? fore) head sweats and I am fearful that the berry poison has me in its grip.

15th April, 1436

My fever grows. I wish I had kept the (? bowl), for I can barely (? crawl, ? walk) to the spring for water. But (? ?) I (?) I have marked this land for my King.

My earlier presumption - that Diogo had been rescued from this lonely castle - ceded away like water from an out-flowing estuary. It seemed that the bitter purple berries had poisoned him.

Despite the passing of time since Diogo's quill had scratched those words, a wholesome sadness enveloped me, for I was reading the final thoughts of a distant brother as he died on that lonely citadel. As these musings passed through my mind, I happened to glance over the gunwales to the sea below. As if sent by Lucifer himself to mark the sombre tone of the moment, the carcass of a dead island bird drifted past.

At another time I would have jumped for my net, broiled the dead bird for dinner and savoured a hot broth for supper as well. But seeing its forlorn, bedraggled corpse reminded me of Bubo when I had first sighted him. Any thoughts of eating the dead bird seemed distasteful. The island birds were survivors, like Bubo and I - except, of course, for the one now bobbing, decomposing, alongside the stern of the *Maris Alarum*.

With a heavy chest, I returned one last time to the document. I had just one paragraph to translate, but I guessed in advance what it would say.

I beseech my most gracious King to grant my family (? whatever) riches he (? deems) ? as reward for my service to his Kingdom.

I could have written the last line without even referencing the script.

May God have mercy on my soul.

With that final prescient line, he was gone.

Diogo's soul deserved a proper burial, one befitting his true and loyal spirit. In the absence of his remains, I vowed to inter his final story to the island. I carefully folded the canvas along the original crease line and rolled it tightly, then returned it to its pot. I spent the remainder of the day fashioning a new stopper from a spare cork.[141]

Monday 21 May

Thoughts of Diogo and the dead bird turned my mind all night like a farmer furrowing a spring field. From outright hostility toward the island birds, I now felt growing empathy. They had lived on this desolate crag

---

[141] The Dean of Maritime History at Oxford was beside herself with joy when she read the preceding section of McAdam's account, for it filled a large void of knowledge about Diogo de Silves. De Silves was a Portuguese explorer who is credited with discovering the Azores Islands in 1427 – Europe's most easterly point. Previously he was known only through a *single reference* on a naval chart, and nothing at all was known about his life or death. Despite the paucity of information on his life, the Portuguese hold de Silves in such high esteem that their postal service issued a stamp in his honour in 1990. (A copy is in Appendix One). The Dean submitted this new information to a peer-reviewed journal (as yet unpublished), where it has generated much excitement amongst maritime history scholars.

for hundreds, perhaps thousands, of years and had somehow managed to not only survive but thrive. Now, because of the tempest that had savaged the *Maris Alarum*, their whole species was in peril. The natural history of these unique birds might soon end; Diogo and Fernando's spirits would not be the only things to die upon that unforgiving rock.

By and by I heaved myself out of my hammock and fossicked about the galley like a truffle hound[142], searching for breakfast. Alas, all that I had in abundance were oatcakes – hard bricks, now green with mould from the ocean's inundation. I boiled one in water and then fried it in hot lard on the griddle, but still found it very disagreeable to taste. Most men would call it poisonous. The mere waft of it near my nose harkened me back to the dark days of Shepton, and I was unsure if I could eat this swill much longer. To swallow it, or to starve to death: this was a closer choice than I could have ever imagined.

After this poorest of starts, I clambered onto deck. Bubo was absent from his perch again, so, rather than impatiently wait for his presumed return, I called to him loudly, in my deepest voice, a dozen times. By and by I was pleased to sight his blue and red feathers beating toward me. As I waited, I noticed that the breeze had roused to a firm wind. I glanced nervously at the new mast, knowing that I still had to set and test the sails.

 "Good morning Bubo," I offered as he touched down softly upon the port gunwale. After a pause, Bubo replied in his now habitual squawk.

Gaard maard.

"How are the birds?"

Again, Bubo paused. By and by he replied simply: *no pea*. Then another silence, before *bird hurt*. I looked into his owl-like eyes; he was not the merry creature I knew, but instead was insular and slow to answer. It pained me to see him this way.

My attitude toward the flock had shifted, but for what purpose? Even though I now wished to help the birds survive, I had so little food that I

---

[142] A truffle hound is a dog (in fact, often a pig) that is used to hunt for a type of mushroom called a truffle. Truffles, which are highly prized for their flavour and aroma, grow underground on the roots of oak trees, and can only be readily located by an animal with a very keen sense of smell.

could not spare even a morsel - certainly not enough to feed a hungry flock. All I had was a shred of beef, a crock of mouldy tomatoes, a bare couple of dozen raisins, half a crate of rotting oatcakes and....

Oatcakes. I still had dozens of oatcakes. They were mouldy and from a human point of view almost inedible. But surely I could spare a few from my cache for the birds, even if only to stave off their starvation until a better solution arose.

"Bubo, Captain Rum will bring food for the birds."

Bubo looked at me with a tilted head and wide eyes - he was confused.

"Oatcakes," I said simply. Without further explanation from me, Bubo seemed to understand the broad sweep of my message. He then flew back to the flock, presumably to deliver some nattered form of bird communication. I fetched a dozen oatcakes from their storage crate and loaded them into the old flour sack. After pulling my tender astern I stepped into it with much effort, for the waves were peaking. With the wind to my aft, I quickly crossed the passage to Bird Rock.

I rowed about the perimeter to my previous berth. The tide was low, making for a long ascent up the island's perimeter cliff. The sea-sprayed rocks made the climb very slippery; with my laden sack in tow, I could barely climb. After a long struggle I scrambled over the top ledge and lay on the grey earth, recovering. The smell of the pungent manure earth filled my nostrils.

Suddenly I realised where the soil that filled this crater had come from: it was not sand, or even earth, but *guano* from the birds themselves. The entire island was nothing more than a hollow crater filled with bird droppings. I struggled to appreciate the aeons of time it would have taken for the birds to fill this hollowed rock with their excrement, only for much of it, including the vital plants and seeds, to be washed away by a single violent storm. Now all that stood between the flock and extinction were some mouldy hard cakes.

I looked across toward the flock. As before, my presence agitated them and they screeched at me aggressively. Wanting to quell any uprising before it began, I quickly shook the oatcakes from the sack, crumbled them into small pieces and pitched them to the ground in front of the birds. The mood of the flock quickly changed from hostility to disorder as they scrambled after the morsels. As the healthier, faster birds claimed the oatcake portions, I cast the remainder toward the periphery so that the poorest birds would have a chance of procuring a prized crumb.

At first, everything progressed as I had expected: amidst a squabble, each bird secured a morsel. Thankfully, they were soon too consumed eating to be agitated by my presence. But then - somewhat unusually, I felt – the birds flew to separate areas to eat. It seemed that each bird wished to have space in which to protect its bounty, for they spread themselves over much of the plateau. But then, just as I began to feel some pride in my offering, these rude birds felt fit to insult me: instead of eating their dinner, they spat out the oatcake as if it was nothing more than tobacco spittle.

I knew that the hard-cakes did not possess the finest taste in the Kingdom. I also conceded that they were tough, mouldy and barely palatable to my human tongue. But if I were a bird, having not eaten even a seed for weeks, I would not have emitted such sustenance even if my beak screamed murder at me. These ungrateful birds had wasted my gift of 12 valuable cakes. If they now starved to death, it would not be upon my head.

I watched, increasingly disdainful, as the ignorant birds spat and scratched at an earth made from their own faeces; even a sty pig was not so ignorant. Annoyed, I shunned the birds, and even turned away from Bubo who was flitting about the flock, seemingly enjoying himself. I was in no mind for frivolity for I had just wasted precious rations and felt not an iota of warmth for doing so. Despite the low tide and the stiffening wind, I soon departed the island.

Tuesday 22 May

I lay awake, before dawn, as Mother Ocean rocked me in my swaying hammock. My feelings toward the birds had twisted again. I now felt more irritation than sympathy, for they had wasted rations in needless fashion. A sailor would earn himself 20 lashes for such a slight.

The thought of snapping a bird's neck again passed by me, but, like a washed-up fishing net, this notion entangled itself with my promise to Bubo that I would not kill the birds. Just as I had this thought I heard a warble from the deck. *Gaaard Maaarn*.

Despite my annoyance yesterday with the birds, I was pleased that Bubo had returned. We shared some fish, and even had another lesson. Bubo was very attentive so I extended him with a task; after only two hours my clever bird learned to tie a knot in a rope, producing a mother-in-law's hitch! I attempted to correct his technique to produce a true reef knot but he became agitated. Perhaps it was fairer to Bubo that I confined my expectations, for manipulating a rope into a knot was a skill that even a trained monkey, with fingers and thumbs, would struggle to master. For Bubo to achieve this feat with just his beak and two talons spoke not only of the sharpness of his mind but his dexterity. He certainly seemed to have a natural affinity with rope, heightening my suspicion that he used vines in his natural environment.

I was so impressed by his attentiveness that I petted him for a good part of the remaining morning. Whenever my movements slowed, he ducked his head down low, almost as if he was bowing before the King, exposing the back of his neck; this movement seemed to indicate that he wanted more petting. I obliged. Sitting with Bubo in the gentle breezes on deck helped to mellow my thoughts as well.

Later, with Bubo's help, I rigged the halyards. This task took a small fraction of the time that it would have taken without his assistance. My previous training paid a handsome dividend for I did not have to climb the mast at all, and rigged two sails without a single splinter.

After tightening the stays and re-checking all knots, I carefully hoisted the mainsail to half height. This sentence flows freely from my quill and I concede that a task as simple as pulling on a halyard is not usually difficult, but in truth it was a torment. I fretted for many minutes, and had a few pulls of rum, before committing the act, for I feared that the joint might crack again. I was out of options if this repair failed.

It was afternoon before I finally mustered the courage, fortified by another good splash of rum, to cast away on a downwind run to test my carpentry. I hoisted half of the headsail and set it wing-to-wing against the mainsail to stabilise the lateral load. Again, my gills filled with dread from imagined problems, but I knew that there was no other way to assuage my worries than to press forward.

I soon gave thanks to Providence, because after a light tack to windward the mast remained upright. Although it buckled ever so slightly at the join, I heard no creaks or groans, and the black cord stayed fast about it.

However I was not ready to set sail for Africa just yet, for the breeze was only five knots. This light weather was not a true test of what lay ahead. I would do further tests when the wind was stouter. Even though this rock was desolate, its presence reassured me, and I did not want to sail further with the risk of another snapped mast hanging above my head like Damocles' sword[143]. As soon as the wind reached 20 knots, I would test my repair further, and then set sail for the African coast.

At least my ship was now functioning, albeit poorly, but in such a vast ocean, two half-sails were vastly superior to two oars. I also had access to ample fresh water, and the fishing was fair. My luck had flipped to the finer – I could feel it in my sinews. If I had a barometer for Providence then I am sure it would have predicted the same.

My mind still vaulted with the thought of taking some birds. I thought that I should try to talk about this with Bubo, but he had flown back to the island and didn't return in the evening. Yet I doubt that his mind could grasp such concepts, or even that he could understand my words in such a complex discussion.

~~Thursday 24 May~~[144] Wednesday 23 May

I dreamed all night of roasted turkey. I could not remove this thought from my mind. But when I looked down at my forearm and saw the scratches from Bubo's talons, they reminded me of my promise to him. As I lay in my hammock, gently rubbing those same scars to relieve their itch, I asked myself a question: what man, with no-one to judge him other than a bird, would resist life-giving sustenance for the sake of an oath given on just a moment's thought? An oath given to a mere bird.

---

[143] Damocles is remembered in history for a story in which he offered to swap places with a rich King (Dionysius) in order to luxuriate in his wealth and fortune. However Dionysius hung a sword above Damocles' throne; the weapon was suspended by just a single hair that could snap at any time. The anxiety soon became too much for Damocles, who begged Dionysius to swap back. The story became a metaphor for the pressure that comes with positions of power.

[144] The original date was crossed out and replaced. The reasons for this change will soon become apparent.

To hold this promise under such conditions would be piety for no sake other than itself, in which I had always seen no point. Such holiness was as shallow as ceasing work on the Sabbath in case it offended some unseen, imagined deity.

The island birds would soon die anyway – a long, slow death of starvation - so to take away their pain swiftly would be a blessed relief. I would be doing the flock a service because there would be fewer beaks to feed if food became available. Yes, it was clearly beneficial for all if I killed a few birds – not just for my plate, but also for the advantage of the flock. But would Bubo understand? The birds were his family, his species, while I was neither of these. I dared not raise the question of a mercy killing with him for I feared his answer.

Nor did I wish to insult Bubo with betrayal, for he could depart my ship forever with a few beats of his large wings. I enjoyed keeping him as my pet, and he was starting to prove himself useful for a variety of simple tasks. Despite me being his master, it was true that he had a power over me, for he could depart in an instant if he felt so inclined, yet I could not leave him even if I wished to because he could easily fly after me, or perch atop the mast out of my reach.

I realised that I would have to kill a bird without Bubo's knowledge. Perhaps I could distract the flock with some oatcake crumbs and then smite one on the edge of the flock in the cacophony. No alarm would be raised, for one bold swipe of my sword would silence a bird forever.

Even though Diogo had described them as 'tough', the smell of roasted turkey, fresh from the coals, again filled my mind. I pictured the bird's gleaming flesh shining from the basting of its own fat and the succulent crunch as I sunk my teeth through the browned skin. Again I asked myself: what price a promise? Especially one made to a bird.

By and by, the imagined smell of a roasted bird held more sway than my fleeting promise. With my scimitar concealed beneath my breeches and another dozen oatcakes in the old sack, I rowed for Bird Rock. The sun's first rays were heralding its arrival as I climbed the perimeter wall.

My first vision over the plateau revealed an odd sight: the arrangement of the birds. Each time I had seen them previously they had been huddled in a flock, generally in the lee of the rock wall. They had spread themselves across the plateau in a loose grid, as though sitting upon the squares of a giant chess board[145]. The birds sat on their rumps looking down at the grey dirt, and barely a sound passed from their beaks - a welcome change from their irritating chattering. It was as if they were sinners at a Sunday sermon, seated evenly in the pews with their heads bowed in contrition. Perhaps they prayed for forgiveness for wasting my oatcakes in such needless fashion two days before.

Bubo. Where was he? I looked about and saw that he was perched on a rocky outcrop on the southern wall, his head tucked under his wing, asleep. I hoped he would stay that way so that he did not witness me taking a bird. I continued watching the flock, planning my swoop and my subsequent exit.

The birds soon noted my appearance. They responded with consternation, but thankfully not the outright hostility that earlier been my welcome. I scooped some oatcakes from the sack, crumbled them and broadcast them about, saving a few cakes in the sack in case I later needed them to distract any hostile birds. With the attention of the flock now elsewhere and Bubo asleep, my moment was upon me. It was time to strike swiftly and strongly. I looked down to retrieve my scimitar from my breeches, but as I did, something in the earth caught my gaze. Something green.

I looked down again with new purpose, and saw what appeared to be a small green shoot protruding from the soil. I bent low to examine it more closely. It was indeed a tiny shoot and even had two stalks. Had I discovered a plant that, in time, would grow and provide food? I looked again: yes, two small green stalks had twisted their way from the earth.

A loud sound interrupted my inspection - a high-pitched, melodic trill, followed by a deep series of hoots. One of the turkey flock had thrown its head back and was flapping its tiny wings and hooting rapidly. The other birds soon crowded like seagulls around an old bread crust, intent upon viewing whatever had excited the first bird. The cacophony woke Bubo, dismissing the thoughts I had of taking a bird during the rabble. He flew over, and by dint of his working wings he was able to view the source of the excitement without jostling among the throng. By and by

---

[145] Chess as we know today was developed about 1500. It was a popular game in the early 19th century in Britain.

the rabble dispersed, and Bubo flew over to me and perched upon my forearm, his sharp talons again digging into my bare skin.

"What happened, Bubo?" I asked. "Why are the birds excited?"

He launched himself from my forearm and flew ahead, leading me to the source of the commotion. The last of the oatcakes in my sack soon cleared the flock as they chased the vital crumbs, and soon I could see, curling from the guano earth, a tiny green stalk about as long as my thumbnail.

"That's good news Bubo," I said in truth, for the plants might help to keep the birds alive. "Where did the seed come from?"

Bubo widened his eyes.

"The seed," I repeated. "The seed for the plant. Where did the seed come from?"

Bubo's eyes widened again and his head tipped sideways.

"Where did the seed come from that became the plant?" By and by, after many gestures and repeats of my question, he seemed to understand, for his eyes narrowed and his neck straightened. Yet his carked answer made no sense.

Captain Rum.

Clearly, Bubo had misunderstood me.

"From Captain Rum?" I queried. "The seed came from Captain Rum? Captain Rum has no seeds."

Bubo squawked a simply reply, which again surprised me.

Oatcake.

As soon as Bubo conveyed this notion, I instantly knew that it wasn't true. First, in making the hard cakes, the baker would have crushed the oat seeds with a mortar-and-pestle and then mixed them with salt and melted fat, which in most cases renders them lifeless. Although I had known an occasional oat seed to sprout from a hard cake – in fact, it had happened once earlier on this journey – such germination was rare. Second, the seeds had been in the guano-earth for only two days. I am no farmer but I knew that oats took up to a week to germinate, even under fine growing conditions. So it was clear that the sprouts were not

162

from the oatcakes but from pre-existing kernels that had simply lain dormant in the soil and had survived the ocean's destructive purge. These latent seeds had chosen a most opportune time – for me - to make their burst for life.

Were they weeds? Or useful remnants of fruit-bearing plants? Regardless of the plant's edibility, it was better that the birds thought that I had provided it; I would rather a tainted hero than a dead saint. So despite the absurdity of his belief, I kept my doubts private from Bubo. If the birds believed that I was their saviour then I would be a fool to dent my own crown.

Amidst the cacophony, I had forgotten about the two small stalks that had appeared near my sack. I showed Bubo the stalks – were there now three? On closer inspection, it seemed to be a different plant to the other one; despite being taller, it was finer in blade, and perhaps a deeper green. I did not tell Bubo that this finding confirmed my suspicion that the sprouts were from dormant seeds. If this plant was different to the other one then I could not have supplied it, because I had provided hard-cakes that contained only oat seed. But in their happy ignorance the birds trilled excitedly, and now seemed to regard me not as a dangerous interloper but, I admit with only a minor pang of guilt, as a provider. Their aggression toward me had certainly diminished.

With Bubo now awake and by my side, I no longer had the opportunity to kill a bird. But I did not fret, for I had time aplenty to hunt surreptitiously, satisfying my hunger without damaging my relations with my pet.

I returned to my ship, where I simply sat in the sunshine near the port gunwale. My mood eased as the rising morning sun soothed my stiff back. Slowly my mind relaxed and then wandered about like a fluky breeze. I no longer worried about testing the mast or fretted about taking a bird for a meal. My eyelids felt more comfortable down than up, so I retreated to my hammock where I simply swam along in a field of my own imaginings. Although I had been awake for less than an hour, I drifted into a pleasant morning siesta.

*

I did not know how long I slept and had difficulty in reckoning it. In some ways it was though I had been resting for barely half a day, for the sun was just past noon and the waxing moon had dipped downward only a quarter of an arc compared to when I first laid down. However, when I later returned to the island, other observations showed that I had been sleeping for far longer: in particular, the two tiny plants that I had discovered earlier were both now half as long as my forefinger, having almost doubled their previous size.

My confusion amplified as I wandered around the plateau. I saw a dozen tiny sprouts where earlier there had been nothing but bare guano. Had I slept for an entire turning of the clock? It seemed so implausible - to have lain for just a morning nap yet slept more than 24 hours without so much as a flinch - but the alternative – that a dozen seeds had germinated and the other plant had grown an inch in just one morning – seemed impossible. So I was left with nothing but the highly unlikely, and so I was forced to admit to sleeping through an entire day!

True, I had lain in bed for an entire turn of the clock before – this occurred many times after my dear Beth departed. But that slumber was due to the heaviness of my body and the lead in my bones, not the tiredness of my eyes. But this was the first time I had truly slept through noon, sun down and then sun up without so much as blinking open an eye. Should a man feel proud of such an accomplishment? Or should I feel ashamed of the very laziness in my blood? I thought the former, and as there was no other man to judge me, I registered a sense of satisfaction at the length of my uninterrupted dozing.

After I gifted them another feed of crumbled oatcakes, the birds seemed even more accommodating of my presence. Perhaps they still thought of me as their saviour for supplying seed. I alone knew that the rapidly growing plants had not come from me, but my current standing with the birds was a vast improvement on the earlier possibility of being pecked to death, so again I kept my lips and my thoughts apart. In truth, it did not matter, for even if I were able to somehow explain my thoughts to Bubo, the birds would not be able to fathom such concepts.

I looked about for Bubo and soon spotted him at the far edge of the plateau, merrily hopping among the flock. It now felt right to see him spending time with his kind, which I conceded was a change from my thoughts only days ago. Perhaps the long sleep had pushed my mood toward the convivial.

I wandered aimlessly about the island, although apart from the newly germinating seed there seemed little to explore. Some birds were still plainly suffering from hunger and looked poorly, but at least now there was hope for them, although I feared that the harvest from the new plants might arrive too late for some, despite the oatcakes to stave off death for now. Yet I was surprised and in some ways impressed to note that the birds had not eaten the young plants. Either the new plants were unpalatable to them, or they had developed instincts to let them mature before eating them.

I drank some water from the spring, pausing briefly to acknowledge Diogo and Ferdinand. I filled my flask and decided to return with my water crocks for a refill, as my ship's supply was stale and dank.

Thursday 24 May

Again, the wind and seas were slight, so I spent the morning sorting through my remaining rations. A hint of dismay wedged itself amongst my temporarily lifted spirits, for little remained of any foodstuffs. With the local fishing providing reasonable returns (my catch last night provided two solid fillets with very few bones) it seemed pointless to ration my meagre stocks further, so with the last shards of my original provisions I prepared a feast.

Ah, but how sea life had changed the meaning of the word 'feast'. In London, a feast would have meant some bread-fried oysters to begin, then a large bowl of minted pea soup, followed by a hotpot of baked lamb shanks, finished with a treacle pudding. Here, moored in the middle of a vast expanse of ocean next to an unidentified rock, a 'feast' referred to a tortured, leathery slice of dried beef, a handful of hardened peas, a crock of old tomato pulp and a handful of wizened raisins.

Yet after this meal, my plate would become even more monotone: fish, fish and more fish - and perhaps, I still debate, some roast bird. If I was prepared for a long wait at this outpost, perhaps I could harvest some island leaves or fruits - if the birds did not eat them first. This meagre situation would persist until I found land - real land, arable land - not some isolated crag with weeds shooting from old bird droppings.

I packed the food into the old flour sack, along with another dozen mouldy oatcakes for the birds, and tied it with a rope around my shoulders so that I could scale the rock face with unencumbered hands. The tide was high when I arrived at Bird Rock, enabling me to easily ascend the perimeter cliff. But when my eyes peered over the summit I was felled by a sight of such surprise that my legs gave like they were made of egg yolks, and it was only the grip of my hands that saved me from a fall.

The plateau was covered in oats.

True, the covering was sparse. But to see such a crop of three or four dozen young stalks where three days ago there was little but grey ashen earth was a vault for my senses. I pulled myself over the ledge and rubbed my eyes – thrice- to check that the devil himself was not tricking my vision. No, everything was as it first presented: a youthful field of oat seedlings, each a few inches high. I walked to the nearest plant and touched it gently. My fingers too, must have been in cohorts with the devil, for they also confirmed that the oats were real.

I sat slowly to the ground, like a boy's toy top losing spin, as I struggled with the truth of what lay before me. I looked and looked again but in the end, I was left with one clear reality: Bubo was right. The birds, in their island crater full of dung, had grown a small crop of young oats from old hard cake seed! Even a Grampian farmer[146] would concede bewilderment at such a feat.

I simply sat in silent wonder and watched the birds. A field of oats was growing on this barren, isolated, dung-filled island rock! My mind spun.

I knew that some Lords in England would pay a pretty pound for bat guano to fertilise their crops; the farmers revered it as the best plant tonic available. But this soil, this bird dung dirt, seemed miraculous in its powers. I simply sat where I was, still stunned, and watched the birds go about their tasks.

---

[146] The Grampians, in north east Scotland, is a fertile area known for its high volume production of grain crops.

The longer I observed their habits, the more awed I became. They were not immobile sentries as I had first presumed, but instead were constantly active in some small way: scratching extra guano over a furrow, perhaps scraping some away, or testing the earth with a probing beak. I noticed that occasionally a bird would waddle across the plateau and fill its long beak with water from the spring, then use it to moisten the earth around the plants. Sometimes it seemed that the birds were using their small wings to fan the plants, or spreading them out to provide shade. These clever birds had learned to make the most of their environment, and were farmers *extraordinario*.

Distantly I recall reading some Lamarck[147] – Reverend Butler's preferred naturalist. Here, on Bird Rock, his theories could be seen in action. As each bird had learned the skills of farming, its forms had changed so that its beak and talons better suited its purpose. Over many centuries, the birds had gradually grown the tools to be skilled workers of the earth rather than flyers through an unproductive sky. Out here, on this isolated rock, where would they fly? If those doubters of Lamarck could just glance at these birds, then their objections to his theories would evaporate in an instant. [148]

By and by I wondered about that other clever bird, Bubo. I looked about and saw him diving for fish, not far from where I now sat. After observing him for a while, it was clear that he too was very skilled in his craft. He would glide high above the water, staying aloft in the up-winds from the island cliffs with barely a flicker of his grand wings. Then, when

---

[147] Jean-Baptiste Lamarck (1744-1829), a French naturalist and botanist, was the first scientist to enunciate a clear theory of evolution. His theories, now discredited and replaced by those of Charles Darwin, contended that repeated actions gradually changed an animal's shape. It then passed this acquired change to its offspring. For example, if a giraffe frequently stretched up to reach high leaves, then its neck and legs would gradually elongate. It's offspring would subsequently be born with similarly long neck and limbs.

[148] Charles Darwin's generally accepted theory of evolution would explain the birds' behaviour in a different way: those birds who were *born* with minor variations that helped them adapt to their limited resources – i.e. the small isolated plot of fertile land - were more likely to survive, and would then pass these natural variations to their offspring. Conversely, flying was not a very useful skill on this isolated rock, meaning that this trait slowly, over many centuries, became redundant. Gradually this endemic flock developed the habits and mannerisms that McAdam interpreted as 'farming'.

his keen owl-like eyes spied a tasty fish swimming too near the surface he would flap his blue and red wings frantically, then turn and speed down toward the ocean. Then he would pull his wings tightly to his body, using just their tips to curve his flight path sharply along the water's surface, plunging his talons under, usually emerging with a small fish between his talons. Then, I noted after long observation, he would turn his prey about to the fore-aft direction, perhaps to carry it more freely against the wind, before flying to solid ground where he would then devour it with his sharp beak.

Fishermen and farmers – the birds were advanced in their respective abilities. Yet it was clear that the island birds could neither swim nor fly, and Bubo would not know how to plant a seed even if taught. So each bird, although accomplished in its own art, would perish if it found itself alone in the other bird's world.

While feeding the birds more oatcakes, I discovered something that yet again surprised me. The three separate shoots that I had discovered earlier were small wheat stalks, not oats. But from where had the wheat seed come? The hard cakes could explain the oats, but the discovery of the wheat presented a different conundrum. I had not provided the seed, and there was nothing but seawater and empty ocean air for hundreds of leagues in every direction. From where had the birds procured wheat?

Later, I decided that rather than return to the *Maris Alarum* I would spend the night on the island, for the evening was warm, still and clear. When I eventually depart Bird Rock, my cloistered hammock will be my only choice of bedding, so I felt that it would pay me to use the available variety now.

For supper I ate the last of the beef strips, which proved to be a long labour for my jaw, although I did enjoy their wizened flavour. Bubo also brought me two sardines that I ate raw. After the fresh fish, my palate was not in the mood for mouldy tomatoes, hard dry peas or even the shrivelled raisins. I hoped that my mouth would never have to chew on such fare, for if I was forced to eat such swill it would be a sign of low times. As the evening star rose in the east, I emptied my sack of the remaining foodstuffs and pushed them aside into a crevice in a rock. I cleared a hip hole[149] in the earth, and then laid the hessian sack down as a thin bed sheet. At least it would keep my nose from the guano.

As I drifted to sleep, the answer to the question of where the wheat seeds had come from hit me in the face – literally. The old sack! Of course! The lazy London miller who had ground the wheat for my flour had done such a poor job that he left some seeds unmilled. The kernels must have fallen from my sack as I shook out the last of the oatcakes. Now, here they were, not ten feet from where I lay, growing toward the star-filled heavens. If I ever meet that miller again I shall not box his ears as was my earlier vow, but will shake him warmly by the hand in thanks for his laziness and ineptitude.

Friday 25 May

I slept poorly because the earth felt as though it was waving and rolling beneath me throughout the night. Although my sea legs were strong, I feared that my land legs were wasting away like a calf-palsied cow's[150].

The plants had grown further overnight and were now almost ankle high. Three inches. Astounding.[151]

I returned to my ship and spent the morning on simple chores. I wanted to test the mast again, but the wind remained light, so I did not even weigh anchor. Instead, my attention turned back to Diogo's pewter plaque and canvas note, which had so consumed me earlier. It was time to put them to rest.

---

[149] A hip hole was a small indentation, about the size of a soup bowl, dug into the earth. It increased the comfort of sleeping on solid ground by accommodating the lateral pelvic and hip bones.

[150] Calf palsy occurs when the nerves in a cow's hips are over-stretched during delivery of her calf. This nerve damage causes weakening and paralysis in the cow's hind legs.

[151] I was originally sceptical of McAdam's reports, for it seemed unlikely that the grains could grow to approximately 8 cm (3 inches) high in only four days. I checked with the director of the Oxford University Herbaria, who assured me that while such growth was unusual, it was not impossible. He cited one species of bamboo that grows up to 120 cm (four feet) per *day* – roughly *sixty times* the rate of the grain! He added that the fertile guano soil, with virtually unlimited elements such as nitrogen, would have been extremely conducive to growth. Before the advent of modern agricultural chemistry, guano was prized as a supreme plant fertiliser.

I had already decided that the canvas note belonged to Bird Rock, where it could rest with the spirits of Diogo and Fernando. I took the little urn, complete with its newly carved stopper, and wrapped it in oilcloth. I then smeared the package with thick white lard from the griddle and then wrapped it in oilcloth again, and then bound it with some twine. It was now as likely to last the ages as the sailors' bones themselves.

My mind tumbled on what to do with the plaque. Should I return it to its place within the rock crevice on the island? Inter it to the earth? Or should I hold it as a keepsake of my journey? No answer seemed to be a completely correct one. By and by I realised that the King of Portugal — was it John?[152] - might take a keen interest in it, for it did indeed claim this land for him. Perhaps such a relic would gain me an audience with his Highness should I ever venture to Oporto, or one of its sister towns, again. At the very least, it was an interesting historical trinket. I retreated to the hold and prised up a floorboard, and into this safe area I cached the plaque. It would be safe from pirates or buccaneers, even if I were not.

Next, I fetched four short lengths of elm from my spare supply. I chiselled opposing shallow rebates in each length and then bound each pair together, forming two crosses. Using the tip of a sharp leather punch, I scraped each sailor's name firmly into the crossbeam and inked the channels. This simple task took me deep into the afternoon.

I packed a large portion of fish for dinner (and some more rotted oat cakes for the birds' supper) and also carried some supplies, including a small spade and a new crock of rum. I dressed in my full captain's uniform, including my vest, boots and hat. Upon arrival at Bird Rock I was again surprised to see that the oats had grown even further. The three wheat stalks were now half as high as my knee, with the oats in close pursuit. The birds continued to tend to the plants with maternal care, like ewes suckling spring lambs.

For the burial I chose a patch of bare earth near the spring, which I guessed was where Diogo lay as he passed. Below a rocky ledge, I dug a hole. Twelve inches deep would have been sufficient to bury the urn, but I honoured Diogo and Fernando's spirit by digging as far down as my

---

[152] The Captain was correct. The King of Portugal in 1821 was João (John) VI

arm and spade would stretch, for a shallow grave was a sign of a wretched life.

I interred the urn containing the canvas note and then refilled the hole, tamping tightly as I shovelled. When the hole was no longer, I used the back of the spade to hammer the crosses in place. The stakes penetrated easily into the friable soil, so I drove them deeply to keep them firm throughout the ages. I then sprinkled some water from the spring onto the graves and wished them good Providence in the afterlife, wherever and whatever that entailed. Then, following seafaring tradition, I spent the afternoon in the company of my rum crock, dipping my hat to my deceased kin with every swig.

Later, as the rum took hold and my mind loosened, my thoughts turned, unguarded, to Beth. My memories dragged me over her death and, in particular, her burial. I wallowed in despair as the fatal hunting trip seared through my mind, each scene flashing like a grotesque painting. That crack of the sapling ... I will hear it in my nightmares forever. That stag ... as big as they grow, it antler plunging straight into Beth's heart - a heart so large and kind and generous that its size made it unmissable.

My rum-addled mind vaults forward two days. I see Beth's body being lowered into the earth, a priest mumbling unintelligibly over a Bible. Beth's mother is hysterical, and makes no contributions apart from relentless sobbing, but the sounds, in my vision, are distant. Her father, stern and ashen faced, pitches some earth onto her breast. I see myself step forward and toss a handful of salt into her coffin[153] but I feel nothing in the numbness of the moment. As Beth's coffin lowers, I catch one final glimpse of her twisted blue face. Even the embalmers, with their lotions and powders and cotton wool, could not conceal her final expression of fear and pain. That face now lives in me every day. Even this far at sea I cannot escape its torment.

Yet that day also haunted me for another reason: I alone knew that Beth had a secret; one that she had taken with her to her grave. Unfortunately, I had discovered it too.

I knew that the rum was the cause of these thoughts. But rum was also the medicine. I took another long swig.

---

[153] Throwing salt in the deceased person's coffin was an old custom that signified the hope that his or her spirit would be preserved.

Saturday 26 May

I woke slowly. The rum crock was nearly empty – oh no. Too much, McAdam, too much. I took many pulls of water at the spring to quell the rasping of my dry mouth, yet my gills stayed green for many hours. I didn't know if it was the excessive rum consumption or that my land legs had deserted me that caused my queasiness - perhaps it was both. By and by Bubo flapped over to me. I had distant recall of talking with him deep into the night.

Gaard Maarn.

"Morning," I mumbled weakly.

Rum ... rum ... rum, he trilled, his repetition implying that I had partaken of a large measure. *Cucule insolens* indeed.

I did not acknowledge his quip - he was like a mother-in-law with such talk. I sat silently, for I was not in the mood for chatter or lessons. But by and by Bubo said a word that very much surprised me, and also startled me, for I had not taught it to him specifically. *Beth.*

I had no clear recollection of our conversation, but it did not surprise me that I had mentioned my dearly departed last night, for she had indeed been in my thoughts. Bubo was now repeating my nocturnal chatter back into my ears like an audible looking glass. I sighed.

"Beth was Captain Rum's friend." Despite knowing Bubo would not understand, I felt that telling him about Beth might lift some lead from my heavy heart. "Beth was my friend," I repeated.

Bubo's eyes widened.

"*Friend* is a hard word to explain," I said with another retiring sigh, and leaned back against the rock wall. His hackle feathers raised a little, indicating his frustration at my lack of effort. But even a simple word such as "fish" had been hard to convey to him, so how could I possibly explain even a tiny nuance of such a complex and broad term as "friend"? "The birds are Bubo's friends, Beth was my friend."

Friend, he eventually repeated. I doubted that Bubo understood the meaning, but he nonetheless seemed satisfied with my explanation. We then sat quietly and he ducked his head down, seeming to indicate that he wanted a pet on his hackles, which I duly obliged, as much to soothe my own soul as his.

Sunday 27 May

Having slept on the *Maris Alarum*, I spent the morning casting for fish and was rewarded with two fine fillets for lunch. It was a shame that my feathered first mate was not about, for he would have provided the same result but in minutes, not hours. Yet another part of me was glad for the solitude. Sitting in the warm sunshine, bobbing gently on the calm waters, flicking a line out then retrieving it steadily –these activities lull the mind. Fishing like this was like a poultice for my soul. I conceded, however, that the pastime was far more agreeable when my life did not depend upon the outcome.

Because the wind and the seas remained slight, I still could not retest the mast. By and by I returned to the island with the aim of refreshing my water supply from the spring. I carried half a dozen empty four-gallon crocks with me. All went to plan until I encountered the cliff face, and soon discovered that scaling even a modest wall while carrying a heavy crock was not easy. I realised that it would be even more difficult on the return journey when each crock would weigh another 30 pounds.

I retreated to my ship, fetched a length of stout rope and then rowed back to the island. I scaled the cliff, attached the rope around a rocky knob and lowered myself down. I then wrapped the rope around an empty crock and hitched it tight, climbed back to the top, and then pulled the container up using the rope. If the crocks had handles I might have accomplished this task more quickly by lifting three at a time, but I nonetheless used this simple but laborious method to raise all six jugs to the plateau.

I carried them to the spring and set about filling them, listening to the bubbles as they gurgled from the jar's mouth. As I filled the jugs with the precious fresh water, I contentedly watched the birds as they buzzed about their crops, like butterflies dipping for nectar over a spring field. They continued to watch, water, shade and even fan their beloved plants, directed by some instinct that was beyond my calling to even imagine. Their well-tended crops had grown by an astonishing amount.

The sun now was high and hot, so I sat in the shade by the spring. Bubo later joined me, landing on my forearm. I ruffled his hackle feathers, and by and by we commenced a lesson in which he learned two more new words.

He continues to surprise me with his understanding of my sentences. I am sure that when I say, for example, "Hello Bubo. Would you like some fresh fish for dinner?" he hears only the words "Bubo" and "fish", yet he responds, in his limited way, as though he comprehends each and every word. Perhaps it is like my understanding of Spanish – my command of it is poor, but by latching on to a few key words in each phrase, I can make some sense of most conversations.

During lesson breaks (of which we take many, for Bubo's concentration span is short) I watched the island birds as they hopped and flapped about the plateau. At one point during the morning a bird seemed to have thieved from its companions, for it nibbled at a stalk of precious oats. Later, another bird helped itself to a similar portion - those conniving scoundrels! Like the insolent lad who stole away with my crate of goods from the Holborn Street Tavern, I felt like delivering them a stout clip with the back of my hand, for their kin had laboured long and hard, and did not deserve to have the fruits of their labour pilfered before they had ripened to useful seed.

The longer I watched, however, the less concerned I became, for it was soon apparent that each bird was taking a tiny piece in turn. At different stages of the morning, each bird approached an oat stalk and used its beak to cut away a small length to eat. During my observation I think that none helped itself more than once, although I concede that recognising one bird from its neighbour in a moving flock was difficult. Yet this behaviour was so far removed from the scrapping seagulls at Southampton, who squabbled and squawked over every miserly stale crust, that although both species had wings and feathers it was as if they were different creatures altogether.

I realised that while the gulls had developed instincts to fight for individual survival, the island birds had grown instincts of kinship, promoting the livelihood of the flock for the ultimate benefit of each. In this respect, the island birds acted more like ants than gulls.

Despite understanding the basic ideas behind Lamarck's theories, I found it incredible to observe, first hand, these simple creatures picking

174

at only a small off-cut of oat stalk, when surely their first instinct would have simply been to devour the whole plant. Over many centuries their survival on this tiny island no doubt depended upon overcoming this urge, which would help ensure that seed, and therefore food, was available in the future. I am surely the unwitting envy of every natural philosopher in the Kingdom such was the uniqueness of this display.

Such sights demonstrate the value of my journey over the oceans. Despite my isolation and all that has befallen me so far, I am increasingly pleased to have taken it.

Monday 28 May

The summer winds remained slight, again preventing me from testing the mast repair. My patience to complete this task was thinning. An imagined goblin sat at the back of my mind, interjecting its rasping voice each day to remind me that the repair may yet break when tested in stronger winds; reminding me that I was not yet free. It was clear that this annoying nag would not cease until I completed the tests, but alas, I could do nothing to hasten this process except to sit idly by and wait for a stiffer wind. At least Bird Rock was close by, fish were plentiful, and the plants were growing while I was forced to wait. Perhaps they would even yield a small harvest before I departed. Although such a taking would be minor, I would welcome even a half a mug of fresh oat porridge as if it was Mrs Harlesden's pumpkin pie.

Tuesday 29 May

No tasks or chores called at me, so I spent the day relaxing on deck in the shade of a half-raised headsail, prising apart the water-glued pages of my Spanish book and reading aloud in an effort to sharpen my tongue. Toward evening I returned to the island, bringing with me a wrapped portion of cooked fish for supper, and a good portion of the remaining oat cakes to fortify the birds. The moon was full and large, so it seemed a fine night to sleep among the growing crops and below the shining stars; the landlubber in me still existed, even if he was a weakly soul in need of an outing.

Bubo flew to me and ducked his head toward the crook of my leather-padded arm, no doubt aspiring to a neck ruffle, which he duly received. I offered him some fish but he declined, saying *Bubo fish fish fish*. This simple repetition seems to be his method of implying "lots" as in "Bubo has eaten lots of fish."

By and by I laid out my sack and settled into a comfortable hollow in the guano-earth. I lay, peering at the heavens, gazing admiringly at the rising full moon and counting the shooting stars (six) until my eyes grew heavy.

Barely had my lids shut when a haunting melody filled my head. At first I could not discern its origin for it seemed to appear inside my mind without first channelling through my ears; it was as if the tune was not travelling through the air, but was originating in the space inside my head. I sat up in awe, whereupon it became clear that this wonderful, lilting tune was being sung by the birds.

I had not heard them in this voice before. Did they sing in thanksgiving for the new grain crops? Or perhaps a ritual homage to the full moon? I had no way of telling. Yet the cause mattered little for the birdsong was a fine and wonderful sound, and I would have enjoyed it as much even if it were paying tribute to shark dung.

Although each bird whistled a different tune, each part was in harmony with its neighbour – like a symphony in which each musician played a different melody for the benefit of the whole piece. In and out of my mind the birdsong swept, like slow waves rolling up and then receding down a gentle beach, hypnotic in its quality. At times the tune sprung sideways, dancing with merry limbs and sweeping around like a jaunty summer breeze. I lay still, mesmerised, letting that melodic breeze carry me away.

I cannot guess for how long I listened – perhaps a minute, perhaps an hour – but, by and by, my eyelids grew heavy. Drowsiness seeped through me like warm honey, for although the day had been light on labour, the warm sun and gentle breeze had done their becalming work. So it was, with the mellifluous birdsong filling my head and my torso lying upon the warm soft earth, that I fell into the deepest, most restful of sleeps.

Wednesday 30 May

I awoke with pleasant memories of last evening's birdsong. The wind remained slight, only 5 knots from the north west. The wheat and oat stalks stood proudly. Their rapid maturation was truly astounding.

My day was lazy, slow and warm. I had completed every task and chore, except of course a full trial of the mast. I intended to sleep upon the island again in the hope that the birds repeated their song.

Thursday 31 May

Unfortunately, the birds did not repeat their musical chorus last night, but I nevertheless slept soundly on the island. My land legs had already strengthened.

The wind was even calmer, barely a 5-knot nor-wester. So again my day was filled with little but waiting for the wind to lift. I was like a coach driver lingering for a passenger that he could not see and who had no specific arrival time. My frustration grew, for as my strength and condition returned, my patience left me in equal measure.

Sunday 3 June

For five nights I have slept on the island, hoping for a reprise from the birds' choir. Unfortunately, they were silent. During one of our regular lessons, I asked Bubo about the song, but he didn't understand my request, despite me humming the tune to the best of my recollection. I admit I am no Callcott[154] but surely a fair judge would register that my melody could be described as a 'song'. I even whistled some tunes, but to no advantage.

The oats stalks were already starting to form into seed heads[155]. I was tempted to harvest some grain, but knew that patience would provide far greater returns later, both for me and for the birds. I hoped that I could take enough to bake a few small oat-bread loaves. I wondered if, or when, the birds would harvest the crop?

The wind has not lifted itself. I am now full to the brim with rest, and am craving adventure, but the still wind blocks my path to freedom. This afternoon I stood on the rock and faced to the nor' west. I loudly pleaded with Mother Ocean to grant me a good blow, but to no avail. Twice I took the *Maris Alarum* for a short run, but with her low sails in

---

[154] McAdam was probably referring to John Wall Callcott, a musician and composer who wrote a number of short pieces that were popular during the period. Callcott was born in 1766, and died on 15 May 1821, ironically only a couple of weeks before McAdam unknowingly penned this epithet.

[155] I was again sceptical of McAdam's claim that a plant could seed in just a few short weeks. However the Herbaria chief backed McAdam's assertion with some scientific credibility, explaining that some species of plants – for example, Duckweed (*Wolffia microscopica*)– could produce seed within 30 hours.

these light winds she did little more than float. Time and again I implore myself to be patient, for the temptation to forego the mast trial, and take my chances with Mother Ocean, was growing stronger by the day.

Monday 4 June

I slept on my ship again. Just after dawn I rowed to the island, as much for the bracing exercise as for any other reason. Whilst there I was privileged to observe a natural spectacle the likes of which I have never sighted before and doubt that I will witness again. Just as the sun began tracking upward into the eastern sky, one bird emitted a tuneful fanfare: *tu-whit-tu-whoo, tu-whit-tu-whoo*. It followed this melodic blast with some unintelligible chirping.

This sound galvanised the flock to activity. I watched with interest as the birds fluttered into action. As each bird approached an oat stalk it pecked a kernel or two from the ear, then took it to an open space, scratched the ground, and spat the seed into the furrow. Then followed the other habits that the birds had already demonstrated: watering, shading, probing and above all, watching. In short, the birds were farming.[156] Had I not already observed these incredible birds I would have thought that I was hysterical with the fever.

By and by they had planted a good portion of the plateau with oats. (Later I must write a fuller account of the birds' actions before the detail slips from my mind, for I am certain that the Society would be most interested.[157]) The birds amazed me with their endeavour; how difficult it must have been for them not to just eat the seed but to plant it for future use. I know many men who would choose one apple today rather

---

[156] Animals that farm are rare but not unknown in nature. Beavers "farm" fish in self-made dams, allowing them to propagate rather than eating them immediately. Some species of fish plant mosses and seaweeds for later consumption, and termites have even been known to "herd" aphids like cattle. An ornithology professors at Oxford was not aware of similar traits among any living birds, but suggested that this behaviour was an evolved endemic survival trait.

[157] Unfortunately this log book does not contain any such account. I scoured the original shelves at Old Bod library, but found nothing. If you ever come across an account of some island birds planting a field of grain, please let me know!

than 100 next year, yet these simple birds had learned that to act in this way on such a tiny island would be to perish.

Bubo flew to join me. He perched on a rock ledge by my side, thus saving my forearm from a talon scratching.

Seed he chirped. I nodded with a slight smile on my lips. *Seed seed seed* he added, and flapped his wings in what I took to be a show of excitement.

"Captain Rum is happy that your bird friends will not die," I said, and truly meant it - it is hard to accurately describe the feeling that comes from saving not just a single bird, but a whole species. Even though the birds were unable to speak of their gratitude, their trills and hoots demonstrated it. My cockles[158] felt full and warm; a later glance in my looking glass showed a man with a hint of a satisfied smile.

Eventually, the birds' sowing activities slowed. Of immediate interest to me were the ears that remained unharvested. When taken together the grains would fill a bowl —enough for a few small bread buns.

From the *Maris Alarum* I fetched my scimitar for harvesting, a mortar & pestle for grinding, a lidded bowl for storage, and a large tin plate to help with the threshing[159]. I spent the day earning myself a pound of grain flour. The birds seemed oblivious to my presence and certainly did not interrupt me; they had their own tasks to attend. As I worked I heard a vaguely familiar sound from the farthest reach of the island – a high-pitched, melodic trill, followed by a deep series of hoots – which I had not heard since the very first oat stalks appeared many days ago. At this call, many birds fluttered to the far plateau and appeared to be pleased with what they discovered, but I was deep at work milling the oats and so did not pause to investigate.

It was bracing to be active and useful again. By sundown I had a full bowl of roughly ground and loosely threshed oat flour. I returned to the

---

[158] A "cockle" is a small heart-shaped marine mollusc. McAdam was no doubt referring to his heart. The word survives in the modern saying "to warm the cockles of my heart".

[159] Threshing is the process of sorting the grain seed from the fibrous husks. McAdam probably achieved this by tossing the crushed grain into the air. The lighter husks would drift away, while the heavier seeds would fall back into the plate.

Maris Alarum, and with great anticipation I fanned the oven coals to a cooking heat. I rooted about the hold for the yeast packet and upon locating it, I congratulated myself for not pitching it overboard after the storm, despite its seemingly useless contribution to ship life. I peeled back the many layers of greaseproof paper and wiped away the layers of lard between. My foresight was rewarded for the yeast was unspoilt and, I hoped, still viable.

It was. I wasted little time in baking a small batch of bread. The aroma as the buns rose in the oven was, to my nose, sweeter than a Beethoven symphony was to the ears. Freshly milled oat flour, sweet island water and sun dried ocean salt, all freshly baked into tiny warm loaves - I salivated at the thought and somehow managed to bide my time until the dough had risen and the crust had browned.

When I bit into that first bun – well, I must wonder if any man had ever set such fine fare upon his tongue. I could not have anticipated in London that I would write in such raptures about something as simple as bread, but the words that follow barely do justice to my enjoyment of this first taste. The loaf had a toasted crust that crumbled readily under my teeth. The flesh was full and tasted sweet but with a hint of saltiness. I could imagine it being equally at home sandwiching some peppered beef, or being coated with sugar for a child's birthday treat. As I chewed, the roughly-milled grains softened and then slowly dissolved away in my mouth, leaving me pining for more.

A broad smile pulled across my cheeks as I reached for a second warm bun. They say that a pleasure denied is a pleasure doubled, and in this case both my previous pain and my current reward were multiplied by many score. Rarely have I felt so content.

Tuesday 5 June

I enjoyed some more bread and water to start the day. Although this fare was also my sustenance while in the clink at Shepton Mallet, to give both meals the same name is a crime upon language, for they describe things that are as far apart as the poles of the earth: one is earthy, sweet and nutritious, while the other is vile, poisonous and dank. Yet both are labelled as 'bread and water'.

Although the breeze remained slight it occasionally gusted toward 10 knots, and I sensed that it was on the rise. Perhaps I would soon be able to test the mast repair with a view to departing soon thereafter. With the oat bread now in my belly, I thanked Mother Ocean for her timing and withdrew the vitriol that I had previously spat toward her.

With both sails hoisted to half height, I tested the mast on a windward run. Observing that the join held firm I performed a jibe, forcing the mast to show its strength from all sides. Again, it passed the test. Later, when the breeze stiffened, I coaxed the *Maris Alarum* into a sharp tack, and again the repair held firm. I now had realistic hope that soon I might be able to depart Bird Rock. The world and her people were waiting for me.

With a heart full of optimism, I rowed to Bird Rock and informed Bubo of our likely departure. He seemed disappointed to be leaving his kind - I think I can now read his thoughts in his owl-like eyes and the movements of his body. Like a dog wagging his tail, or a wolf baring its teeth, Bubo says much to me without words: his wide eyes and tilting head, his bowed neck, and his purring beak grind all have meaning. Even his position on board my ship – whether it is the contentment of the port gunwale or the defiance of the mast head - says something. Now that I have learned to read these signals, our communication is stronger still.

In some ways I can comprehend Bubo's mind better than I could read a man, for humans clutter their messages with false chatter and deception. But Bubo, with his limited vocabulary and paucity of word use, did not camouflage his thoughts in this way.

I watched the birds for some time. Most of their activity was again at the far end of the island, with the fields of oats and wheat now tended by just a few dozen sentries. The birds' spirit of cohesion continued to amaze me. Like bees working for the benefit of the hive, they laboured for the commune and not for themselves. The notions of Thomas More's *Utopia*[160] spring to mind.

---

[160] Sir Thomas More (1478-1535) was an English philosopher. He wrote of Raphael, an adventurer, who discovered an island called Utopia whose political system was based upon communal ownership and labour.

As I climbed down the cliff and stepped into my tender, I wondered whether I would ever place a foot on Bird Rock again. Perhaps not, for if the wind was favourable and the mast held firm during its final test tomorrow, then I planned to weigh anchor at the first opportunity. But I would not forget these remarkable birds. Despite the angst of our first meeting, they had earned a permanent warm space in my memory.

Bubo returned to the *Maris Alarum* with me. I wanted him to help me fish, in the hope of preserving some fillets before departure. While we were on deck, Bubo mentioned the words *pea* and *raisin*. I told him clearly that we had no more peas or raisins, and that all the food was gone except for fish. But he repeated the words many times – *pea pea pea raisin raisin raisin* –like a child begging for boiled sweets that didn't exist. By and by I lost patience and simply ignored him. As usual, his hackles rose at my indifference, but I did not want to reward him with a petting for his whinging, so it took a while for his feathers to drop.

We spent the rest of the day and evening fishing, and after I finally pulled in the last line we had seven large fish, and two dozen sardines courtesy of Bubo's talons. I stored the small fish in a jar with salt and the remaining vinegar. I then smoke-dried the larger fillets overnight. To this end, I placed dried firewood bark in a pan on the hot stove, over which I suspended the cuts on a wire rack, and then contained it all within a wooden crate. The smoke not only added a delicate flavour but would also help to preserve the fish for many weeks, sustaining me until I reached Africa.

Wednesday 6 June

It is morning, and I am pleased to write that the wind is up. Yesterday's breeze is now a stout wind of 12 knots – not quite enough to turn white caps, but blowy enough to billow the sails. My greatest fear is *not* that the mast repair will crack – although that would be insufferable - but more specifically that it will crack when I am away from the safety of Bird Rock. It is now time, *finally*, to test my carpentry against the elements, and then be on my way. My next words shall be written *en route* to Africa – I hope!

*

I hoisted both sails to half height. The *Maris Alarum* seemed to groan a little, and then she sighed as if to say "at last", before heaving herself into a torpid downwind run. Yes, it was slow, but at least I was sailing again. Soon thereafter, with fortified confidence, I hoisted the sails to three parts up. The *Maris Alarum* took on another degree of heal[161] and forged ahead more swiftly. Not even a kink appeared at the mast join, so I tugged on the halyards and gave her full flight. A large gust filled the sails, and sent my ship slicing through the chop like a merry porpoise.

I let out a whoop of joy, for feeling the salt spray in my face gave breath to my sailor's soul. At this speed, I thought, it could be no more than a few weeks to the African coast. Emancipated by this knowledge, I again whooped for joy – a loud and long crow - for my troubles were ceding into my past.

I wish I had saved my breath for a curse. A loud and long curse.

It was soon thereafter that I put the *Maris Alarum* into the wind and took a hard tack to port. All I heard was a single loud crack. But that one brief sound took away not only my optimism, but all of my hope as well. The once tall and true beam started to bend and buckle like a crooked elbow.

Later inspection showed a complete fracture in the mast extension rebate. The problem was as clear as it was insurmountable: the mast was broken. Again. The repair had failed.

I am stranded on Bird Rock. *Forever.*

---

[161] A *heal* is a nautical term for the tilt of the boat.

Thursday 7 June

Forever. Forever forever forever forever forever.

Never again shall I set foot in England. I shall never know the delights of a fine meal, or of boisterous company at a tavern. I shall never read a new book, accept the applause of a grateful audience, or father a child. Never shall I embrace a woman, or even lay eyes upon one. I cannot outrun Beth's ghost any longer, for without wind in my sails she can haunt me without distraction.

I would welcome the sight of a boatful of plod sailing over the horizon toward me, with their hard truncheons and cold irons in hand. I would more gladly finish my stretch in Shepton than just sit on my ship waiting to die.

The rum bottle is my only solace.

Friday 8 June

Besides destroying the mast with a pick-axe in a drunken rage yesterday, I have done nothing but sit in the galley, drink rum to silence the clamour from inside my own head, and curse at the world. I ate nought but a bread roll, which suddenly tastes stale and sour, and a fistful of pickled fish that I pulled from the jar. Today I did not even climb up to the deck, for the very wind, which I had waited so long for, now taunts me with its presence.

Saturday 9 June

Bubo visited me from the island today. He continued to cark about peas and raisins, but I have told him firmly that there are no more and that I will clip him if he asks again. I scatted him away, for I had no want for cheap talk, especially with a bird. I ate nothing but loaves and fishes - I am sure Reverend Butler would be proud of me for my biblical puritanism.

In my early morning sober moments, and then the drunken ones for the rest of the day, I pursued every thought on how to make the mainland, but each idea withered like an untrestled vine. My only viable plan was to weigh the anchor and drift, hoping that the currents propelled me landward. But this path was tempting a slow and painful death at sea, tantamount to slowly roasting my hands over hot coals rather than just singeing them on a flame.

At one point my addled mind was so wrought that I contemplated rowing my tender for Africa, and even went as far as timing myself over a furlong to give a reckoning of the trip. It took a full night's sleep to alert myself to the idiocy of this thought.

Again my barrow was stuck in the mud, but this mud was thicker than ever before; for the want of a tree it fixed me like Roman cement. Was I destined to complete my days as a bird watcher and bread nibbler, wrestling with the memories of things, and people, long gone?

I emptied a near-full rum crock last night, and careened about the ship for hours to try to escape visions of she who was no longer here.

Sunday 10 June

I stayed in my hammock almost all day. My only activity was to chop up the rest of the mast for firewood. I felt some small level of revenge as I burned it in the evening.

Elizabeth's ghost taunted me mercilessly for the fourth day in a row. I see that stag flay her ragged body from side to side, her arms flapping like torn sails in the wind. I watch myself lunge at the beast, but my strikes and kicks achieve nothing. After an eternity that was probably no more than a single tick of the clock, the beast flicks my beautiful Beth from its antlers and bolts. The brown earth mixes with the red sticky liquid upon her white blouse as I push my hands into the gaping wound, trying to stem the wretched flow....

Then her wailing stops. The silence is worse than her shrieking. Her eyes turn to me but they are blank. In my fairest dreams she mutters "I love you" with her dying breath and we share a final tender embrace, but my memory knows that no such thing happened. Instead I stare into her blank eyes and watch them turn upward. With a sickening, guttural groan from her chest, she is gone.

That laceration, that evil, bedevilled cut – I can still see its detail: a ragged, gaping hole from her ribs to her abdomen. I push my hands more deeply into her wound, forlornly trying to stem the out-flowing blood that has already killed her. Then ... *I touch it.*

Monday 11 June

I gave the rum a flogging last night. Sick in my hammock all morning. I haven't yet cleaned it up. Sick over the gunwales all afternoon. Drank rum in the evening.

My life is a waste of the ocean's air. All I now want is to see Beth again.

Beth and....

Tuesday 12 June

Awoke in the hold, my body cramped and stiff. My knuckles were cut and bruised – I could not recall why, as the rum had stolen away most of yesterday. I could not make a fist, such was the swelling.

Later in the day, my hands started shaking by themselves. I did not know if this was nerves, or due to the swelling. They stopped later.

The smoked fish was very dry. I knew that I could catch some more, but my bones felt too heavy to move for any activity except fetching another crock of my medicine.

During the night, my Water Wings dream returned. This time the wings sprouted from the mast before flying me away over a calm ocean. Oh, but I wish I could dream something useful, for without lumber for a mast I can fly nowhere.

Wednesday 13 June

Again I awoke on the galley floor with an empty rum crock beside me. I am grateful that the rum steals away my memories, for it shields me from my own actions. While rum's medicinal cushioning is useful, its amnesia is a welcome side effect.

This afternoon, as I lay in my hammock, I had my water wings dream again. This time the mast grew up from the ship like a tree. Then it sprouted wings and flew me away. If only my ship could grow its own mast.

I re-read Diogo's entry in my journal. One line stood out: *I expect Henrique to send another ship soon.* No one was going to send a ship for me. Not a soul on the Earth knew that I was here.

After noon, my hands started shaking again. I could not make them stop. It was only later in the evening as I sat on deck with a crock of rum that they ceased.

Saturday 16 June

I cannot remember what I did on the past three days, apart from waking from time to time on various parts of the ship, for the rum truly stole every moment. But I am pleased that I cannot remember, because the blue bruises in every limb and the rasping raw skin on my knuckles tells me that I was, at the very least, an angry man.

My hands were shaking badly by mid morning. I sat on them to still them but they shook nonetheless. Perhaps the devil himself had taken residence in them. I tried to chase him away with some rum, which seemed to work, as the shaking stopped after just a few mugs.[162]

Sunday 17 June

They say that Sunday is the Lord's Day, but yet again I found proof that he did not care for this notion: I awoke to discover that my rum store was empty. If this was the work of the god of the church, to deprive me of my medicine on his own day, then he was an evil deity indeed. Now I was not only stranded and alone, but had no medicine to soften the landings from my evil dreams. Nor could I chase the devil from my shaking hands. Maybe I will suffer from the scurvy as well. I hope it happens soon, for I am serving no purpose on this earth.

Monday 18 June

---

[162] McAdam was no doubt suffering from *Delerium Tremens*, which is caused by withdrawal from excessive alcohol consumption. Although imbibing further rum would have temporarily eased the Captain's symptoms, it would have exacerbated his underlying problem.

I could not countenance this ship any longer, but nor did I want to go to that rock. I was stranded in a void of hopelessness with no door out. Perhaps it is time for me to blow away into the wind, and make room on this earth for another soul to take my place.

I heard Bubo on deck today, carking about raisins again. He was lucky that I stayed in my hammock with the hatches battened closed or I would have clipped him firmly. I did not wish to talk to Bubo or to see the birds. I could talk to Bubo next year for I had a lifetime left for that. I did not want to pack all of my joy into this month.

Tuesday 19 June

This morning I chanced upon my own reflection in the tin looking glass. My eyes were sallow, my chin was matted with fibrous whiskers and my cheeks were drawn and hollow. My hands jumped about as if they had the shaking palsy[163]. My hair was bedraggled, my eyes red and angry, and my skin blotched and jaded. I covered the looking glass with an old square of burlap cloth, for I didn't want to see this pathetic shell of a man again.

My salted fish store was already low. I knew that I should cast my lures for fresh flesh but I could not see the point. I had a few handfuls of bird flour that would keep me alive if I wished to remain that way. As I stuffed another floury fistful into my mouth, I wondered if there was any point to eating at all. The food was sustaining me ... but for what purpose? I could not tolerate this hopeless, mindless, rum-less existence for much longer.

I found myself playing with a rope. Before I knew it, I had formed a hangman's noose, complete with 13 coils. I found myself walking toward the hatch, down to the galley, where I knew a high exposed bearer would provide a firm anchor point. But something deep inside me stirred, and I cast the noose over the gunwale before I could follow through my desperate thoughts.

---

[163] The shaking palsy was described by Dr James Parkinson in London in 1817, just a few years before McAdam's adventure. The disease is now known as Parkinson's disease.

Wednesday 20 June

I took to sitting on deck to watch for passing driftwood. If I could spot a stout log then perhaps I could make a mast. I haven't seen any so far.

Bubo returned for another visit. He brought with him two purple berries. At first I was very surprised, for I had seen no food other than grain or fish for many sunrises. Just as I was about to consume the fruit, I recalled Diogo's tale of the purple berries. The berry-vine must have germinated from dormant seeds in the soil. How many berries had Diogo consumed? Six, my journal confirmed.

I did not give Bubo my reasons but asked him to bring me four more. I was unsure if I would swallow these poison pills or not, but I wished to keep those cards in my hand should I wish to play them. The noose ... it was too difficult ... too many opportunities for a change of mind. But the berries, once swallowed, would take me away. To Beth.

My hands still have the shaking palsy. I searched the entire ship in case I had misplaced a crock of medicine, but there was none.

Thursday 21 June

Again, I watched the sea all day for driftwood but to no avail. I stayed past dark for I feared that if I went below deck I might miss a log and squander my chance of escape.

In Shepton Mallet, at least I held the comfort that even if my escape failed then time would eventually free me. Here, next to that desolate rock, I did not even have that certainty, regardless of how slight that luxury may have been. A man could not consume his life without hope, just as a fire could not consume wood without air.

I searched again for rum. There was none. I turned out all the pots in the galley onto the floor and the tools from the hold, but there was no rum.

I had just two smoked fillets left. Perhaps, I thought, I should ration them.

Friday 22 June

I ate the last of the fish for breakfast. Now the only food I had was a few handfuls of grainy flour. I sat all day watching for driftwood. I spotted nothing.

In the evening Bubo brought me four more berries from the island. I stowed them in a galley jar. I now had six - an elegant sufficiency to cause my end.

Later I fetched a half mug full of dampened grain flour, but soon realised that I was not in the mood for chewing. I pitched the slurry overboard and watched as it floated away in the darkness. By and by some hatchling fish ate it. The mangy panhandlers[164].

Saturday 23 June

I awoke on deck, for I had decided to sleep outside so that I did not miss a passing log of driftwood. I used a sail to rig a small canopy under which I sat during the day. Like me, the sails were now useless for any other purpose.

My knuckles remained very sore. It was still painful to close my hands. I had no medicine kit and no rum so I could do nothing but curse the pain. At least the shaking palsy seemed to have abated. How it did this without the rum I do not know.

As the high sun passed noon my mouth felt parched. I needed water. I tried to climb down the ladder to the galley but my weakened legs gave way and I tumbled to the floor. I lay there, unwilling and unable to move from exhaustion and pain, until nightfall. Many times I cast my eye toward the berries on the shelf, and it was only weakness of my body, not my intent, that stopped me.

By and by I fell asleep, and awoke later in darkness. The panic of missing a drifting log spurred me, so I hauled myself up and through the hatch. As I lay on deck in the dark, my mind twisted and vaulted from one pained vision to the next. Later my water wings vision returned; it came to me even though I was awake, such was the ferocity of its vision. But this scene was different to my previous visions.

---

[164] *Panhandler* was an old term for a beggar

I saw the *Maris Alarum* bobbing upon calm waters. Then, from the hold below deck, a small sprout appeared. Steadily it grew until it pushed its way through the old mast hole in the deck and reached toward the sky, its round trunk and stout branches revealing it as a conifer pine. Up it grew until it reached the height of a true mast, whereupon it sprouted wings that grew as big as sails. Then the *Maris Alarum* flapped her way lazily across the wave tops, calmly and smoothly carrying me toward the eastern horizon. To land. To freedom.

I tried to ignore the vision for I knew that Beelzebub himself had sent the thoughts to taunt me. But I had no rum and so was at the mercy of his cruel tricks for many hours.

Sunday 24 June

I did not spot any passing driftwood. Once I saw a shark's fin slice through the water. I contemplated throwing myself at it to finish my days, but my fear of the shark was greater than my fear of death.

Bubo continued to chirp at me to go to the island but I didn't have the strength. I asked him to look for driftwood but he refused. I asked him for a better plan but his bird's brain could not stretch that far. He brought me half a dozen ears of wheat – the grains must be growing strongly. I ate a few, and thought to use the grain as a burley trail to attract fish, but I did not have the strength for casting and retrieving. Maybe next week. If I lasted that long.

Bubo also brought me two more purple berries. I stored them with the others, which are now starting to shrivel. I looked at them often.

Maybe another ship will rescue me.

Monday 25 June

I spent the day with my telescope, scanning the horizon for passing ships. I did not see any. It was very hot on deck, even under the sail canopy. My mouth was constantly parched, even though I took frequent small sips of water, which gave me a tiny measure of pleasure as the liquid touched my cracked lips and rasping tongue. I looked for ships. I mumbled to myself. I pined for rum.

These long, empty days are interminable. Yet the hours seem to take even longer than the days; they trudge past like sloughed mud. Yet cruellest of all are the minutes; each seems to take an eternity, and is filled with either ghastly visions of Beth, or the ungrantable wish to be somewhere, *anywhere*, else.

The clink was insufferable, but this life is worse, for it is like a prison but without the distant promise of freedom. Without this hope, I am like the drying purple poison berries that beckon me from the galley. I am but a shrivelled raisin of a man.

Tuesday 26 June

I awoke mid morning with a thought that I hoped might change my heading. I recalled that when Bubo had become lost while looking for fish I had lit a signal fire to guide him back to the *Maris Alarum*. Perhaps, I thought, a smoky fire would alert any passing ships to my presence.

Feebly, carefully, I climbed down to the hold. My legs were weak and bruised from my previous falls, and they trembled unsteadily as they lowered me down the ladder. As I foraged about for some green sticks to smoke the fire, I noticed the crate of tinder containing pine cones. Those cones contained *seeds*. Seeds from conifer trees.

Ideal mast building material.

Only a furlong away was an island of the most fertile soil imaginable. Suddenly my water wings dream made sense.

It used every ounce of strength in my failing body, but within minutes I had rowed to the island and somehow scaled the cliff. I am not sure from which well I dredged the vigour for these actions, but the prospect of rescuing myself from a lifetime of unmitigated drudgery pulled energy from a very deep recess.

"Bubo," I yelled across the plateau.

My faithful pet, ignoring weeks of rudeness and antipathy on my part, quickly flew over to meet me, causing me exquisite pain as he gripped onto my emaciated forearm.

"Bubo, we're saved." I held up the pinecone for him. His big eyes and tilting head conveyed confusion, so I explained: "Captain Rum can grow a tree from these seeds. With the tree Captain Rum can make a new mast."

Even if Bubo had understood what I had explained, he certainly didn't share my excitement. In time he fluttered off toward the birds while I set my fingers to work on the pod, prising precious seeds from beneath its chain-mail-like exterior. By and by I had liberated nine little pods of hope from the cone, and squatted low to the earth to plant them.

I am no farmer, but for many weeks I had watched creatures that excelled at it – a brief apprenticeship of sorts. Just as I had seen the birds do, I scratched three furrows into the guano soil. I was uncertain of the best germination depth for conifer seeds so I dug one furrow deeply, another very shallow and the third between the first two. Into each furrow I dropped three seeds at intervals, and then scraped some earth over as a cover. Using my hat as pot, I fetched some water from the spring and irrigated my new nursery.

My job complete, I took a pull of water myself from the spring and then sat, exhausted, with my back against the rocky ledge. Although fatigued, a deep peace settled over me, unlike any feeling I have ever experienced. This was peace that rode pick-a-back on hope; hope that one day I would live again.

I caught sight of Bubo flying high above the plateau. I followed him as he swooped downward and flew across the fields of oats, past the wheat and then....

Not for the first time on Bird Rock, my own eyes startled me. In my narrow determination to plant the conifer seeds I had failed to notice the changes that had occurred on the plateau in my absence. At the far end, near the northern edge of the rim, was a tangle of new plants. I hurried over as swiftly as my wretched constitution would permit, stumbling past the ever-scurrying farmer birds, to inspect the new crops.

At first I was disappointed, for it was obvious that the first two vines, which grew along the ground and climbed up the rocky walls, were laden with clumps of tiny purple berries – the very same berries that Bubo had brought me. Further, I knew the poisonous nature of these plants from Diogo's message and hesitated even to touch them lest they infect me.

194

Yet as I walked alongside the vines they steadily began to look familiar: large irregular green leaves, dozens of small green tendrils weaving their way along the earth and up the rocks, desperately seeking a notch or protuberance around which to wrap themselves, and small bunches of deep purple berries. I was increasingly sure I had seen their like before.

Tentatively, I picked one of the fruits and held it to my nose. Its smell was sweet, fruity and familiar. Hesitantly, for I was keenly aware of Diogo's fate, I squeezed a small drop of juice onto my tongue. It was sugary and fragrant, not at all bitter like Diogo had described. The taste was also familiar. But could these really be....

Without further hesitation, I popped the fruit into my mouth and chewed down upon it. An explosion of flavour burst onto my tongue. Yes, this was as I had guessed.... a grape. A purple-skinned, white-fleshed, delicious *grape*.

I looked further along the creeping vines and noted half a dozen small bunches, each ripening under the warm island sun. I plucked a handful of fruit from a nearby bunch and delighted in the warm sweetness as I devoured them. How my fortunes had changed in just an hour!

My mind quickly turned to the obvious puzzle: from where had the birds obtained grape seed? I had not pondered this question for long when a second new plant caught my attention. This growth was also a creeping plant, and like the grape vines, it had wound along the earth and then clawed its way up the rocky walls. It had long, lithe tendrils weaving out in many directions, which twirled themselves confidently about any foothold they encountered. Clearly this plant was happy to scale upwards toward the clouds rather than slithering along the earth. It had dozens of small budding blue flowers and tiny oval leaves. I nibbled at a leaf, but found it nondescript in taste. I could not yet identify the plant but held hopes that it would provide nutrition. Perhaps the blue flowers would also form fruits.

Laughing loudly, I helped myself to a few more grapes, saving the seeds aside as I encountered them. Bubo arrived but could not fathom my excited celebration regarding the new discovery. This was understandable as he had already provided eight grapes to me on my ship, which I had mistaken as Diogo's poison berries. I did not have the want, or the need, to explain myself to him. The wryest of smiles spread across my lips as I pictured the harmless grapes, still sitting in a jar on the galley bench, awaiting my ingestion if I had irrevocably tired of this world.

What a fool I had been! Why had I not trusted in myself, knowing that Providence would avail me of an opportunity if I stayed alert to her offerings? One small idea – to grow my own mast – had changed my hope, my outlook, my fortunes, in but a trice. And now fortune had smiled on me further with the new plants. I vowed to lock away this message, for I was sure that at some time in the future I would encounter dark days again.

Although the conifer tree had not yet even germinated, and I was many moons from sailing on Mother Ocean again, I now carry that most precious cargo: hope. While I have her in my soul I cannot be defeated.

Wednesday 27 June

As if to celebrate my emancipation from the awful abyss into which I had cast myself, the bird choir was in full voice last night. They began as the full moon rose, confirming my earlier suspicion that this was the reason for their singing[165]. As I lay on the warm, musty earth, listening to this most harmonious of melodies, my only regret was that there was no other person with which to share my experience. How I would have enjoyed having my Beth beside me on this night.

I did my best to lock away the birds' glorious tune in my head from where I could call on it in future. But in my head the tune must stay, unable to be shared, for I possess a voice fit for only sea shanties, lips that can barely whistle and fingers that could no more play a pianoforte than they could hold Beth's hand again. Was it unjust, I wondered, that such a godly melody was wasted on just one simple man, especially one who had no method of passing it to another?

---

[165] Moon-orientated events are well documented in the animal kingdom. For example, some Australian corals spawn five nights after the first full moon in November. Shellfish renew their shells in harmony with lunar cycles. Even the humble hamster has documented physiological changes that vary with the moon's phases. I enquired to Oxford's zoology department on how animals are able to identify this cycle but the mechanism remains poorly understood.

If only I could capture the sound with a contraption, so that another person's ears could experience it. But I knew that this was not possible, for to harness something so untouchable as a sound was as impossible as flying to the moon[166]. Yet that birdsong sent my soul soaring as high as that celestial body and beyond.

Thursday 28 June

I awoke to a sight that sparked fierce joy inside me: a pine seed had germinated. Although it was just a tiny speck of white and green in the grey earth, it represented my future and hopefully my salvation. I sat in front of it, motionless and entranced, as hour by hour the tiny seedling uncurled itself from the gritty earth and reached toward the heavens. I could now understand why the island birds appeared so thrilled, and broke into song, whenever new crops germinated.

By nightfall it was nearly an inch high.

Friday 29 June

This morning I returned to the island, where I inspected and watered my conifer seedling; I was delighted to see a second small shoot now pushing its way up from the guano.

I ate freshly caught fish with Bubo and took many long pulls of fresh water from the spring. My health was soaring by the day. My feeble, weak-legged climb through the hatch only days ago seemed a distant implausibility.

One puzzle still intrigued me: I still could not fathom from where the birds procured the grape seeds. It remained a mystery, albeit one that I was very pleased to have, for I ate another half dozen. The birds immediately used the newly available seeds and planted another row. Their instincts continued to amaze me for they somehow deduced to plant the seeds near the walls, allowing the future vines to climb up the rocks. How they reasoned this knowledge without books to guide them was yet another unknown.

---

[166] It was still 56 years before Thomas Edison would invent the gramophone record. Of course it was 1968 when human beings finally flew to the moon.

The other plant exploded in blue flowers. I was still unsure of its type, but waited with anticipation.

Sunday 1 July

My stocks continued to rise like a June thermometer. After just four days, the Conifer pine tree was already as high as my shin bone. If I watched it carefully, which I often did, I could almost see it creeping its way upward, like a tide eking up a sand bar. Its little brother has also fared well and was just two inches behind it.

The blue flowers were withering from the new plant. Small light green buds protruded through the browning petals, raising my hopes of fruit.

The birds continued to flutter about, constantly attending their plants. I slowly realised that these birds did not just farm the land – they were *of* the land. And the land was *of* them (literally!) To lose their plants in a storm was not like a Cornwall farmer whose summer hay was destroyed by locusts; to the birds, losing their crop was more akin to losing a child. The loss was permanent and cut the birds to an almost fatal depth. Now, that departed child had returned from the dead they could not hide their delight. Nor did I wish them to, for I could understand their pain.

Monday 2 July

I should not have written of the departed child as I did yesterday, for it unleashed a cruel cavalcade of demons within me. So I shall not write of the torment I endured from within my own mind last night, except to say that my voice is raw this morning because of my screams. For once I was thankful for my isolation so that no other man saw my raving, of which I am ashamed. Instead, I shall focus on what is right with my tiny corner of the world.

The pine tree was now knee high. The second tree was also doing well, and I realised that I must transplant it soon for it was competing with its sibling for light, nourishment and water. I should have thought of this when I planted them.

Small green pods now covered the blue-flowered vine. I pulled one from the vine and sniffed it - it hinted of woodiness with a sweet overtone.

Tentatively I bit through its centre. It had small green seeds inside it and tasted fibrous; perhaps it was the fruit that Diogo had mentioned. .

The green-budded vines must have arisen from latent seeds in the soil. It followed that the grape seeds, too, had been lying quiescent in the soil. Yet this scenario seemed unlikely on many counts. First, how had they avoided being washed away by the inundation? Second, it was most unlikely that the grapes, in particular, had previously grown on this isolated rock. Diogo made no mention of grapes in his letter, but perhaps my long-deceased kin had carried some of them aboard his ship? Despite my earlier mistake on the genesis of the oats and wheat, I could not think of any other explanation for the origin of the new plants.

Tuesday 3 July

My mind now turned to the next stage of my plan: how to fit the mast into the ship. To move such a large piece of lumber would be a tidy job for six men, but near impossible for one. But I knew that I would find a way, for I had scaled far higher peaks on my journey. The mast fitting problem was but a mere hillock on my path compared to the mountains I had scaled so far.

Wednesday 4 July

My mind turned all night with the mast-fitting problem and I awoke with a plan. I could not judge if it would be sufficient to complete the job, but I prepared in the expectation that it would be.

I walked around the island perimeter, peering over the cliff edge toward the ocean below. After one circumnavigation, I returned to the spot that best fitted my criteria: the cliff dropped steeply into the water with a vertical gradient. In fact, this precipice even projected over the water by several yards, making it admirably suited to my envisaged method of locating the new mast.

I carefully uprooted the smaller of the conifer seedlings and replanted it close to the cliff edge. I watered it tenderly and checked it often to ensure that it survived the transplant. Initially I had fears, for its leaves and branches drooped weakly. But by nightfall the little pine was again standing tall and true, so I was confident that it had adapted to its new location.

Thursday 5 July

I returned to the blue-flowered bushes, where the sight of the long green pods on it not only sparked joy inside me, for I knew immediately that they were edible, but also answered the mystery as to where the seeds had come from. The small green buds had elongated so that each was now the length of my finger, tapering to a fine point on both ends. I stripped one open along its length revealing eight small, round, green seeds. *Peas*.

Of course! I suddenly realised that the peas and the grapes had been provided by none other than ... Captain Fintan McAdam. The seeds had come from the last of my original supplies that I had packed to eat on the island. I had emptied them from my sack; the birds, in my absence, must have discovered them and somehow coaxed the two dozen raisins and a handful of dried peas into life. In just six weeks, these conjurers had cultivated old seeds into vibrant rows of young plants. Bubo's incessant messages of *peas* and *raisins* suddenly made sense. I was pleased that I did not clip him, for he was simply trying to convey news of this fortuitous growth.

I dared not eat any peas, for it was clear that this was just the first crop. Staying skint now would provide a larger harvest later. I hoped that the birds appreciated my moderation, even though they could not convey it.

Friday 6 July

Overnight I slept upon Bird Rock. During my dreams, a thought of such importance struck me that I arose immediately and set out searching the island. The clouds obscured the waning moon, but the stars were bright enough to give the grey ashen soil an eerie silver glow. Within a quarter turn of the clock, I had located what I was looking for: the old crock of tomato pulp. I settled back into a restful sleep knowing that I had secured yet another seed source on which the birds hopefully could work their agricultural magic.

At sunrise, I felt of regal importance as I emptied the pulp onto the guano earth. The birds instinctively realised that the red sludge contained a precious cargo; a dozen birds pecked their way through it, each pulling out a seed or two. As was their habit, each then fluttered to a separate part of the plateau where they planted and tended their new crop.

I had developed strong empathy for the birds' love of their crops. The joy and pride I felt as that conifer seed sprouted and raised its seedling eyes toward the sun must be like that of a mother or father with their child.

Oh the pain. My kingdom for a bottle of rum....

Saturday 7 July

I thought again of my Mama today. Had I given her moments of pride? Yes, I am sure I had. I will never forget Mama's beaming face when, even though I was only ten years old, I first read aloud from a book. It was she who thereafter insisted that I read a page each night. It was she who stitched me a vest from an old dress so that I could attend Reverend Butler's school. Of the three-score children in our village, I was one of only four whom attended school. It is thanks to her patience and determination that my quill moves across this page now.

I do still miss her – and my papa. But I am sure that I am right to feel this way - it would be strange and wrong if I didn't miss them at all, so the pain tells me that all is well. I have tried to think about Beth in this way, but I cannot. Perhaps it would be easier had her life not ended in such a way. I know that I must keep trying to forget her, or her spectre will poison my thoughts for eternity. There is not a day, even now, in which she does not pass through my mind at least once. That gruesome, gruesome blueness; even the colours of the deep ocean remind me of her.

Sunday 8 July

I checked on the main conifer pine this morning. It was growing tall and true, and will make a wonderful mast. In just 11 days it was already approaching my growth of 27 years.

I whetted my tools in readiness for work, and was anticipating the labour as a child approaches a birthday. To save toil later I trimmed branches as they appeared, for one swift hack of my scimitar now would save me hours of tedious sawing through thickened branches later.

I tied some of the cut braches together to form a trellis, staked it in place behind the growing peas, and then trained the vines along it. Already they looked healthier to be up from the ground rather than dragging their thin limbs through the guano.

Wednesday 11 July

Despite five days in the soil, the tomato seeds have not germinated. Normally this period would not be unusual, but on this Atlantic Eden such a wait seemed untenable. Perhaps the salt preserve ruined them. The birds were scratching and probing as before, but they seem devoid of life. It was a great pity because a fresh salmon and tomato loaf was in the offing.

Enough peas had sprouted that I felt justified in harvesting a half a dozen of the sweet pods. It had been many months since I had tasted such crisp, fresh food. It reminded me of what I sacrificed to be at sea.

To keep Beth from my thoughts during the idle and rum-less times, I concentrated on lessons with Bubo. They were now a habit and one that we generally enjoyed. As I sat with him on the breezy green plateau with the hot morning sun on my back and the gay birds chirping merrily in the background, my thoughts often turned to Reverend Butler's school. The contrast could not be greater.

We had no breezes or greenery, but instead took our lessons inside a dank windowless stable. The walls were bare and grey, because Reverend thought that bright colours would distract us from our learning. The building was always cold and damp, even in summer, and had only a single fire to warm us during the long winter months. The room was not open and free like the Bird Rock school, but was crammed with students tucked behind tight rows of adjacent desks.

My first two years were very unpleasant. A stroke of the Reverend's cane met every misspelled word or faulty calculation on my slate. Every quip – even if uttered in jest to lighten the mood – was dealt with harshly. I felt six stings in response to a simple jibe on many occasions. Yet the old Reverend must have seen some potential in me, for he offered that I stay on past my 12th birthday to help him tutor the younger students.[167] He even allowed me to write a story with a quill on paper (that I could keep!) rather than on slate. Mama cried when I gifted it to her, rolled into a scroll and tied with a strip of old cloth, at Christmas that year.

The old Reverend always instructed us to "surround ourselves with the Lord", by which he meant the vestments and adornments of religion, such as a crucifix, portraits of a bearded Christ on the walls, and daily attendance at services. As a lad I had no choice but to comply, but felt no benefit or warmth in doing so. Yet here on Bird Rock, I am surrounded by what the Reverend would consider as his God's creations: the ocean and its fish, the sky and its birds and stars, and the myriad of creatures that scutter and plants that grow on his earth. I have, in reality, done exactly as the Reverend instructed – I have surrounded myself with the Lord - although I doubt he would see it as such. It was a pity that he did not look past the Bible at the end of his own crooked nose, for the wonders of the world lay just beyond it had he cared to lift his eyes.

Thursday 12 July

Success this morning: a tomato seedling sprouted. True, it was just one small stalk from but one seed, but I had no doubt that these birds, with their genius for horticulture, would nurture it to robustness. My dream of a salmon and tomato roll lived on.

Today I uncovered the square of burlap cloth from the tin looking glass in my quarters. It was not a handsome sight that greeted my eyes, but

---

[167] In the early 1800s, most children attended school for only a year or two before being put to work. Very few students remained past their 12th birthday, which was a privilege granted only to those who were scholastically gifted.

at least it was an improvement on the sallow monster who saluted me in this very spot a few weeks ago.

I stropped a razor until its edge gleamed, and then took to my matted beard. My welted chin was soon bleeding from half a dozen razor cuts, forcing me to fetch a blotting cloth. Then I trimmed my hair, though a blind man could have done a neater job. If only the dandy barber from Billingsgate could have sailed a little boat to Bird Rock I would have gladly tipped him thrice his price.

I had not bathed properly since London. I foraged about in my quarters, eventually locating my Pears[168] bar. I heated a large pot of spring water (for I could easily replenish it) and then scrubbed myself with a clean rag until I was pink. Later, when Bubo flew to my ship, he looked at me with a tilted head. I took this evident confusion to be a bird form of a compliment.

Thursday 19 July

For a week I have done little but rest, nibble on fresh produce and teach Bubo his lessons. The single tomato shrub produced two tiny fruits already. The birds stripped every seed from their cores and carefully replanted them. I had no doubt that leafy tomato bushes, each sporting bulbous red fruits, would soon cover the island.

The birds dug in a second crop of peas and the grapes were fruiting in abundance. The trestles I rigged for them to creep along were sagging under the weight of fruit, so I fetched some tools from my ship and built a stronger frame for them with some cut-off branches.

The mast tree is now nearly twice my height. With each extra inch of growth, my anticipation grows. In my mind I can see an imaginary finish ribbon at about six yards high. Sometimes it seems that the tree is racing toward it like a hare, while at other times it seems slower than a dull Liverpudlian winter.

Rum. I have not taken a drop for weeks – perhaps my longest ever stretch without it - and feel stronger for its absence. Yet I will also be

---

[168] Andrew Pears (1770-1845) was a London barber who invented soap bars. His original company, Pears, continues producing soap to this day.

honest with myself (for who else is to know?): was a draft available here and now, I would drink it in a trice.

Friday 20 July

The wind was very strong this morning, and remained that way all day. I spent my time on the island harvesting grapes, which were now plentiful. I filled two large crates, but left a fair portion for the birds. I now turned my mind with how to best use or preserve this profusion of fruit, for I couldn't eat them all before they rotted. I could not salt them, use them for bait, nor could I pickle them. It would be a shame, I thought, to waste them, because they had high nutrition that I could not readily source from the oceans. Perhaps I could juice them.

Saturday 21 July

I decided to juice the grapes, for I had plenty of empty rum crocks at my disposal for storage. It was a long labour with only a mortar and pestle at my disposal. Yet my time was free, for the mast-tree still had some way to grow, so I set about my task with quiet determination. Like a plodding mail horse, I steadily covered the distance.

After crushing each bunch of grapes, I strained them through an old square of calico into a mug. When the mug was full, I poured it into a rum crock. By day's end I had filled two crocks – nearly eight gallons – with deep purple grape juice. Before I stowed them in the hold I added a dash of yeast to each, which will turn the juice into wine, which I do only to help to preserve it against mould.

It was again windy all day, and the temperature dropped sharply. My old sailor's bones told me that another blow was nigh. I hoped that it was not as fierce as the last.

Monday 23 July

Deep black clouds covered the sky from dawn and a storm was soon on me – my first real blow since the typhoon. My heart beat fiercely in my chest at the first crack of thunder, for I had not yet even repaired my ship from the previous damage, much less my nerve. As the wind whistled higher my angst grew but, with the *Maris Alarum* tucked tightly into the lee of Bird Rock, it rocked me only like a nasty child pushing another too high upon a rope swing, rather than like an angry bull.

It rained heavily all day so I didn't venture out from my cabin. Bubo returned from the island and slept on his perch rather than with his brothers on the island, which spoke loudly for how gruesome it was outside.

To pass time I re-read Diogo's account in my journal. Among all men, I am one of the few who could fully imagine his fear as the waves smashed his ship into Bird Rock. Twenty-seven men dead. Twenty-seven brave lives lost - their pasty, rock-gored limbs strewn for many leagues over the ocean, achieving naught but to feed the scavenging shark-devils. I made both anchors fast and checked them often, for I had no wish to emulate the fate of Diogo and his men.

I shuddered and slept little, if at all, for I found it hard to toss this image.

Wednesday 25 July

The storm has continued unabated for two days. The sailor in me was nearly broken once before but I somehow survived the ordeal. But I had no wish to test myself again, so I beseeched Mother Ocean to take her fury elsewhere.

As a large wave smashed into the starboard hull, a thought chanced through my mind: should I leave my ship and wait on Bird Rock until the storm passed? The ground there was firm, but the lodgings cold and wet. At first I decided to stay on my ship, but as the storm continued I wavered; every wave that tossed my sloop about pushed my thoughts toward the sanctity of the rock. It was safe, secure and sound. The lure of solid land should never tempt a true sailor, but on this occasion it called me loudly with its promise of solidity. But after further thought I realised that if my ship went down, there would be no joy in watching her perish from afar, thereby sentencing me to a lifetime of isolation and despair, just as freedom had called. I would rather be beaten by Mother Ocean than by myself.

Bubo was still with me. He had not left my ship since the storm started. I sense that he, too, feared what nearly killed him previously, for, like mankind, he appeared to be cursed with a strong memory. But I was pleased for his company, because to share such an experience was to halve the pain, even though he was just a bird.

In the evening I lay in my hammock, listening to the rain thrashing even harder than previously. A loud crack of thunder brought haunting memories into my mind, but, bereft of rum, I had no easy way to quell them. It was difficult to know where to turn in such a situation, for when you fear that a tempest will destroy your ship and you are on that very vessel, a man has few options.

Yet just as I despaired, I heard a faint sound above the wind. The gentle distant noise had no right to reach my ears through the squealing winds and rolling thunder. Yet in time I heard it as clearly as though it was emanating from my hammock itself. It was the birdsong, lilting its way above the crashing white tops to bring soothing music to my ears and peace to my addled heart. Even Mother Ocean's fury could not stop the birds from singing to their moon.

Lulled by the distant bird choir, I dropped into a peaceful slumber. I have not worried about the storm since, for each time the fear assailed me, my imaginings of that godly choir soothed the beasts within.

Friday 27 July

The storm has raged for five days. I have spent my days mopping up the wetness with rags and trying to keep the holds as dry as possible. I kept a strong coal fire burning in the galley to ward off the damp, and to dry the rags so that I could use them again. The galley looked far better for the scrubbing and shone like a new bell.

My hips were sore, for whenever the *Maris Alarum* lurched I collided with the bulkheads, benches or bearers. But whenever I felt the fear creep into my sinews I let the birdsong play again in my head and continued with my swabbing.

Saturday 28 July

After six days, the clouds finally broke this morning. At first light I returned to the island, for I had missed its open gaiety. Immovable earth felt good under my knees. (Should I resign my sailor's hat for scribing such heresy?)

The rain provided a fillip for the conifer tree. It has grown remarkably in my absence, and was now more than thrice my height. I shall let it thicken for just a few more days before I fell it.

Freedom was whispering her enchanting invitation to me again. I hoped that soon she would shout and sing with me from the masthead.

Sunday 29 July

After breakfast on the island, which included a newly-harvested tomato, I returned to the *Maris Alarum* and spent the day dissembling the old mast fixing plates and so forth, and rigging guides to set the new mast into position.

This task was simplified by the fact that I had previously chopped the mast away in a drunken fit of revenge. Never before had a rum rage earned me such a providential keep.

Monday 30 July

The mast tree was now sufficiently high, and with broad sunlight shining on it from all directions during its life, it had grown straight and true. I went to cut it this morning, but at the last tick I decided it would be better to wait another day, for I wished it to broaden another half an inch or so.

I spent the afternoon with Bubo trying to explain how I intend to attach the new mast. He will have an assisting role to play so I instructed him as patiently as I could.

Tuesday 31 July

I again rowed to the island with the aim of cutting the mast tree. Everything else was ready, but again I shirked at the thought. Instead I whetted my axe and adze again and rechecked the fixing plates. And repeated Bubo's training for the task.

If I had just a single mug of rum to get me on my way, all would be well.

Wednesday 1 August

I was torn. I could not wait any longer, yet nor could I bring myself to cut the mast tree. I was riddled, like a plank of old timber, with the knots and nail holes of previous failures. I tried talking to Bubo but he didn't understand. He simply could not understand human emotions such as fear and anxiety.

I wondered if grape juice had turned yet.

Thursday 2 August

This morning's wine tasted bitter and green; it had not yet fully turned, and will need at least a week before it becomes drinkable wine. However it lightened my head enough to get me on my way, and the first bite of axe in wood felt grand. The blade bit deeply into the timber, and after the second swipe, a good wedge flew out. My strength was up and it took me only a few minutes until the fell swoop brought down the trunk.

I then turned to the log with my adze and rasp, stripping its bark and shearing off small braches and nodules as I encountered them. By noon the trunk was clear and smooth. After that I cut half a dozen thick round branches from the second pine tree and trimmed them to form stout cylinders. These I placed under the mast to act as rollers, which would enable me to move this heavy piece of lumber across the chalky earth.

I spent the afternoon trimming the base of the mast to fit into the existing fixing plates, and also attached some sail and boom riggings. It was a grand feeling to be working again. Rest is a fine tonic for a chore-filled life, but the reverse is also true: too much idleness makes the soul slothful. I am sure my papa is looking down on me from his afterlife, proud and pleased at the products of my labour. I have felt his firm hands guiding every stroke of the adze.

I hold warm memories of my father, but, like all memories, they come at a price: regret and sorrow. I feel, as I have for years, a sense of guilt that I was not there to comfort him in his dying moments. But I know that I cannot change this fact any more than I can fly like a bird, so instead I whistle the birdsong inside my head, and think of him contentedly rasping timber in his shipyard.

Friday 3 August

As I sat on deck, bathing in the morning light's gentle glow, the breeze turned to a favourable gentle southerly. I sensed that conditions could not be better for affixing the new mast. I was about to begin what I hoped would be the final major repair for the *Maris Alarum* – ever. Nervous anticipation surged through me for I understood the difficulty of the task ahead. I (yet again) revised my plans with Bubo, and then set myself to work. I packed a sack with assorted parts - tools, a long spare rope, a large pulley and a spool of wire – and commenced the most difficult and important job that I had ever undertaken.

I rowed around the island, clambered up the cliff, and then heaved the prostrate mast across the plateau. I had expected this task to take many hours, but I was pleasantly surprised at the efficiency of the roller system. Before long I had the mast in its place under the cliff-side conifer. In preparation for lowering it, I affixed three black ropes to the mast including one from the tip, and then looped each around a strong overhanging conifer branch.

Next, I had to position the *Maris Alarum* to accept her new mast from above. Using twists of wire, I affixed the pulley to the conifer tree, which I would later use in this endeavour. Then I reversed my earlier path and rowed back to the *Maris Alarum*.

Then I tied a long length of rope to the ship's bow and gave the tag end to Bubo. After numerous lessons he knew his role and played it well: he took the rope in his talons and flew it to the conifer pine tree on the island. It was a difficult trip for him because the rope grew heavier as it lengthened, but with some mighty flaps of his grand blue and red wings he covered the distance admirably. He then rested for a few ticks before threading the rope through the pulley and then returned it back to me.

210

I weighed the anchors. By pulling on the fore rope, I could, via the pulley, move the *Maris Alarum* toward the island. At first I was liberal in my heaving, but as my ship approximated the island I became cautious, because although the waves were small and the southerly was slight, hard rock could do awful things to a ship's hull. When she was just 50 feet away from the cliff face I set two stern anchors and made the ship fast. Now I required great caution and precision. By simultaneously playing out the anchor ropes and pulling upon the bow rope, I inched my ship toward the cliff.

Within an hour I had manoeuvred the *Maris Alarum* until her bow was just a few feet from the cliff face. I pulled both the anchor ropes as firmly as possible, and tightened the pulley rope with two taut haymaker's hitches. My ship was now tethered in place, bobbing patiently on the gentle sea, ready to accept her new mast from above.

I hurried back to the island proper. Again using the rollers, and accompanied by a great deal of my own cursing and grunting, I pushed the mast until it was jutting over the edge of the cliff, balancing delicately above the *Maris Alarum* below. With great vigilance, I played out the black ropes one by one, gradually lowering the mast toward my ship. By and by I cut one black cord; later I cut another. After an excruciating hour, just one black rope, the one in the tip, held the mast aloft. The timber was now positioned exactly as I had planned: it was vertical and hanging amidships, directly above the guides through which it had to pass. After waiting for a passing wind gust to quell, and beseeching Providence to grant me good fortune, it was time to make the final adjustment. I loosened the final cord and let the mast drop steadily down toward the hole.

In my nights at Blackfriars Tavern, I had seen many a rogue betting on a game called 'darts'. The navvies wagered a pretty penny on whether a player could throw his dart into the target bullseye. I wish those dart-playing scoundrels could see me here and now, for as I played out the last cord, the mast dropped directly through the deck hole and fed itself snugly into the steel guiding loops below. *Bullseye.*

Not wishing to waste a moment, for a rogue wave or a gust of wind could disturb the mast's alignment, I ran across the plateau, scrambled down the rock face and rowed with feverish energy to my ship. In less than one hour, I had bolted the new mast in place, and after a few further hour's work Bubo and I had fixed six stays. My new mast was in place. At last, at last, at last.

Saturday 4 August

My sleep last night was aflutter, for my freedom was hopefully just a day away. Over a mug of breakfast tea I gazed up at the mast in wonder, like a man who had lost a limb only to see it grow back overnight. It was a fine piece of timber. The mast was three parts as tall as the original and even slightly thicker in parts. My papa would have been proud.

I recalled Papa's voice as he chided me over a small slight in a ship's wheel that he had commissioned me to carve. Yet I could see that despite his stern words, his gills were bursting with pride at the workmanship I bestowed on that wheel. From when I was just a young lad, it was his hands that had guided the saw, that positioned the chisel, that pressed the spoke-shave in the right directions. I have now fitted a mast carved from a single tree - I am sure he is turning about in his own dust with pride. I wish that he could see it.

I spent the morning rigging the boom and, with Bubo's help, threading the halyards. By early afternoon all that remained was a test sail. I demurred, scarred by the disappointment of the previous trials. Instead, I rechecked (for the fourth time) the fitting plates in the hold, and tightened (for the fifth time) the mast stays. By and by I could no longer check or tighten anything without wasting my time. All that I had left to do was to hoist the sails and cast away.

Bubo was perched high on my shoulder as I hoisted the mainsail to half-mast. In the light breeze, we barely moved - but at least we were sailing again. In short time, I hoisted half the headsail as well and found the mast to be more than a match for the light buffeting. It fitted tightly in the plates and wriggled nary a sixteenth. I hesitated to lift the sails higher, but I knew that to tarry was to invite the devil to play inside my head. Without any further graduations, I hoisted both sails fully. The breeze billowed, the boom swung, and the *Maris Alarum* pulled herself to a heal and cut through the waves.

A few minutes later I spotted a wind shift as it shimmered across the wave tops, and turned my ship for the gust. The sails gave a flap as I steered her across wind and then tightened to a neat curve. The *Maris*

Alarum sped even faster and was now past 8 knots. I completed a jibe that the mast handled without objection. I then threw her into a tack, first to starboard, then to port, all without so much as a groan from the new timber.

As the sun set, I furled the sails in the lee of Bird Rock. The new mast had passed every test I could conceive. The *Maris Alarum* was ready for adventure.

And so, most assuredly, was I.

Sunday 5 August

Before departure, I harvested a large sack of grain, and a crate of green peas. I also took a box of red and green tomatoes, and four crates of plump purple grapes.

My larder has never bulged so far; I look forward to my stomach doing the same, for it is thin indeed after months of disregard. Perhaps soon I will be able to discard the cords that still hold up my breeches.

The sun had almost descended through its full arc before I finally weighed anchor and sailed due east. The birds, a couple of whom had sat upon the cliff-top as we departed, quickly ceded to specks as we made good speed. I realised that I would miss their gay chatter, but at the same time I felt content and even proud that their natural history would continue. I found it odd yet satisfyingly true that a few oatcakes and some rotting seeds had saved this species from extinction.

Adios, Bird Rock. *Saludo*, adventure.

Monday 6 August

Some say that Monday can be unlucky but for the *Maris Alarum*, Bubo and I, this day was as fine and unfettered by low luck as can be. The sun shone brightly, Mother Ocean was calm and the wind blew steadily from the west at 15 knots. I took advantage of the tranquil conditions to juice the remaining crates of grapes, for they would not last unless I did this. Again I added some yeast to the mixture in the hope of better preserving them.

At sunset, we spotted a school of salmon. I had just one spool of fishing line – the other I had wasted on the second mast repair – but managed to land three thick fish in an hour. I baked a small batch of bread, and my tomato and salmon loaf became a reality. Never have I tasted such fine fair: fresh, grain-meal bread loaves, red tomatoes, and ocean salmon just plucked from the sea. I felt truly at ease after such a feed, and allowed myself to luxuriate in that feeling like it was a hot spring bath.

Tuesday 7 August

I still cannot adjust my eyes to the sight of the tall mast. Since the typhoon, the *Maris Alarum's* amidships had been adorned by nothing but a weak, bandaged half-mast with limply flapping sails. Now the sight of a grand, tall spire with its sails billowing in the breeze appears abnormal.

For two days those sails have produced good speed eastward. The easy passage gave me time to reflect on the island birds. Even in hindsight I continued to be impressed, not only by their horticultural instincts but also by their devotion to the commune. They were like a tight band of brothers, working not for themselves but for the flock. It was a pity that more men could not see this display and take the lesson from it.

I thought back to my final days in England and compared it with Bird Rock. I compared that wretched banker Peathorne, who could earn a £50 commission for being nothing but an ignoramus, to the dandy barber who so skilfully and merrily cut my hair but earned only two pennies for his craft. Wasn't this an injustice? Surely the birds' system was more equitable than one that allowed a scoundrel to earn a thousand times more than an honest toiler. I will think on this notion some more, but the answer already seemed clear.

Thursday 9 August

I have taken to scanning the eastern horizon at sunrise, noon and sunset, hoping to spot a silhouette of land, for my ever-present hope was that I was now close. The seas were rougher today and the wind turned nor'west. Yet by sailing hard, I made fair progress.

This morning, as I sipped on a mug of tea, I thought further about the birds' orderliness and whether it was a good system for mankind to live by. By and by I realised that it required the abolition of two traits: greed and laziness. If rations were scarce and just one bird had been greedy and taken a larger portion of the seed than its entitlement, then another bird would have received less. In this case, no bird would wish to be last to eat, which could be resolved by no means less taxing than simply sharing the food equitably from the start.

Similarly, if one bird shirked its duties but received its usual rations, then the other birds would soon see that they could garner rewards without effort. This, too, would lead to anarchy. I concluded that neither greed nor laziness had cursed these birds, and that such a system of work would fail abjectly for any creature that was. Communal existence may benefit ants, bees and birds, for they had no self-indulgence or slothfulness in their bones. But as soon as one human being exploited these weaknesses then any such system was doomed. Perhaps More's *Utopia* needed a rethink.

Bubo and I chatted a little, but I sensed he was missing the birds. I tried to discuss the birds and their communal habits with Bubo but he could not fathom my arguments. It was a shame that Bubo could not grasp such ideals, for I would have enjoyed a robust debate.

Friday 10 August

Friday 6th April –126 days ago - was the last time I laid my eyes on another human. I remember sailing out of the harbour at Oporto with my eyes straight ahead in case I inadvertently saw the brown-eyed girl whom I had embarrassed at the tavern.

How I wished I could replay that night. In my fairest daydreams that I now regularly entertain, I turn and look back from my ship to see her at the foot of the quay. She waves to me. I wave back and holler a greeting. She runs along the pier, keeping pace with the *Maris Alarum* as I sail closer to the pier and hold out my hand. She takes my hand at full stride and then jumps aboard. We embrace. Then the *Maris Alarum* sprouts her water wings and we fly off toward the rising dawn.

But in my dream on this day, I looked at her again. Her brown skin paled, and her brown eyes transformed to emerald to green. She was Beth.

I fought to wipe the dream from my mind, but failed, and soon was in the throes of another vision. An awful vision – among the worst I have experienced. I saw the stag's antler pierce Beth's blouse. I hear that groan; that ghastly, beastly grunt that surely came from the devil himself. I thrust my hand into the jagged, open wound. And then ... and then I feel it. If feel it, but I do not let my hand dally upon it.

Then I see it. Just once. Having seen it, I shall never forget even a tiny detail of it. That gruesome wound, opening a portal to her abdomen... to another being. To my own flesh and blood. I touched and saw, for but a brief few seconds, a limb of my unborn child.

Its tiny arm was no bigger than my finger, its hand smaller than my thumbnail, its fingers the thickness of matchsticks. Did they move? Did those tiny fingers grasp and curl around my thumb? Was it reaching for something, anything, in a desperate last lunge for life? I cannot recall.

Whether the wine had fully turned or not was suddenly irrelevant. I fought my way down to the hold, and lunged for a wine crock. Spilling nearly as much as I swallowed, I poured that bitter medicine down my throat.

Saturday 11 August

Last night's alcohol was tart to taste and left a bitter sting. The birds may have been fine famers but I had no affection for the flavour of their wine. But I had needed its medicine to loosen my mind, and by and by it had sent me into a deep slumber. Unfortunately, my head was heavier this morning by a commensurate amount. I realised that I must find company soon, for I was fighting my own memories again.

I asked Bubo to fly high and look for land, but despite his fine vision he didn't see any. He was acting quiet and withdrawn, and spent most of his time atop the mast today. This worried me, as it was his preferred position when he was feeling threatened.

I had no energy for chores, so I simply lay in my hammock. Later, I realised that without any rum I might contract scurvy. I thought that perhaps a tipple of red wine would keep the bruises away[169].

Sunday 12 August

During the weeks following the typhoon, I fretted too frequently to allow my mind to crave company. I was distracted: repairing my ship, my ongoing hunger, the birds' crops and the *Maris Alarum's* mast all demanded my energies. Now, all was well: my ship was stout, my provisions were fresh and plentiful and the weather was fair, so my mind had little on which to focus. Instead it meandered onto problems of its own making. For the first time on my journey, and despite the proximity of my companion Bubo, I felt alone. Very alone.

Of course, I expected solitude. But I did not expect to feel such a longing for she who was departed, for I had thought that the time and space afforded by an open ocean would drive a wedge between my longings and me. But it seemed to be having the reverse effect.

Later, I realised why this was happening. In the evening I went to light my galley lantern. I lit a stick of kindling on the oven fire, and after igniting the lantern wick, I extinguished the splinter with a quick huff. Then I returned to the fire where, in order to hearten it, I blew upon it fiercely. It struck me that blowing on a flame has opposing effects depending on the size of the fire: a strong blow will extinguish a small flame, yet enlivens a strong one.

As I sipped upon a jar of stringent red wine, I realised that separated love was the same: putting time and space between you and a mere acquaintance extinguishes the relationship; in contrast, absence causes a deep love to grow stronger.

---

[169] Although McAdam was erroneous in thinking that the rum would help his scurvy, he was more correct with the wine. Grapes are a source of vitamin C, whose deficiency causes scurvy. The citrus fruit that he added to his rum stores would have caused a similar beneficial effect, although it should be noted that there are far less harmful ways of ingesting dietary vitamin C than adding a quarter of a lemon to a crock of rum!

Perhaps my journey so far had been like trying to quench a forest fire by blowing wind upon it. Instead of extinguishing my bonds with Beth, I had been feeding them so that they blazed ever hotter.

I gulped down some more wine, and tried to douse the flames inside.

Monday 13 August

My head this morning was cloudier than a London winter sky, and again I had no appetite for breakfast, for work, or even in being upright. Instead, I slept intermittently for most of the morning. Perhaps I have dosed myself too heavily with medicine again.

Bubo was outside, and initially did not respond to my calls. I had faint recall of talking with him deep into the night, and drunkenly chastising him over his lack of knowledge on bird societies.

By and by my head cleared and later Bubo came down from his perch, so in the afternoon I taught Bubo some simple games in an effort to cheer him, for he seemed to have withdrawn from me. Although the pastimes were childish, he seemed to gain amusement from them, and I found them a simple distraction from my torrid musings.

At first I tried to teach Bubo "I spy", but soon learned that he had no notion of written letters or spelling. Even after a long lesson, he could not grasp the idea that lines drawn on a page represented sounds from the tongue. He will never understand this concept. Although he is very clever in many ways, there are simply no connections in his bird-mind that can associate a line to a letter, a letter with a word, a word to a sound, and then that sound to a meaning.

When I reflected on this chain of knowledge necessary for reading, it struck me as remarkable that *any* person could perform such a complex skill. Perhaps Reverend Butler's commission was harder than I first imagined.

I next attempted a simple dice game with Bubo, but, like his spelling, he could not add. To Bubo, when one object had another added to it there were now two objects, not one plus another one. The concept of 1+1=2 just did not exist in his mind and no amount of lessons would change this.

We eventually found common ground in a card game that I called "Pairs" in which I placed playing cards face down on the galley table, and then from memory we alternately attempted to select a pair of identical cards. It took me a couple of hours to teach Bubo the concept (rewarding him each time he chose a pair) but once he grasped it, he quickly excelled at it. Bubo had amazing recall, and once he sighted a card he did not forget its position. I sense that he gained some pleasure from beating me, which he did 10 times in a row. At times I had to take stock of myself: I was playing a card game with a *bird*.

His cleverness still occasionally surprises me, but I have gradually gained an appreciation of Bubo's full intellect. He was a quick learner in many areas, especially remembering words, yet I have just learned that he was as vacant as a simpleton when confronted with spelling. He could never learn to write words even if he grew hands and fingers. He had a fine memory, especially that associated with graphical features such as landmarks (or, of course, picture cards), yet he could not understand that a picture of a fish was a representation of it, rather than the object itself. Similarly, although he was ignorant of the purpose of a map, he was a fine navigator and knew the directions of all eight major points without even consulting a compass. Perhaps everything that he needed to know was contained in his head, so pictures, maps, alphabets and the like were unnecessary.

Bubo could count to ten, but he could not perform any mathematics, even of the simplest variety. Yet he understood logical thought and followed basic instructions like a faithful first mate. He even had some knowledge of the physical properties of simple things and of how they worked, such as a halyard that would hoist a sail when pulled.

He was a good companion with which to share my journey, and I was pleased to have him by my side. I was just pleased to have *someone* by my side.

Tuesday 14 August

I arose early, for I had consumed only half a quart of wine last night before falling asleep. Bubo was more talkative today. I think he enjoyed the card games that we continued to play. I still could not beat Bubo at the "pairs" game and probably never will. Perhaps when we find a tavern we can furtively form a team, and set wagers that I know I will not lose.

Each day I saw a little more of Bubo's personality. He seemed to have some feel for human emotion, and like a good pet dog he had a natural loyalty in his blood. However I doubted that he fully understood my mood swings or frustrations, and certainly could not fathom the logic behind complex thoughts such as communal living. I sensed that he had a sly sense of humour, and I sometimes wondered if my nickname, Captain Rum, was a deliberate comical moniker rather than a simple misappropriation. I like to think the former.

Bubo respected me as his provider and master, and I cared for him in the way that one might love a favoured pet dog. As affirming as this kinship was, it was different from the feelings one has for a close friend or relative.

Or wife.

I again turned heavily to the wine bottle last night. Oh, how I still miss her.

Wednesday 15 August

My morning was again slow, and Bubo was again withdrawn. He spent much of the morning atop the mast. I vaguely remembered arguing with him for many hours last night. I vowed to avoid the wine for a few days to give myself a fresher head, and to ensure that I did not further insult Bubo.

Just after noon, my hands started shaking by themselves again. I had no idea why. But I had no medicine chest and no rum, so I lay on them to still them.

Last's night thoughts had left me feeling down. Had I found myself in this situation 30 days ago I would have whooped for joy, but instead I have focused on what (or who) is missing and am more miserable for the effort. I knew that it was normal to miss someone, but, like a fire enflamed by air rather than extinguished, the time and distance were simply exacerbating my grief.

Yet I knew that I could not sail east forever without encountering someone, somewhere, who would help distract my addled mind. So I tried to steer my thoughts toward the good, and whistled the bird song inside my head to help cast the demons from my mind.

I touched a little more wine in the evening to help to chase away my final misgivings. I initially didn't want the drink, preferring a clear head, but in the end its call was too loud to ignore.

Yet I have since deduced that banning myself from the drink was unnecessary. Like a fire that is brightened by a wind, or the love that is emboldened by time and distance, my want of liquor seemed to have grown stronger in its absence. So, I concluded, the drink must be a true friend rather than a passing acquaintance. My vow melted away in the face of this logic, so I retreated, alone, to the galley, and spent another afternoon and evening with my friend and doctor, the wine bottle.

Thursday 16 August

Bubo startled me awake with a loud but welcome cry: *Captain Rum .... Land.* From a hazy, sluggish hammock, I dragged myself, dry-mouthed and nauseous, to deck. The sun was already approaching mid morning as I took up my telescope.

"Where is the land, Bubo?"

He clucked, pointing with his wing.

"South south east?" I confirmed, although heavy-headed and weary, I was galvanised to action by the tantalising prospect of land. I trained my scope to the horizon but could see nothing. But I trusted Bubo's navigation and held the bearing ... and held it ... and held it. Just as the sun was reaching its noon zenith, my patience was rewarded when land finally came into view. Rarely have I felt such joy.

I could make out a tall peak, like a cathedral spire but cut flat about three parts of the way up. At first, I was unsure if the mountain was part of the mainland or an island in itself, but I dearly hoped it was the former.

It wasn't. After a further hour of sailing, I was disappointed to observe through my scope that it was just an island - I had so hoped for a mainland town with a butcher's market, a tavern with gallons upon gallons of rum, and women of any race or even any colour[170].

221

Nevertheless, I kept my sails tight and by early afternoon I approached the land. I noted that it had far more vegetation than Bird Rock, and my hopes remained high that it was inhabited. I have heard lascivious tales of Cook's crew in the Hawaiian Islands, and hoped for a similar welcome[171].

I dropped my sounding lead over the side, for an early warning of a shallow reef was better than one discovered a trice too late. I had spooled out 12 fathoms until the lead hit the bottom. This suggested that the island was, like Bird Rock, the tip of a steep underwater mountain, with nothing but its peak jutting above the deep surrounding waters.

I circumnavigated the land mass and made a simple chart of its coastline. Upon completing the survey, it was clear that if this island was not the older sibling of Bird Rock then it was certainly a close cousin. Towering black cliffs – well over 20 yards high - formed the perimeter, and like Bird Rock it had no natural harbour in which to moor my ship. The mountain was tall – by reckoning it with my dented sextant I calculated that it was over 100 yards from its base to the cut-off top of the cone – and rose out of the ocean above the western cliffs. The rest of the island flattened and stretched out for about 400 yards to the east. The whole island, when viewed from the north, gave the impression of being a gigantic boot. I named it *Boot Island*.

The seas behaved erratically around Boot Island. At the western mountainous end, the waves crashed into the rock with relentless ferocity. The sea was not simply tossing idle chop onto the rocks, but was bearing down onto them with one powerful surge after another. The roaring sound was exhilarating and the salt spray filled my lungs with the ocean's spirit, but I nevertheless kept a good distance; it would

---

[170] The phrase 'or even any colour' would today be considered very racist and narrow minded. However in McAdam's time such a notion would have been liberal to the point of being scandalous.

[171] Captain James Cook arrived in the Hawaiian Islands in 1778. His party was welcomed by the natives, whose females were very uninhibited, trading sexual services for the simplest trinket (even a nail!) For a band of crewmen who had been trapped together on a ship for months without female company, this layover was very welcome indeed. Cook, however, apparently stayed true to his marital vows, despite the wanton approaches of the island women who were eager to bed the Captain.

be a poor finish to my journey if the *Maris Alarum* ended her days as a multitude of splinters. I noted that a lot of debris from the island – timber, plant material, and even some old vines and the like - had collected at the base of the cliff, and I had no wish to add to it.

I was not sure from where these powerful waves arose but suspected it was from the meeting of two ocean currents. Perhaps the sea floor might also channel the water here to breaking height. Whatever the cause, these mighty waves crashed with unceasing rhythm into the black western cliffs. Even Bubo watched them with seemingly grim fascination.

Conversely the eastern, low end of the island – the 'toes' of the boot – was far calmer. It seemed that the western mountain shielded the rest of the coastline from the waves and wind. By the time I had completed my circumnavigation, I was disappointed that my observations did not match my imaginings; a welcome to match Cook's party's would have to wait. I could see little of interest apart from the tops of some tall palm trees that grew at the mountain's base.

I sailed to the southern border in the lee of the peak, edged closer to the shore until my anchor found ground, and then furled the sails for the night. I planned to explore the island more fully the following day. I toasted the land sighting with some wine. Time had not improved its flavour; it still had more than a hint of vinegar to it.

Friday 17 August

I slept turbulently and arose late. The wine had a strong fist, such was the pain it gave my head after last night's quart. I vowed to drink less of it today, for I needed respite from its morning vengeance.

I had intended to explore the island before moving forward. Several times I tried to raise myself, but failed. I felt in no condition for activity and instead instructed Bubo to fly over the island, explaining to him that he must report to me what he could see. He seemed oddly recalcitrant – perhaps he didn't understand, or maybe I had cruelled him with my tongue again last night. But by and by he obeyed my orders. He returned later and through a vexing account – my poor condition had my patience at a low ebb – he seemed to be indicating that the island was filled with water. Maybe I misinterpreted him, or he misunderstood my questions, or perhaps the island had an inland lagoon. Either way I did not learn as much as I had hoped. I asked Bubo if he saw any men (or women – he does not know the difference) but he said no. On this point I checked thrice for I wished to be sure.

I looked across at the sheer black cliffs that jutted out of the water. They seemed impenetrable. Now that I knew that there were no human inhabitants, there seemed little point in exploring it. Particularly not this morning. *Especially* not with a thumping pain in the back of my head.

My curiosity nagged at me. Perhaps Bubo had missed something ... or someone. But another glance at the foreboding rock walls soon extinguished that feeling. My tired head insisted that nothing of interest could possibly live in such an inhospitable place. With a heavy sigh, I dragged up the long anchor rope, tugged on the halyards with resignation, and again set sail for the African coast.

By midafternoon, my headache had not lightened. My hands were shaking uncontrollably again. To quell these symptoms I poured a deep mug of wine, and nursed it through the afternoon. Slowly the shaking eased; the medicinal wine seemed as useful as rum to chase the palsy from my hands. By the evening's fourth mug my head pain was also ceding.

Later I tried to give Bubo some bread dipped in wine, but he shunned it. I have a dim memory that I grew agitated at him for not accepting my offer and of chasing him about the cabin.

Saturday 18 August

I awoke with yet another headache and more regrets. Bubo would not talk to me at all. He left me in no doubt that my wine-tongue had savaged him the previous night.

"I'm sorry Bubo," I called to him at the top of the mast, despite having poor recollection of my sins. He did not reply, and continued to shun me.

The wind had swung to the east, meaning that I spent much of my day tacking into the breeze. I still mulled over the disappointment of Boot Island - the desolate and barren thing. So I searched, yet again in vain, for more land. I saw nothing. I asked Bubo to look for land but he refused outright. A sailor would be flogged for such insubordination.

Later that morning I opened another wine crock, for my hands were shaking again. I still didn't know what caused this malady but I had discovered that liquor was the best medicine for it. After lunch, I remember trying to coax Bubo down from the mast with a handful of grapes. But he remained obstinate so I threw them at him, before falling asleep on deck.

I awoke in the early evening, my mouth parched. Bubo saw me stir and flew to the top of the mast. Again he would not listen to my entreaties or accept my apologies. That damn bird – he could be so frustrating. I took another mug to soothe my mind.

Sunday 19 August

I awoke mid morning with more crust than an old loaf. My eyes were clouded, which was an advantage as I passed the looking glass. I barely made it to the galley for water before retreating to my hammock.

By noon, my head had cleared sufficiently that I was able to climb to the deck. I carried a handful of grapes with me as a token of redemption for Bubo. But he wasn't on his perch, and nor was he atop the mast. This absence was most uncommon and unwelcome. Had I chastised him too harshly last evening? I fetched my telescope and scanned the skies but could not see him.

But my regrets grew with every passing hour. I would hate to lose Bubo now, but surely he could understand that the ill words were not mine, but were from the wine. Yes, I concede that my lips had formed the sounds, but the thoughts had come from the liquor and not from my heart.

I had known since I first untied the string from Bubo's leg, just after he arrived on my ship, that he could fly away at any time. But as we had journeyed together our bond had grown. Not only had I taught him lessons but also I had fed him and housed him. Surely even his bird-brain could see that one or two slights, coming from a liquor loosened tongue, should be forgiven and forgotten.

It was late afternoon when I finally caught a glimpse of his majestic wings silhouetted against the deepening sky. I called to him and held out my leather-patched forearm as he glided toward the *Maris Alarum*. But rather than land on my arm or on the port gunwale, he docked atop the mast; he was clearly still angry with me. I tried to coax him down and made offerings of grapes and peas, but to no avail. In time Bubo carked two simple words – *No Land* –but then shunned me again. I sensed that he might not have returned had he found somewhere else to perch for the night.

By and by I left the food in a bowl on deck, and retreated to my hammock. I was pleased to have Bubo back, but sensed that he was close to departing forever. I vowed not to touch a drop of wine that evening.

As I lay, sober and relieved that Bubo had returned, my mind searched for direction. I knew that I had treated Bubo poorly, but told myself that the words had come from the wine, not from me. Yet I had to concede that it was I, Fintan McAdam, who had poured the drink down my throat.

Much of my drinking, whether rum, gin or bird-wine, had been necessary to soften the blow from the loss of my beloved, and to slow and steel my heart after the evil visions. But as I lay contemplating the near loss of my bird mate, I gradually realised that the cure was giving rise to more troubles than it was solving.

Many examples sprang easily to mind: stealing the rowboat in London - I was only larking about after a few drafts of rum, and the vessel was all but sinking from neglect, but that one act of tomfoolery changed my life for the poorer; the lad who I nearly killed outside Ye Olde Mitre Tavern; falling from the pier in Oporto; drunkenly sailing into a waiting typhoon after the debacle of the brown-eyed girl at the bar.

Numerous times I had awoken with bruises and bumps, but with no knowledge of how they occurred. On many occasions I had only a distant recall of sullies and slurs that I had delivered from rum-loosened lips, or arguments settled with liquor-fuelled fists. Frequently on my ship, I had suffered grazed knuckles from fights with no-one but myself.

The drink had been like the old square of burlap cloth that I had once hung over my looking glass: it had prevented me from seeing myself as I was. The more I drunk, the more loosely I behaved, yet at the same time the liquor hid my actions from me by wiping them from my memory. I was a man who had never faced himself in the looking glass; I had never called myself to account for my own drunken deeds because I could not recount them. But this did not make them disappear; on the contrary, it encouraged them to mount. Now even Bubo was tallying my sins against me.

Suddenly I had a moment of clarity. I remembered that Papa used to say that if a friend betrayed you once then you should forgive him. If he betrayed you twice then you should give him a firm clip across the chin to see that it did not recur, but forgive him again. But if that friend betrayed you again and again and again then you should cast him away forever, because no good would come of the alliance.

It occurred to me that my relationship with liquor was like the third friend. Yes, the drink had helped me through hard times, softened some landings and provided a solace of sorts. It had also helped to ease the shaking palsy in my hands. But the drink had betrayed me more times than I could count. Even worse, it had not only made me betray myself, but had hidden those betrayals from me.

Acting quickly, before I could demur, I took the remaining crocks of wine and cast them into the sea. The liquor would enslave me no more.

Monday 20 August

I was pleased to see Bubo atop the mast when my morning head poked through the deck hatch. Although he still wasn't talking to me, at least he remained aboard my ship. I noted with relief that he had eaten my peace offerings.

The wind was still blowing from the east, so I took to the whipstaff and tacked often, trying to maintain the east in my bearing. For much of the night my mind had assailed me with a plethora of misgivings. Now, under the mottled blue skies and with the wind in my face, much of my journey came into stark focus.

My thoughts curled through a trellis of my recent life, starting with my time in the clink. After escaping Shepton to the sanctity of Liverpool, I foolishly made the decision to return to London, somehow reasoning

227

that returning home might stop my widower wounds from weeping. But the familiarity only made my mental cuts bleed more deeply, and the most accessible relief was to flee again.

But I can now see that trying to sail away from my memories was a haphazard way to recover from my loss. True, I had to leave in haste with the plod all but ensnaring me as I fled, but my plans were well set before Sergeant G. Jones first came knocking on Mrs Harlesden's door. Perhaps I pined for the sea because it had been like a balm after the deaths of my Mama and then my Papa.

Those spice runs had distracted me from my sadness. The ribaldry of ship life had been like a tonic to the despair that overcame me on both occasions. The daily rum rations, the bawdy singing and even the occasional fist fight took control of my meandering senses. In hindsight - which is now so clear it is as if I am peering through my telescope - I see that to launch solo across the oceans was a very different undertaking from crewing a merchant navy clipper. An evening draft of rum with a lively crew was a different beast to a crock taken solo in a cramped galley.

As the afternoon crept by, I thought further about my journey. When I had first arrived at Bird Rock, I had nearly bypassed it without more than a fleeting glance because of the lingering effects of the rum. I had gone ashore only to find Bubo and if not for his absence I would have missed it altogether. I would not have experienced the remarkable birds, their amazing plants, Diogo's tale, or repaired my mast. I probably would have starved to a slow and undignified death at sea.

Now I had similarly bypassed Boot Island after just one circumnavigation, ruled by a mind that had been pickled by wine. It seemed improbable, but there may have been something of interest in its interior. Although my clouded head had told me at the time not to waste time and effort in climbing those high walls, I had plenty of both 'time' and 'effort' at my disposal, for my constitution was strong and I had no chronological limits upon my journey. So despite having only a small chance of gain I had nothing to lose. Was this another poor decision by a liquor-dulled head that might cost me?

I had let better options in my life pass by me, or had fallen into them only by chance. I was not going to make the same mistake again.

I turned my ship about, set the downwind sails wing-to-wing, and made fast for Boot Island.

Tuesday 21 August

Some say that if at first success does not find you then you should look for her again. Others think that only a fool would repeat his actions and hope for a different outcome. After arriving back at Boot Island this morning I unfortunately saw most truth in the latter; nothing suggested that it held anything of interest.

I again circumnavigated the island and made minor adjustments to my earlier chart. Despite this unremarkable second look, I had already decided that I would be a fool not to explore further, so I anchored in the southern lee and rowed my tender for the lowest cliff.

Before commencing the climb, I donned my Fisherman's Friend cork jacket. The ascent was long –at least twenty yards of steep rock. Despite the assurance of the floating jacket, my ever-present fear of sharks and other sea-devils, not to mention the terrifying fall, ensured that I clung grimly to the rock face.

The August summer sun had baked the black rocks warm – not enough to cook bread by, but certainly enough to make the climb uncomfortable. My fingers sought crevices for they not only provided sure grip but also were cooler to the touch. Little by little, I forged my way up the cliff. I cursed good-naturedly at Bubo, who had simply flown to the cliff top and was awaiting my arrival.

By and by I heaved myself over the ledge. The cliff top upon which I sat formed a ridge perhaps thirty or forty yards wide. It was very uneven, with many loose rocks and boulders forming its surface. The ridge surrounded a large inland lagoon (Bubo was right). The water looked inky black from above, no doubt due to the deep reflections of the high, dark rock walls that surrounded it. It was as calm as a millpond, except in a few areas where bubbles broke the surface.

The lagoon lapped gently onto a small sandy beach below the western hill. Behind the beach, nested into the crib of the mountain, was a narrow green hinterland. It contained many trees, the taller of which I had earlier sighted from my ship, and a thick growth of other low vegetation. I clambered and climbed down the steep drop from the ridge to investigate this area further.

The beach sand was fine and white, and it squeaked as my boots trampled on it. The trees in the hinterland area were of three main varieties. The most common species was a type of clumping bamboo. I had seen similar specimens in the southern oceans on my previous travels. Their stems were thick and yellow, and were adorned by short green leaves. Many of the stalks had cracked away at the base, but the lagoon's rising tide must have floated the timber away because there was no detritus lying about. In fact the whole area looked neat, almost as prim as an English rose garden.

There were also a few dozen stout trees, each possessing a thick canopy of oval-shaped leaves. Some of their branches sported bulbous nut-like fruits, of which a small taste proved were bitter and vile. Even Bubo found them distasteful. Their thick trunks were most unusual for they displayed long, downward-spiralling scars in the bark. Perhaps some type of insect or parasite had attacked them, for each of these thick trees had a myriad of such peculiar marks upon it.

Finally and most strikingly, there were some extremely tall, thin-trunked palms. These trees stretched toward the clouds and were so supple that every wind shift made them rock and sway. Despite their age, they bent in the breeze like young green saplings. Some of the palms bore produce in their high canopies; one specimen in particular was loaded with half a dozen round coconuts. I have seen many varieties of palm on my travels but I have never encountered any as high and flexible as these.

An assortment of low shrubs and bushes nestled below the trees. One plant bore oval-shaped yellow fruit that was ridged along its sides. I plucked one from the bush and split it with my hands. Its cross section was shaped like a five-pointed star and had light green, watery flesh. I took a small bite and was pleasantly surprised at the sweet taste – hinting of melon and perhaps a little of peach. I took another, larger bite and gave the remainder to Bubo. I planned to harvest a crate of these sugary treats before I departed, for they provided a welcome change for my palate.

After exploring the narrow hinterland, I wandered down to the foreshore. The afternoon sun grew ever hotter so I removed my boots, rolled up my trousers and waded to shin height through the cool water. Gratefully, I splashed the water on my face and forehead, noting that it was salty, not fresh. I surmised that the ocean must feed the lagoon, not a spring; there must be a break in the cliff wall somewhere, but I could not see it. Perhaps a more thorough search later would reveal the opening.

One clear difference from Bird Rock was the abundance of natural critters. Dozens of small blue crabs dug themselves into the sand as I passed, and white legged lizards basked in the sun on the rock cliffs until my presence sent them scuttling into deeper crevices. I also spotted a small octopus in the shallows, but it squirted itself away before I could catch it with my hat. In contrast, the only living creatures that I had encountered on Bird Rock were the birds themselves. Perhaps the birds had, over the centuries, eaten all the other species to extinction until all that remained were their precious plants.

I ambled further along the beach. At the far end I noted a large patch of sea grasses and seaweed wafting in the shallows. Some small baitfish darted to and fro amongst the taller weeds. I nibbled on a thick leaf and found it salty and fishy to the taste. I finished eating the leaf and by the time I had devoured it the taste was passably pleasant. I meandered back, stopping occasionally to admire the grandeur of the scenery: the cool, calm lagoon, flanked by the hard black cliffs, which were in turn dwarfed by the western mountain. It was most serene, and it was only the relentless palsy in my hands that disturbed the moment at all. Even Bubo seemed captive to the tranquillity, and despite our recent differences he nestled himself into the crook of my arm.

Something cluttered behind of me, startling me from my reverie. I turned to see that two coconuts had fallen from a palm. Bubo and I retrieved the coconuts and then spent a simple hour stripping the hide from their exteriors to expose the shell inside. With a sharp rock, I punctured the tough casings and we each enjoyed a generous trickle of sweet milk. We then shattered the shell on the rocky cliff and nibbled upon the exposed meat. Bubo was *particularly* fond of coconut flesh. I shall have to harvest more before I depart to keep for him as a treat.

The sun dipped behind the western mountain, casting a long shadow over the lagoon and turning the bubbling water an even deeper black. We ate some more of the yellow star fruit and sat quietly together as the sun disappeared. As the stars came out Bubo flew off to a tree to roost. By and by I set my hat and the fisherman's friend vest on the sand and lay myself down for the evening.

*

Deep in the night, I was awoken by a splash. I bolted upright. Under the light of the near-full moon I could see ripples extending across the lagoon from the shoreline, confirming that I had not imagined the noise. I sat for a long while in the still of the night but neither heard nor saw anything else. By and by I drifted back to sleep, though I was flighty to any further noises and therefore slept fittingly.

Wednesday 22 August

I awoke lying on the soft white sand with Bubo pecking my ear. He had clearly been awake for some time and was pining for company.

Gaard maarn, he chirped.

"Good morning Bubo," I mumbled incoherently, for the night remained in my voice. By and by I sat up and gratefully bit into the star fruit that Bubo had fetched me.

"Would you like to climb the mountain with Captain Rum?" I asked as I swung my arm to the west.

Bubo twisted his neck about and then swivelled it back the other way, and then tilted his head.

"Maybe we could climb the mountain and look for more land," I suggested.

Bubo fly. No land.

I chewed thoughtfully at the last portion of star fruit. It was easy to forget that Bubo could fly – a hard day's climb for me was just a brief jaunt for him. But I was nevertheless determined to climb the peak, and so had soon strapped on my boots and was picking my way up the steep ragged mountain.

I wish I could report that the climb was worthwhile, but the truth told a different tale. After hiking for most of the morning and scrambling up ever-steeper grades, I summited just before noon. I saw little of consequence during my climb: just a few lizards, a nest of honey ants, a small flock of seagull-like birds, and a scattering of shrubs and hardy plants. As Bubo predicted, the view from the summit contained nothing but endless ocean and a hot blue sky.

I did not dally at the top, for my thirst was growing. I traversed to the eastern side, hoping for some respite from the afternoon heat during my descent, but the sun was high and cast only a small shadow. After an hour, I spotted some green lichen growing on the lower northern face and altered the course of my downward trek to intercept it. I was rewarded by a trickle of water that I gratefully cupped into my hands to drink. I followed the watercourse downward and eventually found a small rock pool filled to the brim with clear water that I greedily lapped. The sun was now low in the sky and a cool breeze was up, so I paused for a while to rest my fatigued, trembling knees. When combined with the palsy in my hands, I now shook from top to toe like a fiddler's bow.

After a good rest, I finished the last 50 yards of my descent down to the lagoon. This last walk was undemanding, because nature had contrived to form a series of rocky steps down to the northern end of the beach. They were most convenient. My stomach was growling, for the day's exertions had been taxing, so I plucked a handful of thick seaweed leaves from the shallow lagoon bed and rolled them like a gentlemen's cigar before eating them raw. I followed up with half a dozen star fruits for supper.

I hoped to find another coconut, for its milk was sweet and nutritious. However none had fallen. The nuts were too high for me to dislodge by throwing stones at them, so I tried shaking a tree at the base but to no avail. I also attempted to climb a trunk, but after 20 feet (only 80 feet to go!) it was clear that these trees were far too high and wavering to ascend. I found it impossible to keep a firm grip when the shaft flexed under my weight, leaving me alternately hanging below it or swinging beside it. A stout ship's mast was difficult to climb, but these trees were doubly as devilish; they were nigh upon impossible to scale.

I was contemplating returning to the *Maris Alarum* when Bubo flew to join me. After explaining my problem, Bubo simply flew to the canopy and had soon dislodged two coconuts with his powerful talons, which we duly enjoyed as dessert.

After eating my fill and leaving the rest to Bubo, who was inordinately pleased by my gift, I ambled across to examine the thick-trunked trees further, for their spiral welts intrigued me. With a sharp rock, I prodded into the scars trying to dislodge an insect, for I was keen to see what miniature beast would cause such marks. Some sticky white sap trickled out and ran down the diagonal scar before congealing into a pliable lump. Apart from that I found no insects or other creatures; nothing at all to suggest what had made these welts.

The tide was now high, and tiny waves lapped all the way up to the hinterland as the purple sky deepened to black. I laid my hat and vest below one of the stout trees and settled in for the evening, talking quietly with Bubo in the branches above as we drifted into sleep.

*

Captain Rum! Captain Rum!

I awoke suddenly to Bubo's night-time cry. Instantly I leaped to my feet and sought him from among the branches above.

Captain Rum! He screeched again, sounding even more desperate amidst the still quiet of the lagoon.

"What is it Bubo?" I asked. "What's wrong?"

Aaark!

Suddenly I heard a splash from the beach. I turned sharply to see a dark shape disappear into the shallow water and swim away. If I had been alone then I would have assumed that my dreams had been playing nocturnal tricks upon me, or that I was having a strange vision. However Bubo's warning, and the deep ripples now fanning across the lagoon, assured me that something had definitely been prowling about the shallow waters.

Judging by the size of the splash, the creature was large. Was it an alligator? Or perhaps a marine mammal of sorts, like a porpoise or sea cow? Or even — I hoped not - a shark.

"What did you see Bubo?"

Animal he said, before adding enigmatically *Captain Rum.*

'Animal' was Bubo's catch-all phrase for any living creature other than a bird, a fish, or myself. I had to know more.

"What did it look like? Did the animal have a fin?" I asked, mimicking a fin on my back to aid his comprehension. *No.*

"Or large teeth?" I questioned, pointing to my own. *No.*

"Or a long snout?" *No.*

"Did it have a tail?" *No tail.*

No fins, teeth, snout or tail. So it was not a fish, porpoise or alligator. Perhaps it was sea cow, or even a small whale caught in the shallows.

"Why did the animal make a splash Bubo? Did it jump out of the water? Why did it suddenly swim away?"

I eked an answer, phrase by phrase, from Bubo.

Animal walk ... Bubo call ... Animal swim.

I was now even more confused: the creature could walk? What sort of sea creature could walk? Was it perhaps a large sea turtle coming ashore to lay?

"How did it walk Bubo? Did it use flippers to push itself up the beach?" I asked as I inelegantly mimed the action.

Then Bubo said some words that kept me awake for the rest of the night, and have haunted me since.

Walk legs. And then, even more eerily: *Captain Rum walk legs. Animal walk legs.*

Thursday 23 August

The sky was still a deep mauve colour when I arose. My mind needed answers, and sleep was not a happy bedfellow of a worried mind.

Keeping my eyes trained on the lagoon, which soon began glowing pink in the morning light, I walked along the beach to the southern end. Apart from a few wafting reeds and an occasional bubbling shimmer, it looked still and empty. I could see no sign of the mysterious creature. Yet somewhere in that innocuous-looking pond was a clue as to what had emerged over the past two nights. To find this creature was now paramount in my mind, for it might be either nutritious or deadly, but at present I did not know which of these two extremes.

After climbing the steep rise to the surrounding cliff-top, I walked along the ridge, aiming to traverse its entire length to view the lagoon from all vantage points. The path was rocky and difficult, with its loose boulders making the going difficult. At frequent intervals I stopped to survey the water, searching for any sign of movement. But its inky blackness betrayed nothing.

The sun was high and hot by the time I reached the halfway point at the ridge's eastern end. I sat to rest, taking in the full majesty of the western mountain from this farthest viewpoint. Beads of sweat trickled down my forehead; I was looking forward to a long pull of fresh water from the rock pond that awaited my return.

Bubo flew to join me. I quizzed him again about the creature but he could add little more than what he had already told me. My curiosity grew by the minute, but fear also cultivated itself as well; at this point the former just outweighed the latter, so I pressed on in my exploration. But still I saw nothing unexpected. After another hour or so spent clambering along the ragged ridge top I was wilting from the heat, so I lowered myself down some large boulders toward the lagoon. Although only a fool would swim in unknown waters - particularly with a mystery creature dwelling within - a cold splash of water would be most welcome.

The tide was at its lowest ebb as I dropped onto an outcrop near water level. I cupped the cool water in my hands and tipped it onto my head and neck. I let the water run down my back, enjoying the fresh relief. It was just as I threw my head back that I glanced something unusual just below the waterline: a piece of bamboo.

Ordinarily a length of bamboo floating in a lagoon would be no cause for attention. I had seen cracked bases on the hinterland bamboo trees and so I expected to see some stray or floating stalks. However this piece differed markedly: it was tied to the rock face by strips of rope.

This sighting spiked a cavalcade of thoughts. Why was a piece of bamboo tied to a rock, on the outskirts of a lagoon, on an otherwise barren and isolated island? This was clearly a deliberate arrangement. More importantly, who, or what, had placed it there? And when? With a sudden need for answers driving me, I hurriedly clambered over to investigate.

The bamboo emerged from within a jumble of boulders on the cliff face. From there it angled down, disappearing into the lagoon. This structure was certainly not natural –the bamboo had been positioned with intent, and with considerable difficulty. I used a sharp piece of shell to cut away the tag end of the rope and inspected it more closely. I frayed apart one end and discovered that it was made of woven fibres, probably stripped palm leaves. The strands were covered by a thick whitish substance into which the water did not penetrate, but simply slid off, leaving the surface with a dull, dry sheen. The sap from the bulbous trees came quickly to mind.

Had human beings lived on this island before? It seemed unlikely, but no other explanation was possible.

I cast my eyes along the waterline for more evidence of bamboo. With this purposeful gaze, I soon saw what the tide had previously covered: half a dozen bamboo lengths spearing downward into the lagoon, just below the waterline. With trepidation I followed one bamboo strip through the water with my hands, but felt naught before my reach – and my nerve – were exhausted. I contemplated diving into the lagoon and pulling myself downward along its length, but the thought of the resident creature weighed too heavily upon my mind.

Despite the heat, a deep shiver cut through me as I reviewed my knowledge of Boot Island. First, the visits of the night creature: I had heard it twice and seen the ripples of its water entry, and despite the darkness of the night, Bubo had sighted it with his keen gaze. Second, the bamboo struts: they had been positioned with intent in the water, patently a work of intelligence. Third, the bamboo tethering rope: it was a dextrous piece of weaving requiring great skill to plait, and the knowledge to harvest and apply the waterproof coating.

Suddenly I was certain: mankind had been to Boot Island before. But where had they gone? Had the creature – or creatures, for I now realised there may be more than one - destroyed them? Or eaten them? Were the creatures still here?

Fear suddenly coursed through me, instantly overtaking curiosity as my driving emotion. Without further pause, I scrambled to the ridge top and skirted my way along it as quickly as my inelegant boulder hopping would allow. Eventually, with bloodied shins and scraped knees, I arrived on the ridge-top that overlooked my tender. In a trice I had scaled my way down, almost falling twice such was my haste, and then rowed hurriedly back to the *Maris Alarum*.

I called for Bubo. As soon as he landed I ushered him below deck and battened the hatches tightly. We spent the night cocooned on board my ship, but despite the familiar surroundings I slept little for the second night in a row.

I pined for some liquor to ease my thoughts. But there was none.

Friday 24 August

I sat on the deck of the *Maris Alarum* in morning's first light, waiting for the tide to drop; a lower sea level would allow me to better view the mysterious bamboo poles. I had determined that my best approach was to row around the outside of the island, particularly in the calmer southern waters. In this way I could survey the island more closely without exposing myself to the dangers of the lagoon creature. The bamboo struts that pierced through the boulders must start somewhere, and I was determined to find that source.

By and by the ebbing tide fell away. After donning my cork vest for safety, I rowed with Bubo along the long southern edge of Boot Island. Before long I spotted a length of bamboo running horizontally, just below the waterline. Ordinarily a sailor would pass by it without a second glance, but now that I was seeking it, the cylindrical shape was clear against the black rock. It would have been difficult to spot at any time other than this very low tide.

I fastened my tender. After surveying the nearby seas for sharks or other sea-demons, I slid my hands onto the bamboo, following it along in the water. About an arm's length under the surface, I felt the first of many surprises for this day: this horizontal pole was but one of many. A quiver of bamboo poles ran along the rocky walls, just below the water's surface. My mind twisted and tumbled relentlessly as to their purpose, but every explanation seemed absurd in the extreme.

I rowed further along the cliff wall, and soon saw a deep vertical fissure in the rock. I edged my tender as close as the choppy swell would allow, from where I could see that several of the bamboo poles turned and ran upwards, inside the crack, toward the cliff tops, at which point they disappeared into the jumbled rock atop the ridge. Some further investigating showed a similar arrangement at another fissure further to the east.

I guessed that the bamboo poles were being used as a type of pipe, perhaps to pump water into the lagoon. But why? Surely a far simpler method of filling the lagoon could be devised – simply tunnelling a hole through the cliff wall would achieve the same outcome for far less effort. Perhaps they were to somehow pump water out. But if they were merely to pump water, then why did the horizontal pipes all head to the west? I rowed my tender in that direction where I hoped an answer waited, for this was the greatest mystery I had encountered in all my travels.

The mountain soon loomed large, and before long I heard the crash of waves into the western rocks, and felt the cool fleck of ocean spray on my forehead. The swell grew too intimidating for my little rowboat and I did not want to proceed further for fear of capsizing. Instead I fastened my tender to an outcrop and started stepping my way from rock to rock along the cliff face, much as I had done previously on Bird Rock.

The cliff was slippery from the sea spray, so I was in constant fear of falling into the rough ocean below. By and by I retreated, returned to my tender and tied a long length of rope to my vest and the other to a cleat on the transom[172] so that if I tumbled into the sea I could hopefully pull myself to safety before the waves, or the sea-devil sharks, finished me off.

Anxiety churned inside me as I worked my way around the headland. Below me, the waves crashed into the cliffs, smashing them with increasingly brutal force. Despite my earlier precautions I doubted that I could survive the ocean's maelstrom if I fell from the rocks, for waves would smite me against the cliff face within seconds. Slowly, with fear as my moderator, I inched my way down toward the waterline. My knuckles were white and my forearm muscles swelled due to their overly-firm grip on the slippery rock. Although a possible answer to the mystery lay below me, my terror was so great that I could barely look down.

---

[172] The *transom* is the rear wall of the boat

By and by I reached a small ledge about 10 feet above the ferocious waves. Although precariously perched, the platform was large enough that I could stand freely, so I took some time to rest. As I stood rubbing my weary forearms, I noticed a peculiar hissing noise above the waves, accompanied by a wooden-sounding click. Both sounds were rhythmic and seemed synchronous with the crashing waves. After regaining my nerve I peered over the edge, expecting to see more pipes. Instead I received yet another surprise.

Each bamboo pipe terminated at an odd apparatus that floated just below the water's surface. They appeared to be large bags of woven fibre, each about the size of a sheep. On closer inspection I noted that each sack had a short length of bamboo pipe protruding upward. I estimated that there were perhaps three dozen of these strange structures bobbing just below the surging waves.

I slapped my own cheeks to ensure that my mind was in unison with my senses. Woven bags floating near an otherwise empty island? If I encountered a porpoise tucked into bed at London's Royal Infirmary, or a cow merrily riding a bicycle down Holborn High St, I could scarcely be more surprised. The bags seemed incongruous to the point of impossibility. Yet what else could I do but believe my own eyes? Not for the first time on this journey, I wished for another man to be my witness, if only to reassure me that my senses were true.

After pausing for a while, I realised that I had seen these strange objects earlier from the *Maris Alarum*, but had dismissed them as mere debris amongst the pounding waves. I looked further, hoping for some explanation as to what I was observing, but I could no more discern the purpose of these floating bags than I could open one of Harrison's time pieces and understand the meshing of its cogs and wheels. The hissing and clicking sounds continued, but did not illuminate me any further. After a long delay to allow reason to do its work, I realised that I could not solve this puzzle by thought alone; I would have to examine one of the bags directly.

But how could I reach one? I could not climb down any further, for the surface was devilishly slippery and devoid of further footholds. I could not leap into the water, for the heaving waves would smash my head on the rocks within seconds. I was a mere 10 feet above the ocean's surface but the bags may as well have been in Africa, such was my difficulty in reaching them.

I called to Bubo, who was lazily gliding above the cliffs. He arrived presently.

"Bubo," I said. "Fetch Captain Rum some wire from the ship."

After only a few repetitions – fetch wire - he seemed to understand my meaning, and with a cark he flew off toward the nearby *Maris Alarum*. A few minutes later he returned, clutching a small roll of wire in his talons.

"You're a good pet," I said softly, ruffling his hackles as a reward for his service. "Captain Rum will give you some extra coconut this evening."

Bubo looked on inquisitively as I bent one end of the wire into a hook. I had soon formed the shape to my satisfaction and lowered it toward the floating bags. With great patience, I manoeuvred the hook until it was around the end of one of the bamboo pipes. This task is written simply, but in truth it was frustrating and ungainly, for the waves thundering into the bags made it a true test of perserverence. Not only that, but the shaking palsy in my hands had started again, making delicate manoeuvring all but impossible.

When the hook was finally in place I tugged at the wire and was pleased to note that the bag structure, with its attendant bamboo pipe, slowly rose from the ocean. Deliberately, I raised it toward me and soon the whole apparatus, with its bamboo pipe still attached and trailing into the sea, was safe in my keeping.

I examined the apparatus methodically. The bag was skilfully woven from palm fronds and coated with the white material that repelled water – the same substance that had been used on the ropes. I looked more closely at the repelling material and scraped off a small wedge. It was springy and pliable to touch, and reminded me of a substance popularised by Mr. Priestly[173] in London, which he used for erasing the marks of graphite pencil upon paper. He called it a "rubber". (I had seen their like at Whittow & Harris's Art supplies in Holborn.) Almost certainly, the substance had been obtained from the thick-trunked trees, for there seemed no other source on this remote cay.

---

[173] Joseph Priestly (1733-1804) was a scientist who not only discovered oxygen, but pioneered the use of rubber.

The bag apparatus was constructed in a "V" shape, with timber reinforcing on two sides. The long bamboo pipe entered from one end, and a shorter pipe protruded from the top; its length was sufficient to keep its opening above the ocean swell. A rock weight hung just below the apparatus, no doubt to ensure its correct floating orientation. When viewed as a whole the apparatus best resembled an odd set of oversized fireplace bellows.

I pushed the sides of the V together and heard a small click. As I released the sides, the V expanded to its full width, accompanied by a hissing noise of airflow. The bag seemed to be drawing in air. But why? I had to know more, so I carefully dissembled the bag and peered inside. The sack contained an odd, oblique configuration of sticks, held together by twists of fine rope and thick hinges of the rubber material. It soon became evident that this arrangement functioned as a type of spring to force the V wings apart. The final parts of the structure were two flat discs- perhaps they were shells – that were also covered in the white rubber material, which covered the pipe openings. I soon discerned that they acted as simple valves, alternately sealing one pipe or the other.

An operative trial demonstrated that the apparatus was indeed similar to a set of bellows. When the V wings were compressed –a function admirably performed by the crashing of the relentless waves below me – the bellows pumped air into the long bamboo pipe. Then, as the wave receded, the spring inside would expand, drawing air in through the top opening.

Satisfied that I now understood the workings of the sea bellows, I repaired it to its original condition and dropped it off the ledge, whereupon it fell in among the other floats and resumed its duties. I watched for some time as the waves crashed against the bobbing bellows, shunting them closed and sending blasts of air back toward the lagoon.

I was certainly pleased to have developed an understanding of the mysterious apparatus, but the answering of this first puzzle raised dozens of questions that were far more difficult to answer, particularly: Why? Why would anyone build a system to pump air into the lagoon? Had there been men here in the past who had made it, or did the legged creature from the lagoon create it?

Despite these presently unanswerable questions, two facts lay themselves bare. First, this system was obviously the work of an intelligent and dextrous being. Second, there were no human dwellings on the island - no housing or shelter, not even a cave – meaning that if mankind had built this system they had since departed, or had been wiped out. My mind spun with improbable possibilities and impossible probabilities.

I simply could not comprehend the enormity of what I had observed. I returned to the *Maris Alarum* to think. Like a stomach after a big feast, my head was full with mystery and I could force in no more strangeness until I had digested this lot.

Saturday 25 August

The first task I set myself this morning was to explore the north-western side of the island, to which I had paid scant attention so far. It took only a few hours to satisfy myself that it was similar to the south-western coastline, with an arrangement of pipes and large floating bellows pumping air into the lagoon.

On my return I rowed past the Eastern horn, where I noted a broad gaping hole in the rock face. Above the waterline it was about the size of large horse-drawn carriage, and appeared to extend even further below the surface. The tide flowed quickly through the gap, showing that it was clearly the entry and exit point of the lagoon waters. Without this fracture the interior of the island would be dry, and would more closely resemble Bird Rock.

I returned to my mother ship, where I hit an impasse in my mind. I had fully explored the island from outside, and could learn no more about it from the relative comfort and safety of the *Maris Alarum*. Yet if I entered the lagoon then I would again expose myself to the lagoon creature, which might yet prove hostile.

I looked down my hands and noticed that they were shaking again. I did not think that this was fear, but another case of the shaking palsy. I cursed myself for casting away my medicine like useless jetsam, because I could certainly do with a mug of wine now, both to help my hands and to aid my thinking. I had a cursory search through the galley for any missed crocks, but in my heart I knew that there was none. Instead I made a cup of tea, which helped fleetingly, and then retired to my hammock to think.

I passed the afternoon anxiously. Should I simply leave and sail on toward Africa? Or should I stay and try to discover more about this baffling island and its ominous inhabitant? Although I considered myself a contender for most challenges thrown in my path, I conceded that fear was rapidly cultivating within me and might soon overflow to my gills. The lure of a quiet day at sea, lazily tacking into the breeze, with no dread of the lagoon-creature, called at me loudly. *"The simple life is best for you, McAdam,"* the voice instructed. *"You will achieve nothing but a frightening and lonely death by poking a sea creature from its nightly slumber."*

Several times I moved to cast away, but something stopped me. It was not a reasoned voice with a logical counterview, but just a vague feeling in my cockles that I should stay and not shirk the challenge. Although the feeling was indistinct, in time it balanced the reasoned arguments of the voice. After all, if I had wanted to avoid situations like this I could have staying in England, drinking rum and playing whist at Blackfriars. At least, I thought, my decisions were arising from a sober and reasoned mind, and were not liquor-soaked reactions, or decisions made from a heavy, crusty-eyed morning head.

Yet despite my sobriety, I remained mired in a swamp of inaction. My heart told me to stay, but my head told me to stay *away* from that island. Paralysed by these balancing forces, I barely moved from my hammock all day.

In the evening I sat with Bubo in front of the fire, even though the night was warm outside. We said little. I drank many cups of tea, for its bitterness provided me with some unidentifiable solace, although the persistent shaking in my hands made it difficult to sip without scalding my lips. It was very late before I fell asleep, none the wiser for a course of action.

Sunday 26 August

I spent the morning on my ship, still considering my next action. If I could take just a mug or two of liquor then the answer would appear.

But there was none, so I simply sat on deck and let my mind sort through the rabble on its own.

By and by, some aspects became clearer. If I stayed, then I would have to go inside the island's walls, for I could learn nothing more from the deck of my ship. But to do so would open myself to attack by the creature, who must be growing bolder. If the creature attacked me I was unsure that I could escape the confines of the surrounding cliffs quickly enough, for the climb was a steep one of 20 yards. To place myself in that indefensible position was to invite danger to dinner.

I tried to talk with Bubo – as much to verbalise my thoughts as for any other reason - but understandably he could not appreciate my vexation. I had another mug of tea. In time I climbed to deck, where the sun was bright and the air was clear. I looked across at Boot Island's foreboding walls. They looked so inhospitable. Some white gulls were circling above the cliffs, gliding freely and easily as they searched for scraps of food in the crevices. How serene they looked. I sat for some time just looking at the simple birds going about their day.

The gulls reminded me of my time after leaving Oporto. I recalled sitting in this same position on the deck doing the same thing: observing the gulls as they flew about my ship. I fetched my journal and re-read the passage:

Mostly I now feel happy, for whenever the salt air is in my chest and the sun is on my back, I feel like I am flying as high as the gulls that glide beside my ship. I thought back to the louts and laggards who lined the London alleyways: every man owned such a pair of wings, but it was a pity that most men had not discovered how to fly with them.

Suddenly I realised: I was right. I *had* wings – not just the water wings of my dreams, but a pair of broad feathered wings that would set me free if I let them. I was not a lout or laggard but Captain Fintan McAdam, commander of the *Maris Alarum*. I had sailed halfway across the Atlantic; I had survived a wild sea typhoon as ferocious as had ever beset itself upon a ship; I had not only repaired my mast but had done so with a tree I had nurtured myself. I was strong, assured, and above all, unaffected by the drink.

The answer was suddenly clear in my heart as well as my mind: if I wanted to see the creature, which I most assuredly did, then I had to go back to the lagoon. If I didn't then I was a <u>weakly wingless coward who should have stayed in London</u>.[174]

I packed two pistols with black powder and sheathed my scimitar about my waist. Ten minutes later, I stood upon the white beach sands of Boot Island, with my loyal bird perched on my shoulder.

*

The stars had rotated a quarter of a turn around Polaris when I felt my eyelids dropping. Despite my trepidation, three nights of flitting slumber was taking its tithe. I fought to stay awake, but the heaviness of my eyes had even more persistence than my fear.

"Bubo," I whispered. "Captain Rum is going to sleep. Please watch the lagoon." I indicated as such with my arms until he understood.

It was just before dawn when I felt a pang in my left ear lobe. Bubo was biting me. My eyes shot open and took a while to adjust to the light. When they did, I received such a surprise that I am yet to recover from it. The creature had emerged from the lagoon. It was standing still just 10 feet away looking directly at me.

The creature was human.

Female human.

My head twitched in surprise, which was enough to startle the woman-creature. She leapt back into the water and disappeared below the inky black surface as my startled cry echoed across the lagoon.

Monday 27 August

I sat on the beach until the sun rose. I no longer felt any fear in my bones, for my disbelief would not allow any other emotion to take a foothold. Bubo had long since deserted me, for I could no more carry a conversation with him than jump over a star. To him I must have appeared like a blind deaf-mute; my eyes gazed into empty space, no words passed my lips and no sounds entered my ears. I was, in short, so distracted by my obsession with the woman-creature that it had turned me into a simpleton.

---

[174] McAdam heavily accented this underlining in his journal.

By and by I meandered across the beach and then somehow climbed up and over the ridge to my tender. In hindsight, it was a considerable achievement that I arrived back at my ship without losing my way, for my mind was numb.

I lay on my hammock, trying to comprehend what I had witnessed. A woman-creature! On this most desolate of islands, in the dark of night, she had emerged from a black lagoon, twisting my sensibilities like a thousand tangled fishing lines. *Was she a mermaid*? I have heard of such creatures on my travels, and some old sea-dogs attest to having sighted one, but I had always believed that they were nothing but the fantasy of a deprived mind. Surely my own mind was not so wanting of company that it had invented some for me.

I know I have had the visions of Beth – hundreds of them – but this sighting was different. I was *not* imaging it - Bubo had seen her too. Surely the devil could not be cavorting inside the mind of a bird. Yet if she was not a mermaid and not a fantasy creation of my own mind, then what could she be? Her appearance posed so many conundrums. If she was human, then where did she live? I had seen no sign of shelter, nor was there a boat, or any other sign of transportation or habitation. Was she alone? I had seen no other. Could she talk? *Would* she talk?

At least this creature had answered one question with certainty: I was right to have stayed on at Boot Island. Africa could wait. I needed to learn everything about the woman-mermaid-being, regardless of the cost.

I have risked far more, for less.

*

It was late afternoon before I had regained enough sensibility to determine my best course of action. I packed a square of canvas with an offering of provisions: a bread roll, a handful of peas, some pickled fish and two tomatoes. Carrying my pistols tied in a scarf about my neck and with my scimitar hanging from my belt, I rowed for Boot Island. After scrambling up, over and down the perimeter cliff I arrived at the narrow beach, where I formed a mound of sand at its head. I laid my offering on this makeshift altar, and then beat a hasty retreat back to the *Maris Alarum*. The woman creature must know that I come in peace.

247

Tuesday 28 August

In the morning, I dispatched Bubo to Boot Island. He returned a few minutes later reporting that the woman-creature had partially accepted my offering: she had taken the tomatoes, bread and peas, but had left the fish untouched. I made a small pouch containing another food offering and sent Bubo to the beach with it.

I remained on the *Maris Alarum* all day. I achieved little for my mind remained wrought with the woman and nothing else.

Wednesday 29 August

The mermaid again took the tomatoes and peas from the parcel, but this time she ignored the bread as well as the fish. Bubo ate the leftovers for his breakfast. I hoped that my gifts had demonstrated to the woman-creature that I meant no harm. Tonight I will try to meet her again.

*

I sat on the sand in the deepening dusk. I carried my weapons concealed, but left the food parcel on open display upon a sand altar.

The stars wheeled slowly across the sky as I stared at the black lagoon. A gibbous moon, one week waned from full, rose in the east. Finally, deep into the night, a ripple appeared on the surface. I was taken aback by this simple occurrence. Could it be a sign of the mermaid-creature returning? In a trice I had an answer, for she emerged seamlessly from the lagoon, creating barely a splash as she slid upright. She stood, facing me directly, in knee-deep water.

Against the backing moonlight I could discern only her silhouette - her narrow waist recalled a timing glass. Oh, but what a fine figure she possessed - any man with at least one eye would think the same, but for a sailor alone at sea for months - well, her body stole my vision like a lodestone draws a nail. After a long and breathless pause, she took a half step toward me. I dared not even twitch an eyebrow lest my movement frighten her back to the water. Yet I felt my hand unconsciously tighten around my pistol grip, for I knew nothing of the woman's powers.

She hesitantly took another step forward. She seemed to be trying to make out my features – all the while I was doing the same to her. I saw that she wore a band of cloth around her waist and another strip around her torso. She flicked her hair from her face. Her locks were wet and straight and dark – brown or black I was unsure –and so long that they hung to her waist. It was too dark to discern her facial features, except for her high cheekbones, which caught the moonlight.

Silence washed over the lagoon. Even the lapping waves seemed aware that they should be silent. Neither of us moved - she, perhaps, from fear, and I because this creature utterly spellbound me.

By and by she stepped toward me again. Now she was fully out of the water, so her feet were visible. I saw that she had no fish tail like the mermaids of legend, but human ankles and toes. She had no gills, but woman's nose and mouth and lips. Clearly, this being before me was no mermaid and no lagoon creature. She was a human being, as mortal as I was.

Still entranced, but emboldened by her humanity, I held out my hand toward the small parcel of food. She did not move. I stared at her and she at me.

"Take it," I whispered.

She looked at me, her brow furrowing, but she dared come no closer.

"Take it. This food is for you," I whispered again. Still she did not flinch. Slowly, almost imperceptibly, I stepped forward, and then pitched the small parcel gently onto the ground. Barely had it touched the sand when she had pounced upon it, swivelled, dived into the lagoon and disappeared into the dark water.

I vaulted to the water's edge but could see nothing. In a trice she was gone leaving nothing; nothing but footprints in the wet sand. I watched the water's surface for a long while, expecting that she would surface for a breath, but saw not even a ripple.

Thursday 30 August

I spent my day on the *Maris Alarum*. The lagoon woman imbued every thought and permeated every daydream. I tried to sleep but could not; I performed menial chores but had no heart; I played the Pairs game with

Bubo but was devoid of spirit. The lagoon woman filled my being. She had accepted my gift. I *had* to meet with her again.

But would such a fair maiden fall in with an old jack tar like myself? After six weeks without bathing or grooming, my mirror did not tell a happy tale. I stropped a razor to a keen edge and then lathered my pears bar to foaming. With deliberate strokes, I shaved myself clean, and then used the same razor to trim my hair to an agreeable crop. I washed my vest and jacket in some soapy water, and rubbed a little charcoal into worn spots on my boots and belt. By and by the reflection improved its report, and by late afternoon, under the forgiving light of my tallow lamp, I had convinced the looking glass that I resembled, barely, a gentleman.

I spent the last hours of the day simply sitting on deck, with my back against the mast, waiting. Oh, but how I wished I could have sped the sun across the sky, and cast a net over the eastern horizon and pulled the stars above it. The wait was an impost that I dearly wanted to end, but the stronger my yearning, the slower time seemed to plod.

Finally the sun dropped and the sky darkened. I prepared a food parcel, shouldered my arms, and was soon on the beach, nervously fidgeting with anticipation. I laid my weapons under a green shrub behind me, taking care to prop the pistols up out of the sand, and then set the food parcel in front of me as before. Then, as I had done all day, I waited.

My chin was nodding on my breastbone when she finally appeared. I jerked my head up to see her standing upon the wet sand, her body outlined against the blue starlight. Her splendour hit me like a hammer on an egg. For some time I could do nothing but stare. Stare and desire. Desire and want. Want and wish.

"Hello," I whispered by and by.

Her head cocked at the sound of my voice, but she made no other movement.

"Hello," I repeated, adding a gentle wave of my hand. Then I gestured to the food parcel in front of me.

"For you."

She fixed her gaze intently upon the parcel. In time she took a small step forward, but then hesitated, timid, like an untamed beast. Suddenly her gaze shifted to the trees behind me, and her brow dipped in consternation. I twisted my neck to investigate. In but a trice she pounced on the food, and by the time I realised that she had tricked me she was already in the water.

"Come back," I hollered, futilely. I ran to the water's edge and charged in, boots and all. I dove as far as I could, my hands flailing about for her, but I encountered nothing but water. The horror of my ice-cold plunge into the Thames jolted my mind, but I shunted that vision aside and flayed my way into the darkness. That woman must be in here somewhere, and she could not stay under water indefinitely – I just had to find her.

With my eyes opened widely, I plunged my head under the water, searching for a glimpse of the woman, but could see nothing through the brine under the grey-blue light of the night. I stood to my feet, gasped for air, and then stroked again, floundering through the water like a wheat thresher. However I soon realised my folly, because without my cork jacket I was barely able to float much less catch the woman, who could obviously swim as if she was born a fish.

Suddenly I felt a firm grip clamp around my left leg. I looked down through the shallow water where I saw not the long-haired woman, but two large shadowy figures. I kicked hard with my right leg but one of the shadows locked on it as well. I thrashed down with my fists connecting solidly with, I think, a shoulder. I tried to kick my legs free, but within a trice my ankles were bound by rope. The shadows then pulled me underwater, where I swung my fists in a flurry of punches. But I could not land a telling blow for the water slowed my movements and stole my balance, and the shadows slid and dodged through the water like sea devils.

With a bursting chest I sprung upward off the lagoon floor, propelling myself toward the surface, where I gasped a lung full of air. In the split second that my head was above the water, I saw and heard Bubo above me, wildly squawking and carking in anger. I sensed that he tried to attack the lagoon shadow-men with his beak and talons, but after that I know nothing for I was dragged under the water. Desperately I lashed my elbows and fists wildly downward, but could score nothing but water-softened blows upon my assailants. One attacker latched onto my left arm and soon had my wrist twisted behind my back. I tried to push my attacker away, but the water would grant me no traction. My head was forced under the surface where I could just discern their dark humanoid shapes through the flurry of white bubbles.

I fought with all my being to escape. But with just one untethered arm with which to attack, I was rapidly losing the battle. I struggled upward toward air but could not force my head high enough. Then one of the figures appeared in front of me and twisted my free arm like a spring. Soon my arms were bound; I was now fully trussed like a slaughtered hog.

I could not fight. I could not swim for the surface. I could not breathe. I was utterly at the mercy of the lagoon men. I ceased struggling, for my efforts were achieving naught but wasting my air. Then the two dark figures grasped under my shoulders and mercilessly pulled me toward the depths of the lagoon, intent upon drowning me in this cold black void.

Deeper and deeper into the dark water they dragged me, like two netherworld rowboats towing a broken galleon to Hades. I could not attack or resist. A hand clamped over my mouth, and although I knew that breathing would only fill my lungs with choking water, I shook my head violently and bit at the hand to try to dislodge it. But my assailant's grip was too firm and this final resistance was in vain. I realised the futility of any further struggle and fully surrendered. At this point, I knew only one thing: I was about to die.

We surged deeper. My ears stung, but the pain barely registered. My eyes clouded with grey. My ribs and stomach cramped as they strained to take a breath, but I could not inhale against the hand that clamped around my mouth and nose. Every sinew and bone inside me cried out for precious air, but still the merciless lagoon-men dragged me even deeper. I felt dizzy. My eyes went black. Then my mind started spinning. Then floating. My mind floated free of my body ... I swam free....

Now I felt warm ... warm and comfortable ... peaceful ... calm flooded through me....

Scenes from my life flitted through my memory – not in order like a Shakespearean play, but instead like pictures on a thousand playing cards thrown in the air at once, yet with each being visible to me. I saw my childhood in the shipyards and relived my spice runs. I suffered the spirit-crushing pressure of prison and experienced the lights of Liverpool and the sounds and smells of London. I cried for my Mother, I despaired for my Father. I experienced terror – scenes of sharks and storms and Shepton prison interwove with each other in a horrifying side show.

I opened my eyes. Now I could see Elizabeth. She was surrounded by a bright light. Her face was not blue and bitter like in my usual visions, but was smiling, pink and pretty. She stood before me in a white summer dress, holding a cloth-wrapped babe. The baby wriggled beneath its swaddling as if to greet me. Beth smiled and nodded, and held out the infant for me to take in my arms.

I felt overjoyed, I felt comfortable, and I felt happy. I reached out to take my baby ... my thoughts went black....

*

I have no idea how long I was unconscious; it may have been an hour, or perhaps I was out for a day or more. But when I awoke, my situation was even more mystifying than before. I was in a very dim, musty room that was lit only by a single flickering lamp - I suspected from the smell that it was whale blubber oil. I was lying on a bamboo bed: its mattress was made of woven palm fronds and stuffed with what smelled like dried seaweed. The walls were black rock with patches of red earth, while the floor was covered in loose matting. The whole room felt damp – wet, dank and damp.

There were no windows, and a weak timber doorway barred the room's only exit. Beside my bed was a roughly hewn table on which sat a large shell filled with clear liquid. I dipped my finger in to taste: fresh water. I sat and took a long pull.

I was dressed in only my breeches. My shirt, jacket and vest all hung over the foot of the bed, with my boots and socks underneath. Someone had taken care to undress me and to dry my wet garments as best they could.

I heard a noise outside the door. It opened just a crack – just enough for me to notice the white of an eye peering at me through the deep gloom – before it hastily closed. I heard feet quickly shuffling down an outside passage and then some rapid unintelligible murmuring. I sat up over the edge of the bed, but my head spun with being upright and I could do nothing but steady myself for fear of falling to the floor. Just as I regained my balance, the door swung open. Two dark-skinned men walked into the room.

My head grew light and stars danced about my eyes. I barely had time to steer myself toward the mattress before I blacked out again.

*

By and by I awoke again. The men had gone. I sat gingerly, and inhaled deeply to steady myself. This time my dizziness was less severe than previously, and it eased completely following a few long pulls of water from the shell. I took several more slow breathes, and then paused to recount recent events.

I remembered diving into the lagoon after the long-haired girl – I concede this was foolish, but she was *so* beautiful that I soon forgave myself this impetuosity - then being dragged deep underwater by two assailants. I had very nearly drowned – perhaps I would have if one attacker had not clasped my mouth closed, for my urge to inhale, even though I had been underwater, had been overwhelming - and had passed into unconsciousness. But now I was obviously *not* underwater, for although the room was damp, it was not deluged. So where was I? Why had the men dragged me into the lagoon as if to drown me, and then carefully undressed me and laid me in a bed?

The answer, or at least a possible bearer of it, was close, for I heard footsteps approaching the exit. Soon enough the haggard door opened and the two dark-skinned men entered the chamber. They stood in front the bed, and stared gruffly at me through the dim light. They wore loose loincloths but their torsos were bare. Their hair was unkempt and matted and their bodies muscular and lean. One had a deep scar on his shoulder that looked suspiciously like a talon scrape; perhaps Bubo inflicted this on him during our struggle. Both men were both wet and dripping, so I guessed that they had swum across the lagoon to meet me.

One of the men opened his mouth as if to speak, but no words came out. Nor did his lips move. Instead I heard a high-pitched wailing noise - the sound lilted up and down before finishing with an odd series of gentle, high-pitched *arrk* sounds, like a distant seagull on a windy beach. Then both men looked at me. How should one respond to such a performance? I did not know, so I did nothing.

The second man fixed me in a brusque stare, the whites of his eyes standing out against his deep skin. Again my head spun, but I held his gaze. From somewhere within him arose a sound, seemingly not from his throat or lips, but just from deep within his chest. What a strange voice it was; more like music than conversation. The note began high and swept its way downward with the cadence of a long sigh, but with a series of small steps rather than a continuous descent of the tone. He repeated this scale three times. Then the noise transformed into a series of innocent-sounding yelps, much like a newborn dog might make. Throughout the whole performance his face barely moved a mite. Then he looked at me and raised his eyebrows as if expecting a reply.

Flabbergasted, I merely sat like a simpleton asked to perform Maskelyne's calculations. I shrugged my shoulders to which the men seemed even more displeased. They became animated, directing a myriad of sounds toward me. My quill does a poor service at recording them, but my nearest written approximation is that one of them sang the word "Oh" sharply and through a closed mouth, starting the pitch low and raising it by a tone with each utterance. The other clicked his tongue, and by flicking his lips outward made peculiar sounds that were somewhat like large drops of water falling on a pond.

It was clear that the natives were trying to communicate with me by such means, which I welcomed, for I was sure that when we bridged the divide in our tongues that I could explain my situation and demand my leave. Surely the natives would not imprison me – or worse - simply for landing on their island. At the moment I had no inkling as to the meaning of their curious language.

As their frustration mounted, they steadily became more taciturn. To ensure that I did not further offend them I simply remained still, with a simpleton's smile fixed on my face. Although my stoicism irritated the men, I could think of no action that was less likely to provoke them.

"I beg you to grant me your pardon," I offered after a long and increasingly tense period of unfruitful communication. "I don't understand."

At this utterance, the men stopped abruptly and looked at each other. Another series of harshly spoken clicks ensued. After this brief exchange the men turned sharply and left me alone.

I sat idly for a long while, utterly unsure of what to do next. My senses were overwhelmed: my near death, the mystery of my location and the strange singing men had all combined to rattle my mind as never before. I have read many accounts of the sea voyages of others, in which many a sailor had encountered an unknown tribe of natives; some were aggressive and wanted to fight, while others, like those comely women encountered by Cook's crew in the Hawaiian Islands, were accommodating to the point of wanton excess. Such discoveries, both dangerous and pleasurable and everywhere between, were part of the spirit of such a voyage. But even in my most outlandish dreams I could not have conceived of the bizarre happenings of this day. I only hoped that the men would soon return to the cave, escort me to my ship, and allow me to sail away unimpeded. Despite the adventure afforded by this episode, I was already longing for a quiet day at sea.

My spinning mind demanded that I lie on the bed, cover my head with the rough bed blanket and not emerge until this ordeal was over. But I resisted this temptation for my freedom might depend on the sharpness of my mind.

The weak door hung limply, invitingly unlatched. Although this opening was a low deterrent to escape, it was also a sign that the natives held no fear of this happening. By and by I crept toward this exit and peered out. The door opened onto an earthen corridor about 20 feet long that sloped sharply downward. At the far end was a short flattened area on which sat two roughly-hewn bamboo stools, both empty. The corridor then dropped further downward to the left, from where a dull light emanated. I listened carefully for a full minute, but heard no sounds other than the gentle lapping of water. Certainly I heard no human noises or voices. By and by my confidence grew and I took a single step outside the doorway.

"Hello," I whispered. I heard nothing in reply but a faint echo and my own heart, which was beating loudly and rapidly within my chest. Suddenly I heard a splash. Without pause I swivelled, retreated and threw myself back into the bed. It creaked under my sudden weight, but thankfully did not fracture. A trice later the two brusque natives marched back into the room, this time with an older woman between them. The old woman had long greying locks and she, like her flanking minders, was dripping and wet. Their dark skin glistened in the muted orange lamp light.

One of the men gently prodded the grey-haired woman. She muttered some words - not sing-song or clicking, but real, human sounding words. I was overjoyed to hear such utterances, but unfortunately she made no sense.

"*Jin...do...bray,*" she seemed to say.

I looked at her blankly.

"*Jin- do-bray,*" she repeated, waving her hand. She then mumbled something that to my ears sounded like "*Kat-bya zovut?*" Again I did nothing but sit, for any other movement might incorrectly imply that I understood her.

"*Kak ... teb-ya ... zo-vut??*" she said, clearly enunciating every syllable. Again, to both of our frustrations, she made no sense.

"*Ve govorit ....*" she paused, searching her mind for a word, "*...ve govorit ... por rooski?*"

All three looked at me expectantly. I shrugged. The older lady repeated herself, this time quite loudly: "*Ve - govorit - por - rooski?*" Helpless, I shrugged again.

By and by their well of patience ran dry. Exasperated, the men led the old woman out the door, making harsh clicking and popping sounds to each other as they walked. I heard a splash of water, and then nothing but silence. I found myself alone again.

Despite the musty earthiness of the cave air, I shivered. What was the old woman's message? I could do nothing but wonder at the meaning of her phrases. I repeated them over in my mind to commit them to memory, for they may later prove to be important. I called upon my experiences with the Liverpool bards, in which I often had less than a day between performances to commit a dozen sonnets to memory.

By and by I tired of the linguistic exercises. As I did, my inquisitiveness grew; was there an exit from this Shepton Mallet-like cave? I crept out the doorway, and although I was alone I treaded softly and quietly as I inched my way down the empty hallway. The slope was so steep that at times I turned and crabbed my way backwards for fear of sliding. I reached the plateau on which the small stools sat and cautiously peered left down the branching corridor. It was short and empty, and stepped down to a pool of water at its far end. Dim light filtered up from the pool, but I could see very little except a simple timber platform that bordered the hole. There was no other outlet from this cave, meaning that the men and the grey-haired woman must have dived into that hole to exit.

Suddenly a dark shadow appeared under the water. I scampered back up the slope and hurried to the small room, and again drew upon my acting days, feigning innocence and fatigue as the men returned. As before, the two men were wet, but on this occasion a stout young lad accompanied them. His matted hair, brief clothing and hardened musculature were similar to his senior tribesmen. He stood before me, clearly nervous. This emboldened me, for it was I who should be nervous in this strangest of abodes.

"*Mah ... marhab ....marhaban,*" he stuttered.

Despite gaining no response from me, he nonetheless continued.

"*Show is mick?*"

This phrase sounded vaguely English and sparked my attention. My reaction encouraged him enough to repeat the phrase in an ever-louder voice, which of course did nothing to advance my comprehension. After half a dozen such trials I sat like a simpleton as before, merely shrugging at his utterances. I had no wish to encourage the lad further, for his notion - that repeating the phrase in an ever-louder voice would aid my understanding – was clearly flawed. He tried a few more halting phrases, including something that sounded like "*hal tada arabi*" but the guards soon gave up and escorted him away, their irritability rising.

It was clear to me that the men were trying to communicate in different languages, but I had no idea as to their meaning[175]. Yet I diligently committed them to memory, for I might later have an opportunity to translate the messages – I hoped.

Soon I was alone again. I returned to the corridor, and with confidence gained from familiarity, I turned the corner and eased myself down the steep steps toward the water and its surrounding platform. Light

---

[175] The captain was correct. A tutor from the linguistics department at Oxford analysed the phonetics in the captain's account and suggests that the first two languages were Russian and Arabic. She added that McAdam did a remarkable job in recalling the foreign phrases.

glistened up through the hole, so it was obviously connected with the outside world. But why would these perplexing people enter a cave from a water pool?

Then something in the corner of the platform caught my interest: a stick of bamboo that protruded up through the pool. I gently placed my palm over its opening and felt it expel a gentle waft of air. A candle of thought lit inside my head: the bellows, the bamboo pipes, the watery entrance to this cave ... that must mean I was....

Suddenly three shadowy figures materialised into view, deep below the water hole. I retreated hastily and scampered back to my room, and had barely flung myself onto the bed when three men – the original two warrior types, plus another older man – entered the room. I could not fathom how they had scrambled out of that hole so quickly, for they had appeared at my door as though they had simply sauntered unimpeded up some stairs rather than heaving themselves out of a deep pool. If they knew that I had been prowling about the exit, or that I had spotted the bamboo pipe, they certainly did not seem to care.

At first this session progressed as had the others.

"*Hol-ha,*" mumbled the old man. I said nothing, for this phrase did not come from the King's English.

"*Kwal estu numbray*?" he asked. I rubbed my neck in frustration. Perhaps, soon, someone would arrive that spoke and understood my language. Until then it appeared that I would simply have to be polite, shake my head, and simply try to contain my exasperation.

"*De dondy eresh?*" the old man asked hopefully. I shrugged and shook my head.

"*Hobler espar nol*?" Again, a shrug and a sigh.

The old man turned to his younger companions and shook his head. Just as they were turning to leave the room, a hint of comprehension flickered into my mind.

"Repeat," I said to him. "Repeat your last word." Obviously ignorant of the English language, the old man just looked at me mutely.

"*Repetir,*" I said, this time in my best Spanish. Again my entreaty drew nothing but a blank look. As the trio retreated from the room, the old man's lack of reaction suggested that my guess had been wrong, but before they disappeared, I tried one more phrase.

"*Hablas Espanol?*" I called to the old man. He paused his shuffling gait and slowly turned back to me, surprise etched in his features.

"*Hablas Espanol?*" I repeated.

"*Si,*" he stuttered, his eyes opening wide with unexpected surprise. "*Que ... habla ... Espanol?*"

"*Si,*" I replied. "*Un poco* – a little."

He sighed with relief, and then clicked a message of sorts to his companions, who also sighed. The trio ushered themselves back into the room where our attempt at communication began. The guards fetched a stool for the old man and we sat, facing each other, trying to bridge the wide divide in our tongues.

My command of the Spanish language was, at its best, mediocre. Unfortunately the old man's grasp was even worse: his words were poorly practiced, weakly inflected, and he unfailingly mangled his grammar. Nevertheless, through a combination of half-concocted words and effusive sign language, we limped our way to a loose understanding of each other.

Our initial task – the learning of each other's names – proved particularly difficult. I soon realised that the Boot Islanders constructed their language from high-pitched singsong, which they sometimes combined with sharp clicking and harsh popping sounds. So the translation, first from the Boot-Island language into Spanish, and then to English, proved to be devilishly difficult.

My best description is that the older man was called "Arooo", which he sung with a long, lilting "ooo" sound to finish. The younger men were called "Taa-TA-hoo" and "Lee-BE-nay" in which the final syllable was similarly sing-song, while the middle sound was pronounced with a very sharp, audible click that I simply could not replicate with my tongue, much less my pencil.

I introduced myself as Captain Fintan McAdam. Yet they did little to acknowledge my name or my rank – Arooo did not even attempt to repeat it. Perhaps it was too much to expect this courtesy from natives.

"*De ... donde ... eresh?*" he asked me by and by.

"London," I replied. *"Soy de* London." I doubt that he knew where the Mother City was, for he gave no sign of understanding. Nevertheless, he pressed on.

"Por que?"

"Why? Why... what?"

He fumbled over his word for a minute, before repeating

"Por que..." he then pointed at me, *"...agua*?"

Why *water*? I looked at the filled shell, but he shook his head. He didn't make sense. I shrugged.

"Por que ... aqui?" Ah, that was better. *Why here*. Why was I here?

A thousand answers flooded through my mind, like a waterfall over a cliff. I would have been unable to articulate them in English, even given a whole night and a goodly splash of rum to expound upon them, so to translate my thoughts into broken Spanish was nearly impossible. I could think of many abbreviated replies: to experience adventure on the high seas; to escape English law and its fetid jails; to test myself against and to renew my acquaintance with Mother Ocean. And... Beth. To forget Beth. But how could I summarise these feelings in gestured Spanish?

"Descubrir mi," I settled on.

"Que?"

 "Descubrir mi. To discover myself."

I was unsure if Arooo misunderstood my words or was confused about their deeper meaning - most likely both - but he clearly struggled to translate my reply. By and by he turned to Taa-TA-hoo and Lee-BE-nay and simply shook his head. They clicked their messages back to him, and although I did not comprehend their strange tongue, the shaking of their heads indicated that they did not understand either. I could sense their impatience growing, for they then clicked their tongues rapidly and tersely at Arooo. He shrugged at them in contrition, and then questioned me in a new vein.

"Que ki-ares?"

"Repetir por favor."

"Que ... kwi-air-ez."

"Ah, si," I replied, for I now understood his question: *Que quieres* – what did I want?

The long-haired girl immediately came to mind, but I thought it prudent to keep my innermost desires silent. A more practical answer was also true - but how could I best explain that I simply wanted my freedom? If I explained that I meant them no harm and that I wished to leave, then surely they would let me depart.

Again I fumbled for words, but settled upon *"navegar nave lejos"*: Sail ship away. Arooo seemed to understand. He turned to his companions and clicked a short message. They raised their eyebrows at me and popped their lips and clicked their tongues, and even at times broke into song-speak, formulating a full reply. Arooo sat with his chin in his hands, appearing to be mentally rehearsing the requested translation.

After some time he looked up and pointed his arms high, then spread them wide.

"Arbol grande" he began.

Big tree, I thought and nodded. *"Si, arbol grande."*

"Mani," he added. *"Mani?"*

I shook my head. I did not know what "mani" meant.[176]

"Marron?" he tried, then made a round shape with his hands

"Marron", I thought, meant brown. Big tree brown – he was not making much sense. Perhaps I had misunderstood. I shook my head.

"Marron, marron. Arbol grande marron," he tried again, still forming a circular shape with his hands. Still ignorant of his implication, I shrugged. He rubbed his chin, deep in thought. Then he tried again with a different phrase.

"Marron bola."

His words and gestures suddenly made sense. *Brown ball*. Big tree, brown ball. Coconuts.

"Si, si. Comprende. Arbol grande marron bola ... Coco."

---

[176] Mani actually means "peanut".

"*Si, coco*," he replied, relieved that his translation had been understood. However, his next statement was less convivial. He pointed at me.

"*Robar*." The word was close enough to the English that I had little need for further translation, but he repeated it with emphasis: "*Robar coco*." He was suggesting that I was a robber, a thief – that I had stolen their coconuts.

Suddenly I felt my indignity rising. How dare they suggest such a slur! I quickly moved to calm myself, for to fight these men here and now would be most unwise, but felt my fingers curling into fists nonetheless. The two younger natives stood taller and prouder, showing that they sensed my anger.

Through gritted teeth I explained to Arooo that the island had appeared deserted, and that there were no outward signs that the land was inhabited. Clearly the Boot Islanders had gone to great lengths to conceal their habitation from others, and it was only through Providence that I had stumbled upon it at all. I finished my statement by demanding that they retract their insinuation that I was a thief.

Unfortunately the translation proved too difficult for Arooo to bridge. The men looked unimpressed with my defence, and were unintimidated by my defiance. Again I felt my anger rising, and struggled to keep it in check. By and by I forced myself into an apology of sorts, again citing a misunderstanding. But my contrition fell on stubborn ears, for Taa-TA-hoo and Lee-BE-nay remained taciturn.

By and by they decided that the inquisition had gone on long enough, so the three men left me alone. I lay back in the bed, exhausted, for the conversation had been long and difficult. I had achieved nothing to advance my freedom, but one point was now clear – the natives were not as friendly as I had hoped, and regarded me as an unwelcome intruder. What was their plan for me now? My mind rolled with many possibilities, each more gruesome than the former, until I had truly worked myself into a state.

I tried to rest for a while but could not sleep, for I was angry with the men and anxious about my fate. Oh, what I would have given for a few pints of rum. I could have blurred the pain of my incarceration into a pea-soup haze, and then slept and slept and slept some more. On awakening, I could have again given the rum a touch, giving me the strength to confront my captors when they next appeared.

But of course there was no rum. There was no wine, no gin, not even a pint of apple cider. So I was forced to endure the cold, damp cave, and my anger at being so unjustly held here, alone. Very alone.

After some listless tossing for an hour or three – time was very difficult to gauge in that dark little grotto - I could not face my own thoughts any longer, so I let my let myself out through the rickety door to investigate the possibilities for escape.

Apart from the timber frame and the bamboo ventilation pipes (I spotted a second one), I could discern no other features of the water hole. Curious as to what lay outside, I plunged my head under and looked through the water. Although the light was dim, I could see that the tunnel continued downward for about 10 feet. Eager to see further, I dunked my upper body as far down as my nerve would allow, all the time gripping the wooden frame to prevent me overbalancing into the hole. The extra depth afforded me a slightly wider view, but apart from a few darting baitfish I could see nothing extra. But this inspection proved what I had already assumed: I was being held in an underwater cave, deep in the lagoon. The possibility of escape was nil.

Friday 31 August

I awoke in the clammy cave feeling cold and miserable. My attempt at sleep had been wracked with nightmares, and my lids had barely flickered closed. But at least, I reminded myself, I was still alive; it was better to be a man with cold fingers than a man with no hands.

Despite the uncertainty of my surroundings, I tried to face them stoically. I hoped that the natives would return to emancipate me from this hole, for I had already made it clear that I had no quarrel with them.

I had not eaten for a day. Although I did not feel hungry, I knew that I needed food to maintain my strength. Soon after I awoke, the native Arooo granted my unspoken wish when he appeared with a small package of provisions that contained two raw whole fish: one looked like a large sardine, while the second - perhaps a reef trout – was as long as my foot. There was also a single rolled leaf of thick seaweed. The whole meal was delivered on a thin flat rock, the crude plate making the simple fare even more unappealing. Nevertheless I ate methodically; the smaller specimen I devoured skeleton and all, crunching my way through the bones to draw every bit of goodness from it.

Memories of the sardine that Bubo brought me after being out all night searching for fish flooded back to me. *Bubo*. Where was my first mate? I was sure that he realised that something was terribly wrong. Whether this knowledge was useful or unfortunate I could not say ... probably the latter, for he had worry in his bones and was no doubt fretting about my disappearance. Was he perched on the port gunwale on the *Maris Alarum* waiting hopefully for my return? Or had he long since given me away as dead, and flown away in search of a greener paddock? Surely, I answered myself, he would think that I had perished, for he had seen me wrestled under the water but not resurface. But I could do nothing to alert him to my plight.

I skinned the larger fish barehanded and picked about the bones, sucking off as much meat as possible. Arooo watched, detachedly and in silence. When I had finished the fish, he focused on me, readying himself for more tedious translation.

"*Taa-TA-hoo, Lee-BE-nay ... responsable.*"

"*Si,*" I replied – I understood that Taa-TA-hoo and Lee-BE-nay were in charge.

"*Ellos ... recelo...*" Then he pointed at me. *Recelo*: distrust. They distrusted me.

"*Cocos especial.*" Then, for emphasis, he added "*Cocos* muy *especial.*" His tone left little doubt: the islanders considered that the coconuts were special, even sacred. In their minds, I had not only invaded their land but had stolen four of their precious icons, which they would not easily forgive.

"*Lo siento,*" I offered by way of apology.

"*Recelo,*" he repeated, shaking his head, and then left me protesting.

My mood fell like hard rain as an awful truth dawned on me: the natives were not going to let me free. I was incarcerated. Again.

My thoughts quickly turned to escape, but one fact was immediately clear: even *if* I had my Fisherman's Friend vest and somehow managed

265

to swim out of the tunnel entrance, the natives would soon recapture me as I tried to cross the lagoon. One hundred yards of water had been my saviour at the Thames dock, but here on Boot Island it was my unyielding captor – a captor that I could neither fight nor flee.

Now fraught, I paced around the room with my face buried in my hands. By and by, through my anguish, some logic emerged, like a distant lighthouse beacon above an ink-black sea. I reasoned that because escape was impossible through the existing entrance, I would have to make another. At some point in the past the natives had excavated these caves, so perhaps I could dig my way to freedom. I dared to hope.

A quick examination of the room showed that the walls were constituted from two types of rock: in some areas, particularly the ceiling, fore and side walls, the rock was rough and black, much like the cliffs outside. In contrast, the floor and the rear wall were smoother and a red-brown colour. A quick test of the dark stone showed that it was forged like iron, and would be impossible to cut through. However when I scraped my belt buckle – the hardest object in my possession – on the red rock, it crumbled more readily.

I scoured the room for tools. Soon I had compiled a collection of crude implements: a sharp stout length of bamboo from a hastily disassembled chair, the shell water container, and the thin rock that had earlier served as my dinner plate. With this motley assortment of tools, I wasted no time in chiselling away at the lower wall in the farthest corner of the room, where I could most easily conceal my activities. I planned to hack out a narrow tunnel to the outside of the island's wall, and then, under cover of darkness, climb my way around the ridge to my tender and cast away. I did not know how far I would have to dig, but hoped that it was a few yards at the most. I sensed that this was my only chance to escape.

I soon found that the most efficient digging method was to hammer the bamboo pole into the red earth to loosen it, and then scrape it away using the large shell as a shovel of sorts. As I chipped away at the rock, I soon received a pleasant surprise: the earth became softer and more giving, and by and by I could scoop it with the shell without even loosening it first.[177] My progress was rapid, and within an hour I had forged a hole about 18 inches in diameter and two feet deep.

It was soon thereafter that I hit an impediment– literally. Tunnelling suddenly became difficult, and even my bamboo pick could not penetrate the earth. An inspection under the light of the tallow lamp showed that I had encountered a seam of the hard black rock. I would have to try another site.

Using the flat rock, I tamped the earth back into the hole as tightly as possible. When it was almost full, I moistened the last of the dirt to form clay and pressed it into the opening to conceal my efforts. Once satisfied that the hole was masked well enough to pass a cursory inspection under the cave's low light, I sat back, not just to rest, for the labour had been intensive, but also to study the lie of the rocks. I wanted to choose the best spot for a new tunnel, for I did not want to waste my energy again.

After carefully observing the contour of the black rock, I picked a spot on the middle of the back wall where the soft red rock was dominant. Despite my fatigue I dug quickly, for I had no way of knowing when the natives would return, and I was unable to readily conceal this tunnel due to its open position. My quick progress again surprised me, and in less than an hour I had forged a deep hole of an arm's length. However soon thereafter I encountered the same problem as previously: I struck a face of unyielding black rock, and was unable to dig any further.

Undeterred, I refilled the shaft and commenced another route, this one into the side wall behind the bed. This approach would mean a far longer dig to the outside wall of the island, but I hoped I could skirt the black rock via this approach. Yet again I was disappointed, for another hard seam thwarted me after only a foot of excavation.

Now physically spent, I slumped onto the small bed. My mind harkened back to my circumnavigation of the island, during which I had observed walls of hard black rock, with not a hint of red earth. I realised that any soft dirt would have long-since been eroded away by the wind and

---

[177] An old college friend from the Geology Department enlightened me on the geophysics of McAdam's cave. The black rock was undoubtedly *basalt*, which forms when lava cools quickly, and is therefore very common around oceanic volcanoes. The softer red rock was *tuff* (also called *tufa*) which is formed from a conglomeration of volcanic ash. Tuff is very soft in its natural state, but hardens when it oxidises on exposure to air. This property made it very easy to tunnel through.

waves; it was clear that the red dirt could only exist in seams inside the black rock. I was exhausted and covered in filthy red soil, and the realisation hit me with the surety of a sunrise: I could not possibly tunnel out of this prison. There was no hope of escape. I was completely at the mercy of the Boot Island leaders.

Although the simple bed, meals of fish and fresh water elevated this island cell above the sickly pall of Shepton Mallet, the loneliness and isolation were worse. I was not only separated from the lagoon by the cave walls, but from my ship by the lagoon, and from my previous world by hundreds of leagues of ocean. I was even unable to talk to my pet bird. I was truly, unconditionally, inconsolably alone.

I had fled from the clutches from the London plod and an undeserved stretch in the clink, only to land in another prison barely six months later. Had I not been so desperate I would have smiled at the irony.

My mood rapidly deteriorated as I ruminated on my isolation, the uncertainty about my future, and the squalor in which I found myself. I cursed aloud at my decision to return to Boot Island. If I had simply continued on my way I might have made landfall at Africa by now, and would be sitting in a tavern with a large mug of rum to toast my fine fortune.

Liquor. I needed it. Yes, I conceded that I had cast it out of my life forever, for it had let me down innumerable times. But I needed just a quart to hold me up until the travesty of my imprisonment inside this clammy hole was over. I would trade my left hand for just a quart. Even just a mug would soothe my mind and give the strength to fight again. But there was none. Not a drop.

My low spirits and fatigue lead me down treacherous pathways. As much as I tried to resist, my loneliness enkindled a longing for Beth. That desire inevitably became a vision. With no medicine to fight the apparition, my mind became increasingly hysterical as the demons did their work.

If I could have watched myself, I would have seen a man fail in his bid to rid himself of those demons, for Beth's vision implanted herself inside that cave and would not leave me all night. If I closed my eyes, she was there. If I opened them wide, there she stood in front of me, her bloodied bosom glowing red despite the dim cave light. With nowhere to hide, and no medicine at hand, Elizabeth's ghost had me at her mercy. She replayed that fateful day, from the moment that I cut the tether to ensnare the rope around the stag's antlers ... I shall always see those antlers, those instruments of death, spreading out widely like a whale's tail.

If I could have watched myself, I would have seen a crazed man, bouncing himself off the grimy cave walls, tearing his hair with his hands. I would have seen him running wild-eyed down the corridor to dunk his head into the water pool in order to rid himself of the ghosts of his grisly-killed wife.

For once I was pleased for my isolation; the natives could not hear my manic screams or my desperate pleas for mercy.

I do not think it lessens me as a man, as an English captain, or as the proud son of the late George McAdam, to say that after the nightmare finally ceded, I lay on my bed and wept. I wept aloud. I wept for hours. I wept for Elizabeth. I wept for my unborn child. I wept *for* my child, and *like* a child. But mostly I wept out of sheer hopelessness.

My journey to forget Beth had failed. I could not rent her from my soul no matter how hard I tried, and I doubted that I ever would.

Thomas or Mary. Thomas George McAdam if he was a boy, Mary Elizabeth McAdam if she was a girl.

Saturday 1 September

In the morning I sat on a stool near the waterhole, for its natural light, although dim and muted, drew me toward it as a warm campfire draws a weary winter traveller. My countenance was low but calm; my emotional night had left me exhausted, but in an odd way I felt it had drained the anxiety from me. It would not be a stretch of the truth to say that my weakness - my outburst, my capitulation - did me good.

My thoughts turned with many questions. Occasionally I wondered about the long-haired girl who had lured me onto this island. Where was she? Had the senior natives originally dispatched her to trap me, or had she met with me surreptitiously? Did the other natives even know that we had met? I also recaptured the comely silhouette of her narrow waist, and her proud cheekbones glowing softly in the moonlight. But, I reminded myself with disdain, she was outside, and I was in here, and even though just a few yards of rock wall separated me from the lagoon, it was entirely possible that I would never see her again.

I thought repeatedly about escape, but knew on every level that it was impossible. I could not swim or dig my way free, so absconding against the will of the natives was unfeasible. After much deliberation, I realised that my best chance was to bargain or parlay my way to freedom. Even though I held the natives in contempt for my unjust incarceration, and my preferred course would be to pound the next man I saw until his face turned blue, I knew that this would harm my cause. The natives could easily kill me by drowning, or even through simple neglect. So instead of force and retribution, I would have to play a slow hand and ingratiate myself to them at every turn. I would be alert for any chance to negotiate, and could only hope that the native Arooo, my translator, was about when that opportunity arose. Perhaps I could buy their peace with some trinkets, food, or even some of the non-vital tools from my ship.

The *Maris Alarum* ... what was happening to her? I wondered. Were the natives ransacking her? My mind wandered back to Bubo: how was he bearing without me?

The answer-bearers to my questions suddenly appeared, almost as if by a conjuring trick, from the waterhole. I snapped from my worrisome reverie to see Arooo, Taa-TA-hoo and Lee-BE-nay standing before me.

"*Ven*," barked Arooo, instructing me to 'come' while pointing down the waterhole.

I hesitated. To dive into that water would be as suicidal as throwing myself into a volcano pit. I could barely float in a warm London bath much less swim through a deep lagoon.

"*Ven, ven*," he demanded, my demurral testing their patience. I mentally searched for the Spanish phrase for "cannot swim" but it was not forthcoming. I tried to signal my inability to swim to the three men but they had no tolerance for the grievances of an uninvited foreigner. An astonishingly loud click of Taa-TA-hoo's tongue brought the discourse to a sudden halt. Arooo disappeared into the opening, and I followed involuntarily soon after, with Taa-TA-hoo and Lee-BE-nay physically pulling me into the terrifying brine.

I hit the water in shock. My body twirled and turned as Taa-TA-hoo and Lee-BE-nay pulled me through the water. I was powerless in this most foreign of environments; I would feel more familiar if I walked on the moon. I did not struggle because I knew that it would waste my air and my energy, but my inner demons were clawing at me with the enmity of Lucifer himself. I could do nothing but close my eyes, hold my breath and wish for this horrific ordeal to be over.

My ears popped. I had no sense of my position and no knowledge of whether they were dragging me up or down. But I soon realised one thing: that I needed another breath. *Soon.* I opened my eyes and saw that we were travelling horizontally rather than ascending. Far above I could see the underside of the water's surface shimmering like an evil giant's looking glass. (In hindsight - I had never seen water from underneath before, and I remain amazed by its quicksilver-like appearance, but at the time I had no inclination to marvel at it.) I signalled frenetically to one of the men – I could not discern which – that I desperately needed air. He seemed to understand, and made some whale-song noises to his counterpart, after which they changed course.

A few interminable seconds later, we arrived at a bamboo pipe that was suspended freely from the underwater cliff face. I saw that air bubbled in slow bursts from the pipe's free end, so immediately I reached for it and greedily inhaled. My chest had to work very hard, but by and by I managed to suck in some precious air. As I hovered in the water, Taa-TA-hoo and Lee-BE-nay held me steady until I recovered my breath, and my nerve. By and by I had retrieved what little composure I could summon and we started our ascent. But my terror quickly returned as we left the sanctity and security of the precious breathing pipe.

We had risen just a couple of fathoms when the men suddenly stopped. One of them abruptly pulled my head to face his – it was Lee-BE-nay - and he made some gestures with his hands in front of his mouth. I tried to focus but my mind was crowded with anxiety, which overwhelmed all other considerations. Again I tried to concentrate: Lee-BE-nay had pinched his hands in front of his mouth and then extended them open as he moved them away from his face. What was he trying to tell me? He repeated the gesture, but I was none the wiser.

A small cough of air escaped my lips. As it bubbled up Lee-BE-nay became very animated, fervently nodding his head. Suddenly I understood: I had to exhale. I did not understand why, for it seemed foolish to blow out the very thing that was keeping me alive. But Lee-BE-nay was persistent with his sign language, and we recommenced our ascent only after I had acquiesced to his request. So I blew my air out – and blew and blew and blew. I exhaled an extraordinarily long stream of bubbles as we swam upward, astonished at the volume of air that escaped from my lips. It seemed impossible for my chest to hold so much. The natives clearly had some magic or witchcraft in their breathing pipes, because this air seemed to have almost indefinite supply.[178]

It was to my great relief that we burst through the lagoon's surface. But Taa-TA-hoo and Lee-BE-nay left me little time for pleasantries as they roughly ushered me to the beach.

I glanced around briefly: the small beach seemed an entirely different place to the one I had explored previously. It was now filled with dozens of native people who turned to stare, but I had little time to absorb any details for Arooo soon joined us. I watched as he morphed from swimming horizontally through the shallows to standing upright on the beach in one smooth movement. A flicker of amazement at his dextrous movements somehow registered in my mind amidst the jostle of melancholy, terror and anxiety. The three men then marched me over the short sandy beach to the tree-lined strip, whereupon Arooo translated a stern message from his companions.

"*Arbol grande marron bola cocos,*" he began, laboriously redefining "coconut" for me. I nodded. "*Cocos muy especial*". I nodded again, for this speech was familiar.

"*Robar.*"

---

[178] This phenomenon is well known in modern hydrology and is experienced by SCUBA divers. The ingenious ventilation system on Boot Island used the ocean waves to compress the floating bellows, creating enough pressure to force the air through the pipes. The air that McAdam inhaled was therefore slightly pressurised, and so it would have expanded as he ascended, increasing its volume. Had Lee-BE-nay not insisted that McAdam exhale, the Captain's lungs could have ruptured.

I felt testy. We had covered this debate previously, and I had already explained my position. Did they need to drag me through the lagoon to the point of drowning to hear this message repeated? I felt the redness rising inside me for I was already tired and anxious, and was just a tick away from lashing out with my fists. However I recalled my earlier decision to try to parlay the natives, and somehow controlled my anger. Suddenly Arooo started flapping his arms in a most unexpected way.

"*Ave*," he added. "*Ave robar.*"

He pointed to the rocky beach surrounds around which lay half a dozen shattered carcasses of the precious produce. As Arooo flapped his arms again like wings, I understood: *the bird*. The bird – Bubo - was a robber. Bubo had been stealing their sacred coconuts, stripping them with his sharp beak, and then and breaking them on the rocks. He did love coconut. In keeping with my forced contrition I reassured the islanders, primarily with sign language, but also with a brief ungrammatical statement - *no mas ave robar cocos* - that from now on, Bubo would leave their coconuts alone.

I then turned to the skies and the trees and called for Bubo. Barely had the call parted from my lips when he came swooping down from the western mountain, warbling and carking with what sounded to me like bird joy. However as he neared our party he hovered above us, wary of the unexpected company.

Captain Rum he squawked. Like a faithful pet, Bubo seemed immensely pleased to see me, as I was to see him.

"Hello Bubo," I hollered up to him. "I've missed you." I knew that he would not understand my affection, but felt the need to say it anyway. But now it behoved me to rebuke his ways.

"Men angry at Bubo for eating coconuts." I paused and repeated the statements a few times to aid his understanding before continuing.

Aark. Displeasure. Good –perhaps he was beginning to understand.

"The men are angry. Do not take coconuts. No coconuts." I accompanied my repeated message with hand signs, pointing and head shaking.

Bubo Coconuts.

"I know Bubo likes coconuts. But no more coconuts."

He must have gained the gist of my message, for he screeched wildly at the islanders and then flapped above their heads, squawking ferociously. Then he flew to a perch in a nearby tree and carked noisily at them from a distance. Rarely have I seen him so upset.

I did not think that it was poor for him to act this way, for like a faithful hound he clearly disliked my captors and their directives, and was simply expressing this feeling through natural bird actions. Despite Bubo's frustration, I hoped that the matter was now resolved with Taa-TA-hoo and Lee-BE-nay, so I turned to them, ready with more forced contrition.

My three captors – and in fact all of the natives who were on the beach - were looking at me with bland astonishment. It took me a moment to comprehend the reason for their wonder: they had never seen a man talk openly with a bird before or, in particular, for a bird to reply. This dialogue was now so natural to me that I had not given it thought. The men sang-spoke to each other, with the content of their conversation clear: Bubo had amazed them. Some of them even looked fearful, perhaps suspecting that Bubo was possessed by some dark magic or the like.

"*Ave sin robar cocos*," I assured them, hoping that Bubo would obey my orders and would, albeit begrudgingly, leave the coconuts alone. While the natives continued discussing the bizarre bird that was still carking at them from atop a nearby palm, I stole a glance toward the hinterland, looking for the weapons that I had left under the tree. They were gone.

By and by their incredulous discussion and the disbelieving shaking of their heads dissipated, so I turned, hopefully, back toward Arooo.

"*Bueno*?" I asked. "*Bueno amigos*?

If they thought things were now good, or that we were friends, they certainly did not act that way. Their stern demeanour was barely assuaged. However they seemed to be satisfied that I had dealt adequately with Bubo, for they ushered me across the beach toward the horror of another dive into the lagoon. I resisted, not just because of the petrifying plunge that awaited me, but because I sensed that this could be my only opportunity to negotiate my freedom with Taa-TA-hoo and Lee-BE-nay.

"*Un minuto,*" I begged to Arooo as we neared the water line. "*Un minuto, por favour.*"

Arooo was confused. Even after I repeated my simple request a few times he remained bewildered. Perhaps the Boot Islanders had no concept of minutes and hours. I sought another translation.

"*Un momento. Un momento, por favour.*"

Arooo now understood and relayed my wish to Taa-TA-hoo and Lee-BE-nay, which they reluctantly granted with a pair of terse nods. I had to use this stay wisely, for I had no possibility to influence the natives while I was incarcerated, alone, in that cave. I reasoned that food must be of great important to the Boot Islanders, for their island had limited provisions, so I tried to barter my way to acceptance: perhaps a peace offering would soften their attitude toward me.

I thought back to the gifts that I had left for the long-haired woman. She had left the fish untouched – with hindsight this was unsurprising as they had such fare in abundance – and rejected the bread on the second night. However she had taken the tomatoes on both nights, of which I had a surfeit on my ship that would soon be over-ripe anyway. I had little to lose by offering them as a gift, but much to gain if it encouraged their acceptance of me.

"Bubo," I called. He looked across from his perch. "Bubo, fetch Captain Rum a tomato from ship. A tomato. Fetch tomato from ship." The islanders looked nervously on as I repeatedly relayed my message to Bubo.

Fetch tomato, he squawked by and by, mercifully understanding my request, and flapped off toward where I hoped the *Maris Alarum* lay anchored.

The islanders' suspicions grew, which was apparent as they hurriedly clicked a conversation between themselves, and anxiously looked at the retreating Bubo and then at me. The reason for their agitation slowly became clear: I was talking in a non-Spanish tongue that even Arooo could not understand. Was I planning an attack or an escape? Was Bubo fetching me a weapon? They had no way of knowing. Their patience suddenly disappeared and they man-handled me toward the water, this time with more than gentle persuasion.

"Un momento," I begged, for I not only wanted a chance to parlay them with my gift but also dreaded the impending inundation. I attempted to explain that Bubo was fetching a gift, a gift of food, but in the pressure of the moment my Spanish tongue was as uncooperative as a mule. Soon Taa-TA-hoo and Lee-BE-nay were propelling me through the water, deep into the heart of the black lagoon.

As previously, I could barely open my eyes such was my fear. All I felt was stinging in my ears and panic over my ever-diminishing air. After pausing to allow me three precious breaths from the free-hanging ventilation pipe, Taa-TA-hoo and Lee-BE-nay escorted me at bewildering pace down to my dingy underwater cave. I opened my eyes as we neared the tunnel entrance. My escorts did not slow as I had expected but instead accelerated, kicking their feet and thrusting their hips at an even more frenetic beat. Just after we entered the underwater entrance, we swerved to the vertical and swam upward inside the water-filled tunnel at an ever-increasing pace. Such was their speed that we vaulted straight up through the water's surface and landed, albeit very clumsily, on the wooden platform. I lay on the splintery timber, panting, but Taa-TA-hoo and Lee-BE-nay soon dragged me to my feet.

Arooo followed soon after. He propelled himself upward through the hole and used his arms to vault himself almost seamlessly to his feet, and then ambled after us without missing a stride. These natives had the water skills of fish but their land abilities were unfettered by tails or fins – a truly unique and advantageous combination.

Once the men had deposited me in my room, they made to leave. I called after Arooo.

"Aves dar frutos," I yelled, letting them know of Bubo's impending food delivery. Arooo turned, nodded in vague recognition, and departed, again leaving me alone with my fear and my demons.

Sunday 2 September

I spent another night alone in the cave. I did not think of Beth at all – perhaps my long weep did me some good. I also noticed that my hands have finally stopped shaking. How this affliction cured itself without my medicine I have no idea, but am grateful for the relief.[179]

As he did two days previously, Arooo appeared mid morning and delivered a food package; this one contained a raw fish, three small raw crabs and a handful of bitter berries. He departed immediately without mentioning the tomato.

I nibbled on the produce as the morning sloughed by. Later, I received a visit from Taa-TA-hoo, Lee-BE-nay and Arooo that I hoped would change my situation for the better.

"*Fruta beuno*," stated Arooo, much to my relief; Bubo must have delivered the tomato as I had requested. "*Beuno*."

Taa-TA-hoo and Lee-BE-nay gruffly nodded their heads in approval - they clearly had enjoyed my gift. Their attitude toward me seemed slightly less hostile, so perhaps my gambit was working.

"*Mas fruta?*" asked Arooo.

More fruit? They wanted more tomatoes. Men have paid for their freedom with caskets of gold and jewels, or laid down their lives for the freedom of others – if I could buy my salvation with just a basket of tomatoes then I would have haggled the cheapest of bargains.

"*Si. Mas fruta en la nave*," I replied, pointing to where I guessed the *Maris Alarum* was anchored.

Arooo turned to his companions and relayed my offer through a short sing-song.

"*Ven.*" It was a simple order – come – but for the first time I was almost pleased to follow my captors into the water hole, for I hoped to further sow the seeds of my deliverance outside. My journey through the lagoon was less stressful than previously, and I arrived at the ventilation pipe without undue distress. I noted that even though I inhaled its bubbling stream for five long breaths, Arooo, Taa-TA-hoo and Lee-BE-nay did not take any supplementary air at all. They had obviously developed an outstanding ability to hold their breath underwater.

---

[179] Of course it was the withdrawal of McAdam's 'medicine' – alcohol – that was causing his *Delirium Tremens* (which he misdiagnosed as *Shaking Palsy*) in the first place. After an extended period without alcohol, his body had finally adjusted back to normal.

As we ascended, I fully opened my eyes under the water for the first time. I noted with surprise that the lagoon was not empty and black as it appeared from above, but was dotted with island life. Even to a sailor accustomed to new sights and customs, much of what I saw seemed as fantastic as a fable.

We passed two women folk who were suspended mid water, simply conversing in their whale-song language as though they were chatting in a Liverpudlian coffee house. A group of islander children darted about near the lagoon wall catching bait fish with a small net, while three men swam languidly below us picking rust-coloured seaweed from some deep rocks. The natives seemed as comfortable under the water as Londoners were on the land. [180]

The natives had a remarkable action for propelling themselves through the water. They held one hand above their head and the other by their side. Then they thrust their hips fore and aft with a two-legged kick, much like a porpoise. Using this method they developed incredible speed and manoeuvrability, which when combined with their immense breath-holding capacity allowed them to travel great distances underwater. Unfortunately I did not share this skill.

The lagoon floor steadily came into focus as we approached the beach. It was very steep and dotted with large coral-clad rocks that jutted up through the sand, like the tips of icebergs protruding above the northern seas. One rock formation in the shallows caught my eye: it was round and had a hole through the middle of it. Two tiny islander boys swam merrily in and out through the hole as if they were playing in a Hyde Park tree.

We seamlessly beached ourselves with a grace that belied our humanoid forms. The natives assisted me in this matter, of course, after which I led them up and around the cliff ridge to my tender. It was only then that I noted Taa-TA-hoo had a length of rope tied around his waist, and wondered as to its purpose.

Without hesitation or fear, Taa-TA-hoo, Lee-BE-nay and Arooo leaped from the cliff top, plunging the whole 20 yards into the swirling ocean

---

[180] Readers should appreciate that swimming was not a common skill in the 1800s, and that however incredible the Boot Island community seems to us, McAdam would have found it doubly so.

below. Lee-BE-nay's leap was the most audacious, for he entered the water with his outstretched arms and head first, with his body straight like a sawn plank. Never have I witnessed such a daring leap.

My sailor's body was not designed for such a plunge, so I climbed my way carefully down the rock face, much to the natives' impatience. By and by we packed ourselves into my tender and I rowed toward the *Maris Alarum*, but our progress was torpid under the heavy load of four men. After a minute, the natives' frustration at the slow progress grew until Taa-TA-hoo and Lee-BE-nay leapt over the side and towed the rowboat to my ship like horses drawing a carriage. They showed no fear that sharks might have been prowling the seas. I could not judge whether their actions were foolhardy or brave, but probably a good measure of both. It seemed risky for the natives to have exposed themselves to nature's beasts when my tender would have delivered them to my ship in just a few extra minutes.

I looked about for Bubo but could not see him. He must have been out catching fish. His absence was frustrating because I wanted to see him, if only to reassure him that I was alive and sound. I was sure he would have appreciated a neck-feather rub as well.

The men accompanied me on board. Although this was my ship and I was her Captain, the men left me in no doubt that I was still their prisoner. Taa-TA-hoo uncurled the rope from his waist and lashed it around my ankles, then my right wrist, and finally tethered it around my ankles again. I could barely walk, and had use of only my left arm; clearly I could not fight or flee while the rope remained in place.

I cringed at the indignity of having a native man truss me up like a Christmas pig. But in hindsight the rope bindings may have saved me from myself, for I felt many times like lashing out with my fists, not only a retribution for my embarrassment but in an attempt to escape. However had I done so I most likely would have been subdued and my entire reason for being on the ship - to make peace with the natives – would have been wasted. So despite the humiliation of being held captive on my own vessel, I somehow stilled my temper and my tongue.

After completing final knot, Taa-TA-hoo ordered me down the hatch. The natives followed me, hesitantly, into the galley. Their wide eyes betrayed that they were experiencing a ship's interior for perhaps the first time. Taa-TA-hoo seemed fascinated by the oven, Lee-BE-nay busied himself examining my navigational instruments, while Arooo explored the cutlery, holding each tarnished piece up and gazing at it as though he was holding the King's crown jewels.

"Frutus," ordered Arooo by and by. As I fetched a crate of tomatoes from the hold, I glanced at the breadbasket, which contained a few dozen rolls that would be stale and inedible if not eaten soon. I took three, and proffered one to each man with the invitation to taste.

"Bread," I told them, before adding in Spanish *"pan"*, although Arooo did not recognise the word even after I repeated it slowly, several times. At first the men demurred – clearly they had never eaten bread before. I tore a chunk off one loaf and swallowed it. By and by each native nibbled at a corner and, emboldened, eventually took a bite. They seemed pleased with the taste, judging from their at-first-hesitant smiles. I needed no further indication as to the suitability of the gift and fetched the breadbasket as well, for I had to seize every opportunity to ingratiate myself with them.

The natives continued exploring my ship for nearly an hour. On occasion, Taa-TA-hoo or Lee-BE-nay would ask a question, which Arooo would translate. However my replies bounced off uneducated ears, so they rarely comprehended my answers.

For example, at one point Lee-BE-nay held up my naval chart and through Arooo, asked "What?"

"Map," I replied.

"Why need map?" he asked through Arooo.

"So that I know where I am going."

"Where you going?"

"Across the ocean."

"Ocean here," he said, pointing. "Why need map?"

The natives seemed to interpret that I needed a map to *find* the ocean, rather than plot a course across it. By and by I sighed and simply shook my head - Lee-BE-nay would never make a navigator. I mumbled something about headings, currents, bearings and speed, which in my heart I knew would confuse him. I achieved my goal for he looked puzzled, turned the map about several times, and soon put it back in its place.

I was surprised by the Boot Islander's lack of skill and understanding of maritime matters such as ship building and navigation. But it also occurred to me that they had few building materials, so any ship would be a flimsy affair. Furthermore, they realistically had nowhere to go, for their island was as remote a citadel that stood in the oceans. Even if they had a stout vessel the journey would be so perilous that it would not be worth undertaking.

I should have been pleased that Lee-BE-nay returned my maps with disinterest, for soon each man soon helped himself to trinkets without a request - not even a nod - in my direction. Taa-TA-hoo took a glass bottle, Lee-BE-nay a long coil of rope and Arooo a knife from the galley. Their audacious pilfering angered me but again held both my tongue and my fists in check, for I knew that exercising either would harm my cause.

It seemed that they did not even realise their rudeness, for they showed no inclination toward guilt. They took ownership of my items as freely as they took air from my galley. Yet part of me was also relieved, for if they had cared to the natives could have stolen more than just trinkets. They could have taken the *Maris Alarum* herself. Or my life.

As we returned to shore, Arooo asked me a question using a mixture of broken Spanish, hand pointing and signs: "What tree gives bread fruit?" This question lightened my mood, and Arooo was hopelessly confused after my merrily tortured explanation of the harvesting, milling and baking process.

After leaving the provisions with Taa-TA-hoo and Lee-BE-nay, Arooo escorted me back to my cave. Rather than being pulled along in ungainly fashion as previously, Arooo indicated that I should simply stand behind him and slide my hands under his arms, and then grip the front of his shoulders. This arrangement made our swim far more streamlined; I even contributed some porpoise kicking. I was feeling increasingly comfortable in the water, and was relaxed enough to take in more of the underwater scene.

In the shallows, I was enchanted to see five lithe young children now diving through the hole in the "play rock", darting in and out of it like eels. As we swam deeper and nearer to the lagoon walls, the scenes became ever more curious. Bamboo shafts ran up, down and sideways. Most pipes disappeared into caves or other structures but a couple hung exposed, bubbling intermittent streams of air toward the surface. Like water stations for a Royal Mail horse, these free pipes would allow a swimmer a longer underwater journey than could be completed without them.

The lagoon wall was dotted with caves. Most of the caverns had decorative bamboo entrances at their face, most of which were adorned with shells and corals. Some caves had grand entrances - perhaps they were communal areas - while others, which I reckoned to be dwellings, were more modest. These bamboo antechambers seemed to have little functional use; perhaps they were built to distinguish each cave from the others, or to appease its owner's vanity.

As we swam further around the lagoon wall, I encountered more aspects of island life: smooth-skinned women collecting shellfish from the deep lagoon floor; a child hitching a ride by clinging to the shell of a startled turtle; an older woman, perhaps a governess of sorts, using whale-song speech to teach some young children. Occasionally one of the youngsters would take a breath from a nearby ventilation pipe and then return to their allotted place.

Clumps of seaweed occupied ledges like gardens, while nooks and crevasses in the walls held bamboo-caged fish. The melodic whale-song talk, which seemed to travel readily through the water, filled my ears from every direction. No doubt these sights and sounds were as mundane to the natives as was a horse and cart to a Londoner, but to my eyes and ears each simple encounter was incredible.

Unlike other tribal communities that had been plundered or destroyed by pirates and privateers for decades, I could see that this island had an undeniable survival advantage: invisibility. The natives had no need for the Ring of Eluned the Fortunate, for they could make themselves disappear whenever they chose simply by retreating to their caves. The black surface of the lagoon revealed nothing of their presence, and the lapping tides quickly obliterated footprints in the sand or any other similar traces of their inhabitation. I am sure that all previous sailors who passed this island had dismissed it as I had: a water-filled, uninviting crag, with no redeeming features worthy of exploration or settlement. The natives had no need to learn war craft, for they could vanish like ghosts in the night.[181]

Yet one question remained firmly fixed in my mind: why, and how, did the natives build their homes under water? Was it just for military invisibility? Although important, this advantage was surely not enough to justify such an enormous imposition on daily life. They must have had another reason, but I could not begin to fathom it.

As we swum near my cave, I thought I saw the long-haired girl through the clear lagoon waters. I glanced at her as we turned toward the entry hole, but I had no time to wave or otherwise communicate with her. But this vision quickly vaulted her to the forefront of my thoughts again, and the earlier desire I had felt for her rapidly returned.

Monday 3 September

Again I had much time alone in my cave. My spirits were higher overnight, for I felt that my ploy of gifting tomatoes to the natives had gone well. My thoughts went frequently toward the long haired girl, and my memory of her hourglass shape warmed my dreams. I longed to see her again, for she was indeed beautiful.

I hungrily ate the small food package (three types of seaweed and the tentacle of a large octopus) that a young native lad delivered to me. However it was late afternoon before Arooo appeared at my door, brandishing a stitched square of woven fibre cloth. He made eating gestures with his hands indicating that we were going for a meal; a very welcome development. He then pitched the cloth to me with the instruction *alterar su ropa:* change your clothes.

I was hesitant, for grace dictated that a ship's captain should dress formally for a meal; a vest, jacket and boots would surely be more

---

[181] There are geological precedents to the Boot Island cave system and its ability to hide its inhabitants. The Cappadocia region in Turkey boasts over 200 cities that are entirely underground, having been excavated through the soft, non-oxidised volcanic rock (The *tuff*). One such city, Derinkuyu, has 20 separate levels and is 60 metres deep; it was home to not only 20 000 people but also their livestock! Entry to this cave city was via a single hole, which, when approached by an enemy, could be disguised to look like an abandoned well.

appropriate. But with the thought of remaining sodden throughout the entire meal, not to mention the difficulty of swimming in such attire, I soon saw the logic in changing and was soon clothed as sparingly as the natives. I was pleased that summer lingered in the air.

Arooo and I were soon swimming underwater, using the increasingly familiar porpoise-like stroke. I looked in every direction for the long haired girl, but did not see her. We angled upward and to the west and soon arrived at our destination cave. This grotto had the grandest entrance of them all, with its decorative timber antechamber projecting fully 10 feet from the underwater rock face. We passed effortlessly through its open archway and then swam upward through a passage toward the cave proper.

I soon found myself standing in a relatively dry room whose walls and floor were draped in matted rugs. The aroma was rich and complex - open fields of grass, salty ocean air, and burning whale oil all mingled with each other - and was far more agreeable than my dank and musty prison room. I noted half a dozen ventilation pipes – far more than the solitary tube that serviced my cave – which no doubt added to the fresher feel of this underwater room. A short earthen corridor stepped its way upward, connecting this entry chamber to an even larger cavern.

Dozens of smoky oil lamps emitted flickering orange light that illuminated a large, oval cave hall; a carpet of woven palm fronds covered its earthen floor. The relative grandeur of the room left little doubt that it was designated for formal meals, communal meetings and the like. In the far wall was another arched opening from which the busy sounds of food preparation emanated - a galley of sorts. At the centre of the cavern, about two dozen rough stools surrounded a long narrow table. Large water-filled shells sat in a line down the table's centre, looking like bone china ornaments as fine as you would set upon the governor's table. Most incredible of all were the intricate art works that decorated the walls, including a series of a dozen or so large shell mosaics depicting scenes from island life.

Taa-TA-hoo and Lee-BE-nay sat at the head of the table; their place settings indicated their superior rank among the islanders. They nodded to me – they were not overly convivial, but these simple nods were a welcome change from their previous scowls. I also detected a faint smile at the sight of my loincloth. Arooo ordered me to remain where I was while he engaged them in a staccato conversation, which at least gave me the opportunity to examine the artworks more closely.

The mosaics were very finely detailed. The first piece looked very old, with many signs of fading and deterioration. It was a primitive picture that illustrated natives harvesting crops. Despite the presence of the familiar-looking mountain, I initially doubted that the picture's heritage was from Boot Island, for there was no depiction of the lagoon. Instead the scene showed an island with a fertile tree-filled central plateau - very similar to Diogo's description of the lush interior of Bird Island. It also showed dozens of caves in the surrounding ridge wall. I wondered what this picture meant, for it was clearly a different place to the water-filled island upon which I was now hostage. Perhaps, I guessed, it was a fantasy or a dream of the artist to live in such a nirvana.

The next picture, also clearly aged, showed scenes of a wild storm attacking that same lush island. I marvelled at the fine detail of the artist; from where, I wondered, had he or she procured the deep-blue-coloured shells that so evoked the wretched sea? I empathised with the islanders in the picture, for like many sailors, including Diogo, Fernando and I, these people understood the harsh realities of living life so close to Mother Ocean. She was a malevolent madam when she chose to be.

As I studied the storm-ravaged scene in the next picture, an impression slowly drew over me like a rising moon: *I was looking at Boot Island history*. This third mosaic depicted what was manifestly a pivotal event in the island's passage through time: the moment that the cliff at the eastern horn of the island collapsed – perhaps through a seam of red earth – exposing a large hole in the ridge wall. The picture showed an advancing wall of water flooding in through the new fissure, sweeping away everything and everyone in its path. By the time the surge was over, the island was irreversibly inundated.

My instinct was confirmed by the next picture that illustrated the flooded lagoon, with the water submerging the plateau and condemning the trees and crops to a watery grave. Fatefully, the inundation also filled the natives' caves. I guessed that many lives were lost in this horrid event; just as painfully, the survivors lost their precious homes and all of their arable land as well.

The mosaics so engrossed me that I was oblivious to the happenings in the room behind me, which had been steadily filling with natives.

Suddenly conscious of their company, I turned and saw a dozen pairs of eyes staring at me. Quickly they shifted their gaze down, but it was already clear from this reaction that they rarely hosted foreigners. Yet I was grateful that there was no aggression in their mannerisms. Some sat, while others remained standing and engaged in soft whale-song conversation. I glanced about for the long-haired girl, hoping that she was among their number, but could not see her. To avoid further awkwardness I buried myself back in the mosaics, and their simple charm and captivating historical context soon enveloped me again.

I stared in silence as the island's past played out before me. The next picture showed the islanders huddled on the lagoon ridge, clinging to each other in desperation, trying to shelter from the wind, sun and wild seas in tiny ramshackle huts. It must have been difficult to survive under such circumstances: there was little room for shelter and increasingly less room for trees and other sustenance-providing plants, for the lagoon had filled all but the small patch of hinterland. Building materials were scarce. I could feel the natives' pain acutely, for such despair had filled my early days on Bird Island. To live on the ocean's hearth, with little but a weak bamboo lean-to for protection, would have been a very stern test of a man's mettle; the wind, rain and sun would have taken a heavy toll, and the rocky floor would have provided not a shred of comfort.

Another image showed a young native swimming into an underwater cave – the artist had skilfully rendered the ridge with tiles that were clear, like glass, so that the cave could be seen inside it. For unknown reasons the natives at the surface were saddened and distressed; even their postures showed this clearly. I turned to Arooo, full of queries, but my questions remained unasked because he was pointing me to a stool.

"*Sentar,*" he instructed. I duly took my seat beside him, across from Taa-TA-hoo and Lee-BE-nay, yet my mind stayed with the pictures for some time. Sounds of food preparation, accompanied by a staccato buzz of short clicking and popping words, emanated from the galley. To my ear this sharp quick talk harmonised with the room's whale-song conversation like a drum accompanying a fiddle, providing a background beat to the lilting melodies.

By and by, like a rolling wave breaking inside my mind, the stark implausibility of my surrounds overtook me. I was about to dine *under water,* deep in the heart of a lagoon. I thought of the great explorers of the world - from Drake and Raleigh through to Dampier, Flinders and Cook[182] - each of whom had sailed the oceans before me. As I thought of those great and fearless men, I simply wondered: had any of them ever had such a mind-turning experience as sitting with a group of natives in an underwater dining hall, listening to haunting whale-song speech while dressed in naught but a square of woven palm fronds? Even though I was a prisoner on this island, I felt my wings beginning to bud again. Yet again I dearly wished for another Englishman to be my witness so that others would more readily believe my report of it.

More natives filtered into the room, their dark wet dark skin glistening orange and yellow in the lamp light. I noted that as they arrived, each diner grasped their fists loosely in front of their chests and then nodded to the assembled islanders with a simple but respectful greeting. Most of them glanced in my direction but did little else to acknowledge me. I sensed that my presence was stifling the mood, but again took solace that I had attracted no outward hostility.

I kept my eyes busy for the long-haired girl, but a native lad eventually took the last seat. I grimaced, for the full table conveyed that she would not be dining with us tonight. Soon after that, Lee-BE-nay stood and sang a long, high note, quietening the other diners, who reverentially turned their eyes forward and downward. I mimicked their piety. Then Taa-TA-hoo stood and together the two chief natives talk-sang a short, lilting verse – perhaps a form of thanksgiving. Once they mentioned a word that sounded like "Yapaarta-se." Some faces turned briefly to me, while a few others giggled. I presume that Taa-TA-hoo and Lee-BE-nay had mentioned me but I did not know in what context.

The thanksgiving ended with two-fisted bows, whereupon some young galley-hands transported food to the table. I was hoping – nay, expecting – a feast, for the setting and occasion suggested grandiosity. But only a pauper would consider that meal a banquet, for it was very

---

[182] Sir Francis Drake, Sir Walter Raleigh, William Dampier, Matthew Flinders and James Cook were indeed all very accomplished explorers and seamen. It is interesting to note that McAdam mentions only Englishmen - he omits other highly credentialed foreign sailors such as Marco Polo, Christopher Columbus and Vasco da Gama – perhaps casting a shadow of xenophobia on 19th century Britain's teaching of maritime history.

restrained. Each guest received a skinned raw fish that had been sprinkled with coarse salt and some finely-cut bitter-tasting leaves, a small crab or two, and a large portion of shredded seaweed that reminded me of sauerkraut.

There was no cutlery, so even the women-folk ate with their hands, but no-one appeared to realise that this was poor manners. After each had devoured their meal, a large shell containing star fruits, plus some boiled root-crops that tasted vaguely of sweet potato, was passed about. Each diner took one - and only one - piece of each fruit.

The conversational singing had just reached a pleasant after-dinner hum when Taa-TA-hoo and Lee-BE-nay stood again. The room grew quiet as they spoke; the natives certainly regarded their leaders with respect, for no-one so much as whispered while they held their discourse. Although I could not understand their language it was clear from their gestures that they were talking of me. The crowd laughed as they depicted me trying to swim, my arms flailing wildly through the water, and I again picked out the word 'Yapaarta-se'. At first I felt affronted by this mimicry, but soon realised the stupidity of such emotion and endured my own comedic humiliation with as much grace as I could muster. I sensed the story of Bubo unfolding as they imitated a bird's flying wings. The crowd directed stifled frowns toward me as they described Bubo smashing the coconuts, but this was quickly countered by a broad sweep of Lee-BE-nay's arm that indicated two galley hands carrying large baskets into the room, one full with ripe tomatoes and the other with bread rolls.

I watched as each diner picked a single fruit from the first basket and enjoyed their reaction as they tasted a sweet tomato for the first time. After a lifetime of little more than raw fish and seaweed, it was easy to understand why they valued this new flavour so much. It must have tasted as rich and strange upon their tongues as when the Indian man's curry powder had first invigorated my senses at Billingsgate market. A broad smile broke across each of their faces as they bit into the deep red flesh, and many cast nodding glances toward me.

But I broke out in laughter – perhaps a little rudely, but if I can accept their earlier slur with good grace then they cannot complain if I return one – as they struggled with the taste of the bread rolls. Why? Taa-TA-hoo and Lee-BE-nay had transported the basket through the water, rendering the bread rolls as little more than sodden lumps of dough. Now I understood why the long-haired girl had ignored my offering of bread on the second night.

After the meal finished, most diners departed without further ceremony. A few islanders remained chatting but as I could not understand their song-talk I stood to study the historical art works again. I signalled to Arooo to join me because I wished to learn more about the island's history, but I struggled for the Spanish words to frame my questions. Arooo's irritation quickly grew and he resorted to simply nodding whenever I asked him something. I soon became equally frustrated because the pictures had piqued my curiosity but my questions were too complex for our limited grammar and simple hand-signs to convey.

"If only you could *comprender Ingles*," I said, mixing my two tongues in exasperation.

Arooo stopped nodding and looked at me sideways.

"*Repetir*," he asked.

"I wish you spoke English," I repeated. "*Deseo que usted habla Inglés*."

"*Habla ingles*?" he inquired.

"*Si, si, si*," I nodded. "*Muy bien...* very well."

Without pause, Arooo turned toward Taa-TA-hoo and Lee-BE-nay. He clicked rapidly, to which they replied in similar staccato fashion.

"*Sentar*," Arooo instructed me, pointing to the stool. "*Momento*."

With that, Arooo hurried from the cavern. I heard him plunge into the exit hole, leaving me with Taa-TA-hoo and Lee-BE-nay, wondering what would happen next. I hoped that someone on the island could speak the mother tongue of the Empire, for to hear just a single familiar syllable would be a balm to my ears.

I admit that what transpired next completely overawed me. Arooo entered the room ... he was accompanied by - for this I offer my eternal gratitude to Providence - *the long-haired girl*. My heart flapped about like a fish caught in a net. It was *her*.

Arooo, as if directed by Cupid himself, sat her directly in front of me. Her features, highlighted by the orange glow of the whale-oil lamps, were even more striking than my memory had conjured. She had deep, dark eyes that were slightly narrowed, and high, full cheekbones that had so enraptured me during my dreams. Her brief loincloth and a chest band afforded me an almost unobstructed view of her smooth brown skin. Long black hair hung down her back. She gave me a simple nod, which I returned on instinct.

Then, I saw it: an infinitesimal smile, imperceptible to all but me, to acknowledge our secret nocturnal meetings on the beach. Clearly she had not been sent to trap me but had visited me surreptitiously, of her own accord. Her tiny hint of a smile told the whole story.

Instantly, I was smitten. Yes, I had dreamed and lusted for this girl already, but now I was fully, wholly, completely smitten.

For a minute I could do nothing but stare, for the cog-wheels in my mind had obstinately frozen on the girl and her beauty. I simply could not conjure up any other reaction but to look blankly at her while my mind tried to reaffirm that she was real. Many times I tried to talk, but the words stuck in my craw and not even a breath of air escaped my lips. My mind careened ahead, and was instantly filled with sinful visions of my future with this beauty.

Then, just as my desires and dreams were soaring toward the stars, a stout young man appeared in the doorway. He walked smartly over and placed an arm about the long-haired girl's shoulders in a clear show of ownership. No! *She was his.*

Had I just eaten a dinner of lead? My innards suddenly felt so heavy it was as if they had dropped to my feet. The simple action of that man, that *interloper*, placing his arms about her shoulders had ripped away my hopes in an instant. My chest steeled itself against that dream-thief, and I felt my fingers curl into fists. The long-haired girl's smile had been for me, not him - yet now he had imposed himself on our connection. I cussed and blasphemed at him inwardly – if one could hear a silent curse, this one was loud and long - but I could do nothing to remedy the slight.

If this intrusion had occurred at Blackfriars I would have challenged him outside, put a few stiff jabs on his chin and then swept the long-haired girl away in my arms, for I knew from her tiny smile that she had eyes for me. But here, deep under a lagoon on a remote island, I could do nothing but suffer the indignity in forced silence and false grace.

"Hel...lo," she said by and by.

"He-hel-hello," I stammered back, my countenance further disturbed by the melodic sound of her voice. Then, after an awkward silence, I added "Do you speak English?"

"Little," she replied in sweet sing-song, and holding her delicate fingers close together to indicate the same. *If only* I had thought to ask this simplest of questions earlier.

"I am pleased. My Spanish is poor. Arooo was frustrated."

She nodded and then said, "My name Ki-Ora." She then loosely clenched her fists and raised them to her chest, before nodding her head in greeting. I nodded and imitated her actions in reply.

"This ... Baa-GA-nee," she said, emphasising and clicking the middle syllable of his name. She indicated her husband-of-sorts, to whom I reluctantly and stiffly repeated the greeting.

"You..." she smiled and sang my tribal name: "*Yapaarta-se*."

From her lips, my name sounded like a moniker for an angel, not a scrubby old jack tar. I can hold no more a tune than a ditty, so despite the sweetness of the song-sound as it came from Ki-Ora's lips, I simply repeated my name in English.

"Yapaarta-se."

She giggled. "Yes, Yapaarta-Se," she sang, and smiled again. I then realised why she had been so amused. "It mean *Swim Like Stone*."

I grinned, for it was as true a name as could have been bestowed. I looked into her eyes, and for a fleeting moment I was able to ignore the presence of everyone else, particularly Baa-GA-nee, in the cave. A satisfied smile worked into my face and stayed fixed upon my cheeks and would still be there now but for what she said next.

"Baa-GA-nee speak English too," she said, thrusting a metaphorical scimitar deep into my side. "We talk ... next day." Then she twisted the figurative sword: "Baa-GA-nee swim you to cave".

I nodded painfully, bid good evening to Ki-Ora, then hung sullenly to Baa-GA-nee's shoulders as we twisted our way through the water to my deep cave. He deposited me in my prison with not a word passing between us. Then I lay on my seaweed mattress, without sleep for much of the night, suffering an unquenchable longing for yet another woman whom I could not hold.

Tuesday 4 September

My day began when Baa-GA-nee delivered raw breakfast fish, with a large side portion of heartache, to my dank cave. My sleep-robbed mind had little want of conversation, particularly with that dream thief. I felt more content to ignore Baa-GA-nee than engage him, but he nevertheless watched me disinterestedly as I picked at the fish. By and by I pushed the fish aside and lay back on my bed.

"I am finished," I said and then rolled away from him, signifying that our meeting was over. I heard him mutter and mumble something in crude English, although his exact words escaped me. He then gathered up the picked fish carcass and strode out the roughly-hewn doorway. Although I was pleased that Baa-GA-nee was leaving, the sound of the door shutting sent a pang of anguish through me for I could barely countenance the thought of spending another day alone in this gloomy grotto, particularly when *she* was outside.

"Wait," I called to Baa-GA-nee, more on instinct than thought. And then, "I have more food in my ship."

His dark features re-appeared in the door.

"More food," I said, thinking of the peas. "Green fruit."

"More food," he confirmed, his deep voice a deep baritone— it was the first time I had clearly heard him speak. He then departed without further acknowledgement. I lay back on my creaking bunk, again with nothing to occupy myself; I would even have welcomed a list of tiresome chores.

As the day inched onward my mind intertwined thoughts of Ki-Ora with, inevitably, Beth. Every time that Beth entered my mind I fought to replace her vision with that of Ki-Ora. But then logic would intervene in the form of Baa-GA-nee, spitefully reminding me that I would never hold Ki-Ora close. Then my thoughts would revert to Beth, before I again pushed her aside, reminding myself that I must forget her. I would then turn to the more comforting visions of Ki-Ora's brown skin ... then Baa-GA-nee... then Beth.... In this morose little cave my mind twisted, vaulted and leapt until I was dizzy from thought.

I was uncertain how long it was before Baa-GA-nee returned. My best reckoning was a few hours but it felt as long as a Glaswegian winter, for tormented time moves torpidly.

"Come," he said simply. "Green food from ship." I followed him to the exit hole where I begrudgingly grasped his shoulders and soon we were swimming toward the beach. I looked about for Ki-Ora, but did not see her. We stopped for just two quick breaths at the air pipe, for Baa-GA-nee seemed to regard my need for air as an irritation rather than a necessity. I was quickly learning that Baa-GA-nee regarded me similarly: as an irritation, and a very expendable one at that. I harboured no doubts that he sensed my desire for his woman, and therefore treated me as a threat.

I reciprocated his feelings for precisely the same reasons. One woman could not hold the love of two men without them coming to blows; this has always been, and will always be. If this contest were on my ground then I would win her heart in a trice. But on Boot Island my cards were poor, and I knew that must play every one with the utmost care if I was to wrench Ki-Ora from his bunk.

We surfaced at the beach, which was again alive with activity. I still could not reconcile it with the serene, empty bay that I encountered when I had first scrambled over the ridge wall. We met with Taa-TA-hoo and Lee-BE-nay, who walked with us across the beach toward the southern ridge. The three native men were soon deep in conversation – the staccato, clicking type of talk that they reverted to when hurried or stressed. They stopped frequently as their debate waxed and waned, providing me the opportunity to observe the native workers.

One gathering quickly took my eye, for they were all women. I cast my eyes from one face to the next, hoping to sight Ki-Ora, for even a passing glance of her would fill a gap in my longing as quickly as an end-log fills a posthole. Alas, she was not among them. Despite Ki-Ora's absence, the women's group held my attention as they skilfully wove large baskets from palm fronds. How rapidly their hands moved! One of them was coating the completed weavings with the rubber material that native girls had collected in coconut shell bowls, catching it as it dripped from long spirals in the thick-trunked trees. I guessed that they were making the bellows apparatus that kept air circulating inside their water-locked caves.

We passed a group of male natives who had gathered under the hinterland tress. They worked with long lengths of bamboo and appeared to be constructing, or perhaps repairing, ventilation pipes. Each man brandished a thin spear that had a sharp rock bound to its tip. They inserted these spears into the centres of newly harvested bamboo poles and then used a bow-like contrivance to rotate them quickly back and forth like a woodworker's drill and bit. By this primitive yet ingenious method they hollowed the bamboo, removing the segmental dividers. They then coated the ends of each pipe with the white rubbery sap and then fitted it to a slightly larger or smaller piece so that they achieved a firm seal. Maintaining the ventilation system was obviously an ongoing task for the Boot islanders, and my brief observations showed that they were very practiced in their craft.

After we arrived at the top of the ridge, I carefully climbed down into my tender. The three natives had already leapt from the cliff top and were frolicking about in the open waters when I arrived. They wasted no time towing me to the *Maris Alarum*. I was still amazed that the natives held so little regard for the prowling sharks and other such devils of the deep; if I merely dipped my hand into the water I would be fearful of losing it to a sharp row of teeth, yet the Boot Islanders freely submerged their whole bodies and even their heads beneath the open ocean with not even a dagger for protection.

Bubo was flying above the eastern horn of the island, just above the hole in the cliff face, and sighted our party as we approached the *Maris Alarum*. He immediately flew to us and landed on the top of the ship's mast. I was pleased and relieved to see him again, for in this world of strangeness and isolation he was more like a dear and trusted friend than a pet bird. Yet rather than trill a greeting as we clambered up the rope ladder and over the gunwales, he carked loudly; Bubo was clearly unhappy with the intrusion of the natives. He soon removed any doubt about his intentions, for after we had pulled ourselves fully aboard Bubo darted down, flapping his wings wildly and screeching aggressively. The sound was startling, even to my ears. In a panic, the natives tumbled under the cover of the boom, but Bubo nevertheless lunged at Baa-GA-nee, seeming to aim his talons at the native's face. (Here I admit to unpleasantness of my thoughts: it was a shame that he had not hit his target, because I held that man in little regard.) I had not seen this fury in Bubo before, even the previous day at the beach. By and by I coaxed Bubo to my forearm and tried to soothe his vitriol. I directed the men, who were now cowering behind the mast, into the hatch.

I pacified Bubo for some minutes with gentle ruffling of his hackle feathers and soft words. Yet he was perhaps right to feel this way about the Islanders, for maybe he sensed that they had robbed me of my freedom. However I wanted to play a calm hand and slowly parlay the natives. Aggression held no chance of success, for I was alone and without weapons. Even if I still possessed my scimitar and pistols I could not hope to take the whole population down in battle, and despite their unjustified imprisonment of me, nor did I wish to. A yielding approach was a better option, and was one that was already making gains. By and by Bubo's rage eased. I released him from my forearm whereupon he flew not to his port gunwale perch but to the top of the mast, demonstrating that he still harboured resentment.

Inside the galley, the natives had recovered from Bubo's onslaught, and as on their previous visit they seemed as gay as children in a sweet shop. Taa-TA-hoo was fascinated with the tool chest, examining even the blunt adze as if it was one of Mr Dollond's prized sextants. The metallic elements in particular held his attention, and he stroked and touched the head of each implement as if it was a woman's thigh. Lee-BE-nay continued his wonderment at my navigational instruments, this time attracted to the numbered log scale and the dividers. As before, I was aware that the natives were beholding many of these simple items for the first time, and that even my old cast iron pot was as wondrous to them as the floating sea bellows were to me. So I waited patiently (like Mr Dollond had done as I explored his instrument proprietary) as the men fossicked about my ship. I realised that they had not trussed my legs today, and in time I felt not like a prisoner but almost like a host.

Baa-GA-nee sat on my galley chair, thereby insulting my Captain's sensibilities. He prodded at the oven.

"What?" he asked brusquely, pointing at the cast iron cooker before him.

"Oven," I replied with equal brevity.

"Why oven?"

"It cooks your food."

"What is cook?"

"It makes your food hot."

He shook his head, obviously lacking the necessary intelligence to comprehend my simple answers.

By and by I fetched a crate of peas, and nibbled on a handful as I waited. They were still green but a little shrivelled, and would benefit from soaking in salt water before cooking. I hoped that the natives enjoyed them as they had the tomatoes, for each gift ingratiated me with them and earned me a small step forward on the overgrown and slippery pathway to my freedom. Perhaps, also, Ki-Ora might be interested in a man who could bring her the exotic delights of another world, rather than one who delivered raw kippers.

The natives seemed oblivious to me as they prodded about the galley. I fetched my journal, for I wished to bring it with me to the island. My right hand burned to record the details of my internment before they slid from my mind. But soon a problem arose: I had to keep my journal dry as I swam through the lagoon to my cave for even a few drops of water would run the ink. Bereft of better alternatives, I fetched my unused log books and carefully unwrapped their covers, taking care not to tear the wool-fat-smeared brown paper that Mr Whittow had suggested would keep the damp at bay. I bound all four sheets tightly around my journal and secured them with twine. It was a poor solution, but I hoped the natives would improve on my methods before submerging my precious journal. I tucked my quill and ink pot under the string. After a moment's thought I also fetched my graphite-and-lead pencil, for it would continue to provide service even if it was wet to its core, and was less likely to smudge when wet than was ink.

Meanwhile Taa-TA-hoo had discovered my burning glass and was bemused by its magnifying effect on his hand. He showed it to Lee-BE-nay, who apparently made a droll comment, for all three natives grinned. They enquired through Baa-GA-nee as to its purpose.

"It makes fire," I said, keeping my replies as simple as possible.

"What is fire?" asked Baa-GA-nee after a laborious translation.

"Fire cooks food."

At this Baa-GA-nee stopped and looked at the stove. He then glanced again at the burning glass, then at the stove again before shrugging his shoulders.

By and by, after many such exchanges, we returned to the island. I carried a large crate of peas and my wrapped journal. The natives had again shamelessly helped themselves to some of my possessions: they carried two knives, my blanket, an earthenware jar and the burning glass. Again they did not seek my approval, offered no apology, and did not demonstrate even a mite of guilt. It was as though they regarded my possessions as their own. I felt very aggrieved by this open pilfering, but could do nothing but keep my lips closed and my fists loose.

The sun was low as we arrived at the island and the beach was now deserted. The lagoon looked tranquil and empty, with no suggestion of life in its inky black waters. The rising tide had wiped away all footprints from the beach and the natives had removed their tools and implements, erasing all trace of their activities. It looked like the same empty, uninhabited cay as I had discovered earlier - the transformation was as miraculous as it was simple.

I indicated my journal. "No water," I said to the natives through Baa-GA-nee. Thankfully Taa-TA-hoo appeared to understand my request, for he plunged his head under the water and emitted a brief but melodic whale song. A short time later a native girl appeared from the water carrying three small woven bags that were covered in the white rubber material. Taa-TA-hoo poured the peas into the first two containers while the third, he made clear, was to store my journal for the underwater journey. Then he and Lee-BE-nay each carried a bag of peas into the lagoon and disappeared.

I bound the woven bag tightly about my precious log book but I remained doubtful, for even a slight inundation would ruin it. But even as I started wrapping, Baa-GA-nee took it from me and simply placed my journal into the bag and tied it there with some string that was attached to the bag's bottom. He did not attempt to seal it closed or to bind the waterproof covers tightly about my precious cargo.

"No!" I cried sharply and attempted, but failed, to snatch it back from him. Clearly Baa-GA-nee did not appreciate, or care, that my journal must not get wet *at all*. Despite my protestations he remained firm, and he submerged the open bag, roughly dragging me down underwater with it, silencing my disagreeing voice. I tried my best to fight the bag off him but this lagoon was his territory, and I soon realised that my struggle was in vain.

I held grimly to Baa-GA-nee's shoulders as we plunged through the darkening lagoon waters. Baa-GA-nee carried the woven bag upside-down in his forward hand, yet defiantly, rudely, uncaringly open. This sight sent stakes of anguish through me as I reeled at the thought of my lost words. My hatred of Baa-GA-nee rapidly escalated, goading me to throttle his neck, and the only reason that I didn't choke him was that my own fate would have suffered.

This brute not only slept aside the woman that I desired, but had just destroyed the other thing that was most precious to me. My written words were more valuable to me than a chest full of silver sovereigns, but each yard of this agonising swim was erasing them forever. Baa-GA-nee, the ignorant savage, had not cared to spend even a minute to seal it against the lagoon water, obliterating months of heart-felt logs. I took just a single breath at the ventilation pipe before waving Baa-GA-nee onward, for the sooner I could begin prising open the sodden pages to salvage what I could of my story, the less damage I would have to contend with.

Yet when we landed upon the small platform at the cave's entrance, Baa-GA-nee surprised me. He opened the bag and untied the string, allowing my journal to drop into my waiting palms. Incredibly, it was dry, with not even a drop of water on its greased paper wrapping. I looked up with astonishment.

"Bag upside down," he said by way of explanation. "No water in bag." I looked at him, my features no doubt conveying both my relief and amazement. "Swim difficult, but no water in bag."[183]

---

[183] To understand this effect, the reader should simply imagine an empty glass submerged open side down into a tub of water. The base of the glass would remain dry.

Stunned, I responded with a stiff two-fisted bow as a show of gratitude. He nodded his head curtly in acknowledgement and left me alone. I wasted no time in opening my journal, and was soon recollecting my recent days with ferocity.

Wednesday 5 September

I awoke late – it was nearly noon, judging by the light that filtered through the entry hole. I had slept deeply, for my journal writing had consumed me well into the night, having stopped only when my whale-oil lamp spluttered to extinction.

Again the natives left me isolated for most of the day. In between my sessions of writing I lay on my bunk, where my mind alternated between two thoughts: how to ingratiate myself further with the natives to secure my release, and Ki-Ora. Mostly Ki-Ora. Later that day, toward the evening, Baa-GA-nee entered my cave.

"Food," he intoned. I needed no further encouragement for my stomach was hollow, and despite my reticence to swim through the lagoon again, or to be physically close to this man (despite his delivery of my journal I still disliked him) I was soon clutching at Baa-GA-nee's shoulders and clumsily kicking my way toward the dining cavern.

Many natives were already sitting around the long table. Most of them turned their deep faces toward me as we entered. I performed a respectful two-fisted bow, which the natives returned in varying degrees. They were clearly more accustomed to my presence than previously, for their sing-song chatter quickly refilled the room. I scanned the faces at the table and soon spotted she whom I hoped to see: Ki-Ora. It was an easy task to find her, for her full smile lit the room like a hundred lanterns. She stood and beckoned me to sit by her side toward the head of the table; clearly she held some minor rank amongst the natives. My hopes briefly blazed as brightly as her smile, but were quickly wetted when Baa-GA-nee, ahead of me, embraced Ki-Ora.

If he intended for his action to demonstrate his ownership of Ki-Ora or to dampen my enthusiasm for her then he failed miserably, for even as her chin rested upon his shoulder her gaze met with mine. I am sure that I did not imagine another tiny smile creeping into the corners of her lips.

Soon we were seated on the tiny stools, with Baa-GA-nee and I to either side of Ki-Ora. Shortly thereafter Taa-TA-hoo and Lee-BE-nay stood and delivered what I assumed a ritual blessing, before three young native girls served the food. Again the fare was quite banal: raw fish (two each) and a large shell-full of cold, dark green stew that I could best describe as pickled seaweed. It was very salty and bitter; even sauerkraut was sweet by comparison. Eating took some time, for picking and sucking raw flesh from fish bones was a laborious task.

Ki-Ora alternated between conversing with Baa-GA-nee and me. In truth she simply made chatter; usually such conversation rasps my ears like the squealing of a stuck sow, but in this case every syllable of Ki-Ora's lilting voice entranced me. My replies, suffocated by my longing for her, were by comparison staccato and uninteresting at best. The harder I tried to engage her attention the more I flailed. My conversational skills were as poor as my swimming; after many days alone at sea the flow of my conversation was sluggish, and her limited understanding of my English words exacerbated the problem.

By and by each diner finished their food, whereupon the young girls passed about the two baskets of peas. At first, the natives were unsure how they should eat them, and looked at the little green fruits as though they had been harvested from the moon. Most of the natives hesitantly took a few pods for their plate, but they seemed uncertain of whether to take just one or a generous handful. Nobody ate them. Soon the basket arrived at Baa-GA-nee, then Ki-Ora and finally to me. I felt dozens of pairs of native eyes upon me as I scooped a modest handful of pea pods onto my shell plate, and then passed the large bowl forward.

I picked up a pod and stripped it, revealing eight small round peas. The natives, including Ki-Ora, watched me intently as if I was a stage performer rather than a diner. On instinct, rather than eat the pea myself, I turned to Ki-Ora and mimed to her that she should open her mouth, whereupon I popped a pea between her soft pink lips. She swallowed it thoughtfully and then broke into a grin. I fed her the remaining seven, each sending her mouth into a broader smile.

For a moment I found my head and body simply moving toward her without conscious direction from my mind, and it took all of my restraint to stop from kissing those lips. I somehow kept myself back, acutely aware of how Baa-GA-nee would react to this public gesture, for he clearly liked to exercise control over Ki-Ora.

But then I saw an amusing sight: each native was feeding peas into his neighbour's open mouth. They had interpreted my surreptitious flirtation with Ki-Ora as a normal eating habit, and were imitating my method! Even Taa-TA-hoo and Lee-BE-nay fed each other, oblivious to the subtle seductive power of such action. A wry grin coursed its way slowly upon my face, momentarily curing me of the torment of being unable to kiss Ki-Ora.

I was about to correct the natives' methods but demurred; this lively show was an improvement on the drudgery of sucking flesh from the bones of raw fish. They seemed to be enjoying themselves. I felt satisfied that my gift had been well received, and that I was steadily gaining the trust of the Boot Islanders - a fact confirmed by the humble two-fisted bows I received as each native later departed.

By and by a group of four - the two chief natives, Ki-Ora and Baa-GA-nee - engaged themselves in deep conversation. From the movement of their eyes it was clear that the topic under discussion was one Captain Fintan "Yapaarta-Se" McAdam. I sat idly as they discussed my fate. How I longed to interject and plead my case for innocence, but the speed of their staccato click-pop language left no pause for interruption.

As their conversation lengthened, the departing diners emptied the room, magnifying my isolation. My awkwardness grew so to lift my unease I edged across to examine the art works that had so intrigued me the previous night. I briefly reappraised the first five pictures before my gaze fell upon the next mosaic, which illustrated the construction of the initial ventilation pipe. I marvelled at the skill of the artist, who had used nothing but crushed shells to represent details such as the tiny air bubbles that emanated from the end of the pipe. I noted that this early system was operated by human effort; a line of men sat behind large sets of bellows awaiting their shift on the pumps.

In the next picture, a cut-away vision showed a crew of men working to enlarge the caves upward, no doubt expanding the liveable areas for dry inhabitation. Many rooms were added, each above or to the side of a previous cave, and above the outside water line. Then this history-book-upon-a-wall showed the first of the wave-operated pumps; they must have worked efficiently, because the next picture showed the intrepid islanders fixing dozens of such pumps into place below the western cliffs. The third-to-last mosaic illustrated the island as I had discovered it: a fully functioning community, with the caves now extending high up into the heart of the surrounding ridge wall, but accessible only through the original cave entrances under the water.

I paused to consider the ramifications of such an arrangement and could see many advantages. First, it allowed the islanders to devote the small, protected stretch of arable hinterland to the life-sustaining trees and shrubs rather than dwellings. Without this land for produce, they would surely find it impossible to sustain their food intake.

Second, the cave habitats provided protection that a loose humpy on a ridge top could never equal. To eke an existence atop the rocky walls under the full weight of the unforgiving elements would have been extremely uncomfortable, perhaps even impossible. By contrast, the underwater caves would be immune from the fury of nature; even the most sadistic of storms could not disturb their calm sanctity. The solid rock walls protected them fully from the rain, winds and even the most violent of typhoons.

Finally, the undersea entrances ensured invisibility, which was a mightily powerful defence in the fight to survive what were increasingly dangerous times. My measure of the islanders grew with these realisations, for they had proved themselves resilient against all that Mother Ocean, and other tribes of men, could throw at them.[184]

---

[184] I gate-crashed the Anthropology department's end-of-semester keg to discuss Boot Island with their graduate students. I discovered that there are several historical precedents of a community overcoming such inundation. The most famous, of course, is Venice, whose inhabitants overcame rising swamp waters by hammering long wooden pillars into the sand, building platforms on those piers, and then constructing their dwellings atop the platforms. Another less famous but equally ingenious method was used in the Micronesian city of Nan Madol (often called 'The Venice of the Pacific'). In the 1300s, its inhabitants built stone walls amidst the rising lagoon waters, which they filled with rocks and coral, forming more than 100 artificial islets on which they lived. However the Boot Island community is the first documented example of a human civilisation *embracing* the ocean as part of its everyday topography, rather than trying to subvert it.

Two recent mosaics completed the series. One showed a ship smashed upon the outside cliff – it was an odd triple-masted design that was not English, and nor was it a Spanish Galleon – but it nevertheless confirmed that I was not the first foreigner to visit Boot Island; after all, some of the islanders knew outside languages, which they must have been learned from someone. The final scene depicted something even more odd: a large grey triangle above the lagoon surface. At first I guessed that it was the fin of a sea devil, but it was large enough to be the sail of a small craft and so could not be that of a shark. I wondered at its significance. Had the Boot Islander people attempted to build a sailing vessel? I had seen no evidence of maritime craft. Suddenly and fortuitously, Ki-Ora appeared at my side.

"Like pictures?" she enquired.

"They are wondrous."

Ki-Ora walked closely beside me – so closely that I could sense her presence with my skin - as I absorbed the art works with my eyes and her heady aroma with the rest of me. Once her arm brushed across mine, sending my loins aflutter. She felt smooth, soft and warm - sensations rarely experienced alone at sea.

"Who is this man?" I asked, pointing at the picture of the young lad swimming into a flooded cave.

"He my ...." Ki-Ora paused, clearly thinking. "... grandmother?"

"Grandfather," I corrected.

"Yes, grandfather," she smiled. "Words I forget sometimes. He my ..."she paused briefly, counting on her fingers, then continued,"... grandfather grandfather grandfather. He Ora-Ba-nee. He found air in cave. Save family. Save island."

I did some mental juggling. Ora-Ba-nee was Ki-Ora's great-great-great-great grandfather - six generations. So I concluded that for about a century the Boot Islanders had resided in these unique undersea dwellings. Like the birds on Bird Island, they had made the most of the poor cards in their hand.

"Why are the people sad?" I asked, while pointing to the group of mourners in the same picture and miming a pout.

Ki-Ora, in her sing-song faltering English, and with a myriad of hand gestures, gradually answered my question.

"Ora-Ba-nee swim to cave. Find air in cave. Stay long time. Family thought he die in water. Next day, Ora-Ba-nee swim back. Alive. Family happy."

It must have been quite a moment, I mused, as another question arose in my mind.

"If there was already air in the caves, why do you need the pumps?"

Ki-Ora's look conveyed that she did not understand my question.

"The pumps," I repeated, miming the action of the bellows and indicating them on the mosaic. "Why do the caves need pumps?"

Her eyes lifted, indicating comprehension.

"Air in cave last one or two day, then no breathe. No lamp burn. No water, air still in cave, but no breathe. Pump make new air."

I could not fathom how air could be used, yet remain there all the same. I nonetheless nodded, for despite my years learning natural history with Reverend Butler it was clear that the natives understood things like air and water far better than I did. Maybe someone like Mr Priestly could explain it on my return to London, for I am sure he would be delighted to hear my reports of this unique civilisation[185].

I pointed to the final picture, which showed the large fin-like triangle cutting its way through lagoon waters. "The grey triangle – what is it?" Ki-Ora's countenance subtly changed. Her head tilted downward and she paused before turning back to me, her lips ever so slightly pursed.

"It is past," she whispered before moving onward, motioning a little too quickly toward the second-to-last picture of the stricken vessel. "This ship Russkiy."

---

[185] We now know, thanks in part to the works of the aforementioned Sir Joseph Priestly, that oxygen, which sustains our respiration, constitutes only 21% of air. The oxygen in the caves, if not refreshed, would be slowly replaced by carbon dioxide, maintaining the air's volume but rendering it unable to support human life, or fire. The ingenious pump system would have elegantly overcome this problem.

It was interesting to know that a Russian vessel had been wrecked on Boot Island, but I was certain that Ki-Ora had avoided a full answer of my previous question. She had clearly been unsettled by my enquiry, or the picture, or both.

A deep voice suddenly interrupted my thoughts. "We go." I turned to see Baa-GA-nee pointing me down the corridor toward the cave exit. Reluctantly – for I was enjoying not only the history lesson but also the unfettered closeness of Ki-Ora – I inched my way down the steep slope. Baa-GA-nee then raised my hopes.

"We take you cave." *We*. "We" included Ki-Ora. I stepped across, positioning myself within easy reach of Ki-Ora's shoulders. But Baa-GA-nee responded quickly to my subtle dance, interposing his broad frame between his woman and me. I soon found myself underwater, staring through the starlit water at the woman I so deeply desired, all the while clinging tightly to her betrothed.

I do not know if Reverend Butler's god of the church exists. I do not know if he enters the minds of men looking for sinners to punish. But I hope he does not, for I sinned many times in my thoughts that night.

Thursday 6 September

I awoke late, noting that someone had left a parcel of food on the small table. I unwrapped it to discover half a dozen small crustaceans, a shell filled with green seaweed stew and a small round disc of white flesh that I could not identify. I ate heartily, for although this meal did not offer the same contentment as, say, a hog's head stew with baked apple, it was a vast improvement on raw fish. In particular, the white fleshy disc was most tender and sweet[186].

By and by I heard a splash from the distant corridor and soon thereafter a radiant Ki-Ora and a typically surly Baa-GA-nee entered my dim cave. I greeted her with a bow, before nodding to Baa-GA-nee as an afterthought.

"Taa-TA-hoo, Lee-BE-nay say you leave cave today." My look of surprise must have been earnest. Baa-GA-nee then added, unfortunately, "Come with me". As he trailed me through the water, it still curdled me to

---

[186] A sea scallop?

grasp this man's shoulders and cling to him as though I was as useless as a small child, and needed to be escorted everywhere for my own well being.

I disliked his similarly paternal attitude toward Ki-Ora. He presided over her as if he was her Lord and she his servant, even though she clearly had authority within the tribe. He acted as though he owned her. When I compared it to the love - the equal, bilateral, caring love – that Beth and I shared, I loathed him even more. I has never felt it necessary to intervene when Beth talked to another man, for I knew and trusted that she would not hurt me. Yet Baa-GA-nee barely let her out of his sight, and scowled at her if she appeared to be enjoying my company.

By and by I opened my eyes to take in the full picture of the lagoon's underwater activity, which I did not only distract myself from the animosity that I felt toward my transporter but also from the memories of my beloved. Each trip through the lagoon so far had revealed many surprises and this traverse proved to be no different. The deepest caves had tightly bound bamboo grids at their entrance, and as we passed by one such grotto I saw a multitude of large fish held captive within it. I guessed that the deepest, lowest caves had flooded fully, and had proved too difficult to extend upward to where dry liveable space could be created. Yet the islanders had put these inundated caves to resourceful use, converting them into live fish storage tanks.

Soon we arrived at the beach whereupon Baa-GA-nee disappeared back into the lagoon, leaving me unguarded. I took a deep, satisfied breath of air. I was not yet a free man, but I could almost pretend as much.

My thoughts went to Bubo, for he would supply some welcome familiarity in this world of weirdness. I looked around the skies but couldn't see him. Thinking that he may have been resting on the *Maris Alarum*, or perhaps diving for fish about her, I climbed the southern ridge for a better vantage point. I noted that although the natives had allowed me some freedom on the island, they did not yet trust me completely: my tender was now moored to my ship rather than to the rocks below me. They knew that Mister Swim-like-stone had no way of reaching his ship without his rowboat. I was clearly still a prisoner, albeit on a picturesque island with a warm soft woman in my sights.

I soon spotted Bubo, his red wingtips flashing as he dove for fish. I called for him and soon he was perched on my forearm, the sharp pain from his talons as welcome as an old friend's embrace.

"Hello Bubo."

Captain Rum.

"Have you been fishing? Are there many fish?"

Fish fish. Two or more.

"You didn't touch the coconuts, did you?"

No coconut.

"Good bird. Good bird, Bubo." I ruffled his neck feathers. Then we simply sat enjoying each other's company, and gazing over to where the *Maris Alarum* bobbed patiently in the calm ocean. By and by I arose, and with Bubo perched on my shoulder I climbed down the boulders to the beach.

Just as my soles touched the warm sand, a group of half a dozen children emerged from the lagoon. They looked at us with unabashed awe. I imagined that a white-skinned man was an unusual sight for them, but to see a large blue and red owl-parrot perched on his shoulder must be as extraordinary as an African giraffe poking its head into a London tavern to bid good morning.

I felt Bubo shift and sensed that, although they were mere children, he was uneasy with our closeness to the natives. He did not trust them. I felt him tighten his talons more firmly into my shoulder and I saw a tiny trickle of blood course down my shirtless chest. Yet I ignored the wound, for the children's interest in Bubo presented another opportunity to build a bridge between the natives and me.

"Hello," I said and gave a hearty wave toward the children. These actions achieved little but to increase their misgivings. A few of the most timid children took small steps backward. Chiding myself, I realised that I had greeted them like an Englishman, not like a Boot Island native. I quietly repeated my greeting but this time I accompanied it by a conservative, two-fisted bow. I looked for a reaction and was pleased to see small grins. I repeated my bow, but this time with a low and reverent bend, hoping to gain some comedic traction as Bubo struggled to stay perched. I was pleased to see a few children smile nervously.

I pointed at myself. "Yapaarta-se," I said while feigning drowning, and was rewarded with reserved giggles. I was pleased to have made comedy from my only word of Boot Island-speak. I lifted Bubo onto my forearm and stroked his hackles, and soon I could sense his easing. I motioned to the children to pet him. At first they were hesitant, but by and by one young girl, perhaps a dozen years of age, timidly stepped forward. She inched out her hand and in time touched Bubo's neck. She petted him for just a trice before pulling her hand away in trepidation. But the spell of timidity was now broken, and another stepped forward and petted him for a few ticks. Soon all the young natives had crowded about Bubo and were caressing him with timid glee.

In time, one of them spoke a word in whale-sing talk that I can best record as *yar-yoo-hal-ee-day*. Many of the young natives repeated this phrase as they patted Bubo. I guessed that it was an informal greeting.

Next it was Bubo's turn for a performance. And what a grand performance it was, for he repeated the sing-song word back to them. At this sound the children stopped and cocked their heads. Bubo trilled the words again, whereupon the children repeated it together. Soon they were all smiling and laughing. I simply stood, letting the children enjoy their newfound curiosity: this was not just an unusual-looking, gaily coloured bird - this was a bird that *talked*!

Some adult natives, drawn by inquisitiveness or perhaps by the need to supervise their offspring in the company of such strange visitors, crept closer. They, too, seemed to enjoy watching my little pet, although they were not as effusive as the children were. By the time the young ones had been herded back to the water for another lesson and the adults had returned to their tasks, I felt that relations had turned. The natives had now largely dismissed any animosity that they felt toward us for stealing their coconuts. Aside from the fact that I could not depart, I now felt more like a guest on Boot Island than an inmate.

Bubo flew off and perched contentedly under the cool canopy of the rubber tree. I wandered along the beach at an aimless pace, stopping occasionally to observe the natives working, liberally offering two-fisted bows and saying *yar-yoo-hal-ee-day*. Yet I noted with dismay that the glass jar that Taa-TA-hoo had stolen from my ship was now lying in the sand, cast aside. Similarly, the rope that Lee-BE-nay had pilfered was hanging limply from a palm tree. Why would the natives take such items if they had no use for them?

The morning heat was climbing, so I worked my way up the western rock face to the small spring. After refreshing myself with a long guzzle of water, I lay under the shade of a star-fruit bush (but did not take any) and readied myself for a spell. But any feelings of tiredness were obliterated when I spied Ki-Ora emerge from the lagoon.

"Ki-Ora," I hollered, temporarily taking leave of discretion. "Yar-yoo-hal-ee-day, Ki-Ora."

She looked up and she broke into a wide, glowing smile. "Yah-oo-ahli-dae," she returned (and later confirmed that it simply mean 'hello' and showed me how best to spell it). Soon she was sitting beside me under the star fruit bush, so close that if I reached out I could have touched her.

I have learned that it is easy to write of another man's love, but when talking of my own desires the ink does not flow so freely. (Now, as I write, my yearning for Ki-Ora makes my quill stagnant, like the ink is thick mud.) But as I sat under that bush I discovered that my desires stilled not only my quill but seized my lips and tongue as well, rusting them closed like an old barn door latch. How could it be that I could talk for hours to a bird, yet could barely utter a syllable when sitting beside the women whom I craved above all else? Some rum would have provided a welcome oiling.

Mercifully, Ki-Ora's melodic tone broke my silence. Despite her poor and halting English, she carried our conversation like a lady of the manor. She had a natural yearning for knowledge and wished to know about Bubo, my ship and my homeland. As time passed my tongue-tie loosened, and by and by our conversation flowed more easily. Ki-Ora drew my thoughts from such a depth that I once even uttered Beth's name - something that I have not done freely for years for fear of a vision, not even after a belly full of Blackfriar's medicine. Yet here, next to Ki-Ora, it almost felt comforting to say Beth's name aloud.

"She died?" confirmed Ki-Ora.

"Yes."

I noticed a small tear coursing delicately down Ki-Ora's right cheek. For a while she seemed stifled: her brow drew down and her questions seemed forced rather than curious. Something about Beth's passing had affected her – affected her more so than I would have imagined it should have. Now it was my turn to gently lead our conversation. By and by her countenance loosed, her smile returned and our conversation flowed again. As the sun passed its zenith I learned much about the islanders and their unique life.

I discovered that my arrival at Boot Island was a rare event; only four times in Boot Island history had a ship landed upon their shores. Two of these vessels had been wrecked during storms. Very few men from each stricken vessel had survived: a lone captain from a Russian ship, and three Spanish crewman from another. Each had lived out their days on the island. I did not have the courage to ask whether they lived as prisoners or as free men, for I feared the answer.

The third ship came from a place that Ki-Ora called *Ma-grib*[187]. I have not heard of such a place and nor have I seen it marked on a chart; perhaps Ki-Ora mispronounced it. This small ship held a crew of four who arrived in poor condition, both men and vessel. All of the sailors died that winter.

Years later, another ship had stopped at the island –this occurred when Ki-Ora was a child. This ship was small, and had a crew of only one – an Englishman. His name, according to Ki-Ora, was 'Caapanbar'. He had apparently escaped from a place called 'Dispanash' before ending up on Boot Island, where he had stayed for 'many days' before dying of 'coughing'. Ki-Ora could recall being sat before him with Baa-GA-nee to practice her English.

My mind trawled through my knowledge of Maritime History - a subject on which I was relatively well versed. However I could not recall a sailor with such a name or place of origin. I vowed to investigate this mystery when I returned to London, for, like all jack tars, this sailor's spirit deserved to rest.[188]

---

[187] *Maghrib al-Aqṣá* is the Arabic name for Morocco.

[188] My initial research unveiled nothing. However the Dean of Maritime History emailed me recently with a possibility. George Bass was an English explorer who was the first to circumnavigate Australia's island of Van Diemen's Land

It was from this varied collection of sailors that the islanders had learned fragments of language that had then been passed through the generations. The tribe had entrusted three or four natives to keep each language burning and to practice its tongue. It was luck, Providence and fine fortune that Ki-Ora had been chosen to learn the King's English, and that she had now been encouraged to practice the tongue with me.

Although Ki-Ora knew the names of various countries – England, Spain, Russia and even Portugal – she had no knowledge whatsoever of their location. I scratched a map in the sand for her, highlighting their positions, but like Bubo she did not see the use of such a drawing. Try as I might, I could not eke the native name for Boot Island from her. It was simply "here". I sensed from the sum of her answers that the Boot Island people had no inclination for travel. Their lack of marine vessels was another indicator in this regard. All that they wished for was contained within the lagoon walls.

As our conversation lengthened I found myself inching closer to Ki-Ora. Once I touched her playfully on her shoulder yet she did not flinch. It was a relief and a pleasure to talk with her without the presence of Baa-GA-nee, who directed and protected her every move. Although I knew Ki-Ora belonged to him, I sensed as the afternoon passed that that her feelings for me were growing. It had been many years since I had courted those same looks from Beth, but a man does not forget such eyes.

Certainly, my feelings for her were growing faster than a Bird Rock tree. Was it love? I cannot say for certain, for I have only a single experience with which to compare. If not love, then my feelings for Ki-Ora were certainly a close sibling; certainly more than just a lonely sailor's flesh lust. But what could I do with this yearning? My logical mind was no help. I reasoned that if Ki-Ora and Baa-GA-nee had marriage arranged by a tribal custom rather than free will, perhaps she inwardly held no

---

(Tasmania). On returning from his final voyage in 1803, he and his ship disappeared forever; his fate remains a mystery. One report suggested that he had been captured and imprisoned by the Spanish for illegal trading. Is it possible that *Caapanbar* was "Captain Bass" and that he had not escaped from a country called *Dispanash* but from "The Spanish" before attempting to flee back to England, but only managing to limp to Boot Island? It is a tantalising but as yet unproven theory.

great affection for him. But alas, even if this were true, neither the tribe nor Baa-GA-nee would take kindly to me if I tried to take Ki-Ora as my own. To move on Ki-Ora would be tantamount to sentencing myself to further unbearable imprisonment, or perhaps even death by drowning. Despite the gravity of the punishment, my mind unceasingly sought ways to commit that very crime.

We watched quietly as some native boys harvested palm fronds for weaving. They used plaited ropes to pull the palm trunks violently to and fro. This rocking action occasionally, if they were lucky, dislodged a drooping frond. I was pleased to note that they used my stolen rope for this purpose, so at least it was working for a master and not lying bedraggled on the beach. It must have provided fine service because the boys dislodged three fronds that afternoon - an increase, Ki-Ora explained, on their usual yield of one or two. The harvest system seemed to me to be very inefficient, but Ki-Ora explained in her delicious, faltering English that they had attempted various other methods in the past without success. As I had discovered earlier, the palms were too tall and supple to climb, for their trunks swayed erratically, even under the weight of a small boy.

Later we walked along the beach, nibbling on thick leaves of seaweed. I had seen many islanders do this during the day and I sensed that the weed, along with fish, were the only foods that they ate without restraint. All other foods, particularly the star fruit and the coconuts, were rationed with frugality.

The tide was near to peaking and the workers had departed from their groups. I was pleased to note that both the glass jar and the rope had been stowed away. Perhaps the natives had not been as careless as I had first judged. It seemed that the natives believed that everyone owned all items; they had no sense of individual possession. Bird Rock and Moore's *Utopia* came to mind again. Perhaps this mind-set explains why they took items from my ship with such guiltless impunity. As far as the natives were concerned, *all* people owned my ship and everything on it, so they were not stealing those items, merely relocating them to a more accessible area. It was a pity, I thought, that they did not share this feeling about coconuts, although I conceded that food was an expendable and rare resource, while the jars, ropes, knives and other such tools could be readily re-used. Interestingly, they had not stolen any of my foodstuffs but had waited for me to gift them.

Later, Ki-Ora asked me a question that at first appeared odd, but was to provide me with inspiration.

"Baa-GA-nee say you make food hot? Why?"

"To cook it," I replied.

"Cook? What cook?"

"You make your food hot...." I began, before realising that my explanation was circular. "You put fish on the fire and its cooks it."

"Fish on fire? Why? Lamp go out."

"You don't use a small lamp, you use a big fire."

"Big lamp?"

"No, not a lamp. A fire." Her consternation indicated confusion. "You cook with a fire made from wood. You burn the wood, not a lamp."

"But if burn wood, then no wood left."

"Then you get more wood."

"Where more wood?"

I looked around at the narrow strip of hinterland with its limited collection of palms, bamboo bushes, rubber trees and assorted smaller plants. Ki-Ora was right: Mother Ocean provided whale oil aplenty for lamps, but the scarce land would grant very little timber. The Boot Islanders had to use each twig efficiently, and burning a log each night would not be sustainable.

"Why cook food?" Ki-Ora asked.

"It tastes good."

"Fish taste good with no fire. No need cook."

"It tastes ... it tastes...." I struggled for the words to describe cooked fish. Then a thought dawned in my mind like a rising sun: it was easy to describe how food looked –an apple was round and red and the size of a small fist - but nearly impossible to describe its taste. How could one show a child the taste of an apple? Give her a bite. So it was clear that a better way to show Ki-Ora the difference between raw and cooked fish would be to fry some for her.

It was thus, as the evening sky turned navy, that I found myself presiding over a dinner gathering of sorts. In attendance were the chiefs, Taa-TA-hoo and Lee-BE-nay; Arooo; another women called Gi-Aata who asked me many questions in faltering Spanish; four native men whom I had not met previously; Baa-GA-nee (scowling as ever); and of course Ki-Ora, her tanned skin assuming a delectable burnt-orange tinge under the fire's glow.

Earlier, a small band of men had escorted me to the *Maris Alarum* (again they had simply swum there through the open sea - these natives had no fear at all) and once on my ship I directed them into the hold. We then formed a cargo line and unloaded a large portion of dry firewood into my tender. I also took two cast iron griddles, a large pot, the remaining tomatoes and peas, a small bag of pepper, a bag of flour, and the final three bread loaves.

I constructed a simple fire pit on the beach, and ignited it with a whale oil lamp. (The lamp had been transported through the lagoon in an upturned bag, just as my journal had, but was still burning merrily at the end of its journey. Incredible.) Although the Boot Islanders were familiar with lamps and flame, the look of amazement on their faces as the cooking fire blazed upwards showed that they had never experienced a burn of such magnitude. They observed my every action earnestly and were overtly admiring when I performed even simple tasks such as fanning the coals or positioning the griddles on new logs for cooking.

Most Englishmen would consider that the meal was a simple affair. First, I combined the tomatoes, pepper and some local seaweed into a thick stew. I boiled some peas in a pot of salty lagoon water. Then I filleted, floured and fried a dozen large fish upon the griddles, two at a time. When everything was prepared, I served each diner a portion on a wide shell plate, finishing each meal with a generous hunk of bread to mop the stew.

As with the previous night's meal, the natives watched me carefully, like hounds staring at a lamb leg, imitating my every move as I consumed my meal. At first they were timid, and many dropped the food back onto their plate, seemingly surprised that it was hot. They also struggled with the concept of using the bread, rather than their fingers, to encourage the stew into their mouths. It took some time but, by and by, smiles appeared on their faces. By the meal's end, the happy song-hum of conversation and occasional translations by Ki-Ora indicated that they had very much enjoyed the meal. "Soft," seemed to be the consensus opinion. The white clean surfaces of the shell-plates, on which nary a morsel remained, provided further evidence of their enjoyment.

After dinner, the natives formed loose groups about the fire, with gentle song-conversation passing between them. I positioned myself next to Ki-Ora, with Baa-GA-nee present as always on her right flank. I tried to talk with her but Gi-Aata, who was sitting to my left, persisted in menial questions, wishing to practice her Spanish tongue. I endured her inane queries and statements (what is your name, the sky is blue, do you like fish, &c &c) until my patience withered. I pleasantly bid her *buenas noches*, smiled, performed a simple two-fisted bow and turned definitively toward Ki-Ora.

She enjoyed the meal, she said, but was sad that it could not happen again for they had no wood to burn. I knew that I had more firewood on the *Maris Alarum*, but that it, too, was finite. Was I a fool to have shown the natives something to which they could not aspire in the future? Would I have been kinder to let them remain ignorant of pleasures such as a hot cooked meal, which they could not repeat? Perhaps this was a rare situation where knowledge was not a friend but a foe.

Without warning Ki-Ora took my hand in hers and said simply, "Thank you Yapaarta-Se." This was not a passing brushing of skin or a fleeting contact - *she held my hand*. I can still feel the warmth of her touch now. Even a thousand lonely nights at sea will not fade that memory, and I know I shall feel her soft fingers curling though mine even as I am carted off my deathbed.

By and by she gently withdrew her hand, despite my gentle reluctance to relinquish it. Soon thereafter Baa-GA-nee clicked some terse words to Ki-Ora, who responded in similar fashion. The sing-song chatter slowed, and the click-pop talk demonstrated that the mood was no longer relaxed. Baa-GA-nee dragged Ki-Ora away soon after, leaving Arooo to escort me back to my cave.

It was an unfortunate end to an otherwise agreeable evening. Yet as I lay upon my bunk I could not help but feel a small shred of satisfaction. I had made a cut in Baa-GA-nee's armour – one that I could aim for again and again.

And I could still feel Ki-Ora's supple, soft hand in mine.

Friday 7 September

It was Arooo and Gi-Aata who delivered my breakfast fish the next morning. I declined to travel to the beach with Arooo and Gi-Aata, for the thought of that woman assailing me with innumerable Spanish questions was more than I could politely tolerate. I still had much to update in my journal and thus spent most of the day in my dank little room, writing and dreaming of she who was outside, and lusting for the feeling of her silken hands.

Part of me wondered if my actions were fair toward Ki-Ora. I held Baa-GA-nee in little regard, for he was permanently sullen around me. If a smile formed on his lips they would surely splinter, so unaccustomed were they to that pose. Yet he knew that I wished to bed his wife, so he was within his rights to protect her and fight for her honour. I would probably think even less of him if he did not challenge me. I hoped that he did not treat her badly last night for the sin of grasping my hand. I loathed to think that I had encouraged an act that would have her punished.

In the evening Arooo fetched me for dinner. His appearance was poor tidings, for I had expected Ki-Ora, or at least Baa-GA-nee, to accompany me. When we arrived at the dining room Ki-Ora was already seated at the head of the table, but unfortunately without a vacant stool nearby. I took the nearest seat at which I could sneak lingering glances at her without appearing to stare. During the meal, grace and good manners compelled me to converse in broken Spanish with Arooo and the ever-more-persistent Gi-Aata. I felt annoyed, to be seated so far from Ki-Ora, but was emboldened by a single short smile that she sent me, demonstrating that she was not unduly affected by Baa-GA-nee's harshness.

The meal moved slowly before withering to a merciful conclusion. Some natives, including Arooo, stayed to talk. Thinking that I could make use of Gi-Aata's craving for conversation, I motioned her to the mosaics, for I still yearned to discover more about them and their story. But just as I turned to her with a query, a high-pitched wailing song filled the air.

The noise came not just from people outside the room, but also seemingly from the walls themselves. Everyone else in the room immediately joined in the wailing, amplifying the clamour until it was near deafening. This sound was not a pleasant melody, but a piercing, harsh pitch, rising and falling with a rapid repeating beat.

Confusion reigned. The natives hurried for the exit. Baa-GA-nee grabbed Ki-Ora roughly by her hand and pulled her toward the exit.

"Go," shouted Ki-Ora to me above the din. "Go to cave."

"Why?" I yelled. "What is wrong?"

"Taran-kula! Taran-kula!" she yelled. Baa-GA-nee, from the water, held out his hand toward me. "Now!" he ordered. Clearly this was not a time for pretentiousness. I plunged into the exit and he swam me home, kicking with an intensity that I had not previously experienced. A sense of panic filled the whole commune, dominating all other feelings. Everywhere I looked people were fleeing for their caves. The intense wailing song filled the water in every direction, reverberating into every crevice and filling my head like air fills the sky. It was distressing.

When we arrived at the entrance to my cave, Baa-GA-nee thrust me firmly upward where I landed with an ungainly thud upon the small platform.

"What is taran...." I tried to ask as I regained my breath.

"Stay," said Baa-GA-nee, interrupting me with finality. "Taran-kula is here. Stay."

He disappeared back down the hole, leaving not even a splash of water in his wake.

*

I lay in the dim light of my cave, perplexed and afraid. By and by the greyness faded and my room grew dark, yet the wailing continued. I must have nodded briefly to sleep, for I awoke later and the noise had gone. But it returned, and was still reverberating when the first hint of morning sunlight filtered into my grotto. I do not know what Taran-kula is, but one fact is clear: the Boot Islanders fear it above all else.

Saturday 8 September

The wailing continued intermittently for most of the morning. I remained alone in my cave and dared not even dunk my head through the exit hole to investigate. Nobody visited and I had nothing to eat.

*

There was a sudden splash from the entry hole. I sat bolt upright in bed to see Ki-Ora standing at my bedside, with Baa-GA-nee's presence confirming that this was not a dream.

"Come," she said. Her tone was high and rushed, making it clear that the situation remained grave. Before I could even think, Ki-Ora and Baa-GA-nee had hustled me down through the exit and we were swimming westward, keeping unusually low and close to the lagoon wall. Soon my lungs grew tight but such was our haste that there was no thought of stopping for air. We changed course and ascended the underwater cliff face. Then, in the edge of my vision, I saw it. *Taran-kula.*

At first Taran-kula was a deep grey shadow in the centre of the lagoon, elusive and gloomy despite the high noon light. Then the shadow moved, highlighting its bulk and shape. This beast was as long as my ship's mast, and as wide as a man's height. It had the unmistakable shape of a massive fin protruding from its dorsum, like a dinghy's sail: the grey triangle from the mosaic. Taran-kula was unmistakably a giant shark, not just the largest that I had ever seen, but perhaps the biggest that had ever preyed within the seas.

Without warning Taran-kula turned toward us. Had Ki-Ora and Baa-GA-nee not been holding me I would have sunk like a sounding lead to the bottom of the lagoon, paralysed with fear. My escorts redoubled their efforts, dragging my limp body along like a sea anchor. I managed to turn my head around, only to see the sea-devil coursing toward us; its white underside and snout contrasted starkly against its grey-black body. One flick of its mighty tail lurched it forward, its teeth bared and sharply white.[189]

I gasped in shock and tasted salt in my mouth as the water flowed in, choking me. *Yapaarta-se.* I was coughing as if I was dying of the plague, in the process inhaling even more water into my lungs. With barely 20

---

[189] *Taran-kula* was most likely a Great White shark, one of the largest and most aggressive species of shark. They routinely grow up to six metres in length, although a few specimens have been recorded at more than 10 metres long.

yards to spare Ki-Ora and Baa-GA-nee thrust me through the entry of the dining cave where I landed flaccidly on the timber platform. I lay, coughing out water, not just through my mouth but my nose as well. My arms shook and I blubbered like a sickly child. If Ki-Ora was not nearby I concede that I might have sobbed outright, for one of my greatest fears had materialised: a shark, a giant sea devil, was prowling the lagoon – just yards from where I lay.

Torpidly I flapped my arms and tried to haul myself to higher ground, but I could gain no traction. Suddenly I felt hands grip about my ankles and pull me up the earthen corridor. Whoever it was then lifted me over his shoulders like a calf being carted to the slaughterhouse. I opened my eyes to see Baa-GA-nee straining to carry me up the stairs to a dry plateau. He placed me on a mat where I lay like a wet sack of flour, limp and useless, while chaos ruled about me.

I heard a crashing sound then the noise of splitting timber. It was as though a violent storm was raging just down the hallway. In my dazed state I could barely respond, but I managed to lift my head for long enough to see Taran-kula's giant jaws ripping into the platform on which I had laid just a minute before.

Ki-Ora saw me amidst the rabble and quickly appeared at my side.

"You ... all right?"

I coughed and sat. Was I all right? My mind had never felt so twisted. Of all the creatures in the seas and of all the lagoons in the oceans, why did Taran-kula, this most massive and malevolent of sharks, choose to attack this one? I would rather run into a burning forest, fight a bar-full of drunken navvies, or face a charging bayonet brigade than confront such a beast. I dread nothing more than the sight of a dorsal fin slicing through the water, yet Beelzebub himself had conspired to send the largest and most malicious shark in the kingdom to me.

I steadied my breathing, thought of the black spaces between the night stars, and played the bird song in my head. By and by I had collected myself sufficiently to look about. I was in a crowded room filled with perhaps two dozen natives. It was clear that this was no social gathering; it had the atmosphere of a war council. Many of the natives were clicking animatedly and gesticulating wildly. In time, I nodded meekly to Ki-Ora. Yes, I was all right. Just all right.

Taa-TA-hoo stood and held out his arms. Silence ensued. He spoke to Ki-Ora, who motioned at me to follow her. The crowd gently parted as we made our way forward. There, on a low bench at the front of the room, were my pistols, still tied together with my neck scarf. Next to them was my scimitar. Lee-BE-nay joined us at the head of the room and initiated a rapid stream of clicks for Ki-Ora to translate.

"Taran-kula here," she started. "Taran-kula - big shark - terror on island." I nodded, so Ki-Ora continued, faltering her way through an explanation of the problem. "Every ..." she stopped and appeared to be counting upon her fingers, ".... every about 1000 days, Taran-kula return. Last time kill six men, one child. Before that, kill...." Ki-Ora paused and trembled. A tiny tear welled in her eye and she looked downward to the floor, ".... kill one man."

Although they could not comprehend English, the assembled natives clearly understood Ki-Ora's message to me. Heads bowed in natural reverence. "It is past," she whispered.

After a deep breath, Ki-Ora continued. "Taran-kula strong. Destroy homes, break air pipes. Trap us in caves for many day. No food or water, no see the sun. Smash the gate to our fish store and tear our seaweed crop. After it leave, we have little food. We have no air pipe. "

She paused, settling her nerve. I looked at her, slowly nodding, understanding and feeling the islanders' pain. "Many times we try kill Taran-kula but fail. No weapon hurt it. Bamboo spear not hurt it. Net not tame it. Taran-kula bigger. Bigger. Now bigger. Soon, Taran-kula destroy us." Then Ki-Ora turned to face me directly.

"Yapaarta-Se, can you help us?"

Lee-BE-nay stepped forward and presented me with my own pistols. "Will this kill Taran-kula?" she asked.

I turned the pistols over in my hands. They had been transported through the water, soaking the powder. Their grips were wet and coated in sand, and the trigger mechanisms were rusty. I pulled at each hammer, but they were gritty and jammed. I wriggled them repeatedly but they remained stubbornly locked in place. It was clear: these pistols would never fire shot again.

I shook my head in resignation. A groan coursed through the room, followed by sharp clicking conversation. I picked up my scimitar; it was a fine weapon but useful only against deer and the like. In a duel with a monster like Taran-kula it would be like a spur in the side of a horse, serving little purpose but to annoy and enrage. It certainly was not the answer. I shook my head again.

I looked about at the assembled natives. These people were Boot Island's oldest, wisest and bravest inhabitants, but every face was blank with fear and indecision. They had seen Taran-kula's devastation before, and the pain and angst of the memories were writ deep in their brows. I looked at Ki-Ora, her eyes pleading with me.

"Can you help us?"

I said nothing for I could envisage no way to kill this monster. I had no weapons that could kill it, no net to capture it, and it would snap even my largest fishing hook as if it were a twig. I could think of no way that I could even scratch Taran-kula's hide, much less destroy it. The ocean was its world, not mine. Taran-kula held every advantage.

Then, at this most inopportune of moments, as I looked into Ki-Ora's pleading eyes, my horror returned. An image of Beth, bleeding and blue, fell over Ki-Ora. I blinked and shook my head as I fought to refocus upon the present. I thought of the bird song, I breathed deeply, I imagined the blackness of a night sky – anything to distract myself from my own uninvited imaginings, but Beth materialised before me regardless. I saw Ki-Ora shift uneasily, but I gazed steadfastly at her so as not to betray my inner terror.

Despite my stoicism, my waking nightmare continued ever more strongly: Beth in the forest, helping me to set the deer trap. Beth hiding behind the rock with me, whispering coquettishly as we waited for prey in the early morning sun. As we kiss, her perfume's scent fills my head. The buck arrives. A huge buck. It steps into the loop. I cut the spring rope. The sapling flings upward, snaring the beast about its antlers. Those antlers. Those wicked, evil antlers. I see them clearly, spreading as wide as a man's reach.

Then I heard Ki-Ora's voice overlayed into my visage, beseeching me again with her question: "Yapaarta-Se, can you help us?"

Wretchedly, her voice was not enough to vault me away from the horror inside my mind, which grew more vivid and painful than ever before. Scenes from Beth's life flashed by like a ghastly book of memories that I was forced to read. Beth and I meeting for the first time in the paper shop ... Beth and I lying on the grassy Thames bank ... Beth in a white dress on our wedding day – but then she screams and her face turns blue as that final damning scene from the forest replayed itself again.

Suddenly, the vision changed. I looked at the beast in the sprung deer trap. The rope was not looped about a stag's antlers, but had instead tightened about something very different: a shark's tail.

Taran-kula's spreading caudal fins, with the snare tightened firmly about their base, had replaced the stag's wide antlers. I looked at Beth. She was no longer screaming but was quietly smiling; her lips were not blue and twisted, but soft and pink and calm. Our babe was cradled in her arms; I heard it gently cry. Beth smiled, then simply nodded to me, and faded away.

Thank you, Beth.

I turned back to Ki-Ora.

"Yes," I said firmly. "Yes, I can help you."

The assembly gave a murmur but I heard little, for my mind was already racing.

*

Over the next hour the native council debated my strategy. All the while the human wailing sounds continued outside, confirming that Taran-kula was still wreaking havoc. Despite many potential flaws in my plan, none of those assembled could envisage a better one. But the need quickly became urgent, for reports were being relayed that Taran-kula had already destroyed the largest fish farm and dozens ventilation pipes, and was becoming increasingly more violent. In the end, the council of natives decreed to try my plan to catch Taran-kula in a snare - effectively a giant deer trap.

I had many ropes at my disposal to set the trap, but where could we find a spring of such size and power that it could ensnare this most monstrous of beasts? The spring would have to be extremely tall, flexible and powerful.

The answer soon came to mind: the giant wavering palm trees that lined the beachhead. Their suppleness and flexibility made them perfect for the task. But the natives soon reminded me that the prime difficulty in setting the spring would be knotting a rope to the top of the palm, for the trees were nearly impossible to scale. Even a lithe boy freely climbing would find it impracticable, and with the added burden of a large coil of rope such a climb would surely fail. After much fretting, we were no closer to solving this problem.

It was only when my mind harkened back to my mast repairs at sea that I saw a possible answer: an answer that had blue and red feathers. However I had private misgivings as I wasn't sure if Bubo could be coerced into co-operating with the natives for he still became agitated in their presence. Nor was I certain that he would understand such a complex task. The natives, too, had grave reservations and repeatedly shook their heads in doubt as Ki-Ora explained my idea. But they could offer no other solutions, for they had been trying to scale those palms for many years without success. By and by I gained the natives' uneasy trust. I hoped that Bubo would not let me down; I had enormous faith in the intelligence and loyalty that he had shown in the past.

Timing was crucial. The trap had to be set at the extreme of low tide, when Taran-kula's bulk would prevent it from interfering with our preparations. With only an hour until the turn, we could delay no longer, for a full day would pass until the low returned, giving Taran-kula 24 hours to wreak more destruction and grief.

We needed a distant distraction in the lagoon that would allow us to escape to the surface without attracting Taran-kula. To this end Lee-BE-nay plunged his head into the exit hole and sung a high-pitched whale song that I heard being distantly relayed through the lagoon. Then there was silence until by and by a message was transmitted back. The nervous eyes in the room told me that the diversion was ready.

Taa-TA-hoo gathered Ki-Ora, Baa-GA-nee and me, with my trusty scimitar sheathed about my waist, and led us to the exit. The natives stood aside, their fists clenched nervously to their chests and heads bowed reverentially toward us as we plunged into the exit hole, stepping between the remnants of the shattered timber platform that

Taran-kula's massive teeth had crushed like pine twigs. My heart was hammering like galloping horses' hooves as I was frenetically dragged through the water to the cliff wall above. Through a cloud of bubbles I sighted Taran-kula's shadow thrashing about the far wall of the lagoon, attracted by the release of bloodied fish from a store. Our troupe of five scrambled up onto the safety of a ledge, picked our way up the rocky face to the ridge proper, and then hustled around the ridge toward my ship. As we scampered I could see streams of people clawing up the lagoon cliff walls. We needed a lot of manpower to set the trap, and these brave young natives were willing to risk their lives to assist.

My mind spun with reasons that the trap would not work – there were far too many to list – but I pressed forward all the same.

We were soon at my tender. Taa-TA-hoo and Lee-BE-nay towed the little boat to the *Maris Alarum* where my first mate Bubo was waiting, carking a simple greeting from the gunwale.

"Hello Bubo," I cried, inordinately pleased that he was beside me in such dark hours.

Captain Rum he squawked and flew to perch upon my forearm. Then he twisted his owl-like neck, peering about. As he looked at Taa-TA-hoo and Lee-BE-nay he carked menacingly, but when he sighted Baa-GA-nee he squawked even more piercingly. Despite his earlier rapport with the native children, he clearly still felt antagonistic toward my present company.

I petted him on the neck and spoke to him gently. "Good bird, Bubo," I whispered, stroking him further. However he remained agitated; he carked repeatedly and hopped about my forearm, digging in the points of his talons with each shift. I realised that although my relations with Taa-TA-hoo and Lee-BE-nay had mellowed, Bubo still held them in contempt, for they had chided him over the coconuts. As for Baa-GA-nee – well, Bubo no doubt held lingering antipathy toward this taciturn man. As I petted Bubo I motioned to the natives to retreat, but they did not appear to understand my gestures. I simply continued talking to Bubo in a soft voice.

"Captain Rum needs your help Bubo."

He carked a non-descript reply.

"Do you remember *Thread Rope*, Bubo?"

He simply carked again.

"Do you remember *Thread Rope* Bubo?" I repeated gently.

Aark he finally replied, seemingly in the positive.

"*Tie knot*, Bubo. Do you remember *Tie knot*?" I repeated my question thrice.

Bubo again paused before answering obliquely: *pet.*

He seemed confused. "Tie knot, Bubo," I repeated, miming tying a knot with my hands. He repeated his oblique caw. *Pet.*

"I don't understand Bubo."

Tie knot ... pet.

Ah, yes. Suddenly his strange answer made sense: I remembered back to Bird Island, where I had been so amazed that Bubo had learned to tie a knot that I had petted him for many hours. Tie knot - pet.

"Yes Bubo. You were a clever bird. Captain Rum gave you a long pet because you tied the knot. Could you tie knot again?"

Pet.

"Yes, Captain Rum will give you a long pet if you tie the knot again." He bowed his head down; I knew what to do and gave him another short soothing ruffle of his neck feathers.

The natives stared at our exchange in silence, no doubt still in awe of my amazing bird.

"Good bird, Bubo, good bird. We will give you coconut too." His eyes pinned into what I like to think was a big bird grin.

With no time to waste, I gathered two coils of my longest and strongest rope. The natives helped load the thick heavy rolls into my tender and we were soon back at the Island. The tide was ebbing toward low and the afternoon sun had begun its western descent as dozens of natives, among them many stout young men, gathered on the beach.

I pointed to the top of the tallest palm, which was wavering in the afternoon breeze, and repeated my previous instructions to Bubo. Then I presented him with the tag end of the rope and waited. For a few breathless ticks Bubo simply sat, gazing about. I repeated my orders very slowly and calmly, proffering the rope and pointing to the tip of the nearest palm. To my immense relief he seemed to understand his task. He grasped the heavy rope between his talons, and without further ceremony he flapped painstakingly toward the palm canopy.

Quickly an unforseen problem developed as Bubo struggled with the heavy weight of his cargo. As he flew higher, the length of the thick rope increased, adding to his load. I fed out the line to him steadily, trying to minimise its drag, but Bubo simply could not ascend higher than half way up the tree under the increasing burden of the heavy rope.

I cursed at myself, verbally and harshly, because this problem had first manifested on Bird Rock when I was trying to position my ship to accommodate her new mast. But in the glow of my success at the time I had forgotten about the near-failure of Bubo's attempt to carry the long heavy rope. It now looked like my oversight would cause our plan to fail, and Taran-kula would continue to wreak havoc with the islanders. I urged Bubo to go on.

"Try harder Bubo," I beseeched. "Fly higher."

As Bubo flapped upward the assembled natives hollered encouragement like a bare-knuckled fight crowd. But no matter how vociferously they cheered or how determinedly Bubo flapped his wings he simply did not have the strength to lift the heavy line any higher. Exhausted, he dropped the rope from his talons whereupon it fell to the ground in a tired tangle. Then he flew down and landed heavily upon my forearm. It was clear that he could not possibly fly the rope high enough. Our plan had failed at the outset. I should have done better.

I called Ki-Ora. "Tell the natives that the rope is too heavy. Bubo cannot carry it. We need another plan."

She looked at me despairingly and shook her head. Suddenly I felt the disappointed gaze of dozens of natives boring into my skull. I was embarrassed at the failure and spewed forth the reasons, no doubt far too quickly for Ki-Ora to comprehend. "Bubo cannot fly to the top of the tree with the rope. We cannot climb the tree. Even the young men cannot do this. If we cannot tie the rope then we cannot set the trap. Without the spring, we cannot catch Taran-kula. There might be another way, but...."

My voice trailed away, for as I was ranting Baa-GA-nee had strode from the crowd and gathered the rope. He looped the coil around his shoulders, and with his hands outstretched before him and his legs tucked into his chest, he pulled himself up the narrow palm trunk. Higher and higher he climbed, like an Indian monkey, until the tree started to bend and sway alarmingly under his weight. Still he kept climbing – 15 feet, 20 feet, 25 feet, and soon he was half way up the trunk at 30 feet. But from this height, it was impossible for him to climb higher, for he was now hanging under the tilting, lilting trunk, his feet barely gripping it, rather than climbing a straight pole. To make his position even more perilous, the tree bobbed with a lurching whip. From this height any slip would be fatal.

Fatal. Inadvertently I whispered the word aloud. *Fatal*.

If Baa-GA-nee fell, Ki-Ora would be alone. She would be mine.

Should I encourage Baa-GA-nee higher? My mind devoured the notion for this was a fleeting opportunity for my deepest desires to be fulfilled. I reasoned that either way I would win, because if Baa-GA-nee completed the climb then our plan could continue, yet if he slipped and fell then my dearest desire was nearer to fulfilment. Why should I not encourage Baa-GA-nee to push higher when either outcome would help my cause? I would be a fool to demur.

Yet as I hollered my entreaty under its cloak of encouragement, the words stuck in my craw. I tried again but the words faltered as they left my lips.

To wish the death of another man - a man who had raised my hackles by doing nothing more than protecting his betrothed from an uninvited stranger... No! I could not do it. It was simply wrong to promote the death of such a brave man, even though the prize was so desirable.

"Come down, Baa-GA-nee," I called. "It is too dangerous. Come back down."

I glanced across at Ki-Ora. Her panic-stricken eyes were trained on Baa-GA-nee, and her hands were cupped over her mouth in abject fear. Her whole body trembled. These emotions were not just the worry of a concerned bystander; Ki-Ora was feeling a dreadful foreboding for someone whom she clearly loved. She called at Baa-GA-nee with harsh clicks and pops to come down, yet even after her entreaty he made no effort to descend. But nor did he climb further. Instead he clamped his feet and then his body tightly about the trunk, fixing his position as best he could. Then he called loudly. *"Yah-oo-ahli-dae."*

Hello? Why would he call "hello" from such a precarious position? Then he called again, in his booming deep voice: "Yah-oo-ahli-dae *Bubo*."

Bubo started at the sound of his name and looked up at the palm, where Baa-GA-nee was calling his name ever louder. "Bubo. Yah-oo-ahli-dae, Bubo."

Bubo's cocked head betrayed his confusion, and his owl-eyes opened as wide as I have ever seen them.

"Fly," I said. "Fly to Baa-GA-nee."

Bubo clucked and then emitted a loud cark.

Bad.

"No. I think Baa-GA-nee is a good man, Bubo."

Aaark.

"Captain Rum was wrong. Baa-GA-nee is not a bad man. He is a good man."

I am not sure if Bubo understood, but his head straightened a little.

"Help Baa-GA-nee, Bubo. Help Captain Rum. Fly. Thread rope. Tie knot."

Again, Baa-GA-nee called from the palm, where his trembling arms and desperate voice revealed his fatigue. I lifted my forearm and proffered the open air to Bubo. "Fly to Baa-GA-nee." With a final loud *aaark*, Bubo flapped his mighty coloured wings and ascended toward the man who was suddenly more my saviour than nemesis.

Baa-GA-nee whistled to Bubo and brandished the tag end of the heavy rope to him. Bubo took the rope in his talons and flew toward the palm canopy. Baa-GA-nee, although exhausted, desperately played out the rope as Bubo flew, while the natives, re-energised, yelled support. My determined pet strained and flapped and beat his mighty wings ever harder as the weight of the rope dragged him down. But slowly and with much effort he gained height and finally, perhaps with his last pennyweight of strength, he reached the top of the palm. Desperately he wedged himself into the base of a palm frond and rested.

His task now complete, Baa-GA-nee slid down the trunk in ungainly fashion and thumped heavily into the sand. Ki-Ora rushed to his side and helped him up, and then held him in a close, lingering embrace. Then she kissed him on his cheek and hugged him again. My gills turned green, but I now knew - by the way that she rushed to his side, the way that she hugged and caressed him, the way she had trembled in fear when his life was in danger – that she loved him dearly. *Ki-Ora loved Baa-GA-nee.* I had no place in intruding; I would no longer press for her affections for her heart clearly belonged to another.

But I had no time to dwell on my loss of Ki-Ora, for other matters quickly pressed for my attention.

"Bubo. Thread rope around the tree," I called. Soon Bubo had not only achieved the loop but after only a few prompts from below he had tied a knot of sorts. From afar it looked like a mother-in-law's hitch instead of a true reef knot, but I did not chide him for that!

I took the free end of the rope and tugged firmly on it to fix the knot. Then I handed it to the assembled men, who needed no translation to know what was required of them now: *Pull.* At first the palm bent effortlessly, for its trunk was so supple that it offered little resistance. However as the tree flexed, the resistance increased as its stouter lower trunk started to absorb the force. More of the islanders joined the fray - even Ki-Ora - and soon dozens of people were pulling on the rope. They heaved and hauled with ever more vigour, sweating in the afternoon heat. I beseeched the natives for one last effort and they responded with a grimacing heave. Then, under great strain, with their feet entrenched deeply into the beach sand and their knuckles cramping white about the line, they held their positions fast.

I took up the loose end of the rope and charged into the lagoon, knowing that a few hardy souls were diverting Taran-kula to the far end of the lagoon. I waded out until my reach was nearly gone and then looked under the water for the next element of the trap: the rock that had a hole in its top; the same rock around which the young children had earlier been playing. I soon located it in the clear water and then ducked down and tied the rope firmly through it.

On my signal, the natives released the rope. Firmly flexed, the palm strained hard against its tethering cable, which pulled it so taut that it hummed in the wind. But both the knots and the rope held fast. From knee-deep water I checked my reach, and was satisfied that a man could reach the rope to cut it with my scimitar.

The spring had been set. Now it was time for the snare.

Bubo took the end of the second rope in his beak and arduously hauled it to the top of the arched tree, using his talons to walk up the first rope like a makeshift ladder. He affixed the rope next to the first tether, while I busied myself tying a loop at the lower end. Which knot should I use for this demanding task? I started with a bowline, but barely had I commenced tying it when I decided that a rolling hitch might provide more strength, for the load that it would have to bear was mighty. Yet soon after that my mind changed again, but this time with finality, for I knew this choice of knot was precise for its purpose: a hangman's noose, complete with 13 turns of the coil.

The natives weighted the bottom of the loop with rocks, floated its top with some small woven bags, and tied some bloodied baitfish around the ring of the noose. Finally, our trap was ready. We had constructed a colossal deer snare – one with the size and strength to capture the most enormous and evil of sharks. I hoped.

My head seethed and swam with doubts and misgivings as Taa-TA-hoo, Lee-BE-nay and I marched the loop into deep water and laid it into the lagoon, past the tether point of the first rope. We retreated to the beach where I laid my scimitar at the base of the palm. We would need it soon enough.

Our trap was now set so the plan from here was straightforward, although we all understood that our success was far from certain. We would wait for the tide to rise at which time the baitfish would attract Taran-kula. As its body passed through the loop, the tensioning rope would be cut, allowing the flexed palm to spring up and ensnare the loop tightly around Taran-kula's tail.

So we waited. As the sun dipped behind the tip of the western mountain I lingered nervously at the water's edge, watching Taran-kula menace its way across the distant lagoon; pieces of shattered timber, dead fish and other detritus floated up behind him like a ship's jetsam. The natives gathered in small groups on the beach but their conversation was restrained; barely a sing-song word nor an anxious click filled the afternoon air. Instead everyone sat in an uneasy silence with their hands clenched quietly in front of their faces, with an occasional collective groan when Taran-kula lurched on another destructive thrust.

As time sloughed by the tide seemed to halt its advance. Logic told me that it was rising at its normal rate, but with the weight of the islanders' homes on the scales, it seemed immobile. Yet rise it did, gradually edging everyone from the narrow beach to the hinterland. I sat under a tree with Bubo, saying very little, for I was as nervous as the natives. By and by Ki-Ora edged up the beach and sat on the sand next to me. I nodded and smiled weakly.

"Bird amazing," she said.

"Yes, he is amazing," I replied. "He is a good pet."

She reached out her hand and gently stroked Bubo on the neck the way she had seen me do earlier. He ground his beak in such a way that he purred like a cat, so deep and long was the sound.

"You do good job with trap," she said to me.

"Thank you. I hope it works." I stared at her for a little longer than I should have, because I now knew that she loved Baa-GA-nee and that I must leave her to him. "Your husband did a good job climbing the tree," I added. "We could not have set the trap without him."

She nodded gratefully but appeared confused.

"And tell your husband that I thank him for carrying me to safety in the cave," I added.

Again she looked puzzled, but replied, "I will tell Baa-GA-nee thank you."

We again sat in silence, gazing out over the lagoon. I remembered the tranquillity of the moment as I had sat here in imagined seclusion, weeks ago, watching the sky turn from pink to navy over the glinting water. I tried to soothe my nerve by recapturing the gentle spirit of that solitude, but could not displace my fretting about the possible failure of the trap. The natives had entrusted me to deliver this plan.

Ki-Ora spoke again. "I sorry Yapaarta-se. I not understand something you say. Can you explain?"

"Of course. What don't you understand?"

331

"You say 'husband'. I don't understand."

A pang coursed through me like fired birdshot. The thought of Ki-Ora bedding with Baa-GA-nee gave me great pain but even though I had newfound respect for that man, explaining the concept of 'husband' was an unbearable impost on my psyche. I averted my gaze and could do nothing but bite my lip in frustration.

"I sorry," she apologised, "My question make trouble." I gave her a tiny nod.

"No, your question is sensible," I said in a weak voice. "I will try to explain."

"Thank you," she replied. "My English poor. I thought Baa-GA-nee was 'brother'."

I looked up, startled.

"Baa-GA-nee is your brother?"

"Ye ...yes."

"You and he have the same mother and father?"

"Yes."

"He is not husband? You are not..." my voice trailed away.

"No. I have no husband." She paused for a moment, before adding in a trembling voice, "Husband killed by Taran-kula." I looked at her with anguished empathy, for I knew the grief of losing your most beloved. "It is past," she whispered.

I am not too arrogant to admit that I would have wept – both in sorrow and in happiness – if not for what happened next: a sentry on the ridge emitted an urgent wailing sound. Taran-kula was on the move. The natives stood as one, suddenly alive. I vaulted up, grabbing Ki-Ora by the hand. We hurried to the beach head where Taa-TA-hoo, Lee-BE-nay and a dozen men were in animated discussion.

"What is wrong?" I asked Ki-Ora.

She pointed at the taut spring rope, whining in the breeze above us. Thirty feet above us.

The problem was so obvious that I cursed myself for neither predicting it nor seeing it earlier. As the tide had risen it had pushed us further up the beach, where the rope was far higher. We would have only one instant, one fleeting moment, to cut the rope when Taran-kula swum through the loop of the snare – but how could we do this when nobody could reach it? As the men debated the solution with a rabble of rapid and noisy clicking, sentries on the surrounding ridge called in frenetic reports of Taran-kula's position. I could do little but watch because Ki-Ora could not translate the rapid squabble.

The natives tried to form a pyramid of men, but it collapsed well short of the target height. Someone tied my scimitar to three joined bamboo poles, but it was judged too insubstantial and likely to fail at the critical moment. All the while the sentries called in more position reports: Taran-kula was even closer. Finally, the council passed their ultimate judgement, which Ki-Ora translated: someone would have to go into the water to cut the rope.

"But surely Taran-kula could attack that person?" I asked.

"Yes," nodded Ki-Ora.

"And that person might die?"

She did not hesitate. "Yes."

I looked upon the nervous and crying families sitting below the trees, and then at the brave group of young men haggling over who would do the job. I saw Baa-GA-nee in the midst of the men gesticulating wildly to his own chest. I turned to face Ki-Ora and looked at her directly. She did not break her gaze, but intensified it.

The noise, the panic, the anxiety, all faded to a blur of London fog. Then, as if by the Devil's intervention, Beth's visage again appeared over Ki-Ora's face. But this time it did not distress me. It was not her twisted, blue face, but her happy, spring-morning face. Beth smiled at me. Suddenly my world, my life, and my departed love all made sense. For the first time since her passing, I understood: *I did not have to forget Beth*. Instead, I should always remember her.

In that instant, my life of fleeing from her memory was over. On the contrary, I vowed to store her memory firmly and permanently in a corner of my soul - but I would keep in that same soul enough space for another to occupy. Aloud, I whispered words that had not passed my lips since she died.

"I will never forget you Beth." Then I uttered some simple words that I should have said to her memory years ago. "I will always love you."

Beth's visage smiled at me again, sending a deep and satisfied contentment through my bones. As I reached my hand toward her, Beth faded. Ki-Ora stood before me, my hand now touching her cheek.

At that moment I tumbled completely into love; not just the desire of a lonely sailor for a woman's warm skin, but wanting all of her, to be with me, forever. It was only the second time in my life that I had felt this emotion. I now knew that my journey was over and that my unstated aims had been fulfilled. I had found a permanent place in my heart for Beth, but also room for another. I had found myself. I could die a contented man.

I smiled warmly at Ki-Ora and proffered a calm kiss on her cheek. Then I performed a deep, reverential two-fisted bow. Without further hesitation I turned and ran. I ran liked a man possessed by a crazed devil. I seized my scimitar from among the rabble of men and charged into the lagoon. The shouts and screams quickly faded behind me as I ploughed deeper into the water. I heard Bubo squawking above me but his noises, too, rapidly grew distant. I could focus only on only one thought: *kill Taran-kula*.

I followed the slanting taut rope until it was low enough overhead that I could swipe it with my scimitar. Danger was now acute, for I was only 10 yards from the baited loop. I dug my feet into the lagoon sand and braced myself to swipe, for I knew that once Taran-kula's body was inside the loop I would have only a trice to cut the rope. Should I fail....

I squinted across the lagoon for my nemesis but could not see it in the dark black reflections of the low afternoon light. The ridge top sentries were gesticulating wildly but I could not understand them. Then, I saw it. A fin. Taran-kula's giant dorsal fin was slicing through the water, heading directly for me. Unfortunately, it was approaching from my side. A realisation suddenly hit me more sharply than a cannon-ball.

Taran-kula would not pass through the loop first.

334

I flailed to move, but knew that I could not possibly adjust my position in time. Taran-kula closed upon me with the speed of a four-horse wagon. I could see its tail whipping like a grotesque serpent and its pointed nose slicing toward me like a monstrous eel. I had no way of outswimming it and could not defend myself with little more than a dagger. I was nothing but shark bait. I stood, facing Taran-kula, and prepared myself for the pain. I prepared myself to die.

In the few seconds that passed before it struck, one thought bridled me more than my looming death: that Taran-kula would not accompany me to Hades. My death would be in vain. I was going to Hell without that beast and the islanders and Ki-Ora would continue to suffer. Taran-kula closed on me. I braced, knowing that I was mere seconds from extreme pain, unbearable fear and a horrible, bloodied death. I hoped that it was swift.

Suddenly a blue and red plume of feathers shot down from the sky. *Bubo*. He plummeted low along the water between Taran-kula and me. In a trice he shot back up, screeching and squawking like the devil himself. Then he speared into the water again, this time to Taran-kula's eastern side. With a thrust of his mighty tail, the shark changed direction, swerving after this enticing new prey. Bubo flew further out into the lagoon then plunged his talons into the water again, surfacing further east. Taran-kula trailed Bubo but gained upon him quickly. Yet Bubo was undeterred. He bravely flew low along the water, taunting the great beast with his fluttering wings, leading him away from me.

Taran-kula again swiped its tail and with an awesome surge it burst out of the water, launching its carcass into the air as it lunged at Bubo. Its gruesome teeth bared out in pointed rows and its evil jaws snapped shut as it disappeared below the water.

Suddenly Bubo was gone. I cried out instinctively, but could do nothing but watch as this ghastly scene played before my eyes. The shark lunged from the water again, with an unmistakable blue feather poking from its jaws.

"Bubo!" I cried, the scream emanating from the pain of losing not just a pet, not just a crewman, but also a friend. "Bubo!" Instinctively I tightened my grip on the scimitar and charged forward, but the water quickly deepened until I could advance no further. I floundered, tilting my head upward for air. I flayed my arms above for the taut rope and felt it just above my head. I pulled myself up just in time to see Bubo dart out of the water, minus a handful of tail feathers. He flew directly toward me, directly over the snare.

Instinctively I thrust my scimitar toward the rope and hacked down hard. But the rope barely frayed. Bubo was now just 10 feet away, with Taran-kula just behind him.

I slashed again but could gain no traction in this deep water. The rope remained firm. I sunk into the lagoon and in the desperation of the moment, time slowed almost to ceasing.

My mind sprung back to the Thames dock where one cut of a rope with this very sword had saved me from a life worse than Hell in Shepton, and granted me the freedom of the oceans. I thought of the typhoon where I had slashed through the rigging ropes to right my ship and save my life. And now, yet again, just a single strand of rope stood between me and a looming, unthinkably horrible death.

Everything seemed to go quiet as emotions and memories ricocheted through me. I thought of Beth, and of the fear and agony she had suffered in her dying moments ... the years of pain I had since endured, trying to escape her memory ... my mama coughing blood, and my papa sweating as he succumbed to his broken leg ... Diogo and Fernando, isolated, alone, and dying painfully on Bird Rock ... the terror of my near-drowning in this very lagoon.

I thought of the countless times I had betrayed myself and everything I stood for with liquor. I imagined Ki-Ora's husband in the clenches of Taran-kula's massive jaw. Finally, I thought of Ki-Ora.

I mustered these emotions and channelled them into a vengeance as great as I have known. As anger rose through me I exploded from the water with a yell that emanated from the core of my soul, and hacked down on that rope with every ounce of strength that I have ever drawn. The scimitar hit the rope and then tumbled from my grasp. Bubo flew past me, just above my still-outstretched arm. Spent, empty and drained, I dropped back into the water.

I turned and through a cloud of bubbles I saw Taran-kula's evil face materialise in front of me. I saw its pointed white nose. I saw its eyes. Its jaws opened wide so that I could see every tooth arrayed into the most evil and ominous of grins. Yet I felt calm for this shark could scare me no more. I was a free man - in body, soul and mind. I grinned back.

Suddenly Tarn-Kula's menacing teeth disappeared from view. I felt a heavy thud on my chest as if a charging bull had hit me, knocking out my wind. My head smashed on the lagoon floor. I spun, disorientated, as bubbles and sand and water forced themselves into my eyes, ears, and nose. I saw blood welling about me. Confused, I groped for the bottom, but could connect with nothing but water. I spun again but could not discern up from down.

I felt a firm grip upon my legs, vaulting my mind back to my first impetuous plunge into this lagoon. But this time the two dark shadows were not here to capture me, but to rescue me. Taa-TA-hoo and Lee-BE-nay quickly lifted me to the surface, where I gasped deeply for air.

"Yapaarta-se." One of them said my name. *Swims like a stone.* I opened my eyes to the sight of Taa-TA-hoo and Lee-BE-nay's deep dark faces. Through water-muffled ears I heard howling in the distance. The natives pointed toward the beach, where, through blurred eyes, I saw the tribe careening about their nemesis. Thrashing on the beach, with the snare loop tightly trussed around his tail, was Taran-kula. Ensnared. Captured. Already defeated. He would torment Boot Island no more. The islanders, and Ki-Ora, were safe.

Bubo flew to me, flapping his torn feathers in ungainly fashion. He perched, exhausted, on my forearm. I could sense his sharp talons digging far deeper than usual, but they did not hurt at all. As Taa-TA-hoo and Lee-BE-nay carried me high toward the beach Bubo bowed his head, so I stroked his hackle feathers in the way that I knew he liked best.

"Thank you Bubo," I whispered in his ear. "Thank you, my friend."

Captain Rum, he cawed, and then ground his beak into a rumbling purr, seemingly very pleased and at ease with himself.

The natives surged into the shallows to congratulate us. I was lauded by all, and my name, Yapaarta-se, echoed over the lagoon. The natives showered Bubo with gifts of coconut; he will be feasting for a month.

Then I saw her. Ki-Ora. She was smiling and holding her arms outstretched toward me. We walked toward each other, and despite the bleeding wound on the back of my head, we embraced. Then she kissed me - strongly, lingeringly and passionately. We did not leave each other's side for the rest of the evening.

The natives fetched firewood from my ship and enkindled a large blaze. They hurled the gutted carcass of their nemesis upon the fiery embers. Later, large platters of Taran-kula's baked flesh were passed about, the ultimate privilege of the victor.

When all had eaten their fill, the natives broke spontaneously into song; their natural melodies were as wondrous and uplifting as was the bird choir. Later, coconuts and star fruits were fetched from a store and we feasted again. The moon sped far too quickly across the sky, for it was as fine a celebration as man (or bird) could wish for.

As the night lengthened the natives gradually departed, and even Bubo flew wearily away to roost. As the black sky lightened in the east, only Ki-Ora, Baa-GA-nee and I remained. We sat quietly for an hour or so, barely talking, simply letting the tumultuous events of the day cede away. Baa-GA-nee looked at me intently and often as I held his sister's hand; he seemed to be thinking. By and by he stood and bowed deeply to Ki-Ora, then turned and repeated the two-fisted bow to me. Without a word, he slid silently into the lagoon, leaving Ki-Ora and I alone on the warm beach.

Ki-Ora's cheek bones glowed warmly by the light of the embers. We lay down in each other's arms on the same stretch of sand at which we had first met eyes, many nights ago. The dark sky turned mauve too swiftly, for I wished this night would continue without ever ending.

As the sun's first rays edged over the horizon they beamed through the hole in the eastern ridge, illuminating the natural fault that had created this most unique of lands. The day now broken, Ki-Ora took me by the hand and escorted me to her cave.

Whatever ill twists of fate that Providence has dealt me in the past, I wholly concede that she has now squared the ledger.

The End

Epilogue

<u>A final note from the editor</u>

So ends the wondrous account of Fintan McAdam, a.k.a. Captain Rum. I am pleased that we left him in a (very) happy place.

After finishing my initial reading of the journal, two questions came immediately to mind. First, where, geographically, are the enigmatic Bird Rock and Boot Island located? Second, how did the journal end up in the shelves of the Bodleian Library, Oxford? On the assumption that the reader harbours similar curiosities, I have attempted to answer these two questions.

The captain's last reported position before the typhoon was 36.90°N, 13.6°E, placing him off the coast of southern Portugal. His subsequent movements can be estimated as follows.

(a)   The *Maris Alarum* endured four days of extreme cyclonic weather, which could have pushed her hundreds of kilometres in any direction. But we know that cyclones rotate anti-clockwise in the northern hemisphere and so may extrapolate that her most likely path was south-west. I estimate that the winds may have pushed McAdam's vessel 500 km, although I concede that this is merely an educated guess.
(b)   McAdam's journal tells us that he then floated aimlessly for nine days, during which time the prevailing Atlantic currents would have bobbed him about 50 kilometres south.
(c)   After repairing his mast, McAdam spent 12 days sailing slowly east-south-east, during which he would have travelled an estimated 250 km.
(d)   Finally, McAdam spent a few days under Bubo's navigation, sailing south-south-west, covering say 50 km.

Using these estimates – which I again concede are loose approximations only – we can place McAdam somewhere between the Islands of Madeira and the Canary Islands, roughly 750 km from the coast of Morocco.

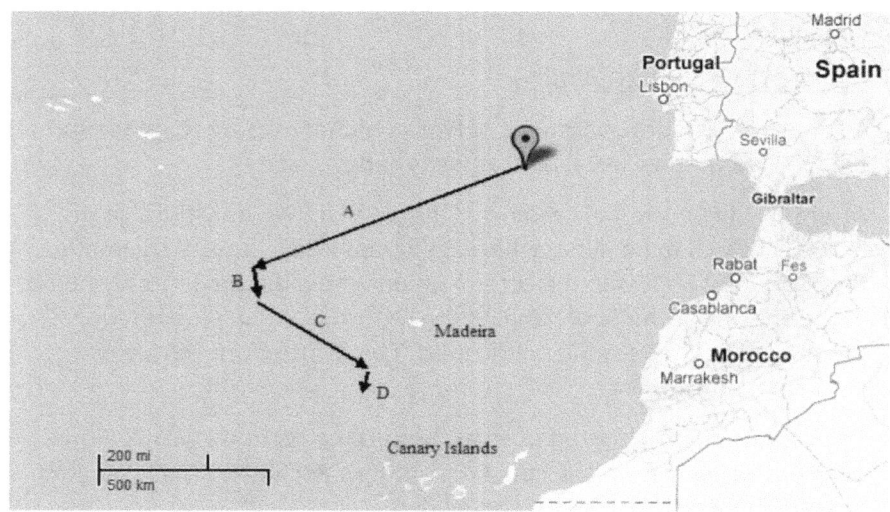

Figure 1. McAdam's possible route from his last reported position

In this large expanse of otherwise empty water is a tiny archipelago known as *Ilhas Selvagens,* the Savage Islands. Is it possible that two of the rocky cays from within this group once hosted the *Maris Alarum*? The evidence is tantalising.

The Savage Islands were formed by volcanic activity about 70 million years ago. Many of its islands are the tips of undersea mountains, thus fitting McAdam's geological descriptions. One island, *Selvagem Pequena*, visually resembles McAdam's Boot Island. Furthermore, the islands were uninhabited throughout the 19th century and used only as occasional way points for Madeiran maritime journeys. In short, I believe that their geographical location, features and history mark the Savage Islands as prime candidates for McAdam's Bird Rock and Boot Island.

Intriguingly, the Savage Islands have long held a reputation as a "Treasure Island". Early explorers traversed this area searching for the famed "Atlantic paradise". Did the existence of the mysterious Boot Island people initiate this reputation? At least four serious dig attempts have been made (in 1813, 1851, 1856 and 1948), but nothing of value was recovered. Perhaps in light of McAdam's diary, another sortie should be considered, for the islands remain largely uninhabited and unexplored to this day.

Regarding the passage of McAdam's journal back to English shores: I would like to report that I had an epiphany that led to the answer. But I cannot claim this achievement. Thankfully, Ms. Lucille (Lucy) Mitchell, a graduate student of the Oxford Faculty of English, did have a moment of such enlightenment. Her investigative leap was to focus upon the only surname that, in the absence of heirs or descendents, would have held ongoing relevance to McAdam. That surname was *Harlesden*.

Lucy discovered that Mrs Harlesden, McAdam's land-lady in London to whom he had forwarded all of his absentee mail, was, in fact, *Miss* Edna Harlesden. She died a spinster in 1841 leaving no direct descendents. However she had a sister, Winifred, who married Mr Charles Winning (becoming, most alliteratively, Winnie Winning.)

Winnie's grand-daughter later became Mrs Gladys Bell, who bequeathed a large portion of her estate to Oxford University in 1895. Lucy somehow procured the original consignment note which read, in part, that 'chattels received from the estate of Mrs Gladys Bell, including ... 27 old & rare books, on a variety of subjects, including history, poetry, pottery, maritime history...."

Despite further intrepid detective work, Ms Mitchell was unable to locate any more detailed references to Mrs Harlesden's great-great-niece's bestowment. So the prospect, despite being far from proved, hangs tantalisingly in the air: did McAdam send his journal back, perhaps from a distant port, via a passing ship, to Mrs Harlesden?

Ms Mitchell also discovered what might be a co-incidence, but an intriguing one all the same, in the inventory of the *Essex*[190], *which* docked in London in 1845. Captained by Thomas William Pixley, this ship had traversed the globe en route to Calcutta and back. Listed among the imported goods at disembarkation was one "... private consignment, small wrapp'd package, Mrs E. H."

Could it be that Mrs E.H. stood for the recipient, Mrs Edna Harlesden? A large part of me hopes that this is true, for it would show that McAdam had at least one moment of passing contact with the western world. Perhaps we will never know. My academic opinion is that the evidence

---

[190] Registered ship # 265 393, for those who wish to pursue this line of enquiry for themselves.

is too unreliable and uncorroborated to make definite assertions, but in my heart I do believe that McAdam took to the oceans again.

Maybe somewhere, perhaps on a dusty bottom shelf in a distant library, another nondescript little book awaits discovery that has the answers.

H.D. L.

Appendix one

Diogo de Silves

Until McAdam's discovery of the artefacts on Bird Rock, very little was known of Diogo de Silves' life, or how it ended. In fact, he is known only from a single reference on a naval chart. Nevertheless, in 1990, Portugal issued a stamp commemorating the explorer.

Portuguese maritime history scholars have requested a copy of McAdam's journal to study its contents. The Oxford team await their findings with interest.

Appendix Two

Below is a digitally restored copy of the crudely drawn fish that McAdam rendered in his journal while trying to teach Bubo the word.

McAdam conceded in his own hand: "I admit I am no Constable". With all due respect to McAdam, I concur.

More books by John Perrier
JP Publishing Australia

"Back Pain: How to get rid of it Forever"

- Self help/back pain/self treatment
- Adult/Young Adult readers
- Available as print edition or two-volume E-Book

"Campervan Kama Sutra"
Around Australia with a camper trailer, three kids and a dog*

- Travel/comedy
- Adult/Young Adult/Teen
- Available as print or E-Book

"A Few Quiet Beers with God"

- Science fiction/comedy
- Teen/Young adult/Adults who are young at heart
- Available as print or E-Book

"Using Your Brain to Get Rid of Your Pain"
A simple, common sense guide on how to manage stress, reduce pain, and think more healthily.

- Self help/healthy living
- Adult/Young adult
- Available as print or E-Book

You can find more online at
www.JPpublishingAUSTRALIA.com

"Back Pain: How to Get Rid of it Forever"

The title says it all: this book will help you permanently banish your back pain. In three logical sections, it shows you how to feel better.

The first section makes it easy for you to understand your back pain. Using simple, clear language, it explains the structure of your spine, and demystifies many common pain-provoking conditions. The second part offers a unique quiz that will help you to classify your injury into one of four types. In this way, you will learn how to cure your pain, not someone else's.

In part three, the advice flows thick and fast. You will learn clever techniques that will help you to use your spine more efficiently, and discover how to think, eat, relax, and sleep away your pain. You'll also find useful information on exercises, x-rays, medication and muscles, plus some tips on how to choose a spinal health practitioner. Of course, all of the advice will be tailored to your specific problem.

Because the cure uses well-proven techniques, your relief won't just last a few days or weeks. You will feel better forever.

*

"The best self help back book I have ever read."
Dr Keith Charlton, Chiropractor, former governor of the Australian Spinal Research Foundation.

"...a regular dose of humour that will undoubtedly help to lighten your back pain."
John Miller, Physiotherapist with a special interest in back pain.

"One of the most informative surveys of back pain to date."
Graham Sanders, President of the Qld Osteopathic Association

More information on *Back Pain* can also be found at
www.physioworks.com.au

"Campervan Kama Sutra"
Around Australia with a camper trailer, three kids and a dog*

This true story tells of one family's hilarious journey through Australia's rugged outback countryside.

Our intrepid adventurers work their way through numerous mishaps, including, but not limited to, an ill-advised river crossing, an inappropriately packed roof rack and some truly horrible singing.

During their journey, they stumble across a motley assortment of characters such as a confused check-in clerk, a grey nomad with an eye for detail regarding torches, and several Crazy Germans.

While reading Campervan Kama Sutra, you'll not only fall in love with Australia's vast, ever-changing countryside, but you'll also delight in the tragicomedy that arrives with unerring regularity.

You'll laugh until something hurts.

*P.S. There was no dog.

"A Few Quiet Beers with God"

Set in Australia in the year 2031, this story is science-fiction comedy at its best.

When Dave, a hopeless but lovable 34 year old, meets Alexandra, the girl of his dreams, he feels as though his luck has finally changed. But due to his ineptness with technology, he tragically loses contact with her.

Meanwhile, the lust for supremacy of two powerful Americans ignites a bitter feud. Their fight reaches around the globe and soon entwines not only Dave and Alexandra, but also a superstar football player nicknamed 'God'.

Their final meeting precipitates an event that *no-one* saw coming.

"Using Your Brain to get Rid of Your Pain"

A simple, common sense guide on how to manage stress, reduce pain, and think more healthily.

This book will help you to feel better. You'll not only learn how to reduce or cure your aches and pains, but you'll discover techniques that will help you to relax away the stresses and strains of everyday life.

However, this book does not contain masses of complex psychiatry, nor is it a collection of old wives' remedies. You won't have to use any drugs to achieve amazing results, nor will you be required to burn incense or wear mystical healing crystals in an ankle bracelet.

Instead, you will learn how to relieve your pain using the most natural cures known to medical science. Furthermore, the treatment will have beneficial spin-offs rather than unpleasant or dangerous side effects. Better still, it won't cost you a single penny!

INCLUDES COMPLIMENTARY AUDIO TRACK!
See www.JPpublishingAUSTRALIA.com for details

What other health professionals have said...

"This is an easy-to-understand guide to stress and its related symptoms. The author explains these sometimes difficult concepts by using simple, relevant examples, and enlivens the discussion with a touch of humour along the way. Most importantly, it shows you in simple terms how to manage your own problems. I heartily recommend this book to all sufferers of chronic pain."

(Ian McKenzie, Psychologist, Chronic pain clinician)

"What a wonderful, simple-to-read book! It's funny, insightful, and does a magnificent job of combining theory with practical management. Anyone suffering with chronic pain or stress should read this book."

(Hilary Thomson, Occupational Therapist, Former head of Relaxation Unit at the King Khalid National Guard Hospital in Saudi Arabia)

Connect and Contact

Your comments, criticisms, typos, praise, offers for movie deals, and suggestions are all very welcome. Please contact us by any of the links below.

Email: JDPpublishingAUSTRALIA@gmail.com
                (Please note the extra 'D')

Facebook: https://www.facebook.com/JPpublishingAustralia

Website: www.JPpublishingAUSTRALIA.com

Mail: JP Publishing Australia
                56 Quirinal Crescent
                Seven Hills, Brisbane
                AUSTRALIA   4170

www.ingramcontent.com/pod-product-compliance
Lightning Source LLC
Chambersburg PA
CBHW070331030726
47505CB00004B/1166